NORSEMAN'S OATH

By

Jason Born

WORKS WRITTEN BY JASON BORN

THE NORSEMAN CHRONICLES are:
NORSEMAN'S OATH
NORSEMAN RAIDER
NORSEMAN CHIEF
PATHS OF THE NORSEMAN
THE NORSEMAN

THE WALD CHRONICLES are:
WALD VENGEANCE
WALD AFIRE
THE WALD

COPYRIGHT

NORSEMAN'S OATH. Copyright © 2015 by Jason Born. All rights reserved. No part of this book may be used or reproduced in any manner without written permission.

ISBN-13: 978-1508492689
ISBN-10: 1508492689

DEDICATION

To Greg Fleming and his outstanding family.

ACKNOWLEDGEMENTS

Several folks deserve much praise for their work on this project. Each of my novels starts with a bit of history, an idea for a story, then a lot of sketching, typing, and retyping. However, so much more is involved in getting a book from my head into the hands of faithful readers. I hope these few words of gratitude I offer are read by many fans so that it is clear that any success I've been fortunate enough to garner is chiefly due to my associating with patient and talented individuals.

Maps have become a staple in my tales. I have read some historical fiction authors who've said that they choose not to put any maps in their work or to use only the bare minimum. They have sound reasoning, for these men and women believe it is their job to create the settings with words alone. For this, I commend them and support their endeavors. My approach is a little different. I believe that maps can only enhance the readers' experiences with the characters and their actions. They make my work richer.

Nathaniel Born made his second appearance as cartographer. His work, like the writing of his dad (hopefully), improves with each go 'round. Thanks, Natt.

Michael Calandra continued his string of marvelous covers. His best work comes when I shut up and allow his imagination, pencils, and brush to do the talking. This cover took a little longer than normal to come together. I had one idea. Michael had another. In the end, we went an entirely different direction than what either of us originally wanted. It is all for the best, I think, as I love the action demonstrated by the still drawing. Despite already painting for decades, I believe that Michael's talent continues to deepen! Thank you, Michael.

Finally, the most challenging of all positions on the team is that of proofreader and editor. In addition to fixing my many glaring errors, Priscilla Bersee offered tremendous insight in her notes and in person. She gave her heart and mind to the tale, inspiring me to carry on and write many more in the future. She was a voice of support and challenge. Her attention to detail made this work sharper. Priscilla's informed perspective on things military made the yarn fun to build and read.

Thank you, all!

CAST OF MAIN CHARACTERS

Colbain - *Leinster-born, servant in Dyflin*

Crack-a-Bone - *Norse sea king*

Gormflaith - *Leinster-born, former Queen of Dyflin, current Queen of the Ui Neill*

Halldorr - *our hero*

High King Mael Sechnaill - *of the Ui Neill*

King Kvaran - *of Dyflin*

Lady Gytha - *Norse noblewoman and sister to Kvaran*

Norns - *fate spinners at the foot of the Yggdrasil Tree*

Ottar - *Icelandic skald*

Ox-foot - *sea king's lieutenant*

Prince Iron Knee (Gluniairn) - *of Dyflin*

Prince Silkbeard (Sitric) - *of Dyflin*

Princess Aednat - *of the Ui Neill*

Tyrkr - *German thrall*

And a host of warriors, tradesmen, and more . . .

NORSE WESTERN EXPANSION

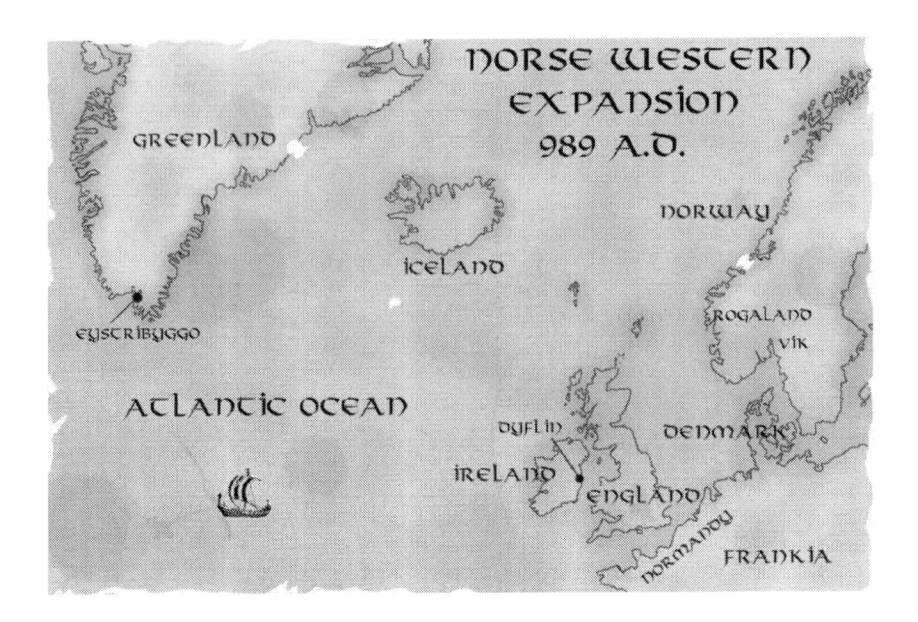

THE IRISH SEA

DYFLIN & HINTERLAND

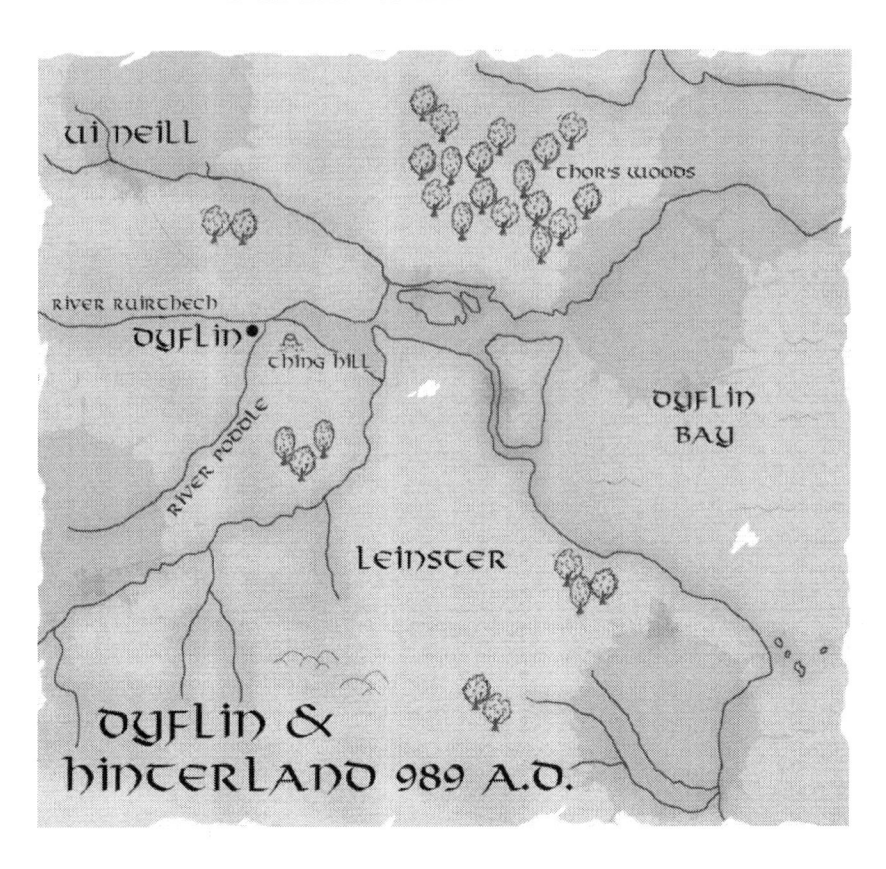

PROLOGUE
989 A.D.

The earth, Midgard, is populated with the vilest of creatures. They slither from one pond, across the shore and over mountains, to simply slip into another sea in order to spread their mayhem. The beast of which I speak is mankind, of course. Wait, you protest. Perhaps you are a Christian and moderate in your drink, dress, and words. You would never say such a thing out loud. You may realize in the deepest recesses of your heart that men are wicked, but you have the hope given to you by the One God and the Christ. At the time of my tale's events I did not yet have the new faith. I said these contemptible things about men, for I did these things.

But you are judicious and not prone to excess. Therefore, instead of calling all men loathsome and in the spirit of building a bridge to my reader – I don't know a single person who would spend even five heartbeats reading my words – I'll merely say something reasonable, something that which even a Christian could agree. All men are liars. From the time we are able to speak, we lie. Did you fill your pants again? No, says the toddler with stinking shit seeping from his trousers, oozing down his bare ankles. Were you working behind my back? No, says the teenage prince who cavorts with the enemy for some make-believe slight the king has given him. Then we have an accord of peace and friendship? Yes, says the warlord whose true plans are to ram a blade an ell deep into the other man's chest.

I am handsome am I not? Yes.

All men are liars.

So I'll continue my version of the tales. Let this be your warning. Much of what follows is the truth. Some of it lies. I don't even know the difference anymore.

• • •

I was destined to be a raider.

Some men, I imagine, were raised under the tutelage of their warrior fathers, knowing all along that they, when grown, would be soldiers themselves. Not so with me. My first father, dead, was a farmer. My second father, a murderer and jarl, but no fighter with professional experience, was forced to exile me for crimes I did not commit. He banished his true son, Leif, as well. We were like brothers, Leif and I. Leif appears in my tales here and there. But my stories are not about him, they tell of my life, my peoples' lives.

Regardless of my upbringing and forgetting about any goals I may have had for the days given me, the norns saw fit to weave me a life of turmoil. Like a fat man stuffing himself into last year's clothes, those spinners of fate crammed me. They compelled me. They forced me in the direction they'd have me go. Gone were my desires of humping a red-haired wife next to my warm hearth as the snows of Rogaland piled high. Vanished were my hopes for nurturing a brood of children, offspring from my fiery woman. Disappeared were my dreams of becoming a man of property, raising cattle, sheep, goats, chickens, wheat, and barley. All those wishes were gone.

I was woven on the loom in my mother's womb to be a killer, a raider.

My mother! I never knew the woman. She was dead before I pushed out my first tooth. I think she died before I tasted her nourishing milk. I wasn't exactly certain how her life passed away. Even now, in a tale apart from this yarn, a version of her death was told to me. But the source of the information was wretched for a host of reasons. I killed him and his family, finishing a blood feud. Regarding my mother, I knew only that my father missed her when I was but a youth. I know that her absence became a gaping hole in his heart. It was a bottomless dung pit in mine.

You see, the only aspect of my former self that I retained into my adulthood was my weakness, my soft-hearted stupidity for women. Women of all ages, I wanted to take care of them. Or, I wanted them to take care of me. Now past my ninetieth year, I can finally admit this truth. Thjordhildr, my adopted mother? She raised me as her own – before I was banished from her sight. Freydis, my one-time betrothed? I bought her expensive trinkets. She warmed my bed and caressed me with her lightly freckled hands – before she publically humiliated me.

We did not wed. Aoife? The young thrall I'd owned briefly. I tried to take care of her. She was dead, killed much before her time. Aoife slept at the bottom of the sea.

I was a raider by destiny. While I held onto just a small nugget of my humanity in that concern for women, I'd given up all hope of a simple life. I plunged into raiding with a vengeance. I lived for thumping a man on his head and taking what should have been mine. It was easy enough to rationalize my actions. If I tilled the earth, broadcasting seed rather than destruction, then someone else – an Englishman, a Dane, or even a fellow Norseman – would come and take my harvest, kill my children, and rape my wife. What was the point of a simple life?

That question was a load of goat turds that I heard rattling in my head again and again as I fashioned myself into someone I was, or was not, fated to become. But when confusion reigns, plow ahead. Chop. Charge. Take. Conquer. Keep going until something or someone makes you stop.

Thor's Beard! I was a raider back then. I was not yet of the Christian faith, following the One God, with its focus on the meek inheriting the earth. No! I was a heathen, a pagan, a follower of the old gods – the gods of my father's father. We were not a docile people. Instead, we took from the gentle.

After learning my craft under the aggressive, but ultimately very dead King Godfrey, I had found a new leader. He led me on strandhoggs of plunder. We washed ashore with the tide and sacked coastal villages. When we flowed out again, our longships were filled with cattle, silver, and wheat. Chained in our holds were Irish thralls who would work their way through the slave auctions at Dyflin and serve masters all over the world. My new leader was aggressive and bold, like Godfrey. He led us inland on my first, true overland raids. When trouncing the sod rather than the watery swells, I missed the taste of salt from the sea and her pitching waves. Yet, these were much like our seaborne invasions. Sheep, goats, Irish thralls, and the relics of Christian churches made our steps heavy as we lugged our new wealth through the deep forests of green that yet littered Ireland. While my heart still craved fertile land on which to sow and an equally fertile woman to wed, my sinews, bones, and muscles were made for war. My fate carried the seasons of my life. I was a raider. For a time at least, I was a raider.

Iron Knee led his small army inland again. I was at his side. Tyrkr, our German slave, was next to me. We carried heavy, round oaken shields with strong iron bosses resting in their centers. Every man painted his bark in whatever manner he liked. Though, since most men are not creative by nature and prefer to pilfer ideas and goods from others, at least half the shields ended up being adorned with alternating, radiating stripes of red, blue, or white. I'd like to say that mine was unique. In truth, I covered it with blue and red stripes that fanned from the boss out to the riveted, iron rim.

The rest of our band of exiled Greenlanders and other misfits remained back in the Norse city-state of Dyflin to serve Iron Knee's younger half-brother, Prince Sitric Silkbeard. My adopted brother, Leif, stayed behind in the town. He filled out his frame more every day, while using his wisdom to baffle me. Cnute, reliable and quiet to a fault, was with him. As he often did, Cnute likely gambled away the money from his last raid in the alleys or taverns of town. Magnus, Loki, Brandr, and Randulfr each stayed behind to protect Dyflin from the northern Irish clans of the Ui Neill. They took their turns standing on the walls watching for invasions from the southern Irish clans of the Leinster. Dyflin was hemmed in atwixt the two and the relationships – one day friendly, the next belligerent – between our neighbors waxed and waned like the moon.

"You're as nervous as a hare caught in the open!" criticized Iron Knee. It was his name that first drew me to the man. What could be a better nickname for the prince who would soon be King of Dyflin? How could a man descended from raiders – himself a warrior – have a better moniker? Iron Knee earned his label honestly. You see, he had a special way of dealing with men he found objectionable. Whether in battle or during a blood feud, when it was time to spill another man's crimson, Iron Knee would snatch his opponent's head between his hands and hammer it down onto his knee. That knee was forever bruised and bloodied. It was formed into a knotted tool as strong as a smith's anvil. The knee, his right one, was so different from his left that his trousers fit tighter over it. It creaked when he walked.

Colbain, Iron Knee's servant who was granted much latitude and hence armed, glanced down at the sword he carried in his hand and reluctantly slid it into its fleece-lined scabbard. He frowned. "You never know where the Irish will come from. They're wily." We were deep into the territory of the Ui Neill violating a truce. But in Iron Knee's mind, if it wasn't us who sullied the peace, sooner rather than later, it would be the Ui Neill.

Iron Knee scoffed as we pushed over a wooded hill. Though he was a head and a half shorter than me, it was difficult to keep up with him. He pumped his short legs, nearly jumping from one step to the next. His paws latched onto low saplings in order to help pull his weight up the hillside. Iron Knee was fast, confident, and eager – all the qualities I adored in those days. They were usually the same qualities that led young men with sharp swords into trouble.

Our leader paused mid-stride. "Takes a conniving Irishman to know one."

Colbain grinned and followed Iron Knee, who again pushed his way uphill. The slave chatted easily. "My mother was Irish. As was your mother, I might remind you, Gluniairn," said Colbain, using Iron Knee's given name. It sounded awfully Irish to me. I winced.

Iron Knee charged back down the hill toward our group. He cracked the knuckles of his hands, something he often did just before he slammed a victim's head onto his knee. Colbain shuddered as Iron Knee reached out. When our leader snatched Colbain's wineskin and drank a long draught, the servant relaxed. He chuckled nervously.

The wineskin came down. Iron Knee smacked his lips and gave an approving gasp. Drips of red wine slowly worked their way through his long beard. Since wine is the subject here, I shall speak of it further. I've had my share of wine. It's like a dessert. But if I want a sweet drink, I'll take mead. Over them both, I'll take ale – sour, stomach-churning ale. It often tastes like you're swilling piss or sucking on a soggy oak barrel stave, but it reminds me of journeys on the pitching sea. It helps me forget other things. I'll take ale.

"A similarity to be sure, Colbain," answered Iron Knee, playfully cuffing the Irishman on the side of his head. "There is a difference, though. And you know it. My father, I'm acquainted with him. King of Dyflin, one-time and maybe again someday, King of Jorvik. Perhaps you've heard of the man. Kvaran is his name. What's your father's name again?"

Iron Knee smacked the skin into his servant's chest. A fat, sheathed dagger that always dangled from Colbain's neck rocked back and forth at the end of its cord. The next King of Dyflin turned and marched back up the hill. Colbain didn't answer, for he didn't have to. He had no idea who his father was.

I felt pity on the man. I've told you my family's plight, but at least I knew my father. Well, actually I knew my *fathers*. My first father, Olef, was killed when I was a boy. I remember singing songs to the old gods with him as we sowed our spring seed in the narrow fields of Rogaland in Norway. My second father, Erik Thorvaldsson, a scoundrel and murderer, was adventurous and boisterous. He'd taken me across the world. Banished from Norway himself, we went to Iceland. Banished again, Erik discovered and settled Greenland. Fitting, I suppose that Erik wound up exiling me as well as his real son for crimes we didn't commit.

So I knew my fathers. I had that. They were gone from my life, but I had ties of reminiscence to my ancestors. Though my sleep was often troubled with turbulent dreams, my head fell to the pillow knowing that I could list my lineage. I was Halldorr, son of Olef, son of Hrolf, son of Gunnar. All of these men and their women – dead, all of them – had been resilient folk, hacking out their lives in the icy fjords of my former home. Colbain knew nothing of his past. If a man has no knowledge of his history, how does he know where he is going?

Colbain wedged the cork into the skin's mouth.

Iron Knee reached the wooded hill's crest. He gasped and dropped to a crouch. He spun to face us and I knew we fell across the paths of men. Our actual prey, a string of four rich monasteries north of the River Boyne, was still a day's march away. But right now, Iron Knee saw someone – a hunting party, a band of the Ui Neill's army, a troupe of travelling merchants. It could have been anyone. The Dyflin prince faced us with stone intensity. He bounced while in his crouch. His fingers rolled against one another. Iron Knee meant to move quickly. My heart rate increased. My skin tingled.

    Twice, he chopped the air with one hand, cleaving our army into three groups. One he sent out to the right around the hill. One he sent left up and over. The last, my group with Tyrkr and Colbain, went straight up toward Iron Knee. We moved rapidly, but nearly silently. The prince motioned for us to keep our weapons sheathed.

    Nervous soldiers draw their swords much too early, just like Colbain had done moments before. It makes them feel good, I suppose, to have the cool grip held firmly in their hand. Such a feeling is an illusion of control. Carrying a sword or axe out front while you lumber through the forest and over rough terrain is a danger. And it makes a calamitous noise. It is hazardous because the truth is that most men are not skilled with carrying a blade. A fine sword's edges will slice a man's skin without him even feeling pain. I've seen it before. A tripping man can ram the point of a sword a half ell deep into a comrade before either of them know what happened. I once watched a man slip and fall into his best friend who marched next to him. The falling man's sword slammed into the top of his friend's foot, pinning the boot and foot to the ground. The friend died of a horrible rot some days later, but that wasn't the worst of it. The ensuing racket was what got most of the men killed back then. The friend screamed. The enemy was alerted. Our other friends died. The raid was lost.

    At the very least an unsheathed sword can ping and ring off glancing branches. It can clatter against tree trunks and mail. Rather than allow such a foolish warning, it would be better for an approaching army to sing out loud. At least then the men would have a spring in their steps as they marched to a victory in honor of the old gods that were carried in the tunes. But that is a bad idea, too. War songs and loud jeering are best reserved for the open battlefield where two forces fall together in opposing shield walls. No, when advancing with stealth in the woods of Ireland, it is best to keep your nerves at bay and your weapons in your belt until you mean to kill.

We made ourselves small and climbed the hill. I instinctively placed my hand on my old saex. It was a strong blade, not the blade of a child, though it was from my youth. It was the only artifact from my true father that I still carried. Iron Knee looked at my hand as I reached him. He frowned. "You won't be needin' that," he whispered while spinning to lead us over the top.

"Not yet," I answered.

"Not ever on this one," the prince said over his shoulder. "The sight of us will make them faint."

• • •

We silently poured over the hill, crouching. I had yet to lay eyes on what Iron Knee had seen. The thorns behind which I ducked obscured my view. I would know soon enough.

The group of our warriors that went right entered the next ravine. I could see their vanguard skulking from tree to tree. The leftmost group had skirted the top of the hillock and wove their way down the opposite side, almost coming toward us. Whatever was in the secluded spot was well-hidden for a time, but Iron Knee found them. We had them surrounded.

The sun was brighter as we moved down. Clouds hadn't blown away to reveal the shining orb. No, the dense tree canopy above thinned as we approached a small clearing. I heard the light giggle of a woman's voice. She sounded young, happy, bright, and carefree. She was probably also fresh and beautiful – for an Irish woman – I told myself. In moments, her laughter would be replaced by shrieks of terror.

Iron Knee paused for a beat at the edge of the forest. I again put my hand to my waist, this time to my sword. Certainly we wouldn't attack even the meekest of enemies without drawing a weapon. An unarmed man is nothing but despised, after all. The prince peered right, then left and saw that the others were in place. I swallowed the viscous spit that formed in my mouth, trying to conjure more liquid. I silently readied my voice for a battle cry.

Iron Knee locked eyes with our flanks' leaders, pointed to his weapons, and shook his head, no.

The prince then popped to his feet and slowly sauntered out into the clearing. Surprised, we did the same, not knowing if our mad leader would soon cause a matching spear to jut from each of our chests. A single hiss from Iron Knee shut up our babbling confusion.

I scanned the tiny, secluded meadow. A creek ran through its center. Three great, large stones sat next to the ambling waters, obviously set there by the giants during the previous age. None of it was out of the ordinary. The boulders masked my view of whatever and whomever Iron Knee had seen from above. He walked nonchalantly toward the rocks and stopped two fadmr away. We did likewise.

Our flanks kept moving around the sides of the massive boulders. Some of our men stepped into the creek. We pinched our prey with warriors moving upstream and down. A lone woman shrieked. Several of our men answered with evil laughs. Now several women screamed.

It was then I understood Iron Knee's plan. As if we were on a hunt, he sent the beaters into the opposite side of the woods to drive the game our way. All we had to do was wait and our quarry would come bounding directly toward us. Colbain slid his sword out halfway.

"Back home, Colbain," warned the prince. With a gentle whoosh, the blade was sent to rest in its scabbard.

A young woman with naked, bouncing tits came bounding over the rocks. She wore a light linen skirt about her waist. Her feet were bare and dripping. She clutched the rest of her clothes to her belly. Another woman came. The second was in a similar state of undress. So were the third and the fourth. All of them had wide eyes. They were surely ready to cry and outright weep, but surprise and shock kept the tears at bay, for now.

Two more bare-chested women came over the rocks. These two were older than the previous runners. Their pale breasts hung limp like deflated water bladders against a horse's withers. Each of the older ladies clutched the arms of a single beauty of classic quality who, though completely naked, struggled against them as if she wanted to turn around and fight our flanking armies. Her long, curly locks of stark blonde bobbed as she came toward us. The hair rapped against her face again and again as the woman twisted her neck as she struggled to be freed. Her breasts, shaped like the tears that they'd bring to any man's eyes, sprang like a buoyant log shoved down into the sea and released. Water leapt from the ends of her nipples as she ran. Between them, her chest was dappled with light freckles. She thrashed. "They'd not dare lay a hand on me!" she shouted, tugging on one of her arms to free herself.

  The gaggle of undressed maidens who came over first was stricken with horror. We had not touched them. We had not moved because Iron Knee, with his helmeted head, stood holding a single hand up, keeping us, his wolves, leashed. The fleeing women stopped and were using whatever clothes they grabbed in their haste to cover themselves. They were shrinking and cowering back toward the rocks, weeping and mumbling.

  The completely nude blonde woman and her handlers ran into the backs of their retreating comrades. She looked forward for the first time. Her face was covered with alternating strands of wet and dry hair. Some of it clung. Other locks were frizzy. I could see her eyes. I forgot about the dozen or more breasts that stared at me and could focus only on those eyes.

  They may have been beautiful. I don't even recall what color they were. Green, I suppose, like so many of her fellow countrymen. They were intense. That is what they were. They shot daggers from them. It felt like her arrows of hate were directed toward me, but that was just because I stood so close to Iron Knee. They ricocheted off his defiant chest and struck me in the face. No, it was my heart, my soft, weak heart. Her missiles honed in on my yearning spot for women.

  "Say nothing," the young woman ordered. She gave commands like someone used to being in charge. The other women scooted. They formed a shield of mostly naked skin around the speaker. "Don't cry. Give these animals no satisfaction. Stand proud."

Iron Knee gave an approving huff. "Dress yourselves," he said to the women using their native tongue. Then he turned to us. "They may need some help with their wrappings. Do what you will to them, but leave no blemishes. They bring less on the auction block when they are damaged."

"Pig," said the blonde woman, using Norse.

Surprised, Iron Knee spun and gave the woman a long stare. He gave a second approving huff. "I've changed my mind," the prince said. "Give them all their clothes to properly dress. Bind them and don't touch them." He wagged a finger. "Don't touch!" There was an audible sigh from the men, even the ones from our flanks who now stood atop the rocks and behind the group of women.

"Don't touch them *until* I've had a chance to talk with the banshee in the center."

That was more to the men's liking.

• • •

"I've seen you before," said Iron Knee. He sat on a rock near the creek. One elbow rested on his small knee. A tiny heap of rocks the size of English pennies sat on his sizable, right knee. The prince's hand hurled the pebbles one-by-one into the flowing waters, creating circular ripples that undulated down the brook until the small tributary dumped into a larger river where they swirled away.

Giant ancient barrows climbed from among a patch of scrub trees nearby, looming over us, forgotten by time. They reminded me of my very first raid on Anglesey for a draugr's treasure that wasn't there. I once was so frightened of what the ghosts would do to me. Now, older by two years and experienced by countless raids I was confident enough to turn my back on the old grave mounds. It was my way of damning their Celtic spirits.

The now-clothed woman to whom Iron Knee spoke sat amongst the gnarled roots of a tall Irish yew. Her hands were bound at the wrists with leather cord. Those wrists were tied to similar cords wrapped around her ankles. All of it was tethered to the tree behind her. Overkill, but we had a young man among us who was practicing his knots for the day he'd get to go a-Viking over the seas.

Colbain, Tyrkr, and I stood behind the prince awaiting our captive's response. She remained silent. The woman was merely following her own orders of moments earlier. She didn't give us any satisfaction. Her fair skin was not wrinkled into a frown. Her full lips didn't tremble. Stoic. Indifferent, almost. Yet her eyes still sent salvo after salvo.

Iron Knee smiled. "I think at the court of Mael Sechnaill. That is where I've seen you. Not too close to his throne, but not too far away either." One of the stones he tossed skipped with four quick leaps and struck the other side of the brook. "One of his wives probably. Not his first and so not that important. But you're young and handsome. Mael must be forty winters old. Ui Neill or not, he deserves someone new to warm his bed."

"The good *Christian* High King of Ireland has but one wife. I am not she," said the woman. Though Iron Knee was partly Christian himself, our captive used the word as a bald accusation against my leader.

Iron Knee tired of throwing rocks. He took a handful of the pebbles and rolled them between his soiled hands, allowing them to fall to the ground in ones and twos. "Ah, fair point. Then you must be the good Christian High King's concubine. You are comely." Iron Knee used the same, measured tone that the woman had employed.

Her jaw clenched – a small, visible sign of her anger. "The good king has no concubines. He is faithful to his one wife."

Iron Knee laughed out loud. The rest of his small rocks fell in one plop. His belly laugh went on and on. He squeezed his eyes tightly until tears came from either side. Iron Knee tried to speak, but only gibberish came out. He lost his breath, which made him laugh all the more. The prince panted until he was able to rumble to a halt, shaking his head. "Oh, I haven't laughed like that in a long time. Thank you." He wiped away the tears. "You mean *current* wife. He is faithful to his *current* wife. I don't know what happened to his first woman, but…"

"She died," said the bound woman. She fought back tears now.

"His new woman, his *current* wife," Iron Knee began, "was my step-mother." The bound woman furrowed her brow. Only two tears managed to squeak out. They were already drying out on her high cheeks. "Oh, that's right," said Iron Knee. "She left my father when it became opportune."

"Gluniairn?" asked our captive.

"Indeed," said the prince. "I am known as Iron Knee. And Gormflaith, the High King's current wife, is my younger brother's mother. She was given to my father so that she could be a peace-weaver between our peoples."

"A lot of good that did. You're half Irish, too. You invade our lands right now. And in the middle of a truce," the woman barked.

Iron Knee shrugged. "Quite right. The Battle of Tara and Gormflaith's premature departure leave us feeling less than friendly." He stood and meandered around in a tight circle, studying the earth that he kicked under his feet. "Now you know all there is to know about me, Prince of Dyflin, soon to be King of Dyflin, and I know nothing of you. Why do you appear in the High King's court, young woman?"

The woman considered his question for a long heartbeat. Her hair had long since dried. Her attendants, tied up some distance away, had not the chance to fix it yet. The blonde locks stood out in wild kinks. She stuck her chin a thumb's width higher in the air. "I am daughter of the High King of Ireland."

Iron Knee's eyes went wide. "A princess. Forgive my manners." He made a show of bowing to the woman. His hands made childish sweeping motions as he bent low. Tyrkr and Colbain laughed.

"And pagan or not, Norse or not, Race of Thor or not, you'll not harm me or my ladies," commanded the captive.

The prince returned to his steady pacing. He tugged at his beard, which was cut short compared to mine and those of my men.

"Did you hear me or do you have salt water in your ears, you pagan?"

"He's no pagan," I said, defending him. Though he and his father were mostly pagan. I was definitely what she would call a heathen, still following the old gods. It was the way of my ancestors. I would soon accept the One True God and the Christ, but that is a different story, told on separate pages of vellum.

"Did you hear me? You'll not lay a hand on us."

"What will you have us do?" Colbain asked of Iron Knee, ignoring the captive's pleas.

The prince sighed. "I haven't decided yet. Keep her bound for now. Keep the rest separate. I don't want to hear them yapping. Do not harm our princess. The men may have sport with the others, but no striking them. Don't diminish their value at the thrall auction."

"Pagans are always raping," accused the princess.

"Huh!" spat Iron Knee, instantly flashing red. "And when a Norsewoman is snatched from her husband's pastures by your filthy Irishmen is she not raped then tied to a tree with a slit throat?"

"At least they slit her throat to put her out of her misery. Otherwise, she may have to return to her wretched Norse husband."

Iron Knee chewed on his teeth, smiling. "More proof that Irishmen are fools. No mind for business. Fools! They waste what would be good coin from slave auctions by killing their captives. Fools. That is why Dyflin is the greatest city on this island. We've done more in a century than you could do in a thousand years."

The princess scowled at Iron Knee while Colbain tested the cords that bound her. The grinning, lustful servant then moved off to tell the men the good news about the sexual availability of the attendants.

My feet remained rooted in place. I remember thinking back then that it was not the best idea to let the men get started, allowing their licentious hunger to run and then be sated. In truth, my reasoning was twofold. The first had to do with the weaknesses I've already shared. I didn't mind chopping the arm off a man brandishing a weapon. I didn't think twice of taking his riches. But I've told you I didn't want to harm women. That was my first worthless reason for not wanting our men to begin raping the attendants. It was meaningless because I could scream it until I was blue and no one, not any Norseman, Irishman, Englishman, except the most devout, would care. Most women wouldn't even understand how a warrior could be so soft-hearted and softer-headed.

My second reason would be the only one to which anyone *might* potentially listen. Like bloodlust in battle, like mead swilled in the halls, like a spooked horse, like a conniving plot set free, rape was difficult to steer once unleashed. Despite Iron Knee's admonitions, many of the princess' ladies would be struck, punched, kicked, and much worse. They'd be lucky to survive the night. And that would diminish the total value to be had at auction. I wanted to use my argument to stop what would happen, but it was too late. Iron Knee huffed and struck off along the creek. In the opposite direction, the first cries had begun.

The Irish had done it to our women.

Some of our men would do it to theirs.

The princess directed her hatred toward me as I stood alone. The glare hurt, but what was I to do? Time and again for centuries armies had killed, pillaged, and raped their way across territory. It was our time to give the pain. In another place, at another time, the pain would come our way.

• • •

The night fell. We camped in that small clearing with Iron Knee, who was so bold that he allowed us to build fires. We were in Ui Neill lands and our prince was sending a message to his men, his captive, and any Irish onlookers. He and his soldiers from Dyflin were unafraid.

We roasted deer taken from the High King's woods. Water from his brooks wetted our gullets. But it was our own ale that started us on the road, galloping toward drunkenness. The drink helped bring me up from the dark stench of my head's fuming dung pit, but I still wallowed in mostly silent anger. A troop of daughters, sisters, mothers, or aunts was being sullied while they lay pinned on their backs among the forest's litter. I alternated grinding my teeth and gnawing on my cheek whenever I heard the victims' distant weeping.

Others were just as angry as I. They didn't care about women or rape. They gave no thought to honor or profit. No. These men allowed the ale we'd brought from Dyflin to carry them to a new level of unexplained vitriol, which, as a matter of course, led to violence. I imagine you've seen similar examples yourself. Get a few pots of fermented brew into a man prone to enraged fits even while sober. Mix him with a batch of like-minded warriors and soon you'll witness trouble. Several of these Dyfliners fought in scraps around our camp. They cursed one another while clubbing with fists and splattering faces and knuckles with blood. We let them carry on, for by morning most of the wrongs committed during the drunken brawls would be forgotten.

Long into the darkness, Iron Knee proclaimed, "You know the trees here have eyes!" Rather than fury, he was feeling silly from the ale. The prince swung the cup around laughing. Some of its contents spilled onto his trousers.

Those of us around the prince's fire gave a knowing nod to Iron Knee. We'd been ambushed by the Irish devils many times, which is why we had learned to place constantly rotating sentries. Tyrkr, the German thrall, answered in his accented Norse. "Aye, the sly snakes are always slithering. The High King may have forces shadowing us right now, waiting for the right time to attack."

Iron Knee chuckled. "That's so, but, no, really, the trees here have eyes." He pointed to a copse of alder that extended out into the meadow. "Just a year ago I caught some Irish spies," he tapped his knee, fighting to get the words out through a building snigger. The men laughed with him. Even I smiled. "I had their eyes plucked out and nailed to those trees over there. So the trees here really do have eyes."

He gulped down the remaining ale from the pot he held in his right hand. Once emptied, he tossed the container toward Colbain. It bounced off the servant's arm. Iron Knee swilled from the wineskin in his left hand. We giggled like young girls while we watched the scene unfold. Colbain offered an impotent, glowering face in the dancing firelight, but knew his place. He immediately stood and left the light to retrieve more ale for the would-be king.

Tyrkr, too, frowned while we snorted. He jumped to his feet and walked his stocky frame over to the copse of alders. After running his fingers over the bark for several moments, the slave returned. He plopped his rump onto the ground and shook his head. "I didn't believe it," he began. "When Iron Knee said it, I didn't believe that trees could have eyes for real. But they do. Those trees over there do." Tyrkr, I must tell you, was never the sharpest blade in our entourage. He was, however, utterly dedicated to his owner, my friend, Leif. Tyrkr also fought with the vigor of the old frozen bitch, Hel, and the contempt inherent in the new, fiery Hell. His willingness to slit enemy bellies and our opponents' throats was why he was invited to travel with Iron Knee.

The prince led us in a new round of laughter directed toward Tyrkr. The thrall chuckled, too, uncertain, but merry nonetheless. Ale could smooth over many hurts.

The tooth of one of the scrappers flew into the back of my neck. The pair kept right on fighting with renewed vigor. Ale could easily create new hurts as well.

At length Colbain returned from our small pile of baggage with the ale pot spilling over its edges. He fooled with his trousers as if he'd just relieved his bladder. His face was flushed from exertion. The damned bastard of an Irishman had taken his turn on one of the exhausted captives. Their soft cries were occasionally loud enough to be heard over our carousing. I was immediately sullen again.

I thought of the poor woman Colbain just defiled. She had the seed of a dozen men spilled into her that night. If her seed bed was fertile, any one of them could blossom. I suppose it wouldn't matter to her, though for some reason it did to me. I cared whether or not she would carry the bastard son of the bastard Colbain or some other raider. A man ought to know his father. A woman ought to know the father of her son.

Battle and war killed men, that much was obvious. But the pair truly butchered women. These twin pariahs of mankind beat the life out of children and women more than they ever could any man. Surely, men waged war. For our trouble we received wounds or death. We also had the glory inherent in it, win or lose. But mothers, daughters, and babies? When I think about it from their perspective, I shudder. It had been that way since before the first man, Ask, and the first woman, Embla, sprang from the trees and became separate living beings. The giants battled. The gods fought. That night around the fire I thought war would be pure savagery until the Ragnarok's finale or until the One God came. Since that night, since becoming a follower of the One God myself, I realize that it is possible to spare the weakest among us a few of the hardships of war, but that only happens if both sides agree on the same principles. Otherwise, the raping, burning, killing would go on and on into the future.

Colbain handed the prince his cup. "What is your problem?" asked Iron Knee. He swatted me with the back of his hand. Colbain picked up his own ale and resumed his drinking. He seemed at ease. One of the soft cries from the women grew louder until a loud smack shut it up.

"That bastard and the others are my problem," I said, pointing to Colbain. "Many of them have daughters or wives. Is that what they'd want invaders to do to them?" I started with the wrong argument. I should have started whining about profits. I knew this, but I was angry and mostly drunk.

Iron Knee immediately frowned. "No! That's not even a real question! I shouldn't even try to answer it. But I will since you fight and kill like no one I've ever seen. If we don't make ourselves and our presence terrible, what would make the Irish want to come to our terms? Do you think that if we are nice, they'll be nice to us? Rubbish. I'll let them start down that path first." He was right, of course. As I said, our men behaved the same as every other conqueror had acted for eons. And how else would we bring the enemy to their knees other than by being more brutal than they? I was wrong in my sullenness. That didn't stop me from protesting.

"I guess I've never felt the need to strap a woman down and take her like she's a heifer in the bull pen. It makes us weak, I think." I was talking nonsense. Perhaps it was the ale. That was the excuse I gave when asked about it later.

"Maybe that works for you," said Iron Knee. "But have you seen Colbain? How else is he to have the chance? What could he offer a woman? No land. No ships. No riches. Nothing." The prince abruptly stopped talking. He looked up into the trees, obviously pondering something. My conversation sucked every bit of joy from the moment. I could hear as the rest of the men grumbled about me around the fire. I sipped more ale, mumbling about them in return.

A small breeze picked up and blew the smoke from the wet logs into the faces of five men. They coughed and waved their hands. When the smoke persisted, they swore and moved to sit closer to others. Soon the wind and therefore the smoke followed them, blowing into all of their faces. They cursed up mighty storms. My mood improved upon seeing their discomfort. I knocked back more brew and resumed my laughing, feeling vindicated by the gods of that particular glen for defending the Irish women.

"A peace-weaver is what she'll be!" shouted Iron Knee, jumping to his feet.

"Who?" Colbain asked.

"That princess tied up over there! Whatever her name is," said Iron Knee.

"Another bride for your father?" asked Tyrkr.

"No. Me, you simpleton! I take her back to her father in the morning and inform him of her impropriety – bathing in the forest for all to see. His Christian mind won't be able to take it. I'll tell him that despite her errors, I'll take her as my first bride. Make an honest woman of her. The High King will grant me some of his lands because the children that the girl will whelp will be his grandkids. Dyflin will grow without another spear thrust." Iron Knee paused and sipped his ale. He shrugged with just one shoulder. A roguish smile curled beneath his moustache. "Perhaps in a few years Dyflin will grow with a few spear thrusts, too."

He plopped back down to his rump. The smoke blew his way. I saw it as a bad omen, but the prince ignored it. Iron Knee raised his cup with the grey and black curling around him. "We leave for Mael Sechnaill's hall at first light." We answered his toast by draining our mugs.

The prince smiled.

His men grinned. Even I offered a half smile, for at least one woman would survive the night completely unharmed. It was a small victory. I smiled fully.

Colbain frowned. The servant stewed the rest of the night.

• • •

Tyrkr kicked me in the ribs. I'd fallen asleep curled into a small ball, shivering, with my covering only an ell away. I was so drunk the night before, my hazed-over eyes couldn't find it in the dim light. The German thrall did the same to the other men around the fire. He skipped nudging Iron Knee. Tyrkr was accepted by most men, even the prince, as an equal on the battlefield, but he knew his place well enough. It was best for a slave not to kick the next king.

"Bull nuts," I grumbled.

"Sheep's ass," said Tyrkr. We laughed at each other.

The German poked Colbain with his toe. The servant rolled over. His face was covered in his own drool. He smacked the foot away with an aggressive swat of his hand. "Bull nuts," said Colbain, repeating what he'd heard me say while he was half asleep.

"Shut up, Colbain," I said. Tyrkr and I had nearly grown up together. We could call each other names. Colbain had not earned that right.

"Clamp it, weakling," snapped Colbain. I was a full head taller than Colbain. My arms were twice the circumference of his. My legs were like stout trees compared to his spindles. If there was a weakling in our army it was that bastard. My pity for him from the day before had vanished.

"Bastard," I mumbled.

"Both of you shut up," said another man who began stirring next to us. He tipped his head to one side. His neck made a large popping sound and he groaned with pleasure. The man froze, puzzled.

I looked up in the same direction. "What is it?" I asked as I fumbled with my sword and belt.

"Nothing," he answered stretching his neck in the other direction until a second crack sounded. "Nothing of note, at least. It's just that the sun is up, a lot." The man pointed to Iron Knee who was still sprawled out in the dirt. "The prince must have drunk more than I thought. He's usually the first one up, shouting, pissing, and spitting at us."

I looked eastward. Sure enough, the sun was over the trees. The bright ball hurt my eyes and my head. I squinted. "Strange," was all I said. Then I slowly straightened to my full height and grunted, stretching my back. I belched, tasting last night's brew. It was worse the second time, dry and rancid.

Colbain crawled over toward the prince. "The sentries should have alerted us at light to change the guard. They must have fallen asleep," said the Irish servant.

I snapped sober. "All of them?" I asked.

Tyrkr frowned, understanding my meaning immediately.

"Tyrkr, take a few men and check our picquets, now!" I said. I returned my attention to Colbain. "Wake him up."

He hesitated.

"Now," I commanded.

"Sire," said Colbain, gently shaking Iron Knee's shoulder. Tyrkr jogged through the camp, waking all the men with a sharp whisper. He assembled a handful of the most sober and they disappeared into the deep woods.

"Sire," said Colbain, more assertive this time. Iron Knee didn't move. I didn't worry that he'd vomited himself to death. The prince lay on his side and I didn't smell any of the foul retch.

"Sire," said Colbain a third time. He shook the prince.

"Damn it!" I said, jumping up and over the smoking embers left from the fire. I shoved Colbain out of the way with a jab from my knee and seized the prince by his arm. His skin was cold, not cold like the night air. It was cold like a man's flesh when you find him the day after a battle, dead.

I flipped Iron Knee onto his back. His eyes were wide open, glassy. All of his spirit was gone. His life had ebbed fully, many, long hours before. "Dead," I gasped. Colbain dropped to his backside, breathing heavily. The rest of the camp was drawing near to the spectacle. A collective sigh echoed through the ranks.

"Move, move, move," shouted Tyrkr as he and the other scouts forced their way toward us. "Iron Knee, the sentries are all dead. All of them have puncture wounds in their sides. It's in the shape of an "X," as if someone plunged a blade in once, pulled it out and twisted, only to send it in again." Tyrkr froze when he saw the dead prince. He pointed at Iron Knee. "Just like that."

I looked back to Iron Knee. A pool of blood sat in the dust where he rested on his side. On that same side, just below the ribs, I saw a copy of the "X" wound that Tyrkr described. The prince's face was etched with panic. The red mark of a palm could be seen on his nose, cheeks, and around his lips in the skin behind his thin beard. His attacker stabbed him and forced the prince to remain silent. We'd allowed an assassin to come into our camp and kill the next King of Dyflin while we slept or, rather, while we lay unconscious. Our lusts were sated by the groins of Irish women and our heads numb from Norse ale, our vigilance had fled. Overconfidence had killed a prince.

"What do we do?" asked Tyrkr.

"We kill the bitch of a princess," said Colbain. "She must be a witch!" He stood and stepped over Iron Knee's body, fumbling with the sheathed knife bouncing at his chest.

"Tyrkr! Grab him," I commanded. The German had Colbain locked in his grip in less than a single heartbeat.

"You are just a vagrant, a wandering orphan. You don't command us," accused Colbain.

"Perhaps," I said. When I stood and looked into the men's faces I could see they agreed with me. "But I lead this army for now."

"You have no authority to do so," said Colbain.

"I have the authority given to me by these men," I said.

"I serve Kvaran and his sons. Just because one is dead, doesn't mean that I am to be arrested."

"You're not arrested, you horse's ass, unless you wish it. Just don't harm the princess. You'll be free if you promise to stay your hand." I looked at his trousers. "And your manhood. Neither touches her."

Colbain tried to shake Tyrkr's grip. He couldn't. The servant huffed. "She'll be unharmed." I nodded to Tyrkr, who let him go.

"What do we do then?" asked Colbain. He was mocking me. For some reason, wherever I go, I am underestimated. Men think that because I am big, I must be brutish. They are partially correct. On the battlefield, I am a brute. But I am no foolish ogre. Colbain wanted to challenge my wisdom. I was up to the task, having learned about command the hard way.

"Forty men in two groups scout our perimeter. If you find an Irish army, come get us. Don't go far; just make sure we aren't under immediate threat." Tyrkr and another man slapped men on the shoulders, selecting them. The two bands plunged into the forest.

"And with her?" asked Colbain. He pointed to the gnarled Irish yew. The princess was awake, studying us with a defiant glare.

"She's a peace-weaver," I answered as I walked over to her. Upon closer inspection I saw that the strong young woman bore the dried tracks of copious tears. So the princess wasn't a bold woman who was certain of everything. She was in the process of moving from child to adult. At times – like in front of Iron Knee – she was able to build a sound defense. But when she was left alone in the dark, the harsh reality smacked her, hard. She sucked up a rattling wad of snot.

Even Colbain complimented me then. "Use her to buy our way out of here if we're surrounded. Trade her for safe passage. A fine idea."

"No," I said, demonstrating with my head toward the woman. "She's meant to be a king's wife, not a bartering tool."

Colbain frowned. So did the rest of the men who pressed in, listening. It was a foolish thing that I was saying. The Irish bastard stated the obvious. "The prince is dead. Iron Knee is dead. Are you an imbecile? There will be no wedding, not to him anyway." Colbain's frown began to turn into a smile as he finished.

Not to him anyway, I thought, getting an idea. I drew my father's saex. Over my shoulder I called, "Gather up the other women. Feed them and get them set to move." I cut the princess's bindings with the blade.

"I suppose you'll want to rape me along the way," said the princess.

I slapped her face. She yelped. It wasn't a hard blow, but it carried enough force to send her head to the side. I instantly regretted it. When the princess straightened herself she held her cheek with one hand and narrowed her eyes.

"I don't rape. I've never raped and I'll not start now." I didn't apologize for striking her.

"Are you the man who spoke against rape last night in the dark?" she asked.

I stared at her without answering. Tyrkr's group and then the second band returned.

"No sign of the enemy," they both said at once.

"I thought as much. If they had an army and eliminated the sentinels, they could have easily slaughtered us last night." I dragged the princess away from the crowding soldiers. I bent down to her and whispered. "I am Halldorr, Norseman, servant to Iron Knee. If you heard me speaking last night, you likely heard the prince's words. Iron Knee was going to return you to your father and accept you as his wife. That is not possible, now. But if I let you go, I think there is still a chance that you can be a weaver of the peace for both sides."

"Let me go?" she asked. "Just like that? No rape?" Then she added, "I suppose you all will have plenty of fun with the other women that you drag away."

I wanted to strike her again. "We will take them and auction them off in Dyflin. I will not allow any more rape, though. I don't do it to make you happy. It takes men away from the business of war. And like Iron Knee said, it reduces the value in the auction yard."

"How kind," the princess said.

"I'm not trying to be some spineless, kind-hearted man. I'm trying to make the best decision. I am Halldorr. I am not Iron Knee. I don't intend to further provoke Mael Sechnaill by invading inland. Our raids might stop altogether if you are competent at spinning the peace. I return back to Sitric Silkbeard, Iron Knee's half-brother."

"The son of my father's current wife?" she asked.

"Yes. And he is young, handsome, and unwed. I propose to you, and will propose to him upon my return to Dyflin, that you weave your peace with him."

"Marry Silkbeard?" she asked.

I shrugged. It was the best I could do. I couldn't very well go marching the girl back to her father. I was not a man of royal blood. Mael Sechnaill would slaughter us all. I could not take her back to Dyflin. Again, I had no real authority other than making battlefield decisions. Kvaran and Sitric might do nothing but curse, or worse, if I brought back the daughter of their rival in chains. I'd already struck her. That was bad enough.

"So that is what I aim to do," I said. "I cannot control you or your words once you walk away from us."

"Can you keep your men from slinking away and raping me anyway?"

My hand moved an inch to strike her. I didn't. "Enough with the rape talk. You're safe. If any of my men turn up missing even for a moment to piss, I'll slice them from their crotches to the ribs. Now what name shall I give Sitric? Whom shall I tell him is of age to wed and restart the peace?"

"Why are you so interested in peace with the Ui Neill? You were raiding our lands just last night."

"We're ready to go!" called the men. I looked over and I saw that the other women were tied in a neat line. Sure enough, more than half had marks on their faces where the vilest of our soldiers had been brutal.

"You ask a lot of questions for a captive," I huffed before shrugging. "I suppose that if there is peace inland at our backs, I can stop slogging through forests and rivers and over hills and down into valleys. I can turn around and we can face front. I can join a crew of true warriors again. I can ride on the planks of a longship again. I'd act like a true raider. The sea," I said.

The woman smiled. "A true raider, eh?"

"Your name?" I rasped, quickly tiring of the conversation.

The girl studied her ladies. She examined the faces of my men. She looked at the dead body of Iron Knee which was slung over a man's shoulder. At last the Irish princess looked at my face. It was taking forever. "Your name? Or, I could put you in that line of future thralls. You'll be treated no differently than they."

She smiled again, her confidence returning. "You won't do that. My name is Aednat. It means little fire and you'd do well to remember that. You'd be wise to warn Sitric that if he comes to take my hand, I live up to my name."

Aednat turned and marched into the woods with head high. I watched her go, my heart, already softened by her beauty, was made gruel by her strength of character.

"What are you doing?" asked Tyrkr. I heard more questioning grumbles from the others. Colbain, though, grinned happily. He clutched the sheath of his large knife in both hands, turning it between the palms. I believe he plotted my downfall.

Angry or content, mumbling or singing, I owed the men no explanation. "To Dyflin!" I said. Little did I know then, but by showing what the Christians label compassion and letting the princess go free, I was setting up a veritable brawl.

And the fight for Norse Dyflin began.

CHAPTER 1

Kvaran's shriveled body shook. He was an ill man, old and infirm. Yet, it was not a fever that made his limbs and shoulders wiggle. It was mirth. He laughed. The King of Dyflin cackled. This was not in his nature – far from it. Kvaran's normal disposition was one of absolute indifference as if he was thoroughly bored with his long life. Now in my own aged feebleness, I can understand his pain. I pen these words well beyond my ninetieth winter and I've seen everything. I've known the heights and valleys life offers and the climbs and falls between.

So too with Kvaran, for he was past ripened. The last decade of his life was filled with nothing but setbacks, making a series of cringe-worthy exclamation points to his otherwise successful career. He and his father retook Dyflin from the Irish after the latter stole it from the Norse for several years. Since then, Kvaran fostered the city into something truly brilliant.

Dyflin was the richest city I'd ever seen. The natives called it Duiblinn, which means black pool. But it was my Norse ancestors who first built it one hundred fifty years earlier and then made it great. Dyflin's people were packed behind a grand earthen mound some four fadmr tall that was topped with a timber palisade. Traders and merchants loved the town. They came from England, Scotland, Sweden, the Holy Roman Empire, Spain, and Frankia bringing with them manufactured goods from the world over. After barter or the exchange of coins, they took with them fine Irish oak, wool, and thralls.

Peddlers were partial to Dyflin because it brought easy access to and from the Irish Sea. It was tucked between two flowing bodies of water, the curving River Poddle to the south and east and the River Ruirthech on the north. Merchants could beach their heavy laden knarrs on the north bank and enter the town from one of just four stoutly defended sets of stairs that led up and over the fort's walls. The only landward entrance was a single, massive, guarded gate that faced the southwest.

I've said the town was magnificent compared to anything else I had ever seen to that point. It was. Kvaran nurtured markets and trade with all of Midgard. Imports of wine, oil, copper, and tin streamed in from Frisian traders. So many artisans and craftsmen poured into his town that entire streets were becoming famous for specialized industry. For some reason, probably happenstance, hordes of butchers and clothmakers congregated onto Fishamble Street. Tanners and smiths competed against one another for customers. Prices fell, making us happy and forcing those tradesmen to operate efficiently, or starve.

But some years before I ever saw Kvaran, he suffered his one major defeat. The Irish High King, Mael Sechnaill, had beaten the King of Dyflin at the Battle of Tara. Then his woman left him for Mael, scandalous and embarrassing. Kvaran's kingdom was smaller than ever. He was boxed in. No real farmlands were left. They were taken by the Irish. Kvaran controlled the mouth of the still-important river system. He controlled a small forest that was continuously harvested for exporting timber. The Norse king held sway over Thor's Woods, a sprawling woods north of the River Ruirthech where those who still worshipped the old gods went to offer sacrifices and collect favor from Odin, Thor, or any forest spirit that remained in that largely Christian land. No trees were felled in Thor's Woods.

Kvaran wriggled. His thinning shoulders danced as he laughed. It was an annoying, sardonic laugh that was not at all like one man joining in the joy of another. No, it was clearly the laugh of a man who thought us truly dense. Kvaran knew better. He thought we should know better and the fact that we didn't gave him only modest, wicked pleasure. For the most part, our perceived stupidity multiplied his irritation and boredom with his own life.

"Peace-weaver?" he asked for sixth time. Each time he asked the question his sarcasm grew thicker, like the fat on a finished hog's back. One of the legs of Kvaran's throne hovered over a warped floorboard. The stout, oak throne teetered as he had his frustrating fun. Creak, thump. Creak, thump.

"That's what Iron Knee thought," I answered again. Instead of laughing as he had all along and ignoring my answer, Kvaran grew still.

"He's dead by the knife of an assassin, you ignorant goat's balls. By the One God, what will happen to Dyflin now?" Kvaran looked at his remaining son, Sitric, who'd seen about seventeen winters. He was a thoughtful lad. It was too early to tell if he'd turn into a warrior, but to me the signs weren't good. Sitric sought counsel more frequently than he sought his prey on the hunt. "The damn sentries were probably in on the plot to kill the prince. Unless someone inside the camp did it. You perhaps." Kvaran didn't point at who the 'you' was. He could have meant that I killed Iron Knee or that Sitric, second in line for the throne, had his half-brother killed. If it was Sitric, which it wasn't, at least that would show the lad had some fire.

"The guards were all killed in the same manner as Iron Knee. It was an Irish assassin," I said. I had no proof other than the strange "X" marks in the dead bodies, but the Irish were our only enemies inland from Dyflin – unless it *was* Sitric. I glanced at the handsome young man again. No, I thought. "Could be Ui Neill. Could be Leinster," I said with a shrug. The allegiances of the various Irish clans strengthened and faded with the seasons. During my short time in Dyflin, we'd been allies with each clan separately, or against both simultaneously.

Kvaran dismissed me with a disgusted wave of his hand. I spun on the hard-packed, earthen floor to leave the long, rectangular hall. Tyrkr, who stood with me, moved to follow.

"I didn't mean for you to get out. Don't be such a child." Kvaran huffed loudly. "I just want you to shut up. I'm tired of hearing your voice." His red felt shoes, worthless to any man who had real work to do, tapped the raised throne platform in unison. I was told that the dye to make the fabric of those boots was a custom combination made just for the king. All of the ingredients were imported, proving again the cosmopolitan nature of the city. Sappanwood came from Asia. Madder made a long trek from the desert home of the Muslims. Finally, kermes, a bug whose body produced a brilliant red when processed, was imported from the lands of former Roma proper. All three were blended in a tiresome process to get Kvaran just what he wanted. Most dyers used a healthy amount of urine in their work to get the colors just right. I'm sure that Kvaran's felt was soaked more than once. I suppose if he had trouble getting the respect of his young followers by way of his actions, his clothes ought to do the job for him.

One of the king's hands slid down to a great barrel with new, pale oak staves that sat next to his rocking throne. Kvaran rested his hand on the container and caressed it softly with his crooked, aged fingers. The barrel contained thousands of coins. They were English pennies stamped with Aethelred's handsome face in profile. The eye of the King of England that you could see on the coin kept its focus on you wherever you went.

It was those pennies that had propelled me into upper class Dyflin. They were not minted in England. My friend, Leif, and I sold the coin dies we stole from a mint in Watchet, England to Kvaran. He now had a dozen moneyers working night and day, hammering out the first coins ever minted on the island of Ireland. Many silver hoards, gathered up from the never-ending raids conducted against the Christian monasteries, were melted and reformed into the pennies. I never tried to prove it, but I think Kvaran had his moneyers blend in several cheaper metals to make his precious silver go farther. More and more coins piled up around the throne, making the King of Dyflin appear rich.

But he was far from wealthy. The slow strangle of age and the constricting grip of the Irish kings sapped his strength. That is why Iron Knee had been out swatting the countryside. He attempted to demonstrate a little of the past glory of Dyflin. He wanted to project her strength. Iron Knee, of course, died in a drunken heap by an assassin's hand. So Kvaran was far from rich. Leif and I and our crew, however, were all verifiably rich now. Our coin die transaction with Kvaran and our sporadic strandhoggs brought us hacksilver, jewels, clothing, and longhouses. We were much better off than the king himself, for we could leave at any time and carry our wealth with us. He was wedded to a kingdom that, like his body, was in rapid decline.

Colbain could take the silence no longer. He stepped forward to stand next to me. "King Kvaran, I think that Halldorr's solution has merit. Don't discount it just because he is ignorant of the ways of Ireland."

I was not ignorant of the politics of Ireland. I'd learned firsthand of the politics of the Irish Sea while following my first king, Godfrey, nearly to my early pyre. As for the island itself, a thousand kings in a half-dozen clans continually competed against one another for expanded control of more forests, pastures, rivers, and slave trafficking. Every mother of one of those kings wanted nothing more than for her boy to become the High King of Ireland. That's what I knew.

I was supposed to remain quiet. The king had said as much. So instead of calling Colbain ignorant himself and a bastard to boot, I rammed my elbow up and into his nose. "How's that for a thank you in coming to my aid, you Irish puke?" His head snapped back. His blood dirtied the sleeve of the new shirt I purchased the week before. The red liquid felt warm against my skin as it soaked through.

"Damn, you, heathen," screamed Kvaran. "The thrall gives you a compliment. He says he thinks your peace-weaver idea is good and you strike him – in my court!" The king threw his arms up into the air. "I can't get to Iona fast enough."

Colbain used the front tail of his garment to dab up the blood. Normally, the bastard would whine or protest, but that day he seemed to have a mission. His goal ranked higher than his complaints. "Iron Knee meant for Princess Aednat to be a peace-weaver. I can't say that I saw merit in it at the start, but in the last few days, I've reconsidered."

Kvaran rolled his eyes. His gaunt face screamed boredom and disgust without his mouth uttering a word. He rapped his knotted knuckles on the barrel's lid and a servant appeared out of the shadows carrying a pot of ale for the king. "What makes you think I need the counsel of a thrall?"

"I appreciate his wisdom in these matters," said Sitric. He combed his long, fine beard. Though a young man, his beard had grown precociously. It was not gnarled like that of most men. It was straight, fair, fine and made many men envious, hence his nickname, Silkbeard. He was handsome, with strong bones. He was thinner, more graceful than his half-brother Iron Knee had been. Sitric could have used his fashionable qualities to lure many beauties, Norse, Frank, even Irish to his longhouse.

But the lad was pious, a fact that irked the king and Iron Knee. Sitric was a true believer in the One God, so much so that he followed the commandments, even the personally difficult ones. The women, therefore, he held at bay for now. In so many ways Silkbeard was quite the opposite of his father.

Kvaran stared at Sitric, the son he had with Gormflaith, the woman who now warmed the bed of his Irish rival, the High King, Mael Sechnaill. The King of Dyflin sighed yet again. His sighs exhausted me. "Well then, speak," Kvaran said to Sitric. "Speak your learned wisdom and all that you've garnered from this intelligent thrall." Kvaran stared up at the ceiling of his great hall.

"Colbain tells me that the woman is comely," began Silkbeard.

"And so are half the women of childbearing age here in Dyflin. So are the women of England, Norway, Denmark, and Frankia," interrupted his father. "I imagine that even the women of the Muslims are attractive if they'd ever let them travel past their doorpost. Who cares that she's beautiful?"

Silkbeard looked to Colbain, who nodded. The young prince appeared to gain strength. He put the wooden comb away and stood taller. "I was just starting, father. My marriage to her will bring peace."

"Hog shit!" exclaimed Kvaran. He pounded his hand on the barrel, shaking the raised platform on which he sat which, in turn, rattled the great post that held up the vast roof of his hall. On that post hung a thin, tiny sheet of gold about the size of a woman's thumb. It jingled against the post, making its etching of a man and woman in full embrace come to life. As the last of the sound reverberated away, the servant brought a new pot of ale.

Kvaran pointed to the gold leaf. "That's all a peace-weaver is good for. Plowing! You plow. You sow. You're done. The peace doesn't last – a season, maybe. My father posted that sheet of gold there when he married my mother. It was to bring the glory of the old gods to their bed. All it brought was me and my bitter life. Peace-weaver!"

Sitric was stunned silent for another heartbeat. He looked again at Colbain for counsel. Curious, I thought, that a prince such as Silkbeard sought so low for good advice. At that moment, Tyrkr, our own thrall and fellow warrior, cleared his throat. He did it not to speak or to be heard, for the simpleton had a catch in his gullet. The sound was a reminder from Odin that power can come from strange places – even thralls. Colbain waved Sitric to continue.

"It will mean more land for the Kingdom of Dyflin," sputtered young Silkbeard.

"Go on," said Kvaran, finally interested.

"Someday you will die," said Silkbeard.

"Don't get ahead of yourself," warned Kvaran, but he was at last genuinely smiling. I don't know if it was because his son was demonstrating forethought, or if Kvaran was happy that one day his long life would finally end.

"I meant that your generation will pass. Not just you. Mael Sechnaill, too, will be gone one day. I am of Leinster blood and Norse blood. If I marry Aednat and she bears me sons, they will be partially of Ui Neill blood. I will gain lands in my lifetime from the Ui Neill. My sons, your grandsons, will gain the seat of the High King of all of Ireland. Only it will be the High King of old. They'll hold sway over the entire island. No longer will Dyflin have to play Leinstermen against Ui Neill and vice versa. We will rule them. We will be them."

Kvaran held his ale pot to his chest like it was a newborn babe. He wrinkled one eye and brought the cup to his lips. He sipped loudly, brought the mug down, then quickly took another sip. In his mind, the king turned over the words of his son. Kvaran ceased his grinning. At least he stopped sighing, I thought. Kvaran smacked his lips. "It is my experience that only Christian monks and young fools lusting after foreign tits believe that peace is possible through women." He paused; I imagine conjuring images of those objects of youthful desire. "I've had my time with the tits of Irish women. They are plump enough, soft enough, but the peace they bring is fleeting." It wasn't sounding good for the union. "I suppose if I want a more permanent peace, I'll have to move to Iona and become a monk."

Kvaran brought the pot down and set it on his barrel of counterfeit coins. He yawned while pinching the bridge of his nose.

The king uttered a long, low grunt with his eyes closed. I exchanged glances with the prince. We hiked our shoulders high, not sure if that was Kvaran's definitive answer. Absent a direct response, the room waited. Sitric shifted his weight from one foot to the other as he wondered what would be his fate.

In truth, Prince Sitric didn't think about fate. He thought in terms of Providence not destiny – as in what the Providence of the One True God would have in store for him. So many of the Norsemen I met on these shores were Christian, thinking of and talking in the ways of the God and the Christ. Many days it seemed that it was just me and my fellow Greenlanders who were the only remaining followers of Odin and Thor.

But then my own fate changed. Sitric's fortune shifted.

Randulfr and Leif charged into the hall from their places on the wall. They brought with them news that would begin a process. And that course would usher in a man of martial brilliance. He was to be a man who would win glory and riches. He was a raider who would one day plunder the largest of all prizes. He even followed the old gods, zealously. And I would follow him for many years.

But first, as it often goes, a woman had to arrive. The man of whom I speak didn't even know he was coming or for what reason.

Leif panted. "The ships have arrived, King Kvaran."

Kvaran's chin slumped to his chest. His head bobbed as he muttered. "Oh, you Greenlander ox! We were in the middle of a family affair. Knarrs come and go all night and day. What ships?"

Leif smiled. He never let the misplaced anger of Kvaran set him on edge. Leif's temperament was moderate. His mind, however, was as brilliant as his flashing green eyes. "The very ships you told us all to watch for."

Kvaran looked blank.

"Another family affair," said Leif, reminding the old king.

Kvaran closed his eyes. He rested his forehead on one of his hands as if the thought of what Leif said was more than he could take.

Randulfr took over for Leif. "The woman Gytha and her flotilla have arrived from England. Your sister is here."

And with that, talk of Sitric's marriage to a Ui Neill princess faded into the distance. Soon it would be another union that took precedence.

• • •

Dyflin was magnificent. I have said as much already, but you must understand that I truly mean it. My homelands up to this point were humble, tiny, and sparsely populated. Dyflin was a spectacle. People from all over Europe came to exchange bits of coins and goods in what was once a far-off corner, barely able to sustain her own people. My ancestors, well, Kvaran and his ancestors, built her into a commercial house of power. None of his prowess at organizing a city-state enabled Kvaran to rid the town of filth, however.

We waddled like a gaggle of geese eastward through streets to greet Gytha as she walked up the steps from the quay. Only a portion of what we called High Street – because it curved around the small hill within the fortress's walls – had planking to lift us out of the mud. The rest of High Street and all the other streets were left to become muddy bogs whenever the frequent rains came. It rained two days prior and the mud just began to dry into hard, rutted rocks. I looked up at the sky. More rain was coming. Kvaran sat in a cart pulled by oxen in order to keep his finery clean. The dray rattled and bounced its way forward.

A small boy ran out and tugged on a tail of my jerkin. He held out a comb made from the antler of a red deer. There were three comb-makers who plied their trade on High Street. They made just enough precious coins to plant gardens in their fenced yards each year to feed their dirty families. "A half penny," the boy said. He was full of hope, for I bought a comb from him the previous week. I also bought one from him the week before that, and the week before that. I don't know if the boy thought I was forgetful and lost the combs or if I gave them away as gifts. He probably didn't think about what I did with them. The boy knew only that the blonde, very tall Norseman would always buy his product.

I snatched the comb and stuffed it into my pocket. It would join the dozen other ones on a shelf in the small longhouse I shared with my men. The only comb I really used was made from walrus tusk and came from Greenland. "Half penny," the boy said again with a smile. His father would have no cause to add another bruise to match the one around the boy's left eye if he brought home money.

My purse jiggled in my hand. I fished out a handful of coins. Like little legs my fingers walked over the various metals. Several pennies that had been hacked in half sat there looking like the mid-month moon. I passed them. So too, I bypassed two Kufic coins from the Muslim world. I found my target and dropped it into his grimy hand. He didn't have to look. The feel of the full penny meant extra fish for his supper. He laughed as he splashed through receding puddles back to his father's shop.

"Not even a thanks," grunted Randulfr. "The urchin takes advantage of you."

"He probably eats better than all of us," Tyrkr huffed. The boy didn't. We ate like kings.

"You're too soft for every sad story that comes your way," said Leif. "It's been the same with you since we met." Leif's father finished raising me when my real father was killed and I was foisted on the Thorvaldsson family. I was a part of Leif's earliest memories. "The old gods made you strong and ferocious. You fight like Odin. Yet you have a heart that breaks when you see the weak. If I didn't know better, you're primed for becoming a Christian." He didn't know how right he was back then. While it is another part of my story and doesn't fit here, I did eventually become a Christian. So did Leif. He would one day single-handedly convert all of Greenland to the new faith. "Your weakness, at least what Freydis perceived, is why my sister would not have you as her husband." Twice, I thought. Leif's sister turned me down twice.

We passed the street where the town's mead halls and single wine tavern sat. They would come alive as the day died.

Now that the sun was high, though hidden by low clouds, the wood-turners and coopers hammered out their trades. Their idle conversations were interrupted with whack, whack, scrape, scrape, whack. Occasionally, a father would shout angry instructions to his son for incorrectly turning a scrap of oak.

Dyflin was grand.

Kvaran slept on a backless chair in the dray. His elbows rested on his knees. He was bored with the city he'd made strong with ruthlessness and vigor. He was bored with his long life. He was tired.

Sitric and Colbain rode horses at the head of our gaggle. Sitric sat up tall on a strong bay. The beast's black socks were splattered with mud, but its beauty was not diminished. Its black tail flicked in the air. The long black mane rested gently on its powerful neck. Its deep brown coat was shiny even in the misty conditions. The prince, the next King of Dyflin since Iron Knee was gone, was regal in the place of his exhausted father. The servant, Colbain, rode a sorrel with a fat belly that made his thin legs stick out wide. The stable boys liked to over-feed that one.

We passed the tear-shaped marketplace at the heart of the city. The thrall auction was inactive today. It drew large crowds on Mondays. Instead of selling slaves to the highest bidder today, merchants from all over set up their small wooden booths to sell pottery from Frankia or amber from the Baltic.

Our group stopped suddenly, well before the palisade and earthen wall. I peered around the leaders to see a procession approaching from the opposite direction. I was surprised to see a young woman on horseback in the van. Armed warriors in two neat columns followed behind her on foot with spears foisted high.

Tyrkr noticed her, too. "Lovely young thing," he said.

"Must be an attendant to Kvaran's sister," I shrugged. "No sibling of Kvaran could be that young."

"A servant leading Gytha's train?" asked Leif.

"We've got one at the head of ours," said Randulfr, rolling his eyes while pointing a thumb at Colbain.

"Where's my brother," barked the woman when she stopped in front of Sitric. She had dark eyes, serious. Those eyes were narrowed with gentle feet of crows at the corners. Gytha was not as young as we first thought. The woman appeared stern, but not angry. Her guards stood silently in the mud.

"That's Kvaran's sister?" asked Leif. "There must be forty years difference between them."

"Welcome to the Kingdom of Dyflin, Aunt Gytha," said Sitric with a bow.

Gytha's features softened. "Sitric? Little Sitric? You came just to my knee the last time I saw you."

"Little Sitric?" mumbled Randulfr. We laughed at the thought.

"I guess I should have known you'd be bigger. I know you are called Silkbeard these days, now that you can grow one." We chuckled again at the expense of the prince. "The name suits you."

Sitric was eager to turn the course of the conversation. "My father has come to greet you. His cart is coming up now." I looked up at Kvaran who groaned in that annoying state between sleep and awake. The cart's driver snapped the oxen in order to thread them through, toward the front of the line. "We received word just a week ago that you'd visit. We didn't expect you so soon."

"I've got business to which I must attend." She was serious again. Gytha sighed with a resigned, far-off gaze. Her sighing was only remotely related to that of her much older brother. It made her appear thoughtful to his aggravated.

The dray arrived. The driver stopped, buffeting the ride. Kvaran awoke with a start, sitting up as straight as he could. "What do you want, sister?" We slopped through puddles to get close enough to hear. Over our shoulders an argument broke out in the marketplace. A Finn trader was accusing a resident of giving him shaved coins. Kvaran looked over at the two and their bickering. "Oh, the One God has given me many years." He sighed. My muscles tensed at the sound. "Some of them were good."

"Your city does well, King Kvaran," offered Gytha.

Kvaran gently clapped his deformed hands together. "I don't have the kind of time left that you do, young sister. Let's finish this efficiently. Yes, my city does well. Yes, the Irish are constantly attacking. No, Iron Knee is not here. He's dead, killed. Yes, Sitric will do fine as king when I am done. He's too thoughtful, too willing to negotiate. In that he is only somewhat like me." His old shoulders pinched toward his ears. "But, my two sons split my one personality between them. I have both aspects, you see. Sitric got the political facet. Iron Knee got my strength and my brutality. He's dead. So the chances of Dyflin expanding without him are zero."

Sitric and Gytha exchanged glances. Gytha appeared embarrassed, but Sitric shrugged, implying that his father was essentially correct. The puppy prince knew this diatribe well.

Kvaran filled the silence that followed his soliloquy. "I'm tired. You know all there is to know about Dyflin." The bickering from the marketplace grew louder. Kvaran clenched his jaw and pushed himself upright in the cart. He pointed to Randulfr. "You, take a man and arrest the Dyfliner. Take half of what he has in his purse and give it to the Finn trader. Take the other half for my treasury." None in my band had ever formally sworn fealty to King Kvaran and he never asked us for it. I suppose he was happy to have any young, new blood who were foolish enough to follow his commands.

Randulfr and Tyrkr walked off and seized the townsman. Kvaran clapped his hands together like he batted off dust from a job well done. He lowered himself down to his bench.

Gytha stared at her older brother.

"Oh, I have to think of everything. Even for others," said the king, slouching down on his elbows. "I arrest the townsman to keep the foreign merchants coming. As long as they keep rolling in, my city is the envy of all towns in the Irish Sea and the North Sea combined. The cheating Dyfliner was probably shaving the coins anyway."

"I'm sure you know best," said Gytha with a polite nod.

Kvaran lifted his red boot and poked the driver with his toe. "Take me back to my hall. Sitric can deal with this woman. I don't have time for her nonsense. It's cold today." It wasn't.

The driver looked up at Silkbeard, who gave a resigned nod. After much backing and adjusting and moving forward and backing, the cart was turned around and clattering over the ruts back to Kvaran's hall on the hill. The king somehow steadied himself and fell back asleep.

"The king has worked hard all his life," offered Sitric as weak explanation.

Gytha gave a thin smile to her nephew. "Great men have one of only two possible endings. Either they quickly die young while on the ascent with swords in their hands and spears in their bellies, or they fade away long past the peak of their power. Though King Kvaran's health gave him the latter path, he is still great. The skalds' tales will say that much."

Sitric bowed at the neck to his aunt. "Agreed. Now, are you willing to discuss your business with me? Since the Battle of Tara, my father has found many reasons to disappear to Iona and reflect on that long life. Even when he is here, his mind is not. Much of the administration of the city had fallen to Iron Knee. With his death, it now falls to me."

"I am sorry about your brother," said Gytha.

"Half-brother," corrected Colbain.

"Thank you," said Sitric to Gytha, ignoring the servant. The prince tugged at the reins of his bay and the beast began to turn. Gytha slid her horse between that of Colbain and his master. We parted the way and let them file toward the hall. "How do your lands in England fare?" asked Silkbeard.

"The lands are in good hands," Gytha said.

"Surely," said Sitric. "I don't remember ever meeting your husband, but he must be a good man to run so vast a territory in England for Aethelred. Likewise, he must be a good man to have won the favor of my aunt."

Gytha's smile was weak. "He was a good man. He's dead."

Silkbeard studied his aunt while their horses ambled beneath them. "I'm sorry. But as you said, there are but two ways that great men die. Your husband took the first path."

She smiled again. "Thank you for making the attempt to care for my feelings. Your father would have never done the same. But I said my husband was a good man, not great. He died of a fever two months ago, as common a death as any."

Sitric rode on. I wouldn't have known what to say to a grieving widow. If I said anything, it would have been some drivel about love or something. Sitric was young but occasionally wise. He changed the subject. "Your lands are in good hands today, you said. A son? A steward or caretaker?"

"Neither." Gytha held up her hands. They were thin but strong. Two prominent, blue veins snaked over the back of each palm. "My hands are good enough for now."

Silkbeard pointed to her hands. "I should think so. You've got the blood of conquerors coursing through your veins."

"Nephew, I'd say you received the good half of your father's blood. Any man can be a brute. It's rare for a man to have the right words, rarer still, to have both strength and brains." I remember thinking that she was wrong. Not every man can be a brute. I've fought dozens of battles against many men and most want nothing more than to turn and flee. They want to run home and rut with their women. They want to turn the sod of their fields. I wanted those things too, but couldn't have them. So, I became a brute, a fiend in war. And I knew that I was rare. Whether or not I had any brains remains an open question.

"Why have you come to us, then? If you've got lands to run, why are you here?" asked Colbain.

"This blood is true. I do have the blood of conquerors in me." Gytha tapped her heart before waving a hand over her groin. "But I cannot make a daughter spontaneously spring from here. I need a husband to continue our line. I need a husband to protect my lands from the English lords who want to expand their territory. I need a man to kill the wolves like you and your piratical raiders. I come to call a Thing for the express purpose of gaining a husband."

"Why come to us?" asked Sitric. "Why not call an assembly in England. There are plenty of Danes living there."

"A Dane is not a Norseman. I want my lineage to be Norse."

"Why not go back to Norway?" asked Colbain.

"Who is this with the bleeding nose who keeps talking? I've already answered one of his inquiries." asked Gytha. Colbain brought his palm up to find that his nose was again spewing out blood. I grinned at the thought and rubbed my elbow. His blood there had begun to dry and flake.

"He's an advisor," began Sitric. "You met him when he and I were both young."

"He's a servant," I said. "Sometimes he carries dung buckets, other times he lugs them when they are full of piss."

"And that is one of those common, mindless brutes you mentioned," said Colbain, wiping the crimson on his fat horse's mane.

"Children," warned Silkbeard. He looked at his aunt. "Why not go to Norway for a husband?"

Gytha studied Colbain, then me. I don't know what she thought of either of us. She kept her emotions hidden behind that indomitable expression. "Two reasons. The first is that if a Norseman is still in the fatherland, then he is, by definition, not adventurous. I want my children to be ready to sail and to conquer if they must. I want them driven. So I want Norsemen who do not live in Norway. Secondly, I come to Dyflin because it is the city where things can be gotten. You want slaves? Go to Dyflin. You want amber or silk? Go to Dyflin. You want pottery or leather or wooden goods? Go to Dyflin. You want a hardy Norse husband who travels the seas and has built himself into something? Go to Dyflin."

Silkbeard chuckled.

"Because I am a woman looking for a husband, you laugh?"

The prince shook his head. He pointed to Kvaran's hall. "No, I'm laughing because when your ships slid to shore we were in there discussing whether or not I'd marry a local princess. No matter our troubles, we are indeed a city where things can be gotten."

And so the great, wet, sloppy city-state where anything in the known world could be acquired had become the destination for royal weddings.

• • •

    Our crew sat in the back of the great hall where Kvaran held his court. Dyflin's king was known as a patron of many poets. Skalds, especially Icelandic, for they were the best, had come to entertain the king and his clingers. The night after Gytha arrived, these poets of old did their level best to create merry. Two now stood on the raised dais, dueling so-to-speak. One began a familiar tale of the ancient gods and left off in a place of his choosing. The second skald had to take up the yarn and finish it in a most unexpected way. Back and forth they did this all night. Perhaps it was the ale, but it seemed to me that with every passing round of storytelling, the lies got better and better.

    "I should raise my hand as a suitor for Gytha," said Leif. One of the skalds lowered his trousers, showing his rump to the crowd in order to portray some of the action in his story. A nearby spectator threw a slab of beef at the man. It slapped the poet's hairy thigh and adhered for a moment before sliding down his leg. The crowd, thoroughly rowdy, laughed and threw more food at the skald. I suppose it meant that he lost that particular round. The winner, a man called Grouse-Poet, bowed to the crowd.

    "What do you have to offer the lady?" I asked. "You're an exiled runt."

    "I am exiled today, but in a few short years, I'll go back to Greenland. I'll inherit a jarldom someday. I bring that with me to the table," answered Leif.

    It was more than a few years before we could return. We had nearly a dozen remaining. None of them would seem short. "Hmmph! What would a woman with lands in England want with a red-haired cub from Greenland? Your lands are worth nothing to her," I said. "They're worth nothing to me! And I love them."

    Leif waved me off. "You still yearn for my sister. You pine and worry and fret. A woman is what you are!"

"And what is wrong with that!" said Gytha, who approached our bench with a sloshing mug of ale in hand. She sat down next to Leif.

Leif looked at the comely, older woman. I had not once, not ever, seen him tongue-tied, but he was then. "Nothing, I . . ." he began.

I burst out laughing at him. We all laughed at the man/boy. Randulfr and Cnute pinched their lips and turned red while they tried to muscle down their swigs of brew. They shook with silent laughter. I vibrated. Ale from my mouth wormed its way into my nose. It dribbled out onto the moustache of my beard, burning the insides of my nostrils. I swiped a paw at it to wipe the ale and snot away.

Gytha let us sit there for a good many moments. Her playfully disgusted look made us laugh harder. Leif smiled, but sheepishly drew invisible shapes on the table with a finger.

"What's wrong with being a woman? Isn't that what I asked, Halldorr?" said Gytha, torturing Leif.

A cough came before my answer. "Aye, that is what you asked the lad. Apparently, he is too shy to answer," I chuckled, breathing in and out of my nose sharply. I pinched my nostrils, trying to clear away the eye-watering pain.

"Well now I'm asking you," the woman said. "Well, out with it."

The rest of the men, now including Leif, erupted. "I, uh, there's nothing wrong with being a woman, if you're a woman," I said. I thought of more to say, but decided to shut up. There was no sense in offending the sister of our host.

"That's it? That is where you leave it?" Gytha asked. Our crewmen beat the table with glee. They watched me roil like when a young boy toys with an injured fly. Gytha was the torturer. I was the wingless insect. None, especially not Leif, came to my aid.

"Well," I began, stalling for any potential interruption.

"Just shut your mouth, Halldorr," said Gytha. She grinned. Her mouth was filled with straight teeth, a truly rare sight. "It is obviously a question that goes beyond the capabilities of men, at least this bunch of men, to answer."

The skalds on the raised platform finished their duel. The winner was hoisted on the broad shoulders of some of Kvaran's best warriors. They paraded him around the room. The victor drank a long draught from each table that he passed. Gytha offered her cup up as he came by our bench. The poet glugged it down. His handlers moved on to the next.

Our band slowed their chuckles to a halt as Gytha snatched up Leif's hand. "Now young Leif, I heard that you would put yourself up as a possible suitor. I encourage you to do so, but keep in mind that I am independent."

"I'd have it no other way," said Leif. The young man was as smitten as the rest of us.

"Let me finish," said Gytha. "And I want a man with experience on the sea. A warrior, too. He should be a soldier. I know of no good way to hold a claim to land other than with the power enough to enforce it."

"I have all those qualities. I may be young, but I sailed with King Godfrey. I have experience in the shield wall. I bring lands with my name," Leif protested.

"Ah, I see. And since you mean to push your notion after I tried to let you down easily, tell me again where those lands are located," said Gytha.

Leif shrugged. "Greenland."

"A land on the other side of the world filled with nothing but rocks, ice, and fog, I'm told," answered Gytha.

"I am a warrior. I fought beside a king," said Leif, throwing his shoulders back. The lad should have stopped fighting. Normally he was prescient of such things. But it is the truest of all truths that men do foolish things for women.

Gytha grinned with a pretty smile. "And remind me what king and kingdom that was."

"Godfrey. He was King of the Isles," said Leif.

"Oh, the Kingdom of the Isles that fell to ruin within one year of his death," said Gytha.

That wasn't fair. "His entire leadership was killed that day. We were there. We saw it! How could you expect his kingdom to carry on after that?" I asked.

"Because he never should have been in that position in the first place." Gytha rested a gentle hand on Leif's shoulder. While it bordered on patronizing, the woman appeared earnest. "No, you men have more to learn when it comes to war if the only man with whom you've studied was the eager King Godfrey. Leif, you may certainly come to the Thing and make your appeal, but I think you've heard my answer. Word has been sent to every corner of every kingdom. I'll have dozens of Europe's finest vying for my hand."

Leif's shoulders slumped. "Oh, come on Leif, don't start whimpering," said Randulfr.

"Yea, you'll wind up looking like a woman!" said Tyrkr. Even Gytha laughed at that.

A rumbling from the king's platform began to hush the crowd. I didn't need to turn to see that it was not Kvaran who stood to give a speech. The old king never stood to address his court. In the days when Iron Knee yet lived, it was he who ran the celebrations and gave rousing talks about how Dyflin would grow into a more powerful kingdom than it had ever been. Those days were gone.

From his throne, Kvaran prodded Colbain with a stick, literally pushing him to the front. The servant held his hand aloft, further quieting the crowd. "Let's see what this Irish worm has to say," said Gytha. Her eyes twinkled. I liked that woman. She'd make a rare wife of some fortunate husband.

"King Kvaran has given me the honor of conveying great news to this assembly of fine men and women," said Colbain.

"Find me a fine man in here and I'll pay handsomely," called a woman's voice from the crowd. We laughed.

"No, no, we mustn't joke," scolded Colbain.

Gytha mumbled. "If we cannot joke, what's the point?

"I bring news that is too fine to be contained. The king's own sister has come to Dyflin in search of a husband," Colbain continued.

"I've got something for her!" shouted a man. We all, including Gytha, laughed at him.

Kvaran took his stick and swatted one of his lieutenants, who promptly arrested the gabby offender. The crowd grumbled their way to silence.

"Good. Now that we have your complete attention, I'll continue. King Kvaran has sent word to all the proper kingdoms in the lands across the continent. Suitors, rich and powerful, will come for her hand. It will mean strong alliances for Lady Gytha and for Dyflin. Her lands and ours will be secure." The crowd cheered. "But that is not all." Colbain looked back to Kvaran and Silkbeard, who stood next to his father. "The king and prince have agreed in principle to negotiate the marrying of Prince Sitric to Aednat, daughter to the High King of Ireland, Mael Sechnaill."

Colbain had paused after this announcement, expecting applause. None came. You see, most people don't think of the world in a strategic sense. They go through life operating on a day to day basis using common sense and versions of loyalty. They use no strategy. The assembly that night did not see that by marrying off Silkbeard to Aednat, it would mean stronger alliances against other foes. They thought only about recent affronts, honor, and common sense. They knew only that Gormflaith, our king's recent wife, abandoned Kvaran for the High King. The crowd understood only that we'd been off and on at war with the Ui Neill for generations. They sat in silence, trying to work out why they should celebrate a union of their prince to the very people who had killed our sons time and again.

"It will mean peace between our peoples," said Colbain in explanation. "It will mean more lands for Dyflin." There was not even a tepid applause. Kvaran muttered something to Colbain. The servant nodded his understanding. "And, of course, the union will mean a united front against those cattle and wife thieves, the Leinstermen!" This was the applause line for which Colbain had been searching. The crowd clapped and cheered. I did, too. The only thing that might be considered better than a dead Ui Neill soldier was a dead Leinster warrior. In either case, I suppose, it meant another dead Irishman, which was always a good thing.

"And," Colbain continued when the merriment died. "Kvaran is so confident in the blessed union that he leaves Dyflin for Iona, his blessed sanctuary up north in the Irish Sea."

Gytha muttered, "His place of retreat and hiding in order to flee the difficult negotiations that will come with the marriage of Silkbeard. He'll do anything to not have to look into the eyes of his former, traitorous wife." I grunted in agreement. The woman was quick in her gauging of the political landscape.

The servant finished his talk. "King Kvaran leaves the city, the kingdom, in Prince Sitric's able hands, confident that a marriage will be arranged and that peace with the Ui Neill will reign."

It was Silkbeard's turn to mutter orders to the servant. Colbain leaned back to listen. He again nodded his understanding. "I am privileged to offer a series of toasts." Colbain raised his empty hand. No one cared that the worm – I liked Gytha's word for him – didn't drink. The assemblage stuck wooden, silver, or tin mugs into the air as they prepared to swig. Ale sloshed. "To our fine King Kvaran! To his sister, our regal Lady Gytha. A toast to the prince! We offer a toast to Aednat, may she be a peace-weaver. A toast to the High King, may his mind see the wisdom in our plan. To Queen Gormflaith, may . . ."

"That's quite enough!" barked King Kvaran, frowning at the mere mention of the woman who ran away with a more powerful king. The hundreds of cups of ale stood frozen at the ends of outstretched arms. "The prince will now speak for himself since it's clear that the Irish don't know a thing about keeping their tongues." The king folded his arms across his chest and pouted.

Colbain shrunk. Prince Sitric gave him a frown that matched Kvaran's as he stepped to finish the toasts. "What the thrall was going to say in his toast to the former queen of these lands was this. May she find that her groin, frequented by many a king, is made weak. May it be like a fragile bridge with too many travelers crossing. May it fail. May her groin and womb be her ruin." Even Kvaran smiled when the crowd cheered. Clinking was followed by gulping swills.

The pup did have a way with words. He proved that he could take a bad situation and make it good. Dyflin was under threat from the outside. Maybe the city would be able to expand under his reign after all. I thought I might give the whelp a chance.

Sitric shouted over the growing ruckus. Laughter resumed. Palms slapped tables as lies were told. "My first official order is to send envoys to the High King of Ireland's court tomorrow. Those chosen for such a task will be selected from only the most honorable among you. Upon your successful return, we will plan for a royal wedding. We may have two such affairs within the month!"

CHAPTER 2

We'd be lucky to have one wedding.

I single-handedly destroyed all hopes for my own marital union back on Greenland. Twice.

I would probably end up doing the same for Silkbeard.

Our band of exiled Norsemen and scraggly survivors was quickly becoming richer suckling on the teats of Dyflin and the Irish. It was lucrative, but the recent pause caused by Gytha's arrival was maddening. No longer did we raid. We attacked nothing. We sat inside our walls, helping a woman plan for a betrothal to an unknown man. We listened to ideas for Sitric's grand nuptials. Every few days we took a turn standing behind the city's palisade to stare out at the twin rivers or lolling sheep. I swear to you that I even thought about trying to sabotage the prince's wedding, just to spark some life into my boring days.

I wouldn't have to try. It was my nature to ruin love.

You see, I was a warrior. I cracked heads together. I slipped knives between ribs. I rammed on a man's shield until it splintered. Then I did the same to his face. Back then, before the One God came into my life, I was one thing. I was about destruction. I record this reality, not out of pride. No, I write the words as a way to document facts. I was a raider. All of my people of any note were raiders. I did not negotiate. I did not talk. I didn't act as an envoy.

Only I did suddenly become an emissary to the court of Mael Sechnaill, because Colbain, the untitled worm, said I should. The union between Sitric and Aednat had been my idea, he said. The servant further said that the woman Aednat would trust me. I freed her after all. It was I, who in my drunken haze, spoke out against rape. The princess knew all that. Colbain assured us that her trust would transfer to her father and step-mother. All were reasons I should join the negotiations according to the bastard Colbain. In truth, I believe Colbain underestimated me. He thought he could control me.

Unfortunately, Sitric Silkbeard, the puppy prince, agreed with his servant. King Kvaran, too old and disinterested to care, had merely waved his approval as his longship floated away with the current the following morning. He was off to Iona to sit in a burned out monastery with only fluttering pigeons interrupting his peace.

I never swore an oath to become one of Kvaran's chosen men. None of us, the survivors of the slaughter of Godfrey, were officially pledged to Dyflin's king. It is not that we didn't try. When we first slid into shore, bloodied and hungry from our loss at Dunadd, Leif and the rest of his crew marched through the muddy streets and into the famous hall. We had interrupted a celebration with music and skalds. The party stopped when we, bedraggled strangers to most, strode in. A circle formed around us as we shoved our way through the throng. We dropped to our knees. Behind us, our men did the same. Leif began spewing a host of compliments to the old king sitting on his throne. I think we woke him from slumber.

Just once Colbain opened his mouth to protest our barging in. Kvaran shushed him, allowing Leif to go on rambling.

"And so, we are aware of your past agreement to ally with Godfrey. We know that the two of you often made accords on the friendliest of terms. Our last oaths were to King Godfrey. His heroic passing has released us. We come here in order to pledge ourselves to you, to serve you and your rich kingdom, to be your swords," said Leif with his head bowed. All of us sat there exposed, hands clasped. I scanned the room, braced for a blind attack.

Kvaran gnawed the inside of his cheek. "I gave ten of my best men to Godfrey the Incompetent. Good for them that they now reside in Odin's hall. Bad for the future of this city. How is it that none of mine survived Godfrey's final debacle, but you can come limping in here today?" asked the king with a raised eyebrow.

"The slaughter was thorough, lord king. Out of our hundreds, we are all that is left," said Leif, pointing around the room with his nose.

"It would be better that you died with them," Kvaran huffed. The king, rapidly snapping his fingers, turned to an attendant. "Bring me drink. Be quick."

"We are able fighters," Leif began.

"Close your mouth!" barked Kvaran. He sighed. "You may stay, but I'll not have you as my oath sworn men. I don't need to bring the ire of more kings down on me. I don't need to go provoking Maredubb from Wales. He's vassal to Aethelred of England after all. I'm not a fool. Godfrey was." Kvaran paused. He took labored breaths, not from any respiratory distress. No, he breathed the toilsome breaths one would expect from a king that wanted only to die. "Perhaps you can be of service, in a fashion. But to think that I'd have a band of vagrants sworn to me is preposterous."

We slowly stood and looked around the room that day, melting into the crowd. Our embarrassment didn't last long, however. Iron Knee, alive and well when we first rumbled into Dyflin, took us on many strandhoggs. I think originally Iron Knee believed we might be killed early on by an enemy's club or a stray Dyfliner's arrow. Then, he and his father would be rid of us. Perhaps they could even build a bond of friendship with old enemies once he reported our deaths to those across the Irish Sea. Quite the opposite occurred. Iron Knee found that we plied our trade well. We were journeymen butchers. We slaughtered the Irish like fatted calves. Iron Knee came to realize that Godfrey, though foolish and dead, had indeed taught us how to kill and take.

Within that first month, through Colbain, the king graciously reconsidered his refusal. He offered us the chance to swear fealty to him again. Equally as courteously, we declined. We had no fear of royal reprisals, for by that time we learned just how precarious was Kvaran's hold on that sliver of Ireland. The king needed every single body he could muster. We were his bodies. Free to do what we would – mostly.

That was over a year ago.

I now rode a palfrey that was outfitted well enough with richly adorned kit, en route to Mael Sechnaill's hall. Magnus, our helmsman from Greenland, went with me because Sitric allowed me to select one man that I trusted to come along. I would have selected Cnute, for he was as dedicated to me as Tyrkr was to Leif. However, Cnute frequented the alleys. He gambled for anything, on anything. It was as sure as a sinking stone, that as soon as Cnute's head crested the waves and he was again financially sound, that he clutched onto a new set of bone dice that pulled him below. I couldn't risk Cnute getting into a fight with a simple Irish soldier to whom he'd lost his latest fortune. So Magnus came.

Colbain led us. Colbain! The bastard servant led our party. Sitric put a worm in charge. We were a band of Norsemen being led by an Irishman who was but a step above the lowest thrall. That fact chafed me more than if I had ridden my palfrey without trousers.

"We should detour east for a time," I said.

"The High King's court is northwest," protested Colbain.

"So we should go northeast," I answered.

Colbain scoffed. "And you are Iron Knee's fearless warrior. So afraid of what might happen that you run the opposite direction."

"Actually, the opposite direction would be southeast," said Magnus. He was a fine man at reckoning a direction and at putting the worm in his place.

"Oh, you're a fat man's goiter!" said Colbain. I chuckled. Perhaps the worm wasn't as bad as I thought. Fat man's goiter, I still giggle about it today.

I took pity on the servant. "I tell you we should go northeast because that is where Thor's Woods lies." I pointed to our rear where fifty horsemen rode, heavily outfitted for war. It would take a demented or serious Ui Neill war party to make an assault against us. "Many of the men you now purport to lead are followers of the old gods, as are Magnus and I. The solstice is nearly upon us. We ought to go while we have the opportunity."

Colbain frowned. "Sitric wants us to secure a union."

"And we will," I said.

Magnus was nodding. He pointed to a heavy, sloshing skin filled with mead that bounced at his charger's hind quarter. "I brought extra just in case we found the time. What difference will a day make in a marriage meant to last for decades?"

"And with all my kinsmen slowly becoming Christianized in these Christian lands we conquer, our old gods and Thor's Woods may one day be gone. Allow the men this chance," I said. I ought to have just told the men to go and they would have gone, regardless of what Colbain said.

Colbain, to his credit, mulled over my request. At last, he said, "No. We are on a mission from the next king of Dyflin. We don't stray from our task."

I shrugged. One tug on my reins to the right and I edged off the path, heading toward Thor's Woods. Magnus followed. So did our small army, no questions asked. I called over my shoulder, "You had the chance to order the men to a time of revelry and reflection. You could have made friends. Now it is I who has made the army happy." I smiled wickedly to the servant. I was such a child.

His shoulders sank. Colbain peered down the path toward the unseen High King's court. By the time his gaze returned to our band, the last of our soldiers had filed off the road. They offered their thanks as they passed me by. The Irish servant, properly put back in his place, nudged his beast after the men.

• • •

The westernmost reaches of Thor's Woods were filled with scrub trees and grasses. What had once been a thick, old growth forest was now a torched and ragged landscape. The Irish burned it in a raid some years before. Along the narrow path we followed, charred earth, black and scorched, could still be seen. Only the hardiest, occasional mature oak still grew to the sky. Even these were now disfigured with bark torched off and pitch-colored spindles for branches on one side. The other side – it could be said it was still alive – had remnants of ridged bark. Higher up, near where the forest canopy used to be, two or three stout limbs remained, pushing out bright green leaves, the only visible sign that the trees were oaks in the first place.

Further on, the remains of carvings of Odin, Thor, and Freyja sadly guarded the way. The Irish had desecrated them. Thor had criss-crossing axe marks that pocked his face and hands. Odin, my father's one-eyed god of poetry, had his other eye carved out by the knife of a diligent Irishman. Freyja had one of her tits lopped off. In its place a talentless artist had painted the shape of someone's exaggerated manhood. All three of the giant figures were badly burned.

The entire forest and those monuments would have gone were it not for Thor, who intervened back then. It was said that the fire raged for three days until our god of thunder sent in a terrific storm from the east – an unlikely direction – to preserve the heart of his sanctuary.

"Irish dogs," I muttered as I pulled my palfrey up next to one of the vast carvings. I rubbed my hand across its shoulder which was the height of mine as I was mounted.

Colbain curbed his horse. "The Norse have done far worse to hundreds of churches throughout Ireland. Monasteries, nunneries, homes, villages have all been targets of your people."

"What do you care?" Magnus asked. "You serve Norse Dyflin. You benefit when your masters gain."

Colbain studied his horse's dingy brown mane. "I'm Irish," he began.

"An Irish steer," I muttered. "Your balls might as well be lopped off and fried up for dinner."

"And you're a cockless rooster," said Colbain. The more names he called me, the more I was growing to like him. "I'm also Norse, though you don't know that, do you?"

I didn't. I removed my hand from the sculpture and wiped the soot onto my shirt, leaving behind a dark smudge.

"You can't go to Mael's court looking like that," said Colbain as he pointed to my unkempt clothes. I was normally somewhat fastidious compared to those around me. But I had a reason for wanting to appear exceptionally dingy.

"I can. It's what they'd expect of a pagan Norse warrior. I'll let you and handsome Magnus here, be the pretty ones," I said. The worm frowned but said no more on the subject. We pushed past the fire's residue. Slowly the sky slipped away and was replaced by the ever-present canopy. The shade was cool and dark. The forest floor was open as the thick leaves above prevented all but the sturdiest of plants to sprout. "So, bastard, how do you know that your father was a Norseman?" I pretended to study him closely. "I'd be surprised that even the idiot from the lowliest village in Rogaland could sire someone like you."

"You're a bastard," said Colbain.

"No," I said. "You're the bastard. I'm an orphan. There's a difference."

Colbain chuckled to himself.

"What?" Magnus asked.

"I'm an orphan, too. We've got that in common, Halldorr."

I pretended to teeter off my horse. "Say it isn't so." Magnus and even Colbain laughed. "Tell me your tale of woe," I said, feeling magnanimous.

"Aye. It is one of woe, I suppose. But in the end, it's all worked out for good, for me, for Ireland even. You know that's in the word of the One God. It says something like, 'in all things God works for the good of those who love him.'" Since learning to read in the Latin text, I can verify that the One God says that through his word. And I can further say that given enough time, it is entirely true, even though immediate circumstances may say otherwise.

We slowly pushed our beasts up a hill. One more ravine and its creek, then one more hill and we'd be in the most sacred of all spots in Ireland – to a pagan Norseman, that is. "My mother was a young teen pledged to be married to some Irishman of no wealth." Colbain spat a wad of phlegm onto a moss-covered rock. I don't know if it was from spite or a bug flew into his mouth. "He was a tanner who worked in a stinking hovel outside a monastery town in Leinster. The men from Dyflin came. They killed the tanner. A Norseman raped the woman who became my mother."

"At least you can praise the One God for that," Magnus said.

Colbain's eyes narrowed. He fiddled with the bulky, sheathed knife swaying at his chest.

"I mean," said Magnus, rolling his eyes, "at least you weren't raised to be a tanner who worked in stench all day."

Colbain dropped his hand.

"How do you go from being a bastard offspring raised in Leinster to a servant of Dyflin's royal family?" I asked.

We splashed through a winding creek and ascended the last hill. Colbain shrugged. "How does it all happen? My mother died. She had a growth spring up on her chest wall." He pointed to his armpit. "It grew and grew. A cancer the doctor said. He put a poultice of yarrow and herbs on it and gave her a mix of wormwood and basil to drink."

"I thought wormwood was for gas," I interrupted. "What good will it do a cancer?"

"Shut up, Halldorr," said Magnus.

Colbain frowned at me, but continued. "I tried the concoction once. It was terrible. My mother changed the wrap and drank the medicine just as she was instructed. The tumor grew so that she couldn't bring her arm down or forward. In a few months she began speaking in gibberish. A week later I was among the men who threw dirt onto her corpse."

"How old were you?" I asked, feeling ashamed for my earlier outburst.

"Five or six. The monks at the monastery took me in. They thought I'd be good at emptying their piss pots when the winter fell around them. It turned out that I had an aptitude for learning. Within a year or two, I was wearing the robes of a monk, well on my way of becoming one myself." Cobain shrugged again. A man's shrug says much. I've shrugged so many times in my life I cannot hope to count. A shrug demonstrates a certain acceptance of fate. He's resigned to the way that the norns, those spinners down at the roots of the Yggdrasil Tree, have laid out for him. Don't mistake a man's shrug for complete defeat, however. Oh, no. A shrug says that he's at peace with what has happened. It does not mean that a man will cease fighting like a wounded, cornered bear when faced with new adversities. That is what Colbain's shrug told me that day. I was beginning to like him. I wouldn't tell him, though.

"One day I told the abbot that I didn't want to be a monk. I just couldn't do it. The idea of being cooped up in a monastery, praying on the hours was like a prison sentence," said Colbain. "The abbot told me that I could travel the world. I didn't have to stay in Ireland. Irish monks were in high demand all over for their proficiency in God's word and for organizing centers of learning. That's what the abbot said."

"Obviously, you're not a monk," I ventured.

Colbain laughed. "I ran away that night. I meant to head west toward the River Shannon, but I was so young and stupid that I went north. After an evening or two of travel, I accidentally worked my way onto Dyflin land. A rider from Queen Gormflaith's entourage found me crouching among the king's herds – back when Dyflin still had decent grazing lands. I was gnawing on a raw fish I caught in a creek with my bare hands. He dragged me to Gormflaith. She took pity on me and here I am."

"Silkbeard's mother, the woman who is now wed to Mael Sechnaill raised you?" Magnus asked.

"In a manner," Colbain said simply. "She saw that I was fed and clothed. I received basic instruction. I became their servant. The queen is a splendid woman."

"Queen Gormflaith was quite a woman, I'm sure," I said. "But now she ruts with the enemy."

Colbain tightened his lips. "Gormflaith is a superb woman regardless of what man spills his seed into her! She's kind, intelligent, and loving."

We were close to sacred ground. I didn't feel like torturing the Irishman so I held my hands up in surrender. "And now you go to the wonderful queen and her new husband to barter for the marriage of her son to her step-daughter?" I summarized. The politics and family trees on Ireland made my former residence on the Isle of Man seem normal.

"No," said Colbain, who pointed down the hill into the dark glen that held our heathen sanctuary. The servant wore a broad grin. It was mostly tooth-filled except for the single canine tooth that had been knocked out one night by a drunken Iron Knee. "She comes to us."

• • •

Queen Gormflaith sat among the wooden monuments while mounted on a tan destrier. The beast was muscled for war. Its powerful shoulders could have carried two men my size with ease. So petite was Gormflaith that the horse seemed to float as it paced back and forth on the well-worn grounds.

What worried me was not the former wife of Kvaran, nor her spirited warhorse. No, she was surrounded by twenty-five armed riders. They hadn't seen us yet.

"Ride them down?" I suggested to Magnus. The blade of my sword was already drawn an ell. Magnus was nodding.

"Not a good way to make a favorable first impression as a diplomat," cautioned Colbain.

"They are on Dyflin land," I whispered. "We have the advantage – for now."

"Queen Gormflaith!" shouted Colbain. "What a tremendous honor you bring to Dyflin today to come to Thor's Woods!"

My balled knuckles rammed into the servant's cheek. He yelped and tipped out of his saddle. Magnus and I each drew our weapons. The men who trailed behind us down the other side of the hill did likewise.

Gormflaith's Ui Neill warriors seized spears and swords. They kicked their horses between us and the queen. Gormflaith calmly nudged her beast forward among the back row of her men. "Colbain?" she asked. Her voice betrayed no concern. It certainly was not the wavering sound of a woman who just watched a host of mounted Norsemen emerge on the hill above her small band.

Her lack of worry troubled me. "Brandr," I rasped. "Take two men and scout south. Send three others north. Make sure we're not being lured into a trap." He poked the men he selected for the job as he pulled away.

The Irish servant crawled back to his feet. He winced and lightly touched the growing blemish on his face with a delicately extended finger. Colbain groaned. "Yes, Queen Gormflaith. It is I, your servant."

"You're not her servant, you Leinster sewage," I whispered. I wanted so badly to rush the Irish below for having the audacity to stand in Thor's Woods. My feet pressed hard against the stirrups to look up and over the growing line of men to my sides. Brandr was now gone. He would need a few moments to scout out our situation. I chastised myself for not sending a screen out in the first place. Then to save my own ego, I remembered we were on Dyflin lands and should not have had any reason to be so cautious.

"Then why does that monster next to you strike such a dedicated man?" called Gormflaith. She was stalling. I knew it. I thought I knew it.

Colbain climbed up into his saddle. "You'll not answer the traitorous woman," I said, scanning the forest. I saw only oaks and alders, no skulking Irishmen.

The servant opened his mouth to defy me. I raised my hand again. He clamped his lips and leaned toward me. "Listen to me, Norse Raider. I know nothing of true war. I nearly melt in battle. But I am smart enough to know that building a rapport with the woman to whom we are sent in the first place does us no harm." He looked into my eyes. His cheek was turning from red to green. "We talk for a little longer. You've sent your scouts. When they come back safely, which they will, and give their reports, it is then you may make your decision to battle or not. But acting hastily now will demolish Kvaran's and Silkbeard's plans for peace."

I wrinkled my nose and grumbled not-so-silently. The bastard was right, of course.

Moments ticked by. "May I answer the woman without reprisal?" asked Colbain.

It made me happy that he asked. "Do what you will."

"Our band's leader hit me because he, too, is dedicated. While I am faithful to the House of Kvaran and Queen Gormflaith no matter where she rests her head, this man fights only for Kvaran. He is not quick to trust," answered Colbain.

I wanted to redden my knuckles and his chin.

Gormflaith laughed out loud. She prodded her destrier forward another step with a nearly imperceptible flick of her wrist. "For that your companion is wise. Understanding the politics of Ireland takes a deft mind. Perhaps your warrior there is not just a thug." Her eyebrows lifted. "I, however, require more than just an adroit mind. I don't merely comprehend the politics of this island. I control them." Gormflaith pointed to her temple and then danced the fingers of both hands in the air like a puppeteer. Her horse twitched its neck as the bouncing reins tickled its skin. "You know this, Colbain. You'd be wise to inform your violent and intelligent companion." She chuckled again. "You are welcome to come down to your pagan sanctuary, men of Dyflin." Gormflaith finished with a sweep of her arm as if she invited us into the High King's hall.

"I should think so!" I shouted down. "Your words of invitation mean nothing. We are on Dyflin land and we'll move where we please."

The queen smiled thinly. She lowered her reins and rested her hands on the tan beast's withers. "There is no doubt about that," Gormflaith said. "But at the moment even you are on my schedule. When your scouts return and tell you that there is no trap waiting to spring, you again have my invitation to ride down with us and enjoy the coming solstice."

My biceps tensed. The woman, though correct, was belittling me in front of my men. She was belittling all of Dyflin in front of her guard.

Brandr rode up. "Nothing," he said.

"And the other way?" I asked.

"Scouts say nothing," said Brandr.

"Ahem," muttered Colbain. He indicated with his head toward the waiting Gormflaith.

"Don't take too much pleasure in being right, worm," I said.

He did. Colbain didn't use words, for he didn't have to. The smirk splashed across his face said enough.

To Brandr, I barked, "Set a perimeter with rotating guards. It won't be said that I ushered us into an ambush." I straightened myself a little taller in the saddle and called down to the queen. "Make a path! Warriors of Dyflin come." I squeezed my knees into the ribs of my small palfrey. It carefully inched its way down the slope. "Make way!" I called. My men funneled behind me. Brandr set about placing sentinels.

Gormflaith backed her destrier the way it had come as her men glided their beasts to the side of the road. When a trail wide enough for four riders abreast opened, the queen halted her horse and waited for our approach. No Ui Neill soldier sat next to her as a shield from us, the enemy. I could have rammed my heels into my old horse's belly and cleaved the Leinster-born woman in two before anyone could have reacted. It was as if the Ui Neill, seeing us approach so slowly, were confident that once we laid eyes on the woman, we'd discover that her blood was impossible to shed.

It was.

Well, of course it wasn't. I mean that a properly placed spear could end her life as easily as it could anyone's sorry existence. Only Queen Gormflaith was not anyone. No spear or any other weapon would ever come within an arm's length of her lovely form. She and her guard had no true fear because no man would dare kill or injure such a creature.

Gormflaith was not young. In fact, she was quite old for a woman, perhaps thirty-five. I say, 'for a woman,' because as you know, the life of a woman is harsh compared to that of a man. If they survive the tortures of birthing a baby, which many do not, they then raise that child. Women repeat this again and again. Now sufficiently exhausted, they form the children from useless, shitting creatures to tolerable adolescents. With the difficult chores completed, men take over. We take those young adults. If they are men, we thump them into what they must become. We toughen them because life is harsh and cruel. If they are women, we take them as wives. The process for these young women is just beginning, but it is a long, repeating process. All along, the now old and tired mother in the first place, continues her fretting. She worries about her sons surviving a battle. The mother agonizes over her daughter's family, over her grandchildren. On and on it goes. The life of woman is nothing but a gnarled ball of anxiety from the day she leaves home. Gormflaith, old enough to physically show the years of worry on her face, was unblemished.

The queen's hair remained radiant at an age when most women's began growing brittle. She wore her blonde locks in braids as was common among my people. The twin braids were long, very long, hanging far down the middle of her back. A bejeweled kerchief covered the crown of her head. The closer I drew, I expected hints and traces of age to reveal themselves. An age spot? None. Lines etched into her face from laughing? Not one. The only hints of age on her glowing face were two vertical lines between her eyebrows, built from years of scowling at her kings and underlings. Even her hands, the only other bit of her skin I could see, remained taut and fresh.

And don't think that it was just her flesh that was comely. Beneath her natural covering, Gormflaith had a framework worthy of royalty. High, sturdy cheekbones adorned her face. Her jaw was strong and angular, though not masculine. Gormflaith's neck was long and lithe. The queen's muscle and fat was as proportionate as any man could hope for in a woman. Her arms, hiding beneath her long sleeves, weren't the sagging limbs of an inactive ruler. They were firm. Her long dress was bunched up in front of her. Gormflaith sat on her saddle like any man, with her knees on either side. This position accentuated her womanly hips and rump. They had grown wide from age and birthing. I briefly imagined clutching a handful of each hip.

"Thank you for averting your gaze downward, Norseman," said Gormflaith playfully. "But I assure you it is not necessary." She waved a hand around in front of her face. "I am right here and you may look."

It was a lovely face, smart and beguiling with a hint of menace. I could look on it all day as long as her eyes didn't look back. They were too intense, too knowing. "I'll look where I please," is what I said back. It was not the best way to address a queen to whom I was to be polite.

Gormflaith laughed and pulled her destrier alongside my horse. Her beast was a full two hands taller than mine so that our heads bobbed at the same level. My back was already rod straight, but I squeezed in my belly and arched my shoulders, trying to get just a finger's width taller. Gormflaith saw what I did out of the corner of her eye. She pursed her lips, squelching a laugh. The queen flexed those great hips and pressed her feet lower in the stirrups. She now grew a finger's breadth taller than me. "We can do this all day if you like."

I sank back down, surly.

Gormflaith giggled. The sound was melodic. I was enchanted.

I laughed with her. I had been enchanted by the woman who left Kvaran. I was lured in by the woman whose body rested with the hated enemy, Mael Sechnaill. I had been charmed by the wit of the queen who, by her own admission, controlled the politics of Ireland like they were marionettes in her pretty hands.

• • •

We drank sweet mead while the sun fell. Dusk came. Dusk went. We drank more sweet mead. Night fell. It was moonless and dark. With the Ui Neill, we drank mead. A great fire burned in the spot that had been chosen by the first settlers of Dyflin when they claimed these trees as belonging to their god, Thor. For nearly two centuries Norsemen had come here to celebrate, to ask favor, and to ask for victory over our many enemies – especially the Irish. We swilled mead with those Ui Neill Irishmen that night. Torches sputtered around the camp, filling the entire valley with a bright orange glow. The oaks, though straight and still, appeared to undulate. The faces of the monuments, carved by masters and brought in from Norway, stared at us in the light. Their eyes followed us. They appeared to wink or blink from the firelight. From my increasingly drunken mind, the immense wooden gods came alive. They plucked me from the ground by the scruff of my neck. They hoisted me into the air and played a game with me. I was their little doll. One-eyed Odin laughed at me as he watched me careen through the sky. Thor held me with my long hair pinched between is enormous fingers. He blew on me and I swayed. He carried me to the carving of Freyja that had come alive like him. Thor dropped my little body. I plopped to a halt right between Freyja's big tits. I nestled in like a baby to his mother's chest. My movement tickled the goddess. She laughed merrily, bouncing me among those bountiful breasts. I slipped through, down into her dress, plunged past her waist, and slammed into the ground where I was knocked unconscious.

We had way too much to drink with the Ui Neill Christians.

"The starry host is in full splendor tonight," said Gormflaith. I opened one eye. She stood tall next to me, peering up into the sky. Her back faced me. I could see that the queen's long braids dangled to below her rump. We were now some distance away from the light and revelry below in the valley. It was quiet and dark enough to, in fact, see all the stars.

I squeezed my eyes open and shut. I moaned, as it nearly pained me to move my eyelids. I was drunk, mead hall drunk. I was drunk like a man gets when he is safely behind the walls of his king's citadel, knowing he has hundreds of guards to protect him from any enemy foolish enough to assault. Only I was outside of Dyflin's palisade. I was one of the men obligated to protect my city from the Irish and there I was drunk with the enemy.

I craned my neck. I could feel that my hair was stuck to last year's fallen leaves. Somehow I had passed out up on the hill and now lay supine on the forest floor. I groaned as I climbed to my elbows. My trousers were uncinched and pulled down to my knees. Only my long jerkin covered my manhood.

Gormflaith turned to face me. The skin of her face was flushed red as if she'd just run up the hill. The queen's chest slowly raised and lowered itself as she drew in large breaths. The cord that tied her dress closed at the top was loose. At her feet was the tunic that she had worn over the dress. She gave me a satisfied smile.

I had been with Freydis when I thought she would be my wife. I knew what it was to rut with a woman. Immediately afterwards, the fleeting ecstasy always waned, leaving you a lump of quivering flesh. My body and, in particular, groin felt nothing like that. My brow furrowed.

"I imagine that your people love the stars. I prefer land and all it has to offer. On it I can navigate by this tree or that town, this rock or that stream. But I can also know my direction by the stars. I've had an old sailor tell me that he reckoned his course by the stars. He said that you Norsemen are the best sailors in the world. He told me you can guide your ships into uncharted waters, with no land in sight, and find your way home. You use your knowledge of the skies and seas to come here and invade. You discover new lands, Iceland and Greenland."

Gormflaith walked toward me and knelt down. She planted a kiss on my forehead. With her dress undone, I could see one of her breasts. It sagged just a bit, like all women's do who have given birth and had the little creatures nurse. Nonetheless, I felt my manhood stir which was unlikely to happen had I just known the queen as she'd have me believe. Gormflaith toyed with me, trying to make me one of her marionettes. Her face was beautiful. Her games might work.

The queen again stood tall and went about getting fully dressed. "Now, that is done." By 'that,' I assumed she meant that we had rutted. I second-guessed myself. How sure was I that we had not? If we had, my mind didn't remember and my groin had forgotten.

"What?" I asked. A cry arose from the drinking men below. Gormflaith's eyes darted in that direction and returned to me. She shook her head.

"Let's not pretend we don't know what just happened," she said. "You've likely just given me Mael Sechnaill's next male heir." I sat up and looked down at my covered groin. I had too much to drink. Another cry, this one louder and less cheerful than the last echoed from the camp. Gormflaith peered down again and gave a satisfied nod. She pointed to my trousers. "Get dressed. It's time to sprinkle the hlaut."

I slowly stood and tied my trousers back up around my waist. The world spun. "What are you talking about?" I asked. "Stars and Norsemen, heirs and hlaut?" I drew in a deep breath and felt my head clear. "I never gave an order to sacrifice a horse for the hlaut."

Gormflaith, fully presentable again, stepped to me. She reached up, snatching my chin through my long whiskers as she shook her head in disgust. "Your orders mean little here. I make no secret that I control what happens in the north, in the west, in the south of Ireland, and, yes, even in the east in Dyflin. I've found that telling a man I am manipulating him and his friends and his enemies makes it all the easier to do so. Your mind will turn on it. You'll wonder what it is I am doing to rule you with every move I make or every word I utter. Like an ox stuck in a bog, your mind is fixed. You can't escape it now. You are like all the others: Kvaran, Mael, and a man you likely don't know, Boru, and . . ." Gormflaith paused as she looked past my shoulder. "Colbain! I told you to leave us alone."

I spun to see the Irish servant springing up the hill. He looked me up and down, scowling. "Queen Gormflaith, I thought you'd want to know the moment the sacrifices were hung. The blood is still warm. It will still run. Why do we do this pagan ritual? Won't we suffer for it?" Colbain planted his feet, intending to stay. He jealously studied the dress of Gormflaith trying to see if anything was out of place.

"Fine. You've done well, Colbain," said the queen, ignoring his questions. Despite that, the servant stood a fraction taller from her praise. "Now, scurry back to the valley and don't come back. I'll be down shortly."

The dejected servant slumped his shoulders and plodded off. "Yes, Queen Gormflaith," he mumbled to the ground.

When he was far enough away, I said, "I don't know what your game is, Gormflaith." I didn't call her queen. "I don't know why you talk of the heavens or why you seek my seed, real or imagined, for your belly, but I do know that I never authorized any of my horses to be killed."

Gormflaith pushed past me. "It's almost like you don't know your own people's history. I was married to a Norse king for many years. I know what the old gods require for sacrifice! Who said anything about horses?"

The shadows were quickly swallowing her. I came to my senses and had to trot behind her to keep up. "I'll not have Irishmen killing my men, solstice or not! They are too drunk to volunteer."

"But I don't mind having some Ui Neill men hung by the ankles and drained if it means that I am drawn more deeply into the hearts of my former subjects. The High King will think me politically adroit. Your men will believe me to be one of their old goddesses. My men will know me to be the true ruler of Ireland."

I stopped her with a firm grip on her shoulder. "But you are Irish! You are Christian! I've known Christians and that is not their way!"

Gormflaith stood still as a stone. She merely glanced at my hand. I felt it burn under her gaze and jerked it away. "They are Ui Neill. I am Leinster. I will be queen of a unified Ireland. I am Christian, but have seen enough of the old gods to know that your people pay them much attention. You, pagan, certainly do. And now you, Halldorr, pay me attention. I have you right where I want you and you know nothing about it. You can do nothing." She spun and walked down into the bright camp.

I blinked in the darkness. My head was cloudy. I gazed up to the stars. They were bright and I knew what direction each of them meant at different times of the night and at different times of the year. I loved those stars, for they meant the sea. I loved the sea for it meant adventure and raids. The rolling swells had propelled me away from Freydis, the woman for whom I lusted. The sea and the stars were a part of me. By Thor!

I looked back down at Gormflaith's swaying hips. She was right. She had me. The woman, though she laid bare all her tricks, still controlled me. My mind was in her hand. She toyed with me. Gormflaith twisted me around her finger like an errant curl of her blonde hair.

I watched her mount a low tree stump. She spread her arms out wide and called together all the men. And I mean all. Both sides, the Ui Neill and Dyfliners came to listen to her words. Though I couldn't hear what she said, I knew that her tongue could make them dance or sing. A flick of her fingers could make them turn on one another and kill. A mere idea in Gormflaith's head could make those men go to war – bloody, maiming, and raping war.

King Kvaran was nothing. Iron Knee had been a toddler. Silkbeard was but a babe. The High King, Mael Sechnaill himself, was impotent.

Gormflaith had proven to me that she was the power in Ireland.

• • •

    I still had blots of blood from the butchered Ui Neill soldiers splattered across my face when we decamped the next morning. In fact, nearly all of the Dyfliners had chosen to be sprinkled with the hlaut. Such was Gormflaith's influence that men who had renounced the old gods felt inspired to go back. The woman encouraged them to follow her in the ritual. Each of the Dyfliners still wore the now flaking black crimson on their cheeks and chests. Some of these were, in truth, Christian. Likewise, each had a devoted priest like my old, dead friend Killian from the Isle of Man. Had any of these dedicated priests, including Killian, heard of our deeds, they would have rightly called them evil. Had one of the new priests who lived within the walls of Dyflin itself discovered the acts of their followers, they would have demanded penitence. No priests would hear of it, however. Killian had died with King Godfrey and no one would convey the news of our ceremony to the rest of Dyflin's Christians.

    The handful of Ui Neill who partook washed themselves of the blood before we left the valley. Gormflaith, too, cleansed herself of the red blotches before mounting her destrier. She controlled the politics of the island, but even she had constraints. The High King's queen would quickly find her influence wane if she rode into his court with the traces of a heathen ritual painted on her fair skin.

    The holy site was abandoned. We took our horses and our empty mead pots on our journey to the High King's hall. Left behind were the totems of our old gods. Fewer and fewer of us worshiped them any longer, but back then my heart was warmed by the knowledge that such colossal images still existed somewhere in the world.

    Now I care little for the old ways. Sitting in solitude in my smoky hovel, I am Christian, decidedly. When the time came for me to change faiths I did so by compulsion – that much is true. But in the intervening years and with day upon lonely day of study and prayer, I've determined that the One God is the truest, purest description of mankind. His word describes the actions of follower and pagan alike. It talks of the pinnacle of our existence – serving him and others. The words convey the deepest chasms of man's heart – thievery, raiding, greed, murder – all of which I'd exhibited.

I was the last of both bands to surmount the hill. I paused and looked back at the smoldering ruins of the grand bonfire. It was the only sign that remained of our having been there at all. A gust of wind – it was dry for that time of year – rushed through the valley and smacked me in the face. It reminded me that there were two other signs of our night spent worshipping in the manners of our fathers. As the breeze rattled old leaves it also blew the two dangling bodies of the sacrificed Ui Neill back and forth. They still hung from the fat boughs of a single oak. Ropes were tied around their ankles with the sailing knots taught to us by our ancestors. They swayed above the coagulating pools of their own blood with their hands outstretched toward the earth. The upturned corpses would rot there. They'd bloat and stink there in the shade of the forest. Their decay would make the cool woods feel hotter as the summer made their flesh rancid. Birds would be the first creatures to find sustenance from what was left of the Irishmen. Pine martens would sniff their way down from their dens in the hills and snag a taste. By the time the branch sagged and the men's sinews lengthened, wolves would be able to nip at them from below. If I was able to return to Thor's Woods on the next summer solstice, I would find two empty swinging ropes with dry, clean bones scattered below.

"The queen wants you to ride with her," said Colbain, who had ridden back to retrieve me for her majesty.

"I'm sure she does," I said.

Colbain glared at me. "It is an honor and you'd be wise to accept."

I studied the smitten servant. "It is an honor you wish would be given to you."

His face twitched. He swallowed a capsule of anger. "Shall I tell her you decline, then?"

I tugged my reins in the direction of the receding line of warriors, Ui Neill and Dyfliners. "I meant nothing by the comment, Colbain." I shook my head. "I mean the lady has you enchanted as much as any man, maybe more."

He allowed his features to soften, but answered not. We rode toward the group at a slow ambling pace. "Don't you think you should scrub the blood of Mael's soldiers from your face before you enter his hall? Shouldn't you tell the rest of the men to do the same?"

"No," I said. "This queen of yours thinks she controls everything. She may. But I want to remind the High King that the Norsemen of Dyflin remain men who lust after the blood of others. Just because the city has fallen on thinner times since Kvaran lost his battle, doesn't mean that our spines have grown weak. Iron Knee is gone, but our martial ethos lingers."

"We don't need to put up a feigned wall of strength because we don't go to plead for peace after losing a battle. We aren't sent to provoke or discipline them. Our mission is one of marital harmony," Colbain scolded.

I shrugged. "Then I suppose Silkbeard shouldn't have sent a man who has given up on marriage as his emissary. If he wanted us to represent ourselves meekly, the prince ought to have sent only you and not a raider."

• • •

The High King was a man between the ages of the dead prince Iron Knee and aged, King Kvaran. I had never met Mael Sechnaill before the day we entered his hall for our matrimonial deliberations. You'd think that I might be nervous in meeting a High King. I wasn't, for I pledged fealty to one king already and now tacitly served another. The High King of Ireland could intimidate me no more than a fangless wolf.

Of course, Mael was long aware of our approach. We had come across many patrols as we made our way north and west, deeper into his kingdom. When I first laid eyes on him he was standing next to his throne, resting a hand on its back. The other hand relaxed at his waist. His body's demeanor showed a man at peace. I could tell he worked very hard to appear casual. One of his legs was planted firmly. The other was cocked so that the toe of his boot rested easily on the broad stone platform on which he stood.

Mael's eyes were not narrowed in anger, nor were they wide in crazed fury. Yet the two blue orbs stood in stark contrast to the ease at which he forcibly held the rest of his body. They burned with intensity, igniting each member of our delegation as we filed into his presence. I was torched for three full heartbeats before he moved onto Brandr, then Colbain, then the rest. Contempt was carried in those rays.

No other Irishman or woman was in his hall. If I wanted to be High King, I could squeeze the life out of him with my bare hands and sit in his throne in less time than it took for you to read this sentence. I didn't care to be just another among one hundred kings of Ireland, though. I was a raider, meant for the sea. I meant to get his acquiescence to his daughter's betrothal, secure Dyflin's backside, and again be at sea, plundering the weak.

I had moved to the center of the room at the front of our band. The king's eyes returned to me after he finished his razing of the others. We stared at one another for a long while in silence. Sechnaill studied every inch of me, though he was careful to pretend to look only at my face. He saw my dirty boots which had tracked in a dried mud trail behind me. He saw my expensive linen trousers, haphazardly stained with dirt, blood, and sweat as if I didn't care a whip about keeping them properly clean. Mael glanced at my hands with their thumbs tucked into my belt. They were dirty. I usually took pride in keeping my hands clean. It was actually the way of my people. We were much cleaner than the filthy Irish or even the dirty English. We bathed once every week. I've known English who washed themselves just once a year. But that day, I wanted to appear to be the barbarian he expected. My father's saex and my sword hung sheathed from the belt. One of my little fingers played with the sword's pommel.

Mael passed his glance over my chainmail. All of the holes and chinks had been repaired so that it appeared rich, but well-used. My armor was what one would expect of an experienced warrior. The High King returned his intense eyes back to my face, the face marred with the dried spots and blotches of his soldiers' sacrificed blood.

We stared again at one another. I wouldn't give him the satisfaction of addressing him first. I was proud of my men. They stood in a ragged order behind me, also silent. Well, they were mostly silent while I studied Mael. Brandr broke wind. It started as a whisper. The fart grew to a flapping rumble. My men chuckled. I wanted to turn and hug Brandr, laughing uncontrollably. I did not, however. I kept my composure even when the stench of Brandr's gas reached my nose.

"Oh, Mother Mary!" exclaimed Colbain, pinching off his nostrils like he was a true lady of English royalty, refined and unused to such things. "Is that how you intend to greet our host?" The servant's question had been directed to me.

My eyes remained fixed on the High King. "I wasn't sure we were guests just yet since we had not been properly received."

"We're in the High King's presence are we not?" asked Colbain. "Isn't that proof enough?"

Brandr's putrid haze reached Mael. His nose curled. One of his eyes flickered, but he remained calm and quiet.

"Boys, boys, boys," said Gormflaith as she entered from a side door. The heavy iron ring rattled when she slammed it shut. "Still seeing who can piss the farthest, I see." The queen had changed out of her riding dress and into finery that could only be imported from the Mediterranean world. No such craftsmen lived anywhere near Ireland. And if the dress had come from those southern realms, it had come through Dyflin. Everyone benefited from Kvaran's trading capital.

The queen stood between the High King and me. She rested her hands on her hips, those magical hips, and examined her husband, then me. "I'll get this contest of wills over with." Mael Sechnaill's jaw clenched. His face reddened, but he said nothing. He probably told himself that it was his kingly pride that kept his mouth shut. Mael was still waiting for me to address him properly. I don't think what he told himself was true, however. The High King was just as impotent to Gormflaith's power as had been Kvaran, as was I, as was every man in the room. Mael, as High King, was just too proud to admit it. That was a weakness that could be exploited.

Gormflaith continued. "In the pissing contest, Halldorr of the Norsemen wins. You see, High King husband, he is young. His stream is full and thick like his other parts. You are," Gormflaith paused as she mounted the raised platform to Mael's throne. "You are experienced, King Sechnaill." She plopped down in the throne.

Through gritted teeth, Mael said, "Not King, High King. Out of the throne, woman."

I chuckled at the High King's exhibition of powerlessness.

"Wipe that smirk off your face, pagan barbarian!" Gormflaith scolded me. "Just because you can piss farther than an older man, doesn't make you the better! The experienced man lasts longer, much longer. He has staying power. He is relentless. Whether we talk of urine, bedding a queen, or ruling a kingdom, the experienced man wins. So greet the man with the respect due him."

Damn. The woman was good. I was shamed by a woman. It was Mael's turn to chuckle while Gormflaith climbed out of his chair and respectfully offered him the spot. Colbain, to my side, joined the High King in his mirth. I wished that Brandr had more gas to expel at that moment, but his bowels remained calm.

I sighed. "King Kvaran and Prince Sitric Silkbeard send their Christian blessings to you, High King of Ireland."

"Kvaran is no more Christian than you, pagan!" said Mael.

"That has been his past," said Colbain. "But even now Dyflin's king is away worshipping at the monastery on Iona." I glared at Colbain.

"The King of Dyflin is away?" said Mael, intrigued.

"He is on the return trip now," I lied. "Sitric Silkbeard ably runs the city, the trade, the growing army." There was no use in making us sound weaker than we already were.

"That pup couldn't run to the dung pit on time," said Mael. Some of my men chuckled, for it was a fine joke.

Gormflaith bristled at such talk of the son she'd had with Kvaran.

"My son is quite capable," interrupted the queen. Mael clenched his jaw again, but let the matter drop.

"As a matter of course," began the High King. "I negotiate with pagans only on the rarest of circumstances. I will never confer with heathens who come to my hall wearing the blood of sacrificial men splashed across their faces. I've already heard of your deeds." Mael's glance ran from me to his queen.

I bowed. "Then our time here is done. I thank you for your hospitality. I'll convey to Dyflin that you were unwilling to hear what her envoys had to say. I suppose there is always the Leinster clan that will listen." I turned. Colbain appeared green. My men were laughing. They began to lead our way out.

Colbain stuttered. "But, but . . ."

Up on the throne, Gormflaith hissed words to the High King which were incomprehensible to me. It sounded like javelins pierced the air and sizzled into his flesh. My warriors were out of the hall. Only Colbain and I remained.

"Wait," called the High King. "You, in your unlearned foolishness, misunderstood my meaning. I meant that I will only speak to the servant and you. The rest of your band must go." Colbain breathed a sigh of relief.

A smile curled amidst my moustache and beard while I faced away from him. Though the queen and king saved face with their words, I had scored the first point. I closed the hall's doors and the negotiations continued.

• • •

That was to be the last point I scored.

A modest banquet was set for us. The sparse foodstuffs were spread out in the centers of the tables which were arranged in a haphazard manner in the round hall. The tall, thatched roof extended upward from the low, circular wall to a high central peak. Fourteen trees, stripped of bark, but otherwise not altered from the day they'd been felled, were planted deeply into the ground in an arc that matched the room's shape then twisted their way up to support the great roof. Servants fluttered in the dark recesses between the ring of trees and the outside wall, pouring drinks from barrels or gathering dishes from shelves. A few spare shields hung from a loft that was built from the posts to the roof. In the loft was a pile of hides that gathered dust and spider webs. Though the shape and construction of the hall was much different than what my people built, the scene was not totally foreign and could have taken place in any jarl's home.

Colbain and I were the sole occupants seated at a long thick table made from a single slab of Irish oak. It was an ancient piece of wood, the grain darkened with age and showing signs of countless spills from careless maids or drunken guests. We shared a long bench that didn't wobble, a remarkable feat given the uneven, earthen floor. I peeked below and saw that an intelligent servant had rolled up a piece of wool into a ball and wedged it under one of the legs.

Mael Sechnaill shared the head table with his queen, three priests, the local abbot, and his daughter, Aednat. All but the girl eagerly ate venison steaks cut from a red deer. They swilled wine to wash down the meat. Between mouthfuls, the priests eyed us, but especially me. I don't blame them since I had still not bothered to wash my face, even when Gormflaith insisted. The High King, seeing his wife's inability to force me to relent, smiled. I think he reveled in my small victory, even for an enemy, against the cunning woman and said, "Allow the heathen this one thing." The queen wasn't one to stew or huff and she didn't do it then. Gormflaith's mind would already be turning on how she would strike back and gain more ground.

Aednat used her eating knife to play with the bloody steak. Her curling blonde locks were under control as a new batch of attendants had seen to her. I lustfully remembered her naked body and all the naked chests of her maidens from when Iron Knee captured them. It was a most beautiful sight in my mind's eye. I stole many glances in Aednat's direction.

She, too, examined me. Her young eyes didn't convey the suspicions of the clergymen beside her. They should have. I have been a father to a girl. She is now old, strong, and wise – certainly more sensible than I was at her age. There were times, though, when my little girl was young and actually trusted men!

You might think her a fool, trusting men. That is your prerogative. In defense, I offer only that I have seen countless young girls and women put their blind faith in men. Some are born with a developing, innate intelligence that eventually sees the folly of such an act. These women, blessed with the ability to discern, grow into formidable creatures. Gormflaith is such an example. Gytha, King Kvaran's widowed sister, was another remarkable specimen. My little Skjoldmo is one more insensible girl who grew up to be an extraordinary beast — and my daughter is a beast. I've known many more similar women. Others, however, retain hope far too long into their adulthood, in the face of their experience and wits. If they survive, they go on repeating the same pattern of trusting men and being harmed. Aednat should not have trusted me for a moment. It was still too early in her life to know whether or not her keen intellect would surpass her witless wishes.

"Why do we not talk of my marriage?" the young woman asked after allowing her knife to clatter on the silver dish. Flecks of the deer's blood splattered up onto her tunic. Gormflaith shook her head like all mothers or step-mothers would. Aednat peered down at the speckled cloth and shrugged with just one shoulder. The little fire was living up to her name.

The High King glanced down the table at his pretty daughter. His silent face reprimanded her outburst, but he softened the criticism with a grin when Aednat nodded her understanding. "I'm told that is why you are here," said the High King to me amidst the clanking of eating knives and dishes. "The princess has been plain in her description about what happened in my woods. My daughter and her attendants were handled in the roughest manner by the pagan Iron Knee and his soldiers. He takes the princess' servants as captives. He sells them in the Dyflin markets like chattel. Then Iron Knee suggests that he marry my daughter!"

"It would have been a fine match," I said, knowing that, for the most part, it would not have been.

Colbain quickly choked down a dry hunk of bread so that he could speak and keep me quiet. "High King Mael Sechnaill," he began. Both the king and queen acknowledged his address by tipping their foreheads. Colbain beamed from their praise. I thought he might cry as he looked at Gormflaith. "That is but one of the items we come here to discuss, a blessed union under the One God between Aednat and a prince of Dyflin. Sadly," he said the word but didn't sound sad, "Iron Knee has left this world for heaven."

"That man," I said, "spoke favorable words to the One God, but his heart was with the host of strong gods of my people. He did not go to the heaven. No, Iron Knee went to Odin's hall as all proper warriors do." I've told you that I still followed the old gods at that point. I believed men went to one of two places when they died. The bold, energetic men of war ran to Valhalla to celebrate, sing songs, and make war with the chief god for all eternity – well, at least until the Ragnarok. Prince Iron Knee was such a man. Other men – weak, old, infirm, shriveled, spineless – joined the frigid goddess Hel in the frozen depths of Niflheim. From my head and into the core of my being I knew Odin's dwelling and Hel's home to be true destinations. Now, something like a shriveled, aged man myself and follower of the One God for seventy years, I have different feelings.

One of the priests coughed at my mention of the pagan god. Colbain continued on. "But King Kvaran and Prince Silkbeard view a marriage between our two kingdoms as a sign of an everlasting peace between Dyflin and the Ui Neill."

Mael chuckled. He gently set his knife down. His tongue ran over his upper row of teeth, plucking out bits of food along the way. It did the same for the lower row, forcing the short, sculpted beard on his chin to stick straight out.

Colbain waited for the king to speak. When he did not, the servant asked, "What is it, High King? Have I said something wrong?"

Mael smacked his tongue. He took a long sip of wine and breathed out deeply as he set the cup down. "Irishman slave," Mael began, "you speak the truth, yet your years of living amongst the heathens make it impossible for you to see."

Colbain looked to his former caretaker. Gormflaith shook her head.

"Of course Dyflin wants a union. We are the strongest of all clans in Ireland. His power is waning. Kvaran is nothing but a growth on my ass to be pinched off, drained, and forgotten," breathed the king. Gormflaith's cheek twitched. She said nothing. The priests giggled.

"A union would benefit us both, King Sechnaill," said Colbain in soothing protest. I tore into my food, wishing I was on the hunt or in a suitable mead hall.

Mael looked to his priests. All three gave frowns. The abbot, whose followers in his own monastery and his brothers in monk's houses throughout Ireland had suffered greatly from nearly two hundred years of my people's raids, said, "No!"

"My advisors are not currently inclined to agree with you, Irishman," said Mael. He picked up his knife and resumed his meal.

'Not currently inclined to agree with you,' I thought. Oh, the politics of the Irish Sea, the politics of Ireland, the interactions with human beings sapped the life out of me. It was better to die with a spear driven into your belly, bleeding while cradling your innards and crying for your mother than to endure the babbling of diplomats. I wanted to slap my palms against the table, push myself upright, and leave without a word to anyone. Within three days I could find a longship and again be on the waves. I'd leave my friends behind. I'd leave Leif and his knarr, *Charging Boar*, bobbing in the river. I could already feel the salt in my eyes and taste it on my lips. The exhilaration of a raid would be within my grasp.

I didn't do what I wanted. I rarely do what I want. Duty to my father. Obligations to my second father. Responsibilities to my friends. Pledges to a king. All of them forced me to move in directions I'd rather not go. Even when I wasn't fighting on a field of battle, I was a soldier. Soldiers obey.

Don't think of me as a pure sacrificial lamb, though. My actions weren't solely for the benefit of others. The best way for me to again ascend the ocean's hills and careen down into her valleys with true strength at my disposal was to help Kvaran secure his backside. Only then would I have the addition of his wealth at my disposal to go harvest even more silver from unsuspecting, lazy kings.

  I looked over to the fair Aednat. She had sat quietly for a long while as others discussed her future. The way in the icy fjords where I grew up was for women to be hardy. They had to be strong. They were fighters. Even if they stayed at home raising sheep and children, our women had to be fearless and opinionated. "Why don't you ask her instead of those men?" I cocked a thumb in the princess's direction.

  Like a flower blossoms in the sunlight, Aednat came alive. She jumped to her feet and sprang around the head table. The priests gasped. The abbot sighed. Gormflaith's wide, angry eyes locked with Colbain's. Mael wasn't about to argue with a mere girl in front of his enemy and advisors. Rather than lose his temper and scold her, he let Aednat begin her babbling.

  The princess faced me. "Behind me, my father may well be panicking." If he was, Mael was too experienced to let it show. Other than pursed lips, his worry was invisible. Aednat turned and plucked up her father's hand. She kissed it. Stepmother and the princess shared a cool stare before the alliance's bartering chip spun to face us. "The High King has nothing to fear. I am just a young woman. He might think me foolish. I am." She playfully chuckled. "But I am not a drooling idiot. I understand that the daughter of a king has responsibilities that go beyond finding a husband who can provide food and protection so that she may give him a house full of sons." Mael's pursed lips relaxed. He even smiled at the back of Aednat's head. Gormflaith, too, loosened her tensed features. Colbain stared up at her full of hope. I stuffed another mouthful of meat into my mouth.

  "I must marry a man from another kingdom. Otherwise, my worth to my people is wasted. What good would it do for me to marry a Ui Neill?" Aednat asked. I watched her. Her curling long, blonde hair bobbed whenever she came to the end of a sentence as the princess' head placed an exclamation point on every utterance. The woman was right by the way. Her marriage bed would do much to help or harm her father's kingdom.

"I believe I should marry a Dyfliner." So, I thought, Aednat was lovely and wise. I swilled some of the High King's ale.

Colbain grinned and rapped his knuckles on the oak table. Gormflaith rubbed her palms together. The queen said, "High King, your daughter shows wisdom beyond her years. She will make Sitric Silkbeard and excellent bride."

Mael was shaking his head. "Nothing of the sort has been decided. Princess Aednat does me a great honor by acknowledging her duty to the Ui Neill. She oversteps her bounds when she names the union."

By Thor! I was again looking for the door. It was as good as decided and all we did was talk. Prince Sitric wanted to marry Aednat. Princess Aednat wanted to marry him. Talk. Talk. Talk.

"Queen, King," pleaded Aednat. "I have not yet named the union. I believe that I should be wed to a Dyfliner. It should not be an overly pious man, vain enough to be called Silkbeard and related to the evil pagan who captured and abused me and my ladies in the forest. It should be to a man who resembles my father in his vigor and in his principles – a strong warrior, yes – someone with a firm grasp of right and wrong in the Christian sense, yes. Father, I would be honored to be offered to the man, Halldorr, as his wife."

I rolled my eyes. I even chuckled with my full mouth. Aednat was not wise. Her heart led her head. The priests gasped again. The monk sighed. Colbain muttered, "No, no, no."

Mael laughed. It was genuine mirth until he saw that Aednat was serious. He pointed to her chair and opened his mouth to send her back.

Gormflaith stole his words. "Impudent girl! Sit back down where a youth belongs. Just saying such a thing as marrying this brute is ridiculous. He's a common thief." The queen's control was ebbing. Her face reddened. "To think that I would let you marry a man of no consequence shows just how right you were. You are just a foolish girl!"

One of the priests piped up. "And to compare your father's principles, Christian and forgiving in nature, to those of this blood-stained heathen is an affront to your faith and the High King."

"This man," began Aednat, stamping a foot. The gesture made her appear more childlike than she was. "The brute as you call him was the only one among the pagans to speak out against raping my ladies! He was most certainly opposed to harming me in any way. He has strength *and* sense enough to know when or when not to wield it. Are those not principles by which my father would live?" He hadn't thus far. I don't believe he ever raped a woman, but plenty of his Ui Neill warriors had forcibly wormed their ways into the crux of conquered Leinster or Dyflin women.

The High King climbed to his feet. His jaw was clenched. He seized his daughter's arm and ushered her to the side door. It creaked open and she was tossed through it with a less than gentle shove. He slammed the slab of wood shut behind her so that the rafters of his hall shook. A mouse that had built a nest among them, fell the long way down, bounced once off a warm hearthstone, landed on the packed floor, and then skittered in a winding path under the same door.

When he again faced his small banquet, Mael breathed in slowly for four or five heartbeats. "Halldorr of Dyflin, you come into my hall and offend me with my own people's blood splashed on your face. I wanted to drain your own crimson from your neck when I saw you. I did not. You came as an emissary and it is the way of a good Christian king to welcome such men. Furthermore, I thank you. If what my impertinent daughter says is true, you helped protect her. In so doing you made an impression on her feeble young and feminine mind and she takes it too far."

"She does," I agreed. Aednat was fair. She was a princess of marrying age. I had a soft place in my dull head and pumping heart for women. I admired her spirit. I appreciated her wealth. But even if I was searching for a wife at that moment, I wanted a woman with hips made for mounting. I needed one who would survive bearing me as many sons as I had fingers. Aednat, a spirited royal, wouldn't stand for whelping babies and pulling on a cow's tits for milk to make cheese.

She'd say that there were milkmaids for such a chore. Well, then I'll wed and bed the milkmaids!

Mael nodded. "I've now said my thanks. We've had a fine dinner. You and this Irishman may report to Kvaran or the inexperienced young Sitric that you made valiant efforts at pleading your case." Gormflaith and Colbain were shaking their heads, knowing what was coming. "King Kvaran of the Foreigners is ancient," the High King continued. "His mind slips. His kingdom descends. I must merely wait until the old man dies and Dyflin's lands might well be mine without lifting a finger. There will be no matrimonial union. Stay the night and be gone by morning or else you'll be viewed as trespassers and not envoys."

I gobbled down the last bits of bread that sat on the table next to my plate before standing to go. Colbain began mumbling a protest, but I jerked him up by his shoulder and dragged him to the hall's main entryway. Before the great door even slammed shut, I could hear Gormflaith erupting onto her husband. She spewed vitriol like the volcanoes on Iceland blew magma.

Our mission failed. In truth, I expected no less. That's what happens when you send a man who is more comfortable pummeling others than talking with them. Kvaran's Dyflin was hemmed in with no new ally. It looked like I was stuck with the prospect of raiding inland, traipsing over well-worn trails, slouching behind bushes, crouching behind a great palisade in a muddy city. The glorious sea would have to wait for a change in the seasons.

And, yet, I was pleased. At least talk of silly weddings would cease.

CHAPTER 3

Silly weddings were the order of the day. I had to forget about my irritation at raiding on land into the various Irish kingdoms. My exasperation at setting aside triumphant sea invasions was put on hold. Something more vexing had become the dominant season of my life.

The Thing where Gytha, Kvaran's sister, would select her next husband was fast approaching.

Earlier in my tale I told you that Gytha's arrival would usher in some of the most magnificent days of my life. I would end up serving a true king. I would become his most trusted protector. I would have a hand in creating a vibrant city where once only a fur trading post sat. I would become a berserker of yore, capable of frightening an enemy to death by the manner in which I held my sword and gnawed on my shield before battle. I would meet the woman who was to become my woman, my wife. She was the first woman for whom I cared and not merely lusted over. Those were to be brilliant years, certainly the most heroic. That is true. But like all aspects of life worth anything, I did not know what the outcomes of the current drudgery would be. I did not understand that the intense widow Gytha would have a hand in shoving me into the future woven for me by the norns.

The bustling population of Dyflin blossomed. There were always transients. Merchants, slave traders, farmers, warriors, and much more often slid into the banks of the city's water thoroughfares for a day or two before slipping back the way they'd come. Mostly they sailed back into the Irish Sea and into the world beyond. Today, however, to the usual suspects' numbers, our working city added Gytha's suitors and their clingers.

They were easy to spot. An English earl or a Norse jarl would proudly strut along our streets. They'd puff out their chests, confident that they'd be the perfect match for the widow. They'd inherit her lands and live a life blessed with largess, more largess than they already had. Behind these peacocks followed their grim retinues. Glittering helmets, shined mail, trimmed beards, and surly frowns decorated these men. I don't know if they could actually fight, but they looked fine enough.

I stood in the road and watched one of them coming toward me. I was on my third idiotic errand for Gytha that day, preparing for the Thing tomorrow. The crowd of craftsmen and women who usually dotted the streets moved to the side to allow the rich man and his guards to pass, giving them a wide berth. Not me. I was young. I was a warrior, proud in my own right, and irritable. I planted my feet in the muck of the road and crossed my arms. You might think positive thoughts of me. You might think that I was demonstrating my strength of will, character, and arms. That is what I thought, too. At the time, I was showing these blustering, temporary invaders that men of Dyflin were strong. It was a foolish thing to do. Thirty-to-one odds. Youth is the only excuse I offer.

The peacock stopped three paces in front of me. I should have offered him a smile, tipped my head, and stepped to the side. I could have trotted off like the sheep dog I was and completed my task. My words could have been welcoming to the man. I said, "Move aside."

"A jarl does not step out of the road for an ox to pass by," said the nobleman. He was a native Norseman, just like me. We should have immediately embraced, talked of home, and parted, agreeing to drink ale late into the night.

"An ox I may be. An ox does not skitter from a rat. He steps on its back. It takes just one crushing blow from his hoof to snap the fanged creature in two." We'd already gathered a large audience. The merchants, shoppers, and seamen who normally hurried about found cause to loiter along the side of the road. Among them was a group of bedraggled warriors whom I'd never seen. I noticed these beat up looking men in the midst of my verbal confrontation because they appeared rough, mean, and among the saddest bunch of sailors I'd ever seen. Their leader was a man perhaps a half-dozen years older than me. He leaned on a heap of empty crates, his arms, like mine, folded across his barrel chest. The man chewed nuts, only occasionally bothering to spit out the shells. When he did, they became tangled in his beard. He watched me, giggling.

"I'm in a forgiving mood," said the peacock. I'd almost forgotten he and his men were there. For certain, I'd forgotten to which trader I was running for Gytha. "I'll be named as the next husband of the widow tomorrow. My power and influence will grow here and back home in Rogaland." He was from the region in which I'd been born. I should take his offering of peace, I thought. When the peacock offered it, I would smile, extend my hand and make a new ally. "So if you, young man, quit this infantile defense of the mud in which you currently engage, I'll forget your indiscretion. I will move on with clothes unsoiled by blood. You will make it to your pillow tonight, alive."

I grinned. My subconscious mind began to give the commands to the muscles of my arms. Unfold. Extend. Shake the man's hand. I even heard myself laughing about it in the future.

But it wasn't me who chuckled. The downtrodden group of seamen now chatted amongst themselves, giggling. Had they made wagers on the possible outcomes of the confrontation in the street, I would have still yielded. At least, if they made and took bets, that meant that a portion of the dirty sailors thought me worthy of continuing my struggle. They didn't wager, though. They giggled and pointed at me, all of them deciding that I had no choice but to give up. Their stout leader brushed off the scraps of shells and nuts from his hands onto his soiled chainmail. He stood to go, clearly indicating that the show was over.

I was arrogant. My youth made me swollen. I had some money and wealth. They only added to my conceit. Though I didn't strut like the jarl I faced, in truth, I suffered from much more pride than he could ever claim. I lowered my shoulder. My feet, I shoved into the ground and in an eye's blink I was propelling forward. The jarl didn't have time to react. His arms were still wrapped around his chest. My arms cinched around his back as my shoulder rammed into the cross of his forearms. I heaved him off the path, one of his boots stayed behind, lodged in the mud. The jarl's back slammed into the road. I crashed on top of him. A whoosh of air raced from his mouth.

But he wasn't done. He used every bit of his strength to jerk his arms free. My grip at his back broke. Soon the jarl had a thumb in each of my eyes as he scrambled around beneath me. He thrust my head to one side, attempting to lay me out on the road, reversing our positions. I couldn't let that happen. I grabbed his wrists and wrenched my face free. I landed my first punch. It was a glancing blow across his cheek. The jarl managed to strike up at me with a balled fist. It smashed into my windpipe. I coughed and gagged.

The jarl quickly crawled out from under me. I latched onto his leg. He struck my long-ago scarred ear with his knuckles. His other hand was grasping for his sword.

"No!" I shouted. I knew that at any moment I would be struck from behind by one of his men. At the time I thought it was fate that I wasn't yet dead. It was more likely the One God's Providence. He had many other plans for me. Among them was not to be killed by a pompous jarl from my homeland. The jarl attempted to jerk his leg away from my iron grip. I then used his own momentum against him. Rather than tug, I pushed on the leg. He toppled over onto his side. His sword plopped into the street's muck an ell away. I crawled up his body, gripping his clothing like the claws of a marten dig into a tree's trunk. I sensed it then. He was flagging. I was resurging.

I straddled him. One of his arms was pinned beneath his weight. The other flailed. His fist hit my legs and my chest. The jarl got one lucky strike in on my groin. Nausea welled up inside me on that one. I swallowed it down, but allowed my anger to rise. I struck him under his arm with perhaps four rapid blows. When he brought his arm down to guard the side of his chest, the contest was over. I moved my target to his exposed area above his shoulders. A hailstorm of muscles, flesh, bone, and fury rained down on him. One after another, my fists took turns pounding the side of his neck and head. His skull was hard and it hurt my hands. I kept right on wailing him through my pain. Soon his screaming stopped and he grew still. My arm came up for more punches.

It was seized by hands from behind. My other arm was grabbed. I was forcibly hauled off the jarl by at least three men.

I realized that my time was over and the jarl's warriors now had me. I might be able to put one or two of them down. Beyond that, I was as good as dead.

Huh! I am not dead, even now. Many days, now that I ache from dawn to dusk from one set of pains and from the gloaming until dawn with another batch, I wish I was dead. If only a brave man from another village would break into my home, confront me, and kill me with my sword in my hand, I could move on. But no, I sit here scratching out the yarns of my youth, waiting and waiting. I wait and wait.

Back then I didn't want to die and I didn't breathe my last that day. The men who had snatched me up were from the unkempt crew who watched from the side. None of the jarl's warriors were within three fadmr of me. They were kept away by a thick screen of ruffians who had seemed to multiply from just moments before. They outnumbered the jarl's guards by four to one. No weapons were drawn by either side. The thugs merely kept the others corralled.

The leader of the street gang bent over the jarl who I had just thrashed. A stray nut fell from his beard onto the injured man's chest. The leader flipped up the jarl's eyelid and let it slap shut. "He'll live. I've seen worse beatings, but not many." The gang's leader unclipped the jarl's belt with its fine sword and placed it around his own waist, over top of the belt and sword he already owned. He stepped to me with an examining eye.

"Oh, lad, Odin's made you for war, that much is sure. But you still have to use this now and again." He shoved a dirty finger into my forehead. "There's no need to kill that man – not today anyway."

"Who are you?" I asked.

He chuckled. "A drifter." The leader had given enough of his time to conversation. He spun and clapped his hands together. "You," he called to the throng of spectators lining the streets. Get back to your business!" He patted the pommels of both swords strapped at his sides. "Your king and your prince don't want you sitting around idle! Now move!" The townsfolk scurried off to their shops aflutter with conversation.

"Ox-foot!" shouted the stranger. "Get this jarl and his crew to their ship. See that they are well provisioned. Escort them down the river and see that they head north back home. Carry the jarl and see that my doctor looks at him."

"Yes, lord!" said Ox-foot. He, in turn, gave clipped orders to the others. They began to point to the quay so that the jarl's troop would turn back around. I was shocked at how confident were these men. Still, they had drawn no weapons. They used sheer force of will to compel their opponents' actions.

One of the jarl's dedicated guardsmen stood rooted in place. He made a verbal sortie. "Why should we not cut you down? We will call to the soldiers of the King of Dyflin and you will be the ones driven away." The ruffians stood firm, nearly disinterested in the soldier's bluster.

The leader called to the man. "You have no reason to attack me or my crews. We just spared the life of your jarl from this man." He pointed over his shoulder with a thumb. "We saved your lives from Dyflin's warriors for they would certainly come to this man's and my aid before yours. We rescued you from complete destruction." He waved his hands like he scattered chickens. "Now go. Go. Forget you came. Live your lives."

The guardsman allowed himself to be pushed back down the path. "Who are you?" he shouted as he receded toward the walls.

"You'll know in time. All of Norway will know in time," answered the stranger. He again walked to me. "Release him." My arms were immediately free. "Now you, too, go about your business. It must be important for you to take the risk you just did. You must be one of Kvaran's men. Or, you are truly stupid. But I don't think so." He sniggered. "I loved the line about the ox and the rat." The man, my savior, began laughing out loud as he walked off toward the heart of the city. His remaining men filed off after him, intentionally bumping shoulders with me.

A tug at my waist brought me to my senses. I looked down and saw the boy from whom I had purchased so many unneeded combs. He held another aloft, wearing a big grin.

"Gifts!" I breathed, remembering my errand for Gytha. I slapped a penny into the boy's outstretched hand and snatched the comb. I was late picking up a pair of swords from the smith. They were ordered by Gytha and she would present them to the man who would be her husband at their ceremony.

The peddling boy did what he always did – disappeared into the crowd to quickly show his father what a fine salesman he was.

I took a last look at the confident band of warriors who rounded onto a side street to attack one of our town's mead halls before I plunged off to do a woman's bidding. That gang's leader, I thought, likely never accepted the silly orders from women. And if he did, he most certainly never obeyed them. He wasn't worried about Things and gifts and weddings. He didn't fret about kings, princes, or ruling. That man was a raider, I thought, natural and pure. He was probably a bad one, unsuccessful, for his clothes and the armor of his men was a mess. But that man had followers and confidence, two items I admired about leaders back then.

I stewed on all this while I sat waiting at the smith's for the rest of the day.

• • •

Cnute, Leif, and I went to the mead halls that night. Brandr, Randulfr, and our other close friends were taking their turns guarding Kvaran's palisade. While our comrades performed their sacred duty as Norsemen, we crawled, sang, and drank our way from one tavern to another. We swilled while standing on tables. Cnute and Leif kissed the whores. I just curled my lips at them, baring my teeth like a surly wolf. We belted out old songs to the old gods. Some of the tunes were merry, others somber. We drank the bittersweet mead rapidly while bellowing the cheerful chants. We sipped thoughtfully and slowly during the sad ones. It was a bawdy time.

When the night was already very long we, at last, burst into the very same hall that the bedraggled sailors from the street now occupied. Their own versions of the ancient songs went on uninterrupted while we pushed through the crowd to find an empty bench. An Icelandic skald told his many tales to a group of drunken warriors in a nearby corner. Cnute pointed ahead to a table that was mostly empty. We changed our course toward it.

Large mitts slapped against our chests. "No further," said a deep voice. It was Ox-foot from earlier in the day. Finally up close to the man, I glanced down at his feet to see the reason for his moniker. Sure enough, the toe of one of his boots was angled grossly to the side. He likely had the malformation since birth. No matter. It did nothing to his ability to get around. The deformity certainly did not reduce his self-assurance. "These seats are taken," Ox-foot said coolly.

They weren't occupied at all. Only the gang's leader and a handful of other men sat at what was mostly a vacant table. The group took turns arm wrestling their lord. Wham! The confident lord loudly pinned another of his followers' hands to the slab. A third warrior shoved the loser out of the way. The next match began.

"There's plenty of room," Cnute protested.

"There's more than enough room for you three to sit outside with your rumps dangling over a dung pit. Afterwards, you can clean out the stinking trench. That is where you belong." My saviors were now making me angry. "Out of our mead hall," commanded Ox-foot. He shuffled his feet to a firm position, expecting me to fight like I did in the street.

"Your hall?" asked Leif, his words were mostly slurred.

At the table, the leader pushed the hand of his new challenger to the oak. The loser went away massaging his knuckles. The man they called their lord downed a large wooden mug of honey mead while one more adventurous hand rose to the challenge. The new man was strong, tall, and eager. He was a head and a half taller than his commander. His chest was like an ancient maple, knotted with muscle.

"Yes, it's our hall. We own wherever we stand. Tonight we stand here. Go." Ox-foot crouched to receive my attack. Though his words told us to leave, the fingers of one of his hands waved me closer, challenging me.

Wham! The leader beat the bigger man at the table. He should not have. I leaned over the stout arms of Ox-foot that blocked our path. "Strange that an old, tired arm can beat even the freshest of challenges all night." The commander looked up at me. "Oh, that's right," I went on, made immortal by the night's guzzling of brew. "These men aren't permitted to win. They're probably told that they shouldn't pin the hand of their fearless leader."

Cnute sighed. Leif groaned. Ox-foot growled, "That's enough. This is your last chance. Go whining off into the night. Tell your precious king to whom you've sworn an oath if you like. Cry to your prince. I don't care. Just leave before I have to make a fun night turn into work." Ox-foot wasn't taunting any longer and he wasn't joking. He fingered a knife stuck in his belt.

"We're not pledged to Kvaran!" I shouted as if that mattered at the moment. Ox-foot and the other guards pushed us back. His hand clasped more tightly onto the knife's grip.

"Let them through!" yelled the leader.

"Lord?" asked Ox-foot. His extended arm kept me at bay.

"It's alright. Let them pass, gimpy," said the stranger.

"But remember what happened on Anglesey just last month," protested Ox-foot. He still shoved me back.

"That was a misunderstanding," scoffed the chieftain. "Now send them my way or you'll be the one sitting alone with your bare ass over the dung hole."

Ox-foot swore under his breath. He jerked his head, indicating we could move by. I gave his beard a playful tug as I went. Ox-foot jabbed my ribs with rock-hard fingers. I liked him.

"Not sworn to Kvaran?" asked the arm wrestler. "How do you manage that?"

"What happened in Anglesey last month?" Leif asked as we sat down around the table. Some of the stranger's guard sidled closer as they prepared to protect their master.

Our verbal adversary laughed. "Ox-foot, go watch the doors. No one in here means me any harm." The guard hesitated. "And even if they did. Could they really do anything to hurt me? Take your men and go." With visible disappointment, the faithful men abandoned their lord. The arm wrestler wasn't entirely devoid of protection, though. He still had two swords strapped at his waist. He wore battered mail, stained with dirt, blood, and ale. His barrel chest rose and fell slowly beneath copious muscles. This man would take one or two of us with him if we tried anything.

And why would we attempt to injure or kill him? He was unknown to us – good or bad.

"They're jumpy," the stranger began. "To answer the green-eyed one among you, just four weeks ago we tarried at Aberffraw, King Maredubb's court."

The three of us looked at one another. "We know the place," Leif answered vaguely. We'd raided it and stolen half of Maredubb's wealth.

"Were you friends with Maredubb or his foe?" I asked, cutting to the point. The man's answer would tell us much.

"Ha!" he guffawed. "Do you really know if a man is with you or against you until the piss drains and the shield wall is pressed?"

He was right, of course. "But that doesn't answer the question," pressed Leif. Though he was drunk, his mind was still as sharp as ever.

The confident man looked at us. He had kind eyes. They were not the type that indicated over sentimentality. No, his eyes said that he was able. This commander was so certain of his skill that he could afford to offer compassion to others whenever he desired. He owed us no answers. Yet they came with gladness. "I was neither his friend nor his foe the moment we landed. It's my business to reconnoiter every kingdom or town in the Irish Sea in case the future demands I fight on its shores. The norns spin. I follow." It was an attitude to which I could relate. "Maredubb's been feeling heady of late. What, with his complete victory over Godfrey . . ."

The three of us held our breaths. "Oh, I see," he said at last. "You were there." He examined us up and down. "You're the ones."

"The ones what?" I asked.

"Ale! Mead!" he screamed over the growing ruckus in the hall. Somewhere a serving maid heard his cry and she came over with pitchers sloshing. Instead of filling the mugs scattered on the benches, each of us snatched one of the basins and drained it. The stranger did likewise. Out of the corner of our eyes we watched the others, draining faster and faster. Ale tumbled down the sides of our mouths, dripping off our beards. Midway through it became a contest. Men make everything a game. We grinned behind the pitchers and chugged faster and faster. The commander slammed his down first, followed by me, and the other two. "Ahh!" he breathed.

"You may drink on my pennies tonight men," he said. "Anyone who survived the slaughter at Dunadd on the losing side deserves my respect."

"How do you know we didn't just run and hide?" asked Leif. I kicked him under the table. We weren't cowards. We fought to the end. And if a man thought you a hero, it was best to allow him that image.

"Because Maredubb brags and brags. He talks and talks when he drinks the ale." That much was true, for his chattering was how we'd found ourselves on his island in the first place, looking for a draugr's treasure. I've written that part of my story elsewhere.

"Maredubb said that a small group of King Godfrey's closest men fought their way out at the final moments. You escaped certain death. He even described you," he pointed to Leif and me, "in case I ever came across you. Maredubb said he'd pay me if I brought you back, dead. He'd pay me even more handsomely if you came alive. That way he could kill you in a manner he saw fit."

The three of us scanned the room. With a snap of the stranger's fingers we'd be bound and dragged down to his ships. We'd be in Maredubb's citadel within one or two turnings of the sun. The commander laughed us. "Oh, I'm not taking you anywhere. I told you that Maredubb began to believe that he was something other than a turd on the outskirts of a once-great kingdom. He started probing my men for treachery. He found just one who was dazzled by the wealth Maredubb took back from Godfrey. One of my men tried to mutiny."

"What happened?" I asked. It was a dumb question, for clearly the stranger survived.

"I killed the traitor." The dirty lord shrugged. "I dispatched Maredubb, too."

"Maredubb is dead?" Cnute asked.

"That's what dispatched means, lad."

We sat there in stunned silence. There had been many a night that we'd gathered with the small band of followers who'd survived the slaughter of Godfrey and plotted our revenge. At best, we'd decided it would be some years away after we gathered wealth and men and ships. Now, this man said that he'd done it in a manner that was like he stepped on the back of a mouse in the thrush.

"Who are you?" I breathed.

"What do you care about the name given me by my brave, beautiful mother before she even knew what I'd become?" he asked.

"We have to call you something," protested Leif.

"You can start by calling me lord," the man said. It wasn't a threat. It was as friendly a reminder as I had ever heard from a man who deserved the respect of others.

"We have to call you something, lord," repeated Leif.

Without asking, the maid had returned with more pitchers. She'd brought another helper with her who was equally as weighted down with the wonderfully bitter piss that my people crave. This time I seized a pitcher and got a few heartbeats worth of head start. The others followed. We pushed that brew down our gullets. It felt like a balled fist punched down into my throat, I drank so fast. It hurt. My eyes watered, but I kept on. I would win this time. I was seconds ahead.

Wham! The commander brought his pitcher down. I finished a moment later and leaned over to inspect his tankard to see if he cheated. He did not. His vessel was drier than mine.

The stranger gave an infectious grin. "Men with whom I've not yet spent the night drinking call me Crack-a-Bone."

• • •

  We'd all heard of Crack-a-Bone. He ruled the Irish Sea. He'd burnt and pillaged the riches of the east in the Baltic Sea. Crack-a-Bone had first made a name for himself among the Kievan Rus. Historically, those people were Swedes, fellow Scandinavians, but Crack-a-Bone spent his adulthood taking what he wanted from Swedish settlements. He invaded Germany, Wendland – everything, everywhere, was his for the taking. Any king, even the mighty English King Aethelred had to make peace with Crack-a-Bone. The now dead and lowly kings, Maredubb and Godfrey, had been forced to consider the whereabouts of Crack-a-Bone and his notorious band of pirates whenever they sallied from their home ports.

  Now I had spent almost the entire night drinking with a most pleasant man who claimed to be the famous raider. He didn't fit the expectations I'd built from his reputation. A sea king who was richer than most land-based kings wouldn't dress like a common brawler. He'd be taller. Crack-a-Bone would be meaner. He wouldn't spend a night laughing and telling lies to men from Greenland like Leif, Cnute, and me. I didn't believe that this man was Crack-a-Bone. But what young man would care about a detail such as truth when another man offers to pay your mead tab until sunrise?

  We drank. Challenge followed contest which had followed competition. We arm wrestled. The so-called Crack-a-Bone won every bout. We stripped to the waist and sweated through glima matches. Here I actually won most. I threw the commander to the ground once. I tossed Ox-foot over a bench filled with swilling men and maidens. We laughed and I helped pull him upright.

  "What is the next game?" asked Crack-a-Bone.

  Someone barged into the mead hall from the outside. Though the morning light didn't yet show on the eastern sky, I could smell that it was close. I thought of the field laid out by the River Poddle where Kvaran's men would practice for war soon after the sun crested the horizon. "Javelins!" I shouted. My head hurt. My belly consumed itself. My pores oozed stench.

"It's a little tight in here for throwing," said Crack-a-Bone. It was a bad joke, but we laughed like drunkards do.

I stood with my recently filled mug of ale. My hand had to rest on Leif's shoulder so that I didn't tip over onto the tabletop. "Down to the practice grounds before the weaklings of Dyflin wake up. We alternate throws. Whoever hits the target's center in less rounds wins. Simple."

Crack-a-Bone jumped to his feet. He, too, snatched up his mug, but he didn't teeter for even a moment. His men began making a hole through which he could pass. "And the wager?" asked the leader.

We hadn't wagered all night. Each event had been about the sport, claiming victory and nothing more. I shrugged with dim eyes.

"Ten pounds of silver to you if you win," Crack-a-Bone offered. We were pouring into the quiet streets. A cat that crouched near the door hissed and ran into an alley. It darted back out past us a moment later with a barking dog nipping at its tail.

"What if you win?" asked Leif. He was always level-headed. Even after consuming too much drink Leif was looking out for me. "Ten pounds of silver?"

A massive band of men, foundering or clinging to one another so they didn't fall over, wound through the streets with the gang's commander and me at the head. "No," the would-be Crack-a-Bone said. "I don't need another bit of shiny metal. I've got loads and loads of the stuff." We pushed up the steps of the earthworks and palisade. A few men slipped or tripped off the side. They hit the packed dirt with loud thuds, rolled to the bottom of the great hill and laid there, too drunk and tired to bother trying again.

"Stop!" shouted a sentry at the top. He held a spear with the business end facing my belly.

"Randulfr," I shouted. "Invasions from within don't go running over the gates to the outside."

"Halldorr?" he asked. "Who are all these men?"

I slapped a hand on Crack-a-Bone's shoulder. It was overly familiar, but I was feeling happy. "This is the man who will give me ten pounds of silver before the sunrise. We're going to Kvaran's training area to test our skill."

Randulfr sized us up. "Hurry. The garrison will be up and out there soon."

"Oh, go wet your pants," I said, pushing past my good friend. The rest followed after.

Leif scurried ahead and paced off fifty long steps from where the targets rested. He dragged his heavy boot in the dirt to mark the distance. "Does anyone have a javelin?" Leif asked.

No one had thought that far ahead. There was suddenly much discussion. Two men argued about something that sounded like it took place five years earlier. They sounded like brothers. Ah, the poetry of drunken warriors blaming one another for not remembering to bring a javelin. I sipped my ale, waiting for a weapon to show up. I grinned like a fool.

One arrived. Cnute swiped my cup and replaced it with the javelin. The wooden shaft felt cool in my sweating hand. I turned to face the target. Only the small amount of torchlight from the timber palisade shed any light on it. I had to squint to reduce the number of targets I saw to one. I bobbed the javelin in my hand once, then twice before my muscles had fully calculated its weight. I skipped, leaned back, stepped forward, and launched the missile toward the goal.

Thump! The sound echoed across the river water. A chorus of cheers rang out after the thud. I leaned on my knees, suddenly woozy, and blinked until I could again focus on the block of wood. I'd hit the target, the noise had told me that much. I couldn't tell just how true was my aim.

Cnute raced to the target to investigate. One of Crack-a-Bone's men went with him to verify my strike. When they returned carrying the javelin, Cnute's smile and the other man's sour face told me I'd done well. I straightened my back up tall and looked down at the dirty pirate captain. "Looks like it will be a short game," I said. The side bets began in earnest. Cnute, faithful to me, but unlucky in gambling, put up his entire coin purse on the accuracy of my arm.

The would-be Crack-a-Bone smiled softly while reaching out his hand. Cnute set the javelin in place. The commander felt it. He weighed it just as I had done. Then he did something strange. He extended his opposite hand out to the side, palm up. It took only a heartbeat for another javelin to materialize. It was slapped into his free hand so that he held two.

I waved at him. "Choose whichever you like best. The outcome won't change."

"Of course it won't." Crack-a-Bone leaned back with one knee raised. Both hands drew far behind him like they were two separate bow strings and his body was a gnarled yew stave. He thrust the foot back down. His chest and those strong arms shot forward. Crack-a-Bone sent both missiles hurling into the air at the same time.

My first instinct was to laugh out loud. But the reverberating thump from the target told me he'd hit it. "So we're tied," I said.

Crack-a-Bone said nothing while Cnute and his man scurried like rats to the target. There was much discussion. Their shadows obscured the butt ends of the javelins. I sipped my ale, awaiting my next turn.

"Come on, Cnute! Let's get this over with. We'll both be richer," I called.

Cnute came carrying one of the javelins. The pirate carried the second one. I hadn't heard it hit the target. I assumed it fell silently into the grass. Cnute corrected me. "I've never seen anything like it. Both missiles were dead on center. Both!"

Crack-a-Bone's eyes twinkled. His smile gleamed in the dim light. Dawn was just cresting on the horizon.

"Every man gets lucky now and then," I said.

Only it wasn't luck. After the second round of tosses the score was four to two. With each successive toss, I sobered more and more. My vision cleared. My aim got worse as I became angrier. I still consistently hit the target, albeit high or low, left or right. Crack-a-Bone's aim was like drops of water from an icicle. One after another, actually two after two, soared true. After just five rounds, my opponent won with ten strikes to my five.

My jovial mood from the night's festivities had decidedly soured. I set the contents of my purse in his hand. It wasn't enough. Crack-a-Bone didn't bother to count it. He dropped it on the packed earth of the training grounds. A few of the shiny pieces rolled amongst his warrior's feet. They let it sit as if they already had ample money. There was no fighting over my scraps, no shoving. One of his lieutenants slowly bent down and carefully gathered them before setting the pennies back into my hand.

"Keep your silver," the commander said. "You got coins from me if you won. You didn't win. Come back to the mead hall. We'll eat a breakfast feast of pork and eggs to soothe your pride, my treat. Before you come, get your comrades – all of your men who used to serve Godfrey. I'll tell you what you owe when they are all assembled."

Kvaran's men began to congregate around us for their morning drills. They didn't know what to make of the rough group of strangers invading their grounds. They were wise enough to give a wide berth, hoping we'd leave.

"Should I be worried?" I asked

"I'd have it no other way," Crack-a-Bone answered. He gave my back a friendly whack as he left with his cackling men.

"What do we do now?" I asked when the last head had dropped below the palisade.

"We see what he has to say," said Leif. "It's time for a little adventure to find us for a change."

"What say you?" I said to Cnute.

"We go eat breakfast. I just lost the last of my coins on a side bet." Cnute frowned at me as if his ill fortune was my fault. Since I lost, I suppose it was. "I mean to stuff a few hams into my cloak so I have something to eat until I can scare up some more money."

It was settled then.

We owed a debt to a man who called himself Crack-a-Bone. We'd go with our haphazardly assembled crew to his disheveled men to find out what he wanted.

• • •

"What's he doing here?" asked Sitric Silkbeard. I hadn't told him that Crack-a-Bone was in his city. The ever-lingering

Colbain overheard us gathering our men. The Irishman toddled then tattled to his prince.

I stood in Dyflin's royal court, dragged there like a truant, facing Sitric. Leif and Cnute were with me. It felt like we were being scolded, though I didn't know for what.

"The Thing is this afternoon," said Gytha. "There are many rich men around town yearning for my hand." She stood leaning on a fat post. Her arms were crossed at her chest. "Or, at least they dream of the wealth I bring. He's just one more in a long line."

Gytha had come to the hall when she heard the young prince shouting. Perhaps he had inherited some of his father's fire after all – a good thing, mandatory even. Maybe the line of Kvaran would continue on, growing stronger than the last generation. I didn't appreciate bearing the brunt of whatever peeved him at the moment, however.

"He didn't tell me why he came. It's not common for newcomers to check in with me," I said a little too sternly. Silkbeard was worked up as he paced the king's platform. He ignored my outburst.

"Is it common for you to thump a rich Norse nobleman who wants to woo my aunt?" Sitric sounded shrill.

I laughed, remembering my fight in the street from the previous day. My knuckles were still raw. Obviously, word had reached the prince. I looked over to Colbain, who smirked. He'd been angry with me since I sunk any chances for an alliance with Mael Sechnaill and his Ui Neill. Come to think of it, Sitric was angry with me for the same thing. Both of them had disappointed their mommy, Gormflaith.

"It's not funny," scolded Sitric. He tugged at the fine hairs of his beard.

Gytha remained in place. "I'm sure the pompous jarl had it coming. They all do," she said. "I've seen more eligible men marching around this place than if you had asked all the kings of Europe to come. I will have many options from which to select this afternoon. One less jarl does us no harm." Gytha used her back to shove herself upright from the post. She came and stood in front of me. I could smell her and it was a pleasant scent.

"You, however, nephew, aren't as free as am I. You don't have that many options for a satisfactory union."

Sitric grunted.

"No, you're handsome enough. You're pious. The Christian women here in Ireland love that," observed Gytha without looking back to Sitric. She stared at me and pushed a firm finger into my meaty chest. "You are the future of Dyflin, nephew. It will be a short future unless you can come to terms with the Ui Neill or the Leinster clans and find yourself a bride. Otherwise, they will brush you into the Irish Sea."

"That's what I'm saying," breathed Sitric. "This man," he pointed to me, "ruined my chances of a wedding with Aednat."

I rolled my eyes. "We've been over that. Don't send a wild bear when you want a tamed squirrel." I thought myself funny.

"And now you cavort with a marauding pagan in my own city!" said the prince, circling back to his concern over Crack-a-Bone. "How am I to convince the neighboring Irish kingdoms we mean them no harm when my own men slaughter Irishmen and hang them from trees or invite the worst of our kind into our halls?"

"We are not your men!" I shouted. "We've sworn no oaths to you or your father. Gytha is right. You'll soon be swept under the waves."

"Thanks to you!" Sitric cried.

"And your mother!" I added. "She's the one who started the slaughter and spreading the hlaut!"

"Say no more on that," warned Colbain.

I walked over his words. "And, maybe this Crack-a-Bone is not the worst of our kind. He's the best. He is what our fathers' fathers dreamt of being. He rides the waves and carries with him our people and our ways to every shore he touches! Without men like him, you would never have been born. And if you had, you'd be knee deep in hog shit in some backwoods Norwegian Fjord!"

"That's not the point," said Sitric.

"What is the point?" asked Gytha. "If you want to grow into the role laid out for you, start by having a purpose when you speak." She was a fine woman. I've said as much before. Strong features. Smart eyes. Perfumed breast. She was to the Norse what Gormflaith was to the Ui Neill, but without the embedded treachery.

Sitric slumped in his father's chair. He looked small and thin. The young man did have some maturing to do if he wanted Dyflin to last beyond one week of his father's eventual death. I waited. We waited for him to state his purpose.

"I want you," he pointed to me, "to do nothing else to impede this kingdom."

I opened my mouth to protest. I'd fought for his tiny kingdom. I'd bled with his brother Iron Knee for this city-state. No other mercenaries in his army could claim to be as dedicated. Gytha slapped my cheek. "Allow the prince to speak. He is finally demonstrating some thought to his words. Give him and his position the respect it deserves." Cnute chuckled. Gytha's commanding stare shut him up.

I wanted to slap the woman back. I didn't. It would only give her more power. Oh, she was something.

"You and your men will swear an oath to me this afternoon at the law-giving hill. It is sacred ground with the bodies of stout-hearted men resting beneath it. The Thing moot will be a perfect place with hundreds, perhaps more than a thousand witnesses to the faith you place in Dyflin. If you do not, you and yours will dangle from the trees. You'll be a sacrifice of peace that the Ui Neill and Dyflin will share. You'll be the tie that binds. It will be the last human sacrifice in all of Ireland. That will please my fellow Christians, be they Irish or Norse. We'll be counted among the great, civilized nations of Christendom." Sitric liked the words he heard himself saying. He nodded in agreement. "At last you'll serve a purpose for something other than yourself."

Colbain irksomely grinned.

Gytha, too, liked the idea. She re-crossed her arms and walked toward the door, sensing that the joy was spent. "Using the assembly called for my betrothal in order to solidify your seat in that throne is shrewd. It's something Kvaran would have done back when he cared." She opened the heavy door to go. "I wish I would have thought of it. You've done well, nephew."

Sitric bowed to his aunt from his seated position. "Thank you, Gytha."

"For now, you've done well," she cautioned with an extended finger. "We'll see how you govern when the politics of Ireland get truly complicated." Gytha slipped out of the hall.

"Perhaps you should pray, sire," suggested Colbain. "The weight of your responsibility descends on your shoulders. We may yet salvage what this man has destroyed. Aednat and parts of the Ui Neill kingdom may still be yours." The Irishman clutched the ever-present knife that dangled from his neck. Sitric grabbed the cross around his.

"Fine idea, Colbain. Dismiss these men," said Sitric.

We turned to go.

"What are you doing?" asked the prince, feeling strong for having just threatened us.

"Didn't you just tell Colbain to tell us to leave?" asked Leif.

"And did he?" asked Sitric. Colbain thought all this was very fun. Any respect I had momentarily built for the man on our mission to Mael's hall was completely vanished. His eyes were narrowed. His smile was filled with manure from kissing the prince's rump. "Did he dismiss you?" asked Silkbeard.

The three of us looked at one another. "No," I said at last.

Many moments ticked by. Thankfully, neither Cnute or Leif ruined our standoff by fidgeting. They stood as still as did I.

"Be gone," Colbain said.

And, believe me, we were.

We collected the rest of our men. The entire way toward our meeting in the mead hall with the so-called Crack-a-Bone, we plotted just how long it would take to provision the sad knarr that served as our longboat. Not long. Before Gytha's Thing even began we could have enough packed to get us to Vedrafjordr. Once there, we could purchase more supplies and make plans about where to go, where to raid.

Any reason we'd had to stay in Dyflin died with Iron Knee. It took us too long to figure that out.

• • •

If you are a Christian who lives in the heart of the Franks, perhaps you've never heard of the norns. Likewise, if you are a young Beiuthook warrior reading this – wait, the Beiuthook people, who adopted me as one of their own when I was already an old man of over forty winters, had no form of writing. They certainly didn't read. In any case, neither of those peoples has heard of the norns. If you've read my tales this far, you've heard me curse them, you've heard me praise them.

The three old hags who knit together the fabric of our lives, the thread of events that makes up our existence, sit cackling among the roots of the Yggdrasil Tree. The three women – what was, what is, and what will be – decide a man's fate by the cords they weave. I don't pretend to know what drives them to make changes for the good or the bad, selecting this string or that. Perhaps if they eat spoiled meat, their upset stomachs steer their anger onto men. It could as easily be rancid ale that stirs them to take a man's safe path and turn it dark. I've heard it said that once a man passes the age of seventy, that the most important episode of his day is a proper squat over the dung pit. I, for one, past my ninetieth winter, am beginning to understand the merriment of a fine bowel movement. Maybe the aged norns each have a solid squat and their moods turn ebullient. The sisters weave in a positive turn for man. I don't know. It could easily be that one of them has a capricious sense of humor.

My life has had many such turns. I plan to go to work with my father. He's dead. I become accustomed to and love my second father. He banishes me. I serve an eager king in Godfrey, who hacks his way to glory, dragging his followers with him. He's killed when a great war axe splinters his false sword and mashes his helmet. His skull turns to gruel. I meet a fighting Christian priest who teaches me rudimentary elements of his faith in a way that I can understand. He dies with his face splayed open by an enemy's sword. You may sense the theme.

But it hasn't all been for the worse when the norns spin for me a new course. My first father died. I was given to a second stout father who cared. I was exiled by my second father for crimes that were not mine. My path took me into the service of King Godfrey, a fighting monarch. Godfrey falls heroically on the battlefield on a cool autumn morn. We flee. I make it to Dyflin and become wealthy, selling plunder from one of Godfrey's raids. From horrible turns, came fine outcomes.

I understand that life is how you look at it. Does it seem tedious, horrible, or unfair? Simply rearrange your thinking. Is it those things and worse? Wait. Sometimes a single day, other times a year will find you in a completely different place. A moment can also be the difference between depression and ecstasy. It has been the case with me.

We shoved our way into the mead hall that had become Crack-a-Bone's headquarters. Each one in our band was surly. Some had begun to build lives in Dyflin. They'd have to flee unless they wanted to pledge fealty to the House of Kvaran and his puppy, Sitric. None wanted to be officially yoked to a house such as theirs, a house whose foundations sank deeper and deeper into the bog of oblivion with every passing year. They feared that one day the High King Mael Sechnaill would rule this tremendous city of theirs. Others were angry that they had somehow been summoned to face a pirate in order to pay off my drunken gambling debts. But no matter the reasons for their irritation at me, our small crew came as ordered. Our men, Greenlanders and Icelanders, all of them of Norse blood, were dedicated to us. They brought their grumbling with them into the small, dark tavern.

"Sounds like you know how to win over friends," said so-called Crack-a-Bone. He sat wide awake pouring over an expansive map on his mead table in the back corner of the hall. Most of his closest men lay sprawled out on the floor from our night of revelry. A few of his highest ranking guards climbed to their feet as we approached, picking our way over the sleeping bodies.

Leif and I peeked back at our mumbling men. They instantly stopped their angry murmurs. "We are here to honor

Halldorr's debt and no more," answered Leif. We were in a hurry. *Charging Boar* needed to be shoved into the river and rowed out to sea before Sitric decided to demonstrate his fledgling power.

Crack-a-Bone chuckled. He returned his attention to the map, swept an extended finger across a shoreline, and whispered something to a lieutenant. The man nodded. He scratched a note on the parchment with charcoal. The man rolled it up, careful not to smudge his writing, and tucked it into his jerkin. He was soon wrapped under a blanket on the floor. I think I heard his snoring join the rest before the commander spoke again. An entire night of celebration can make even a hardened warrior require a cat's nap the following day.

"Eager and sullen this morning," said Crack-a-Bone. "Last night you didn't have a care in the world and suddenly today you wear frowns and wiggle your feet like you've got a woman waiting back home." He studied our faces in the dim light. "Well, I know you don't have a woman, Halldorr Olefsson. Leif here has no woman. Almost none of your men have women beckoning them back home. You're all as free as the raven. What's the hurry?"

He had done some spying to find out about us. It was mildly impressive that he gathered it so quickly. But most people in the city could name us, as we'd won some victories with old Iron Knee. "Let's complete the transaction," said Leif. He was still growing into his mind. Daily, it seemed, he gained breadth and weight and height to go with the aged wisdom with which he'd been blessed. "We've duties to perform."

Crack-a-Bone pressed his meaty hands into the table top and stood. The bench at the back of his knees slid back. One of its legs caught in a dimple in the hard-packed earthen floor. The long seat toppled onto the side of a slumbering man and a dog. The dog was smart enough to yelp and skitter away. The man remained passed out. The bench rose and fell with each of the tired man's breaths. "I'm an easy man. I am. I command my men by doing what I want them to do. They follow. If they don't, I find men who will, who want to share in victories. That said, I am a raider. I've been called a sea king. As such, I expect men to answer my questions. Before I go hurrying my speech to complete this so-called transaction, I want to know why you men seem ready to run." He jammed both thumbs behind the buckles of his belts. It wasn't an overtly threatening move, but I took it that way. I scanned the room. We were outnumbered over three to one. However, we did have an advantage. Most of our coming opponents were beneath our feet and asleep.

Leif and I drew in large breaths. I crossed my arms. Leif set a hand on the pommel of his sword. Crack-a-Bone's eyes fixated on Leif's twitching fingers. "Oh, let's not end it that way." Crack-a-Bone said it in a sad manner. He showed no fear. "You'd send a fair number of my hung-over crewmen to Odin's hall, to be sure. But every one of you would join them. If there be Christians among you, they'd join their Christ. Perhaps that is what you all wish, to rush to the next life. But most men of worth I know, while they don't fear the transition from here to there, don't rush it. They will fight with every amount of wit Odin has given them. They will use every fiber of muscle Thor has laced into their arms. They'll ram, sack, beat, bleed, and grind opponents before they go jumping into the longship that will launch them to Valhalla." Crack-a-Bone – I truly began to believe that he was who he claimed to be – peeled open his buckles and allowed his weapons to clatter to the floor. "There," he said. "I'm naked as can be. Strike me now without an axe in my hand and I'll not wind up with Odin. You don't wish that for me or any man." He shook his head. "Now settle down. Answer my questions and we'll be done with this transaction, as you name it."

Crack-a-Bone was right. Leif and I exchanged glances. We dropped our belts to the floor. "There's a Thing called this afternoon. It's for Gytha's betrothal," I began. I absent-mindedly glanced to the ceiling as if I looked to the sky to find the sun to know how much time we had remaining. Only soot-stained rafters looked back.

"I've just heard that," said Crack-a-Bone. "Kvaran's sister is looking for a husband. You've got plenty of time to get out to the hill and offer yourselves up." He pointed to me. "Halldorr's already eliminated one of the competitors by thumping the Norse jarl. Our meeting here won't be much of a delay."

"We actually don't want to go," said Leif. "We're preparing to leave Dyflin today. We've no plans to return."

"Ah," said Crack-a-Bone. "Fleeing. I didn't take you men for cowards. That is why I intervened in the street. That is why I drank with you and played sport with you. That is why you're invited back here today. I guess I was wrong." He roughly slapped the recently tipped over bench back into place and sat down. "You may go."

"We're not cowards," I answered. "We're not running out of fear. And we are here to pay my gambling debt. We never agreed on my side of the payment. Let's do so now."

"Why are you leaving in such a hurry, then?" asked the leader.

"Sitric wants us to pledge an oath to him and his father at the Thing," said Cnute. He was carefully shoving a half-eaten roasted red grouse into his pocket in order to compensate for his gambling losses.

"And you ladies don't want to take the oaths," said Crack-a-Bone.

"We do not," I agreed.

"You should. King Kvaran needs able-bodied men to serve him and protect this city from the plundering Irish hordes," said Crack-a-Bone now leaning his back against a wall while sitting with his feet long ways across the bench.

"This city is dying. Kvaran was probably vigorous in his youth, but no longer. He is indifferent at best. Iron Knee was ready to lead and fight and push. Sitric will not be a strong king when the time comes. He's pious," I spat.

"Pious or not, you don't know what kind of king he'll be. He'll be a stronger one with your men serving him," observed Crack-a-Bone.

"He's trying to forge an alliance with the Ui Neill," Leif said.

"So," pushed Crack-a-Bone. "Didn't Kvaran do that once or twice? He did the same with the Leinstermen I recall. King Kvaran did so with success."

"But Kvaran, when he did it, and Iron Knee, when he wanted to do it, were negotiating from a seat of strength," I said. "Offering the Christian olive branch is only palatable when you've got victory under your belt. Otherwise, it's the same as loss and surrender."

Crack-a-Bone sat thinking. He rattled the mail that dangled on his lap with his stocky fingers. "So you men don't want to serve Sitric or Kvaran simply because they are not strong. You want to serve only a king who has already won his place."

"No!" shouted Leif. "We're willing to do the heavy lifting, the work. We don't want to be oath sworn to a house that has no intention of even trying to become strong again."

"We pledged ourselves to King Godfrey when he barely had enough oath bound men to fill a leaky longboat. We saw fire in him, though. He had something he wanted to build and we helped," I added.

"Helped him die," goaded Crack-a-Bone. He was enjoying himself. I wished he would just tell me what we owed. We could be gone from Dyflin forever by the midday meal.

"Godfrey did that on his own," I corrected. "We followed our king. He didn't always listen to our counsel."

"So you want a vigorous leader. You want an eager king who wants to expand his holdings. You want to support a raiding king who is brave, who leads from the front like Godfrey, but one who uses his mind and listens to his men when it is appropriate. Is that all that you want?" he asked.

"It would help if he were rich," said Cnute. His jerkin bulged from all the poultry and bread he'd crammed between it and his shirt.

"And rich," agreed Crack-a-Bone. He slowly climbed to his feet on the bench and then stepped up onto the table. He reached a hand up and scraped a rafter. Soot fell like sleet onto his head. The palm came away blackened from the char. Crack-a-Bone looked at the hand and wiped it in the hair of his beard. "I'm afraid that you want a rare man, an even rarer king. Wisdom and strength. Patience and aggression. Wealth and the willingness to share. They're all qualities so unusual to be considered mythical." He bent down and snatched up a loaf of barley bread. It had just one large bite missing. Crack-a-Bone tossed it to Cnute. "There you go lad. You missed this. Now all of you should get going. I can't help you."

I furrowed my brow. "We didn't come here for your help. We came to repay my debt. I lost at throwing spears, remember?"

"That was a fine display," Crack-a-Bone said. "I've never seen a completely drunken man hit five in row."

"You hit ten with five strokes," I said.

Crack-a-Bone smiled. "I did. Now go. You owe nothing."

"I repay my debts! I have honor!" I said stepping up onto the bench on the other side of the table from which Crack-a-Bone had come. I was much taller than he. Our noses met.

"What can you offer me as payment then, laddy?" Crack-a-Bone asked, not bristling. He glared into my eyes. "I'm rich. I'm so rich that I share my plunder generously with my crew. They're now rich. Nothing in your purse or buried under your hearth could make me happy."

"He's rich," observed Cnute with raised eyebrows, no doubt planning his first game of chance against the pirate leader. He bit into the barley loaf.

"I also plan raids down to the last detail when I face a formidable opponent. When I face peasants I strike with ferocious speed. I use wisdom and judgment – mostly. I'm aggressive when it suits me and my men. I pound my enemies into the dust unless keeping them alive and weak is in my interest. I am a sea king. I am a raider. I have all I need and more. But I don't sleep because of it. I don't nap because I'm not lazy. I don't lounge because that would get these fine men killed. I am their protector and benefactor. I am like their father. Odin gives me wisdom and strength, patience and aggression, wealth and a willingness to share," said Crack-a-Bone through gritted teeth.

Behind me Leif dropped to one knee. He clattered against our dropped swords. I spun to see what he did. His head was bowed. Behind him, one-by-one, the rest of our men did the same. Randulfr, Godfrey's old lieutenant, went to his knee. Loki slid down. Brandr descended. Cnute struggled with all his extra baggage, but soon he, too, was resting on one knee amid all the sleeping bodies. "What are you doing?" I asked.

Without looking up, Leif answered. "We've found our way out of running. We've found our way out of pledging to fools. We've found a way to repay your drunken debts. And you may have found a third father."

I was not always the fastest at picking up changes in the wind. Leif was. He saw the wisdom in what he was doing before he even did it. The swells of his intellect finally rolled across the shores of my mind. I turned to face Crack-a-Bone. "If we serve you, we cannot serve another."

He grinned. It was a warm, handsome smile. "You may not," he acknowledged.

"And you'll lead us? We'll be your oath sworn men? We'll fight for you and you for us?" I asked.

"Yes, to all of it," he said.

"And we won't have to serve Sitric?"

"You'll follow only me. If I choose to help the lad, you'll help the lad. If I ally with another, you'll ally with me."

"But we'll be yours and yours only?"

"I don't take kindly to two-tongued, double-oathed men," he said plainly.

I studied his eyes. They met mine, not once looking away. "Whom will we say we serve?" I asked.

He set a hand on my shoulder. "You'll tell the world that you ride the waves behind Crack-a-Bone's famous longship, *Serpent*. You'll say to every tavern maid that you are pledged to a sea king of renown, a man without land, but one who owns the ridges and valleys of the oceans. He places his foot on the shores of whatever land he wishes and I go with him – you'll say that, too. Halldorr, you and Leif's crew will tell Prince Silkbeard this afternoon that you serve Olaf Tryggvason, the most feared sea captain in the world. I've heard my men say these things and they are compliments to me. I take them as such. But me, when I introduce myself, I say I am a humble wanderer, a raider. Call me Crack-a-Bone, I say." He gave my shoulder a shove and released it. "I and my fifty-nine warships will see that nothing ill becomes of you for your vow."

I almost fell off the bench I was in such a hurry to swear my life for this man. Sixty ships! If Crack-a-Bone led an armada of fifty-nine ships, the men I had seen were a tiny fraction of his followers. In that dark tavern, I eagerly dropped to my knee. Before second thoughts could enter my mind, I blurted out, "I, Halldorr, son of Olef, Norseman, swear by Odin and Thor to serve you, to be your arms and armor."

"And counselor," Olaf Crack-a-Bone said. He waved a golden ring in front of my nose. "You'll swear all that on the very Ring of Thor."

No one had ever wanted me to give them advice. But my new lord asked it of me. I could barely save my own life by listening to the thoughts in my head. I clasped the ring between my finger and thumb. "I swear to give advice whether it is heeded or not and take orders until Odin's hall claims one of us."

"Claims one of us, what?" asked Olaf.

"Until Odin's hall claims one of us, my Lord Tryggvason," I said.

The rest of our men gave similar oaths. They pledged their swords and shields, though many called them blades and bark. Some pledged their spears. Sinews and souls were sworn. All, when they kissed that Ring of Thor, promised that their loyalty would be to but one man, Lord Tryggvason. Their lives were owned by another. When the last man had said his vow, Olaf clapped his hands over and again, slowly waking his slumbering troop. "Now, we celebrate the arrival of our sixtieth crew! We drink. We eat." He pointed to Cnute. "That man there has much to share with his new brothers!" We laughed at Cnute. He joined us, hesitantly, as he passed out the food he tried to steal. "Then the lot of us will pack up and we go to the hill east of Dyflin to attend this assembly. We go to the Thing, not to win the hand of Gytha. No, we go to show Prince Sitric what true leadership is and what followers of worth want to see!"

Cheers rang out. The tavern owner and his family were rousted. They cooked and cooked until they had to send runners to gather more food from the peddlers in the streets. We ate and celebrated. Smoke from the hearth danced around us, clogging the hall and our lungs. The fire's warmth made me sweat. Toasts were called. Lies, one upon the other, were told. Crack-a-Bone's men had faced dragons, they said. They had dived to the depths and fought monsters. With every tall tale, my heart latched on more tightly to those men.

The norns, instead of spinning my thread into a ditch, had seen fit to wind in a most exquisite cord. Perhaps what was or what is or what will be had a clean bowel movement that day. Whatever the reason, and in a most improbable manner, I was now a sworn soldier of the man I would follow for more than ten years. I would follow him everywhere. He would grow to trust me with every aspect of his life. I gave my life to him. He would become my third father.

Now he would swat the infantile Sitric for me. He would spank the smug Irish servant Colbain. Olaf Crack-a-Bone Tryggvason might even teach Gytha a little lesson for smacking my face. In that dark mead hall, my day had brightened.

• • •

And it only got better.

Hundreds of free men and free women made their way eastward to the Thing-mount. The wealthy used their horses or carts to ford the River Poddle. Every suitor who had any hope of winning Gytha's heart and her lands crossed the creek's swirling waters on the backs of fine chargers. Those wooers brought with them entourages of mounted soldiers decked out in finery. There must have been several dozen able men who were prepared to present themselves as future, capable husbands that day. The richness of their dress and that of their warriors was meant to awe the choosy bride.

Folks of middling wealth kept their feet dry by rowing small boats across the Poddle. If they had no boat, they weren't left wading through, however. A few enterprising merchants had lowered small crafts from their knarrs and charged people fares to get them across. Traders were smart that way. The roving peddlers filled their purses with coins on the out-going trip. They then napped on the eastern shore, waiting for the assembly to end and bring them the same customers for yet more clinking pennies. Aethelred's face would move between many hands that day.

The poor walked across. Some men carried the tiniest of their children on their shoulders as they trudged through the Poddle. Women grabbed the lowest sections of their skirts, hiked them over their knees, and splashed from one bank to the other. The women of my people are strong – the poorest among them, more so. They lugged rucksacks full of food on their backs in case the lawgiver got longwinded and their husbands squawked for dinner when the shadows grew long.

Olaf Crack-a-Bone, though perhaps wealthier than King Kvaran himself, sloshed through the creek like a common, downtrodden shoemaker. We, his men, dove in after him, sinking to our ankles in the silt and to our thighs in the water. Even after a half-day's worth of ale, my mind was clear. I already loved my new leader.

Ahead, the small plain was filling with congregants. Prince Sitric had a prominent place on the lush, green hillock that had served as the podium for Things since the first Norsemen settled this foreign land. Colbain was there. So was Gytha. She looked beautiful in a long gown the shade of moss on a rock in a secluded glen. Her hair was wrapped in tight braids that stretched down to the small of her back. They swayed as she talked with the man who had been elected this year's lawgiver. I couldn't hear what they said. But from the way he cocked his head and the way his eyes met hers, I could tell the man was smitten with Gytha. He wore a simple silver band on one finger, though. He was married and by the bare nature of the ring I could see that he could not afford to take a second wife. He'd have to suffice with the thrill of talking with the elegant woman.

"That's Kvaran's sister?" whispered Olaf.

"It is, lord," I said.

"Well, she must be thirty or more years younger than the old king!" he said. "Had I known that, I may have entered the fray."

"You still can," I said, chuckling to myself as I compared my lord's dress to the other suitors. We began to push our way through the back of the gathering crowd.

"No," Olaf said. "We've got other business here. Can you be diplomatic?"

Leif and Cnute both grunted. They shook their heads. Olaf giggled. "Neither can I. It's not my nature. But today, you have your first order. Move to the base of the hill where Sitric wants you to prominently vow to follow him. Wait until he asks you to pledge your oaths. Step forward and explain to him that you'd be honored – say it with conviction, lad – but it is impossible for a man to serve two lords. If he persists, leave it to me." Olaf ended his direction with a wink.

My crew and I left the raider and his band. We sliced our way through to the front. Sitric saw us. "You've chosen wisely, Greenlanders." He called all of us Greenlanders though at least half of our original men lay dead on Godfrey's various battlefields and most of what was left had never seen that far flung land. All of us, however, were descended from Norsemen.

"We have indeed, Prince Sitric!" answered Leif.

"I didn't want to have to sacrifice your muscle anyway. It will be a blessing to have you in my Dyfliner army." He was being gracious. That, for one thing, was a sign of maturity. Perhaps he was growing in fits and starts. I can admit it now.

Colbain tugged at his lord's sleeve. The servant pointed up at the sun that peeked out from behind a blanket of ever-present clouds. The Thing's leaders nodded their understanding. The lawgiver stepped forward with his hands extended.

The crowd kept right on talking as if nothing happened. Neighbors chatted about the scourge of the Irish or Kvaran's taxation or how their favorite son just got his first tattoos or their daughter had her first bleed. My people respected kings and the apparatus of government well enough. But they also knew from time eternal that they were free. They'd scratched out meager existences in the frigid north for eons. The sagas told of heroic kings who fought their way to power. Simple men with vigor could become a king in a season. It was the way of my northern kindred. They were loyal to kings because kings gave protection. They did not dread their kings like the English or the Irish or the Franks. My people were free and a lawgiver holding up his hands to quiet them when they were not yet finished telling about how their daughter single-handedly captured an escaped thrall would cause them no pause.

The lawgiver, chosen for his two most dominant traits of patience and memory, stood mostly still. He waved his hands just once or twice to no avail. He called down to our band. "It might be nightfall before we get going." The lawgiver even laughed about it. Sitric and Colbain wore sour expressions.

"Can I help?" asked Gytha.

"If it's alright with the prince," said the lawgiver.

"A woman doesn't really have authority to open a Thing," said Silkbeard.

"I won't be doing that. Just getting their attention," Gytha said. She didn't wait for her nephew's permission. Instead, the woman stepped next to the lawgiver and began speaking. I don't even recall what she said, it may have been gibberish, but it had the desired effect. The rich jarls and ealdormen who traveled across the sea in order to win a rich bride, began slapping their followers quiet. "The selection is about to begin," the nobles hissed. Their whipped men then gave low growls to the free men in the crowd. In but a moment, the plain was silent except for the occasional and lone whine of a baby suffering from colic.

"The Thing is all yours, lawgiver," Gytha said with a sweep of her hand.

The Thing is a most sacred, ancient tradition of my people. It is how disputes are settled. Once or twice a year our free people gather and attempt to circumvent the power of the norns by deciding their own fates. They vote on leaders. They decide which man swindled which man and how much the fine should be. They do their best to step in between a blood feud before too many die. Oftentimes, banishment of one of the clans is the only way to burn out the hatred between two families. Otherwise, it can go on for generations with countless sons and daughters killed. Divorces are settled, weddings announced. All of it happens in a hallowed grove of trees in Norway or on a mountainside in Greenland or on a grassy hillock in Ireland. It is important to impart the wisdom of the spirits that inhabit the natural realms of Midgard. All the Things I've ever attended, but one, have been held in locations separate from civilization. This one was suitable enough. All the Things I've ever attended had another aspect in common. No weapons were permitted. Nothing ruined a peaceful gathering as when the losing side of a disagreement began spilling the blood of the winners. Scanning the area, I saw that no man carried an axe, a spear, a bow, or sword. Each member of Olaf's band had left his belt back in the mead hall.

"Dyfliners and guests!" shouted the lawgiver. "We've much to get to this day. The king's own sister is here to claim a husband." Cheers rang out from the crowd, eager for a show. "After she has made her selection, as is tradition, I will recite a third of the law so that no man may claim ignorance."

"What about the other two-thirds?" shouted a young man some rows behind. "May I break them?"

"Anyone who can perform calculations in his head that quickly will have no excuse if he says he cannot remember what was listed the previous two years!" called the lawgiver. "You know better."

Friends of the young man who asked the foolish question playfully punched his shoulders for interrupting the Thing. They all giggled like naïve youth are wont to do. The group of teens had such joy. Each of them was just a few years younger than me. It was only when the ale flowed or when I rode the waves on the planks of a longboat that I permitted myself such pleasure.

The lawgiver went on. "Once the law is spoken, we have a host of disputes to settle." The assembled residents shouted and clapped. Entertainment was rare in most of the villagers' lives. Seeing one man's cattle taken and given to a neighbor for some offence was often the most excitement commoners would ever have. Not every Norseman found cause to serve in the shield wall. For that, I was sad. The shield wall, though resulting in piss, shit, and death, was the only place in Midgard where a man truly came alive.

"But before we allow the fair Gytha," said the lawgiver.

"And rich. Gytha's not just pretty. She's rich, I hear!" bellowed another man from the crowd. His friends laughed with him. We all joined. The lawgiver and Gytha chuckled with them. Sitric and Colbain were eager to obtain our oaths. They frowned at yet another delay.

"Before the rich and fair Gytha begins her selection process, our Prince Sitric has an announcement to make." The lawgiver stepped to the side of the hilltop.

Silkbeard stepped forward. He received a smattering of polite applause. The fact that he got any was more than he deserved. I didn't redden my hands to honor him because the pup had never accomplished anything. He led because his father had been shrewd, tough, and bloodthirsty. Sitric was known only for his fine beard and his piousness. Leif elbowed me. "Olaf told us to be diplomatic," he warned. Wearing a sour face, I gave three loud and slow claps. "Good," said Leif.

"Dyflin is a pearl in the Irish Sea," shouted Sitric. It was a first-rate beginning to a speech, for the city, as I've told you, was a genuine triumph of Norse raiding, building, and commercial prowess. "She grows stronger by the year." This wasn't exactly true. Her borders continued to shrink. More Irish moved into the city and married Norse men and women, bastardizing our race. But what else should a Prince of Dyflin say? It was another fine sentence, especially for a pup. "I am pleased to offer a public display of the faith newcomers place in Kvaran's House. Men who have fought battles for my dear, departed brother are now prepared to swear an oath of fealty to my father and me today."

The assembly offered much approval. Calls rang out. Their young prince was giving them a show. If men of valor were to bow before Sitric at the Thing, then maybe he wasn't such a wet pup after all. That is what the collection of free men thought. They clapped eagerly this time.

Sitric could sense the slight, positive shift. He grinned and combed his fingers through his whiskers. "I ask for silence as we receive the vows from these men scattered at the foot of the hill. The Greenlanders have seen fit to yoke themselves to us. Those of you pledging, drop to one knee and state your intentions in turn." Gytha gave her nephew an encouraging squeeze on his elbow.

It was time for my diplomacy.

We did not bow. Our entire band remained standing just like the rest of the assembly. Sitric clenched his teeth in anger, but Colbain whispered in the prince's ear. Sitric took the man's advice. He softened his expression, gathering his wits. "The men at the bottom of the hill," he said, "though valiant and true, strong and dedicated, are all deaf." The prince said it with a smile. The crowd took it for the joke it was intended to be. "Now, Greenlanders, bend to take your oaths."

I stepped several paces up the hill. "Lord Prince Sitric, it is an honor that you would ask this of us. We, all of us, would sincerely wish for nothing more than to serve this great city and this magnificent House of Kvaran." I was proud of myself for the lying words I spun. They came easily since Sitric would know them to be spiteful revenge but the gathered horde would not. "We intend to continue to serve all of Dyflin with our sinews, bones, shields, spears. Alas, these fine men before you are unable to speak an oath to your father. To do so would mean that we defy the laws of our ancient people and even flout the laws of Christendom. I've heard it said by Christian priests that a man cannot serve two masters."

My words settled into the ears, then minds of the crowd. They sniggered at Sitric's expense. "What do you mean two masters?" barked Sitric. He wasn't a bad prince, I suppose. He was young and raw. I wanted to tell him I found a real leader, someone who, if he wanted, could win the heart of Aednat the Irish princess all on his own without sending emissaries. I found a leader who was charismatic and invincible. I found a man who made we want to swear over my life without ever asking me to do so. I wanted to tell Sitric these things.

I held my diplomacy together. "We've bent to our knees this very morning and given our service and our lives to another. It would be a black plague upon us if we turned our backs on sacred vows, especially so soon."

"Did you know about this?" Sitric rasped to Colbain. "Was this before or after I met with them this morning?"

Colbain leaned in to whisper to his furious prince. Silkbeard shoved the Irish servant back into the lawgiver.

We'd made Sitric look the fool. It felt so satisfying. "Who?" Sitric shouted. "Are you so willing to admit that you are a traitor to your own people? Have you sworn oaths to the Ui Neill? Are you in league with Mael Sechnaill? Or is it to the Leinsters? You must have gone beyond the confines of Dyflin for your so-called pledges. No one in these city walls would be imprudent enough to accept oaths when they've no right to do so!" I peered around at all the gathered noblemen who'd come from far and wide. I'd say there were plenty of men within the city that morning who would have gladly taken our crew into their service. "This is my city!" spat the prince.

"This is your father's city, Prince Sitric!" Olaf's voice boomed over the crowd. He said the word prince as if it were a slight.

"Who said that?" shrieked Sitric, nearly completely losing his royal demeanor. It wasn't the patient lawgiver who was being interrupted this time.

The crowd was totally silent. I think the sniveling baby and its upset stomach even stopped their churning. Everyone was looking forward to a round of verbal fisticuffs.

"I said it," answered Olaf from the back of the host. I, like Sitric and everyone else, craned my neck back to see the famous raider. From the moment I made my pledge to Olaf, I truly believed him to be the man he claimed. He oozed strength. Crack-a-Bone was nowhere to be seen. He was below average in height and the heads of hundreds of free men obscured the view.

"Stop hiding among my faithful citizens and come forward. I'll deal with you and these traitors all at once!" demanded Sitric. The prince waited a few moments. When no one jumped forward, he said, "That's what I thought. It's easy to be full of bluster when you blend in with others." Gytha again squeezed her nephews arm. It soothed the anxious prince. He took in a deep breath and blew it out. "Halldorr, you and your fellow Greenlanders are solid fighters. I don't wish to lose you, but if you insist on making a mockery of this sacred Thing, I'll string you up like the pagans you are."

"You'll do no such thing," came Olaf's voice again.

"The prince told you to shut your mouth or step to the hill and receive a punishment," barked Colbain. Gytha and Sitric gave the eager servant scowls. He retreated.

"The man is right," called Gytha, the only one on the Thing-mount who retained anything like a regal carriage. "Show yourself. Don't be a coward. It is not the way of our people."

"Oh, I'm no coward, Lady Gytha. It's just that I am not accustomed to being shouted at. I am not used to being ordered to do anything."

"I am Prince of Dyflin, son to Kvaran, heir to the throne. You'll do as I say."

"I'll do as you ask," corrected Olaf. From the sound of his voice, I could generally tell where he stood. But none of the men standing in front of him attempted to step aside. "There is no need to prolong the assembly with this bickering. These suitors, all but one of them who will lose, are holding their breaths hoping that nothing knocks their plans for a wedding and instant empire into the surf. Now ask in a proper manner. I'll come forward, show myself, and even help clear up the situation with those Greenlanders."

Sitric held counsel with Colbain, the lawgiver, and his aunt. Colbain was hissing about Sitric's authority and image. The servant went on and on about how Gormflaith, the Irish queen and mother to Sitric would be disappointed. Sitric was whining in much the same way. The lawgiver, at last, suggested that the Lady Gytha respectfully request that the stranger show himself. It would allow the prince to avoid begging and thereby save face. The party agreed.

"Dear, sir," called Gytha. "You have me at a disadvantage. You know my name but I do not know yours. Would you please do me the honor of coming to this hill and introducing yourself to this assembly? A man of your obvious breeding deserves to be recognized."

"I'll gladly do it, lady. Will you grant me one request?" called Olaf.

"Oh, I'm afraid I'm not in the business of granting requests I've not heard. Nor am I one who exceeds the authority granted me by the prince," said Gytha, bowing to her nephew. I probably fell in love with the intelligent woman at that moment. I've done so a dozen times since then.

"That's fair, lady, fair indeed. I'll ask the man who runs this city while his father is pouting at Iona. Prince Silkbeard, may I bring my meek entourage, such as it is, when I come to the hill? We are unarmed as all proper free men should be at a Thing." I think even the birds and the distant surf stopped making their incessant racket, waiting to see what Sitric would say.

His response proved to be anticlimactic. Sitric was anxious to be done with this chapter. The Thing on the hill was to be an opportunity for him to demonstrate his position, a simple way to muster support for the eventual day his father passed. Instead, it was turning into a farce. He'd lost every verbal battle. The prince would risk no more vocal forays in public. "Granted."

"Men, with me. Make way!" shouted Olaf. Surprised men and women were roughly shoved out of the way. The crowd stepped one pace to the side to make room for the stranger and his *small* band. A single stride was not enough. The gathering was forced to make an ever-widening path for Olaf. At my place on the hillside, I could at last see the entire extent of Olaf's force. It was many times the number of men with whom we'd drunk. His crews alone made up half of the assembly that day. All of them quietly pushed their way to the hill's base. As Olaf promised, they wore no weapons. They were adorned like their leader, in weathered mail – chain or leather. Their faces showed perpetual frowns won by experience in the knock-down world.

Men and women murmured. This was a most surprising turn. Suddenly, there seemed a rival for Silkbeard's very existence. If he had any sense, he was pissing in his trousers. Sitric's eyes widened. He glanced around the perimeter where his loyal soldiers stood guard, equally as unarmed as the rest. I saw the prince swallow. The normally cool Gytha allowed her face to blanch. Seeing her react thus, made me wonder if I had indeed pledged fealty to a man who wanted to take over all of

Dyflin. Oh well, I thought, at least I'd chosen the winning side early.

Olaf climbed up next to me. He stayed some distance from the prince, provoking no one. "So here I am," Olaf said. "Your mystery is solved. I'm afraid that the build-up was more exciting than the revelation." It wasn't and we all knew it. Olaf Tryggvason was showing that his army was larger than all of Sitric's and we had not even seen all the men the pirate raider could muster. The rest, I came to find out, lounged on longboats strewn along the rivers and out on nearby islands in the Irish Sea.

Sitric cleared his throat. His knee visibly twitched. His voice cracked. "And you must be the man of whom I've heard?"

"Well that, Prince Sitric, I don't pretend to know." I giggled at Olaf's answer. My new lord glanced at me with a serious expression. "We're not making a mockery of this. Are we?"

I clamped my mouth shut. "No, lord."

Silkbeard hesitated, as if naming the man would make the scene real. "Would you be Crack-a-Bone?"

Olaf's natural state resumed. He laughed while slapping his uphill knee. "I am. I am. That's not a name I've given myself, you know."

"What is your business in this grand city?" asked Sitric, forcing himself to grow into his role.

"No, I tell you that it's not even my men who've given me that name," said Olaf, ignoring Sitric's question. He spoke loud enough for his words to carry across the crowd. "There was an incident some years back. It was in the Baltic when I had just finished in my service to the Kievan Rus. I don't want to go into the gory details here, but some of the victims on my first raid saw my method of dealing with dissenters and began calling me Crack-a-Bone."

Gytha stepped next to the prince. The brave woman placed a motherly hand in front of Sitric to shield him from harm. "Allow me the honor of being the first to welcome you to King Kvaran's famous city." Her words, of course, were in contradiction to her actions. "May your stay be a fine respite from all your endeavors." She bowed deeply.

"May it, indeed!" exclaimed Olaf. He returned the bow, first to Gytha and then to the prince.

"Well then, Crack-a-Bone," said Sitric. He pushed Gytha's protective arm away. "I welcome you as well. What is your purpose here? Why are you so involved with a Thing that has mostly local implications?"

"Fine questions, Prince Sitric. I am merely sojourning in Dyflin. My ships, as you've probably already heard, are refitting. We bring waves of money to your taverns, whorehouses, storehouses, and tax coffers. We are doing our part to keep the House of Kvaran in power for many years to come."

"And your reason for attending the Thing?" asked Silkbeard, sweeping an arm across the group.

"Oh, yes, that. These are my men." Olaf slapped a hand on my shoulder. His grip was iron. "They are already sworn into my service. I wish it were otherwise, but I'm not one to make a man turn his back on a solemn pledge."

Sitric had lost us. He'd lost his chance to make himself seem up to the task of running his father's city. All he could do now was salvage a bit of pride and allow Gytha to continue with her husband hunt. "It is good to know that these men have found an able lord to serve." They were hard words for the prince to say, but to his credit he said them. "How long do you tarry, Crack-a-Bone?"

"Oh, I don't rest too long," answered Olaf. "I hope to be gone a-Viking again in a few days. The swells are where I belong."

Sitric's mood brightened. "Fine. Fine. You'll go within days." Gytha made the motions of someone eating. Sitric frowned, but nodded. "Do me the honor of bringing your men. Well, not all of your men." Olaf laughed. Sitric smiled. "Bring your leadership team to my hall tonight and dine."

"As you say," said Olaf bowing while retreating backward down the hill. I went with him. "It is fine that I'll soon be cutting across the rolling slopes of Meiti. It will also be fine to dine with you and your fair aunt."

"My aunt," said Sitric absent-mindedly. "I thank you Crack-a-Bone. You've accepted my invitation which warms my heart. You've likewise reminded me that we've much to accomplish today. So, with your permission?" Sitric made another sweeping gesture with his arm.

"By all means. Continue on. I don't intend to impede such a striking woman from finding her victim." He giggled when he said the last.

"Victim?" asked Gytha.

"I meant no harm," said Olaf sheepishly. He fiddled with his hands almost as if he were nervous. "My experience is that a good woman, like you for instance, marries a man for reasons of the mind – politics, alliances, wealth, land. Then when that new husband is around such an excellent specimen of womanhood, he becomes smitten. It is after his heart is swamped with those feminine emotions that death forces them apart. The same was so with me and my dearly departed Geira. I imagine it was the same with you when your first husband passed. If he were Christian, the man went to his grave hoping for just a day longer with you. If he were a follower of Thor, his pyre came too quickly." Olaf hesitated. I think he even blushed. "That's what I meant when I said victim. Of a good woman, I mean." He ended his talk and pushed his way back amongst his men. Olaf looked embarrassed. His men's faces showed not the derision I expected. Their expressions were that of sympathy for their dear leader, a soft-hearted widower.

Gytha was stunned silent.

We were all dazed.

The heat of my long-simmering anger at life in general cooled for a bit. His words reminded me of my own soft spot for the affections of women. If it was appropriate for a legendary warlord to harbor such feminine thoughts, as he called them, then it was fitting for me. I decided that one day I would go back to Greenland and chase after my fiery enchantress. I'd kill whomever she married in the intervening years and make her mine. It was meant to be.

Or, maybe it was not my destiny to return home. Perhaps I'd meet a fat Irish woman and we'd plow our way through life, in our bed and the green fields of her native land. A Frankish girl would make a fine wife, if I could understand her words. I already had a proposal of marriage from Princess Aednat. I let images of her naked body bound through my mind.

I didn't know with whom or how the norns would see fit to bring me my desired family filled with strong-hearted sons. I only knew that a rough sea king's feminine ideals had convinced me that my goal was within reach.

• • •

The lawgiver's voice at last officially began the Thing. He was almost finished with his introduction of Gytha and her task when his words finally awoke me from my sweepingly romantic feelings about women. I say romantic, but they were thoughts which quickly turned lustful once Freydis, my one-time betrothed, entered my mind. I could almost taste her shapely body. A dash of Aednat and my mind turned truly lecherous.

"Lady Gytha has told me nothing of her plans about the manner in which this Thing, this search, will be conducted. I know only that here today she intends to name the man who will become her husband." The lawgiver turned to face the widow. "The Thing moot is yours." He trotted to the back of the hill and set his rump on a rough bench that someone hauled from the city. Sitric and Colbain were already keeping the timber seat warm.

"I thank you, lawgiver," said Gytha before facing the throng. "Because most of you want a fast spectacle and then get to the disputes as quickly as possible, I'll oblige you in the first."

Gytha began pushing the air in front her like she shoved someone's chest. "Make a space at the base of the hill. Those men who would be my husband come forward. Leave your handlers to the back. It is you who must impress me, not your entourages. I marry you, not them."

Much jostling proceeded as wealthy nobles thrust forward, while the rest of us were forced back. It took many moments for the wooers to line themselves up so that each of them could be seen by Gytha. She recognized some of them by just their faces. To those familiar men, Gytha offered a warm smile. To the strangers, the soon-to-be bride gave a more formal bow.

When the crowd had sufficiently readjusted, I saw that Gytha would have the fortune of choosing from the crop's cream. The jarl I recently pummeled was noticeably absent. Those that did show themselves were more than able to make up for him. Twenty or more men, some ugly, some comely, but all rich – or at least dressed to make Gytha think them wealthy – stood in queue. Whether tall or short, fat or thin, they were a proud bunch. Some had fought their way to wealth. Others had inherited it. All of them held their chins high with the confidence that comes when one has little fear. Half wore mail that glittered, proof that there were many thralls in Dyflin with sore arms from the scrubbing they'd given their masters' armor. The remaining unarmored nobles stood adorned with bright clothing dyed in shades of red, green, and blue. Each wore the deepest of hues decorating their newly crafted shirts or trousers. It is a fact that if a man can afford to pay for the pigments and time necessary for deeply dyed fabric, his riches abound. Gytha and her property were prizes that had brought out the best.

Gytha lifted her chin. "Your coming is most welcome. I ask that even if we are already acquainted that you introduce yourself, your lineage, and what you bring to the marriage contract." She pointed to the man on the left end of the line. "You, sir, please begin."

The suitor climbed half-way up the hill. "Wise and fair, Gytha, I am known as the Count of Eu. My name in your native tongue, in the language of my ancestors, is Vilhjalmr. In the language of the land seized by my great-grandfather, Rollo, conqueror, I am known as Guillaume." The crowd mumbled their approval. I did, too. Rollo had carved out what was nearly his own nation. It had become known as Normandy in France. This man had to be one of the myriad of bastard children of Richard the Fearless. He went on. "I trust my noble breeding meets your expectations. The County of Eu is situated in the northeast of Normandy. We have a marvelous river. Trade flourishes. Agriculture dominates. We are tasked with protecting Normandy from invasion from the east. Our commoners are hardy and able. The county brings in ample income annually and will be an exceptional addition to your territories in England."

"That will be enough," clipped Gytha. "Thank you. Next please." The surprised count ambled down the slope to his place, not so dejected as to lose his pride. No, his shoulders remained back and his chest out.

The next man came forward. His resume, though not as well-known as the count's, was stellar. In fact, man after man, noble after noble, told the tale of his life. Every one of them would make a superb match for Gytha, coupling her lands with theirs, adding a potential alliance to Dyflin at a time when one was sorely required.

When the last man finished giving his qualifications, Gytha gave the long line of men a thorough examination. She eyed them one-by-one. What she looked for, I do not know. I don't pretend to understand women. I know that a man, put in the same position, would look only at his potential bride's face or hips or tits or all three once it was established that the women were rich. Gytha might have looked at her suitors' muscled or flabby chests. Maybe she studied their eyes. You can tell a lot from a man's eyes. I don't know what she did.

Gytha peered back at her nephew who had occupied himself by twisting together a handful of grass sprigs into a braid. Colbain chatted with the lawgiver. The woman now studied those men. When she again faced the crowd it was apparent that she'd made a decision. With both hands, Gytha cinched up the front of her skirts a thumb's length and stepped down the hill. The crowd gasped, wondering who would be named as her husband.

Like a knife heated in a fire's embers can split thick whale blubber, Gytha sliced between two aristocrats so the line of wooers was soon in her wake. The sea of free men and women parted without a word from the gracious lady as she marched her way toward the back. The gathering was crackling with wonder.

"What is she doing?" Cnute asked.

"Coming for me," said Leif. He was joking, but Gytha's path would cut right through our party.

"Maybe she didn't find any of the men acceptable," I wondered aloud.

"Is she returning to the city?" asked Brandr.

Gytha advanced. I moved aside to allow her to pass, but she stopped, facing me. I couldn't believe it. I was in the process of receiving a marriage proposal from a second woman whose titles and power outshined my humble upbringing. First, silly Aednat, now a mature, intelligent, beautiful, strong woman repeated the girl's mistake. I thought that I must truly be a catch. After a moment of being tongue-tied, I said, "Gytha, I offer nothing other than a small hoard of treasure under a hearth. I am sure that any of the men at the foot of the hill would make a better match."

Gytha laughed out loud. Cnute and Leif joined her. I immediately felt foolish. The woman wasn't cold-hearted, though. She stuffed a palm over her mouth to hide the enormous smile emblazoned on her lovely face. "An honest mistake," she began, still fighting off chuckles. "Any woman would be proud to call such a great warrior her man. I, however, wish to speak to your leader. Where is he?"

"Uh," I said, looking around. I found Olaf five or six rows behind me. His back was to us and he chatted idly with Randulfr about this adventure or that. He hadn't even watched any of the proceedings. I led her to him.

"And so the horse trotted around with only one leg for the rest of his life," said Olaf, finishing a yarn. He and Randulfr shook their heads and laughed.

"Lord," I said. "Lord, the lady wishes to speak with you."

Olaf turned. His boisterous mirth fled when he found himself staring at Gytha. His expression turned to one of dignity, respect. "How may I help you, lady? Have you vetted the men? Your victim – you know I jest – has he been chosen?" His clothes were still wet from crossing the river. The perpetual blood and rust stains covered his chainmail.

"Who are you Crack-a-Bone?" asked Gytha. "Who are you, really?"

Instantly melted, Olaf answered, "I am Oli." It was a name I'd not heard him use before that moment. Nor would I ever hear him say it again. Gytha, though, would employ the name for years to come when the pair was in the confines of a longhouse or among the closest of friends.

"Will you have me?" she asked.

Giving the answer no thought, giving the alliances, or any repercussions no consideration, Olaf said, "I'll not say no, but I'm afraid that if you desire land, I've none to give. I am a sea king. My shores are everywhere, but my property is none."

Gytha grabbed Olaf by the wrist. He allowed himself to be dragged back to the slope and up the hill.

By now the young pup Sitric was again interested. His braided spring spun between two fingers of one of his hands. He watched in wonder as Gytha and Olaf turned to face the crowd. "I give you the man who will be my husband."

The assembly loved the twist of events. I adored it. The cheering, once it exploded, went on and on as Gytha basked in the praise. Olaf's dozens of crews shouted and called.

Sitric and Colbain were left twiddling their thumbs, wondering what it meant for them that Gytha would soon be married to the most powerful warlord who ever sliced the raging seas.

CHAPTER 4

I have said that all the talk of weddings was silly. When I uttered such ideas it was out of frustration. I was a dolt. The truth was that Gytha's calling of a Thing to find her a husband had been a part of what led me into the service of Olaf. Without her, I never would have been sent to the smith to get her wedding presents. I wouldn't have stubbornly confronted the proud Norse jarl in Dyflin's muddy streets. Olaf never would have noticed me. I'd be doomed to serve Sitric or flee.

The prince, too, benefited from his aunt's union with so powerful a sea king. At first, Silkbeard feared that Olaf would be a rival. The raider's intentions now sealed with a pagan marriage ceremony in Thor's Woods – much to the prince's dismay – proved to be the opposite of lethal. Olaf was willing to aid Dyflin and his fellow Norseman in word and deed.

"I'm what you need in the Irish Sea," said Olaf, some days after his union with Gytha became official. We sat in Kvaran's hall. A fire blazed in the hearth, spilling flickering light onto our faces and belching choking smoke into the room. The logs came from the bottom of last winter's woodpile and were covered in wet, sloppy mud when they were tossed onto the miniature conflagration. "My fleet is unparalleled. You'd have to sail all the way to the Danes to find a similar armada."

"And you offer it to the prince?" asked Colbain, out of turn. He was, as I've told you, a bastard by birth. And though his frequent words of vitriol toward me were impotent since I served another, I used them to foment anger. He said nothing to me at that moment, but his question was like that of a child.

"Idiot bastard," I mumbled. "Worm."

"Control your man." Sitric scolded Olaf.

"I'll not do it," Crack-a-Bone said. "Especially when he's right. I don't know if this yappy servant of yours is a bastard, or not. I do know he's an idiot."

Colbain opened his mouth to protest, but Olaf seized the man's cheeks with just the thumb and index finger of one hand. He squeezed harder and harder. The servant struggled, moaning. He wasn't getting away.

"As I was saying before this, this thrall, interrupted, I tell you that we have an alliance. I do not offer the fleet I've built one victory at a time to another man." Olaf shoved Colbain back. He tumbled off his bench. "I'm telling you, Silkbeard, that you are free to look inland on this murky island. I'll control the waters that lap your shores."

Prince Sitric rightly ignored Olaf's rough treatment of Colbain. "Will you lend me troops, then, to go off fighting inward? They'd be under your command."

The prince's indifference seemed to hurt the servant worse than Olaf's fingers. Colbain's eyes became glassy with tears as he crawled back to his feet.

Olaf stood and shook his head. He paced on a portion of the floor that was lined with fieldstone. No one had ever bothered to finish covering the rest of the earthen floor in all the years of the mighty hall. "No, no, young prince. My men fight on land if we have to. Even then, it's mostly skirmishes. If we must, we must, I suppose. But I am linked to the sea. My men have salt water coursing through their veins. There will be a day when I have to lead them in great land battles, but they are not ready today. Nor am I. We are simple sea brawlers." Everyone knew that wasn't exactly true. No one dared correct him.

"Come back to the table, Oli," said Gytha. She was the daub that was to hold together the Dyflin and Olaf alliance for many years. Olaf grinned narrowly. He obeyed his new bride.

"So what are you suggesting then?" asked Sitric. The boy was a pup, I tell you. I have been called simple, oafish, stupid, and a hundred other things that meant I was dull in my life. It all seemed so clear to me at that moment, though. Silkbeard appeared to be the dim one.

"He says that you should return to the negotiations with Mael Sechnaill for Aednat's hand. This time, however, you go with strength and confidence knowing that Lord Olaf Crack-a-Bone Tryggvason is on your side," I said.

To my surprise, Colbain agreed. "That is an excellent idea, sire. Gormflaith would be so happy." The servant nearly bounced like a pet eager to please.

"Who cares about her happiness?" asked Sitric. "She chose to leave Dyflin. I think of my city, my kingdom." The pup occasionally showed signs of maturity. He was right about his wicked mother.

"I just meant," said Colbain, stuttering. He fingered the sheathed knife at his chest as he always did when he was nervous.

"It's alright," said Sitric. They were almost like brothers, I suppose, treating one another miserably then soothingly from one moment to the next. Gormflaith had raised them both, one to be a king, the other a bastard destined to be a worm servant. "What do you think about your Halldorr's idea?"

Olaf gave me a wink. "I think it is fine. If there be a woman for you in the High King's court, take her. Make babies come out her eyes until you get a few boys of age so that you can choose your successor. Then, who knows, the Ui Neill may answer to Dyflin."

"That was the plan until your man here dashed those hopes," said Colbain, happily calling me Olaf's man as if I were just as much a servant as he.

"Can't you send him somewhere?" asked Gytha. "Isn't there a dung bucket full that needs to be emptied?"

"Go to the stables, Colbain," said Sitric. "Tell them to have fifty horses ready in the morning. See to it that you have provisions for another mission to Mael's court." The servant bit his tongue and left. He pulled so hard on the knife sheath that the cord dug into the skin of his neck.

"Thank you, Prince Sitric," said Gytha when the worm was gone.

"Anything you ask, Aunt Gytha," said Silkbeard. He was learning how to please those who had the power to elevate or crush him. "Now will you go to Mael Sechnaill, Crack-a-Bone? The mere sight of you and your horde will send urine running down his leg."

Olaf chuckled. He swept up his wife's hand and stood to go. She followed gracefully. "Seeing a High King of Ireland piss in his pants would make my day, but I'm afraid that what I told you was true. I mean to leave Dyflin. We are fully rested.

We go tomorrow. Some of my ships will stay, but Halldorr here and his men come with me. I want to see what they're made of. In any event, I'll not be here to offer up diplomatic talk. I'm not really the man for the job."

"Neither was Halldorr," Sitric sighed.

"Then go yourself," shrugged Olaf. He was leading his woman back to their chambers for a last, amorous night before he left.

"A future king doesn't go and beg for a bride," said Silkbeard.

"I suppose not," Olaf said, caring little for those details. He and Gytha left the room without another word.

"Looks like its Colbain or someone else," I said, filling the void.

"At least it can't be you," growled the pup. "That is a mistake I won't make again."

And I thought, 'At least it won't be me.' No. In just one turn of the sun, I'd be cascading over the waves once again.

Freedom.

• • •

At last our crews left the walls they so tirelessly patrolled for Kvaran those many dull months. Though we were securely leashed to Olaf by our word, we still felt free. With our shoulders pushing and our feet turning, *Charging Boar* was heaved off the shingle. Its red and white striped cloth was hoisted so that the wind and the river's current had us skipping out to sea. With every passing moment the mix of salt in the air increased as we propelled toward the gateway to freedom. The serpent, Jormungandr, whose breathing created the waves that began as swirling ripples, was panting as he encircled the earth. The rapid swells rammed against *Charging Boar's* strakes. We were buffeted. It was magnificent.

"You weren't at Olaf's wedding ceremony in Thor's Woods," said Magnus. He stood on the steering deck manhandling the heavy oak rudder. His face was like the rest of ours. It showed the wonder, excitement, and anticipation of a youth who waited for the glorious tales told around the Yule log when the snows were piled high. Anything was possible in those yarns just like anything could happen when a man and his comrades went a-Viking.

"No," I answered. I stowed the antler comb I'd bought from the grubby peddler boy on my way to the ship that morning. My hudfat was already packed full so the new comb clattered against the one comb I actually used. Two sided, with coarse and fine teeth, my everyday comb was made from the tusk of a walrus taken in Greenland. I pulled it out and ran it through mangled knots that had gathered in my long blonde hair.

"Seems you'd want to make nice to our new lord," Magnus said, shrugging. Leif, Randulfr, and the rest of the crew ran whetstones down their blades. Once a ship was fully provisioned and underway, it took but a few men to see that she ran true. The rest were free to prepare for battle by placing an edge on their blades or spear tips, to mend holes in jerkins, cinch leather mail together a little tighter, or to lounge under the midday sun. Our men were experienced and eager for action. I loved the long scraping sounds made by the whetstones in their hands.

"I don't think Olaf minds," I said, grunting when the last knot in my hair came out. "I ate with him and Gytha in the king's hall. He never said a thing."

Magnus toyed with one of the helmsmen on another boat. The River Ruirthech was widening toward its gaping mouth. Magnus pulled hard on the steering oar, turning *Charging Boar* to starboard. Our fat ship wasn't the fastest, but Magnus knew her like a man knows his woman. She sprang across the bow of the nearest ship. We missed a collision by less than an ell. The other helmsman cursed loudly while doing his best to turn with us. When the danger had passed, Magnus shouted over to his counterpart. The pair made a wager on the spot. It had something to do with who was the better captain. Magnus wasn't our ship's captain. Leif was. It didn't matter. Leif kept right on sharpening his sword while Magnus agreed to the terms. I do not remember who won the contest when it was later carried out in the Irish Sea. What I recall is that Cnute heard of yet another chance to gamble. He joined in on one side or the other, betting coins he didn't have, and no doubt losing those same coins.

"Why didn't you go? The rest of his crews were there. I'd bet there were over a thousand men." Magnus said the last in amazement. We'd always lived at the fringes of the world – Norway, Iceland, Greenland. Only when we were exiled and found ourselves in the Irish Sea did we begin to understand just how many people roamed Midgard.

"The next wedding I attend will be my own," I said. My comb was stowed. I, too, now polished my weapons.

"Ah," said Magnus, guessing my mind, "Freydis has ruined you for love."

She had. Everyone who left Greenland with us knew it. That didn't stop me from acting the man. "Shut up. What would you know about Leif's sister anyway?"

Magnus shrugged. Cnute and Leif giggled at me. Thankfully, though, they all gave it up and went on about their business.

Women, I thought. My whetstone glided down the short blade of my father's saex. I loved them. I cherished them with a heart as weak as a Christian monk's caring soul. At the same time, I thought about Freydis. The emotions that swirled in me alternated between what the same Christian monk called lust and hate. I was twice turned down by Freydis for marriage, publically humiliated on the second round. Women brought out the best and worst in men.

I dropped the whetstone. The blade nicked my finger, but no blood came since the callous it wore was as thick as a bear's hide. I reached down to recover the whetstone and I remembered Aoife. She was a little spritely thrall I'd briefly owned. She'd nearly called down the ire of Thor when she attempted to throw a whetstone overboard while we were at sea. I grinned when I thought of the strong-willed little girl. Her grimy bare feet and the chaff colored hair that was forever in her face belied the fact that Aoife was meant to be a fine woman. She never got the chance as I was unable to keep her from harm. Despite the fact that I missed her, I smiled in the ship that day. Not all women made me burn with desire, melt with pity, or clench my fists in rage. Some women made me proud just to know them. Thjordhildr, Leif's mother, was one. Aoife was another. I thought that Gytha should be added to the list.

"Armor!" shouted Leif.

We hadn't even left Dyflin's lands. Or, so I thought. I blinked awake from my musings and saw that the land we fast approached was foreign to me. I jerked my head around. The sail was down. The crew had long ago moved to sit on wooden chests and man the oars. The rhythmic grate-slap of their work, normally music to my ears, had not even registered in my mind. Surf from the roiling white waves of the Irish Sea splashed up into my face. Somewhere I had lost most of a day's worth of travel.

"Armor!" Leif called again. He was looking at me, for the rest of the men were clad in their thick leather or chain. Those who didn't row were already gathering their shields from the top of the gunwale. "Wake up, Halldorr!"

The ship buffeted as the waves broke. I slapped my saex home and rummaged through my baggage. I was experienced enough to make sure that my mail was at the top. Soon I fished my way into the heavy shirt and re-clasped my belts at the waist. A helmet adorned my crown and my shield was soon held aloft. *Charging Boar's* keel skidded into the shore.

We tumbled over the bulwark, splashing shin deep in the sea. Twenty other longships crashed into the sands at the same time. They released their crews in the same manner. The rest of Olaf's armada lounged back in Dyflin or went their separate ways as their captains searched for easy pillaging.

Some distance to my right, I saw Olaf. He was already far up the narrow beach watching us disembark with his hands on his hips. His trousers were filthy. The sea king's mail appeared as if he'd just finished fighting all of Ireland. Behind him was a ravine that led up to the mainland. He was calling orders to his men. Leif had run ahead to gather ours.

"Where are we?" I asked.

Cnute looked crossways at me. "Leinster," he said. He gripped his spear in one hand while the other fiddled with the last thong tying his leather mail. Cnute could have purchased proper chainmail long ago had he not lost all his wealth, day by day, bet by bet in Dyflin's alleys, taverns, and streets.

"I know that much," I said. I dropped my shield and helped him tie his armor.

Randulfr came to my side. He'd been the very dead King Godfrey's longtime lieutenant. "Viklow," he said. "Our ancestors used to control the harbor over there. Those days are gone and so now all we do is raid."

"How do you know?" asked Cnute, again holding his shield and weapon.

"Godfrey and I raided here a time or two." Randulfr wrinkled his nose. "There are a few men of Norse descent still around, but even they are Irish in manner and custom."

"What is it?" I asked. Leif trotted back toward us. He wore a frown.

Randulfr huffed, guessing at Leif's answer. "There are no rich monasteries here. There's but one or two tiny churches. They have just enough wealth to buy their communion loaves."

"And we don't even get to raid them," said Leif. "Brandr, you and Cnute stay behind. You'll guard the ships with men from the other crews." Both men swore. "Oh, I'd not complain. The rest of us get to go collect cattle for Olaf."

So my first raid on my return to the glorious seas was to be one where I had to watch out for splattering cow manure rather than sloshing blood.

"At least we'll eat well," muttered Magnus as we climbed the ravine behind Olaf and his other followers.

"We don't even get to do that," Leif said. "We'll have to house and feed the creatures aboard *Charging Boar* until we return to Dyflin. Olaf means to sell them."

"Shit," I said.

"Exactly," said Leif. "There will be lots of it."

• • •

The afternoon passed by uneventfully. Except for the occasional terrified farmer, we were mostly alone. We stayed to the path, our weapons held idly. Even then, as soon as the frightened Irishmen saw us clambering over the countryside, they'd drop what they were doing and flee.

"I thought Olaf wanted to test our mettle on this first raid," I said. "Why were we told to go off and hunt domesticated animals?"

Leif shrugged. "Isn't that part of his test? Better to see what a man does with no army facing him. If he's incompetent, then, at least, no one else gets killed."

"But we're experienced. He knows that." I whined. It wasn't proper. "I'd throw us into the thick of the fight. That would show what we are made of."

"I don't think there will be any fighting for any of our bands today," said Leif.

"Why? Where did the other crews go?" I asked.

"The town. From the sound of it, Olaf knows the chieftain. They have an arrangement. Olaf doesn't kill anyone and he's allowed to provision whenever he wishes," Leif said. "Olaf even pays for mead and information. They're probably already drinking."

I rolled my eyes. "We really are just gathering cattle then?"

"Yes, we are," answered Leif. He pointed to a wide meadow below where several dozen head of cattle grazed. They paid us no heed. Leif's shoulders slumped. "Sheath your weapons. Go to that copse of trees and cut long, green switches. We're field urchins today."

• • •

"On, Gudruna!" I called. I named one of the cows after Godfrey's wife. You may think it a slight. It was not. Gudruna had been a beautiful queen before she was hacked down at Dunadd. The cow's eyes reminded me of hers.

Our feet lazily dragged through the grass as we whipped the ground with our switches. "Up!" called Tyrkr on the other side of the lingering herd. His green twig snapped on the pin bone of a nearby beast. She clumsily trotted forward for three quick steps before settling back into her ambling pace.

"Come on!" said another of our herders. Actually, he muttered it. We were thoroughly dejected with our assignment. Our heads stared down at the green turf while our chins rested on our mailed chests. I felt the iron rings of my chain tug at the whiskers of my beard as I walked. Everything bothered me. A cool breeze blew. It annoyed me. A faraway raptor that floated on the air's currents gave its call. My ears split. I chewed on my cheek and imagined how our new leader probably laughed at a mead table in Viklow. Crack-a-Bone laughed at me.

Thunder rolled across the clearing behind us. "Great," said Randulfr. "Rain is all we need."

I looked up to the heavens. It was a rare, cloudless day. The aggravating cool breeze that tickled the back of my arms was bringing a storm upon our rumps. The thunder rolled. Even Thor, like Olaf, was sporting with us. The thunder rolled and rolled.

"It's not thunder!" shouted Leif.

"Thor's beard!" I called. It had been King Godfrey's favorite curse. Bearing down on us was a band of riders. They didn't ride the lazy palfrey of a city woman. These men rode beasts with hooves the size of boulders. The destriers hammered the earth with those natural weapons, churning up sod in their wake.

"Form the shield wall!" Randulfr screamed. Our men had chopped in numerous shield walls. We killed there. We were already assembling the life-taking and life-preserving structure. The cows, seemingly unaware of the approaching danger, kept right on marching in the direction we'd set them.

The riders screamed, "Dyflin!" Some of our shields were adorned with Kvaran's mark. That didn't stop these supposed Dyfliners from attacking. They had spears or swords held high. Strong arms were cocked as their charge approached. I could hear the lead beast's breathing grunts as it trampled on. Even its rattling tack made music. We had but moments.

Randulfr surveyed the scene. He foresaw the carnage that would befall us. We had only fought infantry before. A smattering of men on horseback – that's all we had faced. We'd never locked shields while on foot in front of an equal number of charging cavalry. "Two rows," he screamed. He physically shoved us into place. "Spears to the front. Plant the ass end into the turf." We traded weapons where we could quickly obey. No one questioned his orders. Leif, in the front row, handed his fine sword back and snatched another man's spear.

By the sweet sound of Odin's poetry, what happened next were the most chaotic four heartbeats of my life. I've fought in brawls, scraps, melees, battles, contests, and wars. All of them seemed insane while in the midst. But when the first destrier's chest struck the longest spear, a new version of craziness was unleashed on all of Midgard.

Our entire front row of warriors was scattered. They were sent to the sides. They were hurled back into the second row. Impaled horses' chests rammed against uplifted shields which, in turn, pressed against the stout shoulders of Norsemen. Our line, our magnificent shield wall was broken in just a moment.

Fortunately for us, the attackers were not cavalrymen by trade. Their inexperience meant that they gave all their strength to the first strike when they ought to have used the advantage given them and picked at us. Like a youth squeezes out the oozing contents of a pimple, they could have plucked us from our line one-by-one. They could have lost a handful of men. We would have been eliminated.

So instead of us standing like an eternal cliff against the waves and having their surf break away, we melted. But in our melting, their momentum was spent. Their lead riders shot from their mounts like an arrow skips from a yew bow. Those men landed amongst our second row. Their necks were cut before they could even figure out what happened. The horses that fell in the first line, kicked and rolled. They killed two of their own men when those hammering hooves smashed skulls. One of our men was bludgeoned in a like manner. The horses that remained upright kept going right on through us.

We grappled our way upright. Only half their men were still mounted and alive. We were bruised, but we'd lost only three. "Split them off!" I shouted. "Two men to a horse."

Two of the riders decided that all along they had wished for easier pickings that day. They kicked their heels into their horses' bellies and cut away to the side where a forest came near. I never saw them again. The attackers who stayed behind to face us called curses after their former friends. That's when I realized that they were speaking Norse.

"What do you want?" I called as Cnute and I closed on a rider.

"We want our cattle!" shouted the man. He was blonde like me. He was strong like me. He was as Norse as I.

"These aren't your cattle," Cnute yelled. The rider parried a blow from Cnute's spear.

"They will be when you're all dead!" With Cnute off balance, the man swung his blade down. The tip caught Cnute's leather mail, splaying it open. His pale skin beneath wore just the red line of a scratch. Cnute fell back.

I gripped my sword with two hands and swung. I tried to ignore the rider and take down the beast. The man blocked my blow so that the horse's shoulder was safe, for now. I scurried to the rear of the horse. It was a chance I took. It didn't pay off. The rider skillfully twisted his reins. The beast curled it's rump toward me. Just one hoof from his potent kick glanced off my shield. It was strong enough to send me reeling.

The rider spun the beast again. This time its forelegs crawled their way into the sky in order to trample me. The charger breathed mightily. It loudly pulled and pushed air into and out of its lungs. Its flared nostrils belched liquid snot. In a futile attempt to save myself, I lifted my shield. The beast stayed aloft for a second longer than it should have. Then it let loose a blood-tingling whinny. The rider swore. The beast clumsily hopped to the side and tipped over.

Blood sprayed the ground. Randulfr had come to my rescue and lopped off one of the charger's rear legs. He finished off the rider with the same bloody blade. I sat up panting. We'd captured four men. Three more lay dead. Another had decided to join his cowardly friends and pounded off to the woods.

We panted, sucking in swaths of air like a farmer fells reams of wheat in each stroke.

"We best get moving," said Leif. He favored one side. When he lifted his chainmail to investigate, I saw that his skin was already brown, blue, and green – broken ribs. "Gather our dead."

I stood and helped Cnute to his feet. We caught a couple of our opponents' horses and retrieved our dead crewmen. When all was said and done, we had four dead and one badly wounded. Even the injured man succumbed to his wounds on the ride back toward Viklow.

The cows had remained on the path and were half an English mile closer to our destination when we finally caught up with them. We didn't even bother gathering more switches, for those beasts were better trained than us.

"On, Gudruna," I called to a cow. I was so exhausted that I wasn't even sure if it was the same one I had named earlier.

I was certain, however, that my new Lord Crack-a-Bone would soon have my fist drummed into his smug, drunken face. He'd sent us, undermanned, into dangerous territory that he knew well. It was a test, Leif called it.

I meant to make it a test of Crack-a-Bone's mettle, not mine.

• • •

We met two people on the path back to the ships. One was a stooped-over Irish farmer who was surprisingly unafraid of a band of blood-spattered Norsemen. His spine looked like it was a rag that had been wrung out and frozen in place. He had but a handful of teeth left. The man showed us all of them with a wide grin. "Are you lads heading back to your lord with those cattle?" He stood in our way. A cattle dog with long black, brown, and white fur sat next to him. The beast had whip-smart eyes.

"We are, old man," said Leif, pushing past him. "We're not in the best of moods so mind yourself or you'll get hurt."

Undeterred, the old farmer spun to follow. He had a tap-tap, shuffling gait. His dog trotted along beside him, tongue lolling. "If it's all the same fellas, I'll fall in with you. I need to chat with that lord of yours. What be his name?"

"Crack-a-Bone," I said. Just the mention caused the farmer to miss a beat in his step. He regained his composure and kept marching with us, lips pursed in a determined frown. The dog ran about on his own, helping us move the cattle down the road. We soon forgot the pair had even joined us.

The second man we met on the way was Olaf. His entourage was obviously magnitudes larger than ours even with the addition of the old farmer. That didn't stop me from puffing up my chest. I thought I'd face him. I'd face them all. Olaf's guard wore sturdy mail and helmets. They held their swords at the ready as if they were prepared to meet me in combat. He saw the fresh crimson dripping from our mail. "Trouble?" he asked.

"What do you think?" was my reply.

Olaf ignored my tone. "That's why we came. The chieftain in Viklow said a band of Norsemen has been harassing the area all year."

"And you came to rescue us? We don't need your rescue," I said.

"We came because you are our brothers. My men are my sons and I protect them. I'll not answer the questions again," barked Olaf.

It's funny. His indignant attitude and his words were all I needed. I gave up my idiotic feud as quickly as it had begun.

"That's what's left of the group of Norsemen we met," I said, jutting a thumb toward the captives.

Olaf turned to the men with him. "Take the cattle to the ships. See them loaded. I have business with these so-called Norsemen." Ox-foot belted out a series of orders in rapid staccato.

"Crack-a-Bone, sir!" called the hobbling farmer. "Before the cattle are taken away I need a word with you."

Olaf looked at me. I shrugged. The sea king looked at Leif. Leif's shoulders shot up in the same manner as mine. "That's what the old man told us when he fell in line."

"And you thought it important enough to bring him to me?" asked Olaf.

"He's harmless," said Leif.

"The lad is right," said the old man. He trundled up to Olaf and reached a hand onto the pirate's shoulder. Olaf allowed it. "I've been harmless since the day my mother freshened. The labor was hell. That's what my father said. My mother never said, because she died."

"I'd have smacked your head against a rock," huffed Olaf. "If you killed my woman in such a way, your brains would have been splattered."

"That's what my dad said he should have done. But the word of Christ told him not to. He didn't." The farmer gave a long, low whistle. The dog barked once and ran all the way around the herd. It pattered to a halt next to his owner's feet. "Lord, you certainly deserve all the cattle you've got there. You're strong and mighty. These men of yours dealt with a scourge that's been ravaging our countryside for a year. You deserve a reward and then some."

"What is it, old man? Crack-a-Bone here doesn't suffer flatterers," I said.

"Oh, that is nothing but the shit of hogs," growled the farmer with a wave of his hand. "If a compliment is true and meant with sincerity, every man wants to hear about his own greatness."

Olaf plucked the man's hand from his shoulder. "You're right. I like it as much as the next. Now what do you want?"

"Let me split off only my cattle from the rest. I'll take them and be gone." The man tried to straighten up a little taller, but his contorted spine forced his head further to the side.

Olaf chuckled. He moved to walk away. "I'd do it, old man. Just for your boldness, I'd do it, but I don't have that kind of time. A raider needs to keep moving and I see you move like pine tar in winter."

"I'll not be the one sorting, lord. The mutt here does my work." The dog playfully bit at his master's pointing hand.

Olaf was intrigued. He again faced the old man with balled fists on his hips. "And just how will I know that the dog gets the right cows?"

"And heifers, lord. There are a few heifers in the bunch and a few bull calves. You'll see my mark on my cattle. That is how you'll know."

Olaf furrowed his brow. "And how will the dog know?"

Old farmer threw up a hand. "I don't know. But he does." Sensing it was time to strike, the man asked, "May I send him?"

"Do!" called Olaf. His cheeks were bunched up from the corners of his huge smile. Ox-foot watched the exchange and held up a hand to keep his men from spurring the herd on faster.

Without awaiting further instructions, the farmer flattened his palm and softly set it on the dog's black, moist nose. He said, "Away, to me," then quickly lifted the hand.

The dog shot off like a javelin. He cut between Cnute's legs, almost toppling him. The beast ran into the midst of the herd. He nibbled on the hocks of two heifers. They cut to the side. The mutt hopped from one side of the pair to the other, guiding them to a clearing on the side of the road. The old man scuffled to them and patted their heads. The dog again broke off without instructions. Time after time the beast did his work. In less time than it takes a man to empty his bladder, there were a little more than half a dozen cows standing in a rough line by the farmer. The dog skidded to a halt.

Olaf strode over. "Impressive display, but I still don't know that these are yours and only yours."

The old man grinned with his dirty smile. "Lord Crack-a-Bone, just have a look from hook bone to hook bone. You'll see my mark there. None of the other beasts in your herd bears my mark."

Olaf went and studied the separated cattle. After the first two he stopped. He shook his head. "Take your cattle back, old man."

"Thank you, Crack-a-Bone." The old man knew when he'd pushed enough. He tipped his head and turned to go.

"But the dog stays with me." Olaf tugged at a small gold ring that was securely on a rugged finger. He twisted until it popped over the knuckle. "And here is your payment for the beast."

The old man looked at the gold in his hand. He'd probably never had so much of the metal in all his life. But the gold was worthless to the nearly crippled farmer compared to the dog. He looked down at his trusty companion.

"He'll be good to you, lord," the farmer sighed.

"What's his name?" asked Olaf.

The old man shrugged one shoulder. It appeared an uncomfortable movement. "Dog?" he said.

"Fine, I'll call him Vigi." Olaf mimicked the low whistle he'd heard the farmer use.

Vigi's ears perked. He barked, but then realized the call came not from his master. He peered up, confused, at the old man. "It's all right dog. Go to the raider, Vigi." Vigi trotted the three steps to Olaf and sat at his feet. The pirate roughly patted the dog's head. The beast playfully nipped at his new master.

We all watched the old farmer trundle his way back down the path toward the place where he pastured his tiny herd. The cows lowed as if they were happy to be going home with the familiar voice of their owner calling them. "Up, cow," he said to the one I'd named Gudruna. He was just as original with the names of his cattle as he was with his dog.

Olaf clapped his hands. The dog tensed, but sat rooted in the road. "It's time to take care of these so-called Norsemen you've captured."

The beaten men had already dropped to their knees on their own volition by the time Olaf and his new mutt faced them. "Now," wondered Olaf, "what to do with you?"

One of the men lowered his forehead to the road. I winced as I thought of the open gash that adorned it being mashed into the dirt. "Lord Crack-a-Bone, allow us this chance to pledge our oaths to you."

Olaf laughed. Vigi barked along with him. "That's one of the coward's ways to be kept from the hero's sword. Or, perhaps you fear the auction block in Dyflin even more."

"Neither, Lord Crack-a-Bone," said the man to the surface of the road. He cocked his face toward his comrades and hissed, "Down fools." They obeyed. "We'll take the sword if that be your will. We'll gladly take it before being sent to the thrall auction. That much is certain. But we want to swear to you because of who you are. Your reputation is unrivaled. With our jarl dead back in the pasture, we seek a leader. We are good fighters, lord."

Olaf dropped to a knee and rested a hand on Vigi. He stroked the dog's matted fur. Vigi licked Olaf's beard, slowly at first, but then he tasted food left behind in his new master's whiskers and slathered the hair. Olaf let him go. He studied the backs of the captives' heads. "Not the best fighters, I'd say. These simple Greenlanders handled you. From the horses they brought with them, I'd also say you were mounted. They destroyed you despite the advantage."

"In the shield wall, lord, that is where our people excel," countered the man.

"I should hope so!" exclaimed Olaf. He finally batted Vigi away. The beast took the hint and trotted off. He didn't go far. He stuck his snout onto our legs and lapped at the dried blood. "Every proper Norseman had better know how to live in the shield wall. From the fisherman to the goldsmith, that is how our people have fought and how we will fight."

Olaf reached out his hand and grabbed a fistful of the spokesman's hair. He tugged it. "Up, lads. Now, where is it you're from?"

The man with the gash across his forehead rose, followed by the others. The wound was packed with earth. I winced again. "We are from Vedrafjordr."

"What were you doing all the way up here?"

"Our now-dead lord told us to come and raid. He told us we'd stay," said one of the other men.

"Vedrafjordr hasn't been that active for years," said Olaf. "Why the change?"

The men looked at one another. The spokesman said, "If he is to be our lord, we must answer."

They nodded. The second man continued. "Emissaries from the Ui Neill came to our city. They searched for a band of mercenaries who would attack their old enemy, the Leinster clan. Our jarl raised his hand."

That made sense to me. The Ui Neill, though as Irish as a green-eyed monk, hated their fellow Irishmen, the Leinsters. Olaf spat, "That makes no sense. The Ui Neill don't need to beat the bushes for an army. They are stronger than the Leinstermen in almost any fight."

"Why did you shout, 'Dyflin,' when you attacked us?" I asked.

Olaf furrowed his brow. "You didn't tell me that." I don't know if he scolded me or the captives.

"The Ui Neill told us to spread word that we were Dyfliners. I assumed they wanted to provoke the Leinsters to move to full-out war against Dyflin," surmised the lead captive.

Now it all made sense to me. The Leinstermen would launch reprisal attacks against Dyflin. Mael Sechnaill and his Ui Neill would be there to pick up the pieces of both shattered armies.

"Doesn't make sense," scoffed Olaf, showing that what I thought made sense when it came to the politics of the Irish Sea was a pile of dung. "Mael wouldn't want to allow the Leinster clan to get a foothold in Dyflin. Then he'd have to root them out himself. Better to take the chance of letting Dyflin die with Kvaran when the old man finally goes. Doesn't make sense!"

"Lord Crack-a-Bone, we don't know or understand all the workings of the world at the level of noblemen and warlords. We are just the sharp blades that men like you employ. We will still gladly pledge our oaths to you right now on this road. We will be faithful to you and you only until the day we die."

Olaf stood and turned. "Please, lord," pleaded the second man. "As a sign of good faith, we have a sack filled with gold arm rings on that horse over there. Take them as a gift."

The warlord asked me with a glance if that was true. I shrugged. "You didn't check their baggage?" Olaf asked, perturbed. "You Greenlanders seem to be fine fighters, but you've got a few things to learn about thievery."

Tyrkr scurried to the horse, lifted one of the dead men's head, and pulled off a heavy-laden leather sack. It clattered when he dropped it to the ground. The contents proved to be arm rings. "Bring that to me," said Olaf.

When he had his hands on the sack's neck, Olaf reached in and drew out the same number of rings as there were captives, leaving the bag still bulging. He tossed one onto the ground at the knees of each of the foreign Norsemen. "What kind of lord would I be if I accepted a gift from my new men and gave them nothing in return? Halldorr, cut them free, I've already heard their oaths. They will replace the men on your ship that you lost today. They are my sworn men."

He gave the low whistle taught to him by the farmer. Vigi barked and came bounding toward him. The dog, just like every man who'd ever met Olaf, sensed that he was something special. Vigi jumped up at the warlord's barrel chest. Olaf caught the big dog, kissed his nose, and set him back in the road. The two were forever together after that. Only death would one day separate them, but that is part of another of my tales.

"Back to the ships!" shouted Olaf. "We'll burn our dead on pyres tonight. Odin will have new warriors drinking in his halls after we send them off. Tomorrow, we continue our raiding." He slung the bulging bag of arm rings over his shoulder and hummed.

Never before or since has there been a more excellent man.

CHAPTER 5

Men of any excellence are hard to find.

If the spectrum of men runs from my head to my heel, then excellent men of any stripe are represented just by the portion above my brow. As you might guess, I believe Olaf Crack-a-Bone Tryggvason was at the crown. Below him, from his seat down to my brow would be where other fine men resided. Finding them in the world was nearly impossible.

We'd raided for several weeks after taking the cattle at Viklow. The cows shit on the deck planks of *Charging Boar*. Belly wind burst from both ends of the beasts – mouths and rumps – making our sweating shipload of men smell even worse than normal. None of it bothered us. We slid into shore after shore. Small treasures and goods found their way into our holds. Thin Irish boys and girls found themselves chained within our hulls. They'd be sold on the block in Dyflin's marketplace. And before you, in your Christian mind, begin shaming me, remember that if the Irish could build ships as fine as ours, if they could muster even a tenth of our military ethos, they'd be on the shores of Norway doing the same to us. Back then I thanked Odin for his gifts of shipbuilding and woodworking to my people. Now, as a follower of the One God myself, I question those violent actions of my youth. Nonetheless, rather than any of the old gods, instead I thank him for those same gifts.

Olaf continued to prove himself to be a true sea king. He wasn't some grubby warlord. Even though his clothing and sometimes his words demonstrated the latter, his manner, his way of addressing his men, his boisterous personality all meant he was a king without a country. But Olaf had followers. Their numbers swelled by the week. New men would join a ship. A new ship would join his armada. Olaf was a leader of men and he was excellent.

Sitric had a ways to go before anyone would proclaim his excellence. Gormflaith, I suppose, would eagerly weave tales of her fine-bearded son's prowess at this task or that activity. Such tales would be mere stories made up in her head, though. They'd be like the old Head Ransom poems. You see, when a king captures a man and means to have his head lopped off, it is customary to allow the prisoner the chance to recite an extemporaneous poem in order to save his brains. More often than not the attempt is filled with bald lies about the king, the man's captor. The poems go on about how brave is the king. They tell of his fearlessness, steady resolve, and iron chest. They are all lies. Everyone knows it. Yet, if the lies are bold enough and the man's meter is true, the captive gets to walk away with his head intact. Gormflaith and Sitric, back then when Silkbeard was a pup, told themselves tales of how superbly the prince led his city.

By the time we slid back into the shingle along Dyflin's banks, the political landscape had not improved. It had grown worse.

"I said all the things I was told to say," stuttered Colbain.

We weren't in the King of Dyflin's hall for our meeting. Olaf, upon hearing the gossip aflutter in the town, made the prince come to him. We lounged along the southern palisade of the city, the quiet River Poddle barely audible on the other side.

Silkbeard threw his hands up in the air. "If he says he did his best, then he did." He sounded like a brother sticking up for a wayward sibling.

Gytha was affectionately holding her husband's hand. She let it go and stood from the pile of rotting timbers on which she sat. "Never mind what it looks like to the High King. Forget the fact that your negotiator was a mere servant."

"He's Irish," said Silkbeard. "He has that in common with them. He was raised by Gormflaith. Colbain is a natural choice to speak for me."

"Gormflaith is not the High King of Ireland," said Gytha.

"No, but she makes it her business to wrap all men around her finger and her legs around all men," I laughed. "Mael Sechnaill is nothing but a man."

"She does not!" exclaimed Colbain. His teeth clenched.

Gytha moved one step to the servant. She didn't offer the dignity of a slap with her palm. The prince's aunt whipped him with a broad stroke of the back of her hand. I fell in love with her again. Olaf sat, quietly listening. He smiled at his wife. Colbain retreated next to his childhood playmate, Sitric.

"Even if Colbain did as well as any man in talking with the High King about a marital union between our houses, what possible motivation does Mael have to grant it?" asked Gytha.

"To avoid war," was Sitric's simple response.

Gytha spread her arms wide, allowing them to fall to her womanly hips with a slap. "Oh, it's that easy. How foolish of me." She pointed to the prince. "Why do you think your father disappeared to Iona? He knows that our city is in a precarious spot. He knows that it may fall. It's crumbling already. Even the Leinstermen vultures sense it. They've been raiding us now for weeks. The raids do nothing but increase in severity and frequency. The few Leinstermen we've caught say it is for retribution. But Dyflin hasn't been strong enough to storm into Leinster since Iron Knee died. The Leinsters call it revenge, but you should understand that it is truly because they see we are weak!" Olaf and I exchanged glances, remembering what the men from Vedrafjordr that we captured in Viklow had said.

"There's something to those raids," began Olaf. "Leinster is being provoked by someone."

"I can handle a few raids from Leinster farmers," scoffed Sitric, holding up his hand to end that line of the conversation.

Gytha ignored him and went on. "Your father fled because he knows that the Christian monks at all the Irish monasteries record every bit of history they can. And, Kvaran doesn't want it written that Dyflin fell while he was in charge. That dubious honor will go to you, if you don't convince Mael Sechnaill of two things."

"What's that?" asked Silkbeard. He reached under his beard and clutched a cross that dangled from a chain around his neck.

Gytha rested a hand on her nephew's shoulder. Her tone softened. "The first, you are blindly attempting to do. It is innate in our family and you try. You fail so far, but you try. Demonstrate your cunning, your ability to bend, give, and take. Those are the marks of a king."

Olaf huffed. He clearly disagreed, but said nothing. My lord was all about strength.

"And the second trait?" asked Sitric, appearing hopeful.

Gytha looked at her husband. "He can tell you that."

"Well? Out with it," demanded the prince before Crack-a-Bone had a chance to speak. "And tell me why you made me come out here. The stench of the rotting scraps from the butcher shops is enough to turn my toes."

"Stench?" asked Olaf.

"Yes, the odor. Don't tell me you can't smell it," said Colbain.

Olaf stood slowly. He walked past the prince and slid down the muddy earthen embankment to where the winding Fishamble Street ended. Olaf began walking north toward the center of town. "Where's he going?" asked Sitric.

"Patience," shushed Gytha.

Olaf stepped in front of a butcher's shop. The man plied his trade in the street on a wide oak block. He was halfway through slicing a culled cow's carcass into manageable cuts. The offal lay in a bucket, a flaccid lung spilling over the brim. Olaf pointed to a few unfinished halves of lamb that dangled from hooks. "How much?"

Without looking up, the butcher answered, "Three English pennies."

"They'd be for the prince," said Olaf.

The man's eyes peeked up at Olaf then the rest of our group on the mound. Any life in his face faded. "Then it would be my honor to offer them as a gift for the next King of Dyflin."

Sitric smiled.

"Nonsense!" exclaimed Olaf. "The next King of Dyflin is generous to his followers. You'll deliver them to the great hall." Olaf reached into his coin purse. "You'll take five pennies." He slapped them into the butcher's bloody hand.

"Thank you," said the man to Olaf. "Thank you, Prince Sitric," he called up to Silkbeard.

"Yes, yes," answered Olaf. "Do you have a son?"

"Two," said the man, stuffing the precious pennies into his pocket. "They are both making deliveries right now."

"They sound like hard workers," observed Olaf.

"They are," answered the butcher proudly.

"I know it will mean you are short handed for a day or so, but Prince Sitric wants to invite your boys to train for war. He'll pay you a penny per day for each boy while they are away. They'll learn a thing or two about being men, about what our rugged ancestors had to do to found this city, and you'll be able to afford temporary help. What do you say?" asked Olaf.

Sitric was quietly fuming as his prized counterfeit pennies flowed away into the calloused hands of his citizens. He kept his tongue at bay, proving that even pups could go a few moments without yelping.

The butcher stuck out his red palm. Olaf grasped it tightly so that blood oozed out between the cracks. "Good," said Olaf. "Send them to the hall at first light."

The man nodded his understanding and spun into the building that was his tiny shop and home. I couldn't hear his exact words, but the butcher's tone said that his wife was learning about their sudden good fortune.

"What did that prove?" asked Sitric when Olaf had scraped his way up the embankment.

"If you personally do that with three or four hundred tradesmen in this city, you'll have the cheapest, most dedicated mass of men ever assembled. You'll have their boys, too," said Olaf. "You'll have two generations of loyal followers for the price of a few dozen thralls."

"So that is the second thing I need. I need to breed loyalty?" asked Sitric.

"No," said Olaf, looking at Gytha. "I am sorry to disagree, my dear." The sea king's wife gave a half smile before he continued. "Loyalty is the first thing you need. I don't understand all this cunning that my woman spoke about. I appreciate it when I see it, but I know nothing of it. The first thing you need is to get the men and women who work in this stinking section of Dyflin on your side. They will be the ones who hold tight in the shield wall or behind that palisade."

Sitric was shaking his head in frustration. "What is your version of the second thing I need then?"

Olaf appeared confused at the question. "What a thing to ask. You mean to be a king. You take that loyalty and you form it into a massive ball of brutality. You take that strength and prop it up behind you. You go to Mael Sechnaill and you properly ask for his daughter's hand. You give no threats, for you've no need. He'll be able to see the power in your followers' arms and eyes. Only then will you get your valuable union at terms that you like. And then the raiding Leinstermen will be nothing more than a lone mosquito waiting to be smacked."

The pup folded his arms across his chest. For a moment, I thought he'd cry. "You are right, Crack-a-Bone. You, too, Aunt Gytha. Teach me. Show me what I need to do."

The soft-bearded one surprised me. He wasn't so green that he knew only one emotion, blustering stubbornness. Sitric humbled himself in the mud, placing the future of his kingdom under the tutelage of a widow and a warlord.

• • •

I was again sent to Mael Sechnaill's hall. Although you may think it hard to believe, it is so. At least this time, I would do no talking. Everyone agreed that keeping my mouth shut was of paramount importance. Sitric commanded it. Olaf giggled when he heard how I ate with the High King covered in the blood of his soldiers. But the sea king invited me along, nonetheless. He was to be the prince's negotiator. He took with him his chief lieutenants, our crew of Greenlanders, and his personal skald, a man called Ottar. I couldn't decide which of us, the poet or me, rode with Olaf for his entertainment.

Our large entourage approached the gates of Mael's walled fortress. Trees still covered most of Ireland with only small, thin fields of barley interspersed. Farmers were nowhere to be seen on our trek. We hadn't tried to hide our approach so word that a vast armed band made up of the Dark Foreigners, as the Irish sometimes called us, traveled ahead. Any peasants on our path had long since fled.

"What do you think of the land here?" asked Olaf. The charger he'd borrowed from Sitric's stables nipped at my sad palfrey's cheek. Vigi sprang from one side of the road to the other, rousting rabbits or birds.

"Not as bountiful as the fields I've seen in England," I said. My horse used its rounded jaw bone like a hammer and whapped Olaf's charger. Each sufficiently wounded from their temporary battle, they trotted on without further incident.

"No, I mean do you see yourself here for many years?" the warlord asked.

I was surprised by the question. "I go where you go, lord."

"I believe it," answered Olaf. "It's not always the case. In fact, it's rarely the case. But I trust all of my new men as much as my original army." His face shone with nostalgia. "Oh, those who followed me up out of Holmgard were a frightful sight." And as quickly as it came, his reminiscence fled. Olaf looked at me. "You say things as they are, Halldorr. I trust you. You're simple."

Other men have called me simple and much worse. Oftentimes, such name calling made me angry, for men who used those terms were trying to elevate themselves and shove me in the mud. When Olaf used the word, however, I took it as an honor. The way he meant it was true. I was simple. I pledge an oath to you. I'll honor you as my lord. But you damn well better love your men, care for your soldiers – not just in word, but in deed. Olaf did and so when he called me simple, I stuck my chin a bit higher.

The woods cleared. We forded a small creek and followed the hard packed dirt road that wound around a small hillock. Sheep grazed on the hillside. A shepherd, the first man we'd seen in a day or more, leaned on his staff and watched us pass. Living so close to the High King had made him unafraid of strangers.

He had good reason to feel secure. The massive timber gates of Mael's city yawned open. A hundred mailed men stood in front of them. At least a hundred more heads poked up above the stone and timber palisade behind the greeting party.

"Do you mean to stay here, lord?" I asked as we lazily finished the last dozen fadmr of our ride.

Olaf shrugged. "I've never stayed anywhere very long. When I was just a baby, my mother had to curl me in her arms and flee the man who wanted to kill us both. Greycloak was his name. I've run ever since."

"You don't sound so certain," I said.

"I'm not done raiding, if that's what you're worried about. I'm not going to sleep behind the walls of a fortress. But I'll say this; my father was *a* king in Norway. I'll be *the* King of Norway one day. Harald Finehair's blood runs in my veins. I need just a little longer to prepare and I think that Dyflin might just be the spot to use. Thousands of men and goods come through its gates every day. Not a bad place to build an army – if we can keep it from tumbling when Kvaran dies."

"And not a bad place to keep a wife," Ottar said. He rode directly behind the warlord and me.

Olaf gave a half smile. "Gytha is a woman who deserves fine things. She can get them in Dyflin. If I can help her nephew, the pup, while I am there, I will."

Ahead, Gormflaith's giant war charger was shoving through the ranks of infantry barring our way. "Who is that?" asked Olaf. His voice said he was astonished, a typical reaction to the woman.

"That is Gormflaith, the woman who left Kvaran in favor of the High King. She's beautiful and cunning. If you are Odin and your Gytha is Friggas, then Gormflaith is that cold bitch, Hel. Be careful you don't fall under her spell," I warned.

"Ah, Halldorr, you're a warrior skald. Now that's rare indeed," said Ottar. "You're an enigma." I'd been called that before and I still wasn't certain what it meant.

"I've got my woman, lad," said Olaf. "One is all I need. It's all I can handle. You don't have to worry."

"Where's Colbain?" shouted Gormflaith. "He is always sent to us when the Prince of Dyflin wants to talk." Her head was held high on her spear-straight neck.

"Answer the lady," whispered Olaf.

"I'm not supposed to talk. Even you agreed to that," I hissed.

"I'll not be spoken to in such a way," said Olaf. His voice rasped.

"What is the problem?" asked Gormflaith. "Are you confused? Do you not understand your own language?"

When it was clear that Olaf meant to say nothing, I sighed. "Queen Gormflaith, Prince Sitric does wish to talk. Colbain was ill and so we come in his stead." Colbain was well. In fact, the yammering bastard pleaded with Sitric to allow him to come and chat with his dear adopted mother again – all in the name of peace, of course. For once, Silkbeard was taking advice from true leaders in Olaf and Gytha. Colbain was left behind coordinating all the military training the city's street urchins were to receive. I even saw my favorite comb salesman show up the morning we left.

Gormflaith's momentary concern at hearing about Colbain fled. "Very well," she said. The queen pointed to me. "But if it is to be you undermining the marriage talks again, just turn around now and leave. I don't need the High King's childish daughter swooning over a barbarian again." She looked at Olaf. "And who is that frightful creature? Mud, blood, and who knows what else is splattered all over him."

I peeked over at Olaf. He nodded. I took that to mean I was to introduce him. "This is the man sent by Sitric to enter into negotiations with the High King. I will not be talking."

"Thank goodness," said Gormflaith. "You've done nothing but ruin everything from the start."

I ignored her. The traitorous queen previously tried to suck me into her web when she pretended we'd plowed. She tried to sink in her fangs when we sacrificed the Ui Neill soldiers in Thor's Woods. The woman also tried to swallow me whole with alternating glances of strength and weakness. When I proved to be unappetizing prey, she belched me out again. I did the same to her, acting as if she was nothing more than a messenger. I said, "This man is recently allied with Dyflin. He brings with him to our fair city sixty longships bristling with hardened warriors. Tell the High King such a man is at his gates."

Gormflaith laughed out loud. She took a hand from the reins and covered her mouth. "You and my son, the prince, have a lot to learn about telling lies to demonstrate power." The queen shook her head, laughing. "I'll explain it in terms easy enough for you to understand. The lies you tell to make the other side think you have strength when you do not must be believable. You should have said this jarl or raider or whatever you want to call him has ten ships. That would be a lot, but not preposterous." Gormflaith tugged on her reins. Her horse spun. "You may follow me to the High King's hall. While I don't hold out hope for the negotiations, at least my son is trying. Sixty ships!" she exclaimed to herself. "The only man who commands that large a fleet is Tryggvason."

"Queen Gormflaith!" I called after her. "I present to you, the man sent to negotiate a fair marriage transaction, Crack-a-Bone."

The queen's horse halted. Neither it nor she turned around. "And it's true that the sea king, Olaf, has allied with Dyflin?"

"Yes, indeed, Queen Gormflaith," answered Olaf. "I married Gytha. Her lands are mine. My men and ships are hers. I'll say only that we have a mutual understanding, Sitric and I. We have a mutual goal."

"A turn in the road, that is all," muttered Gormflaith. "Make way," she commanded the frowning Irishmen. "Follow me to the hall."

• • •

Our reception by the High King was decidedly different once he found out that Olaf led us. My new lord's reputation was a like a vast, dark cloud that cast its shadow far ahead. Murmurs and fears sprang long before he even walked into the hall. And when we did finally make our entrance – it was to be at dusk, but Olaf didn't lead us from our quarters until the sun had been asleep for a long while – we were greeted with musicians and entertainers and anyone of note in the Ui Neill kingdom. It was markedly distinct from the spartan meal the High King offered me on my first trip to his fortress.

Every drummer stopped pounding when Olaf pushed open the hall's doors. Every flute ceased its whistling. Every conversation halted. Every face turned to get a look at the man with the imposing reputation. Brows furrowed as the Ui Neill men and women tried to match up Olaf's standing as a great sea king with his disheveled appearance. I marched in on Olaf's left. Vigi trotted in on his master's right. The dog's snout immediately went to the floor. It led the beast to an Irishman's leg. Vigi pissed on it before springing off to where a gaggle of children toyed with a cornered mouse.

"Welcome, Olaf Tryggvason," said Mael from his seat at the head table. He swept his arm over his food. "Do join us for a celebration held in your honor. It is not every day that we are blessed with the fortune of having such a distinguished guest."

Olaf's eye twinkled. His famous smile spread wide. "Mael Sechnaill, King of the Ui Neill, High King of Ireland, I'm humbled to think that a man as great as you would even take notice of a simple man like me. Of course, we'll join you in a time of revelry! But if we are to truly carouse tonight. I demand that you get these lazy musicians blowing and beating!" The High King silently agreed and music instantly began bouncing off the hall's high-peaked roof. Conversations slowly resumed as Olaf made his way between the long tables and benches toward the empty one meant for us.

"What would you like to begin with?" asked Mael once we found our seats. Gormflaith sat next to her husband. Princess Aednat sat at the king's other hand. Our eyes met. Her stare was a reminder that Aednat meant little fire in her native tongue. I was still not sure if Aednat's energy would lead her toward the path of Hel like her step-mother or if the youthful spirit would turn out more like Gytha, intelligent and beautiful, but without the manipulative hatred.

Olaf laughed. His broad chest shook. His small belly jiggled. "The difference between races astonishes me," Olaf said. "Never would a Norseman ask another Norseman what he would start with when celebrating. But we are different and it is fair that you ask." He swatted the table with a wide palm. "Ale!

How else are we to begin a party and negotiations if we don't drink toasts to one another?"

Servants, some of whom appeared to be of Norse descent, scampered about carrying pitchers of ale. Olaf's silver cup was filled. The rest of us were given wooden mugs. They, too, were filled to overflowing. The two kings, one of land the other of sea, offered glowing toasts to each other. Any lies told were mere half-truths and neither side took offense to the liberties taken by the other in their words. More ale was poured. More toasts offered. Olaf toasted Gormflaith's beauty. He toasted Aednat's potential. Olaf toasted Mael's city and his soldiers. He spoke highly of the music. Olaf offered glowing words about a man whom he said had a singing voice that sounded like the haunting calls of those females, the Valkyrie, who led dead warriors to Odin's hall. The imagery was lost on the Christian Irish, but nonetheless, they drank a lake's worth of ale that night with every toast. Not to be outdone, Mael Sechnaill met every one of Olaf's toasts with his own. He praised Kvaran's tenure. The High King commended Sitric's perseverance in the negotiations, how the prince sent man after man to get what he wanted. We drank and drank.

And I should tell you a little about the ale. The ale tasted like the warm piss of a fat man who suffered from the gout. It was brilliant. My eyes involuntarily squeezed shut on the first draught it was so deliciously bad. I winced. I think my teeth chattered. I gulped it down with my neck making a loud creaking sound. By my tenth mug, my chest was so warm, my eyelids so at ease, that I merely smiled. I scanned the room. Aednat had turned into a vision of a hazy Christian angel before my eyes. Gormflaith had morphed into Hel herself. Her hair had turned to icicles, her breasts to snow. Olaf told stories to Mael. I think the High King was actually enjoying himself.

At last the food arrived. Our plates were heaped with cuts of pork wallowing in its own juices and blood. Olaf took his eating knife, sliced off a hunk, and used the tip of the small blade to shove the meat into his mouth.

"Is it to your liking?" asked Gormflaith.

"Without a doubt!" exclaimed Olaf.

"And when would you like to discuss the entire reason you've come to us?" asked Gormflaith. "I'm sure Prince Sitric has certain expectations. I'm sure he doesn't want you just sitting here swilling the High King's hospitality."

"Oh, I'm sure Prince Sitric would prefer that it be the High King's and not his own," said Olaf.

Mael joined the warlord in laughter. He looked at his wife. "We'll talk soon enough." The doting father rested a warm hand on that of his daughter. "We'll get this decided by morning, I'm sure. But for now, I want to hear another story from Olaf. That is, if he'll reward us with one."

Olaf spoke through his chewing. "Or, you can have this man here," he pointed to me, "tell you a tale. He's been farther in this world than I!"

"No," said Mael and Gormflaith in unison.

"Yes," said Aednat. Everyone ignored the silly girl. Her eyes sparkled. I studied them and my heart beat a little stronger.

"Alright, alright," said Olaf. Vigi stuck his nose into his owner's groin. Olaf dropped a fist-sized hunk of ham onto the floor. It landed with a splat. The dog attacked it with vigor. "Let me see, what is a good one?" Olaf asked himself.

"Klerkon?" asked Ottar.

"Who's Klerkon?" asked Mael, eager for a good tale.

Olaf waved him off. "No, no. That's a boring tale. Klerkon's the man who killed my mother and sold me for the price of a cloak. I saw him in the marketplace in Holmgard one day when I was nine. I chopped him to pieces with an axe." Several proper Christian ladies at the table next to ours gasped.

"Valdamar?" suggested Ottar.

"The king in Holmgard, yes?" asked Gormflaith, remembering her Scandinavian history from her time as Queen of Dyflin.

"Yes, that's the one. Over there, some of his subjects call him Vladimir. He was more powerful than just Holmgard, though. He was king of all of the Kievan Rus. His territory went from the Baltic up the rivers nearly to the great Constantinople," said Olaf.

"Sounds like a promising story," said Mael.

Olaf frowned and shook his head. "Naw," he said. "Not much to tell. I joined Valdamar's army. I was just a scrapper, but the men saw fit to elevate me to command. I became a captain over many men. I fought in countless battles, all of them victorious. Valdamar began to fret that the men loved me more and that I'd take over. He had nothing to fear, however. I had bigger plans. I left him."

I could see what Olaf was doing. Even in my addled drunkenness, it was plain that Ottar and Olaf were subtly threatening the High King. They were explaining his martial prowess without saying a word. They were doing just what they told Sitric he'd have to do to get a fair set of terms in his marriage to Aednat.

"I've got it, lord," said Ottar. "Burizlaf and Geira. That is a tale you'll tell."

"You must tell me this one," demanded Mael. "He's the King of Wendland. I don't know the man, but I know he fought against the heathen Danes in the past. Tell me."

Olaf gave his skald a playful wink that went unseen by the royals. "If you insist, I'll do it. I had left Valdamar with a few crews. We sailed the Baltic in those early years. We raided. After we sacked Borgundarholm storms came. The winds and rain tumbled us here and there." Olaf leaned one way, then the other, acting out the scene. "But Thor was gracious that night." The priests lining Mael's table frowned at the mention of our old god. "Red-bearded Thor blew us to the shores of Wendland."

"You must have attacked King Burizlaf," wondered Gormflaith. "Since he was against your cousins the Danes, I mean."

Olaf chuckled. "No, Queen Gormflaith. I take each man as himself. I didn't even meet Burizlaf at his shores. We were driven into a small district of his kingdom. Now, Burizlaf was unfortunate enough to have no sons. Three daughters, can you believe the ill fortune?"

Mael looked at Aednat. He again tapped her hand. "It is not the best fortune to befall a man." Aednat turned the corners of her mouth downward.

"Oh, but it's not the end of it all, you know," said Olaf. "One of his daughters was called Geira." Olaf paused and quickly wiped a tear away from his eye. "She was the military governor in that particular district."

"A woman?" asked Mael.

"That's what she told me when she came marching out, leading her men to oppose us." Olaf faced his skald. "Ottar was there. She was a woman, right?"

"Aye," answered Ottar. His smile was sad.

"Geira rode out in front of her men by herself. Right between our two armies, she went. And as cool as glacial ice, Geira sat there waiting. I said to myself, 'what is this,' and stepped out of my shield wall. I rarely ride a horse like I did today, you see. So, I walked up the beach and met Geira," said Olaf.

"Did you kill her? You killed the woman, right?" asked Mael, clearly wanting it to be so. It would help confirm in his mind just what a pagan Olaf was.

"Kill her?" Olaf huffed. "I stared at her. My mouth was agape. I looked at her under that heavy mail and shining helmet. I couldn't see her face clearly, but it didn't matter. Any woman who presented herself in such a way was beautiful. I proposed that we marry one another. Geira agreed. We rode to her father, Burizlaf, and made it official."

Mael slapped his knee. "That was quite a story, Olaf. I didn't know that about you."

"That's not the end, just yet," said Olaf, wagging a finger. "Once I married Geira I became wedded to her father, to her family. His problems were my problems. His friends were my friends. His enemies, mine." Olaf paused and his face grew stern. "I am now married to Gytha." He picked up one of the large leg bones from the hog that sat on the table. Olaf broke it in two. That wasn't the impressive part. He moved the two, short pieces next to one another in his hands and without any effort snapped them simultaneously. He took the now four short sections and broke them at once. "Do you mean to be friend or enemy to my new family?"

• • •

Mael Sechnaill clumsily rose to his feet. His legs were wobbly, for he'd consumed as much ale as Olaf. The High King was far more used to sipping a few cups of wine with his midday meal and dinner. Olaf used one of his men as the back of a chair, leaning back while seated on his bench. The warlord looked as fresh as the moment we'd come to the celebration.

Mael lifted his silver cup for the one hundredth time that night. By then it was already morning, just before the sun sped above the horizon. This time, his toast was not boastful or meaningless. It was to announce something of importance. "Noblemen, noblewomen of the Ui Neill, visitors from the other Irish clans, I am proud to stand before you with news. All these hours spent drinking the drink of these Dark Foreigners hasn't been for naught." The crowd chuckled. Everyone from the king to the lowest slave was exhausted. Vigi was curled up under the warm arms of children who slept on the floor.

"My little beloved Princess Aednat is to be wed to Prince Sitric, son to Queen Gormflaith within the month." Tired applause began. It started slow, like a longboat begins to move when the men first stick their oars below the waves. Soon, the gravity of the declaration sunk in and the High King's hall was again alive with cheer. Gormflaith looked as pleased and satisfied as a man who'd just finished his time with the village whore. Aednat's jaw was clenched, but the young woman wasn't foolish enough to cry, whine, or complain which proved she was becoming wise. It is important to know your place in this world.

The clapping faded. "Along with my daughter's hand and my blood which will run through the couple's children's veins, I happily grant lands up to and including the River Boyne to Dyflin's future king." Olaf folded his arms and leaned his head back against the other man. He closed his eyes while wearing a grin. Mael continued, "Please once more, let us drink. We toast peace between our two peoples." Mael sipped the ale and set down the cup. He lowered himself into his chair using both hands on the table to steady his body.

Olaf's eyes snapped open. He downed another mug of ale. He tapped the rim and pointed down so that a wandering servant could see he wanted more. Even I was done drinking by then. "You know I've got this name Crack-a-Bone. People call me that. Most don't even know why."

Mael blankly stared at the warlord beneath heavy eyelids. Aednat spoke up. "It's because that's how you kill people, right?"

Olaf smiled. "Many people say that, don't they, Ottar?"

"They do, lord," answered the skald.

"By Hel's frosty crotch, I've even been known to give that as the reason." He leaned in and acted like he shared a great secret. "The truth is that I foster the idea because it makes my opponents nervous. I got the name because breaking bones is my favorite method of telling the future," he giggled.

"That's not nearly as terrifying as thinking you snap people in half with your bare hands," said Aednat.

"Oh, I've done that, too," joked Olaf. "But I break bones when I want to divine the future. Well, I shattered one earlier in the evening . . ."

"And what did you see?" asked Gormflaith, prodding Olaf to the point. Even she was fading, I think.

"I'm glad you asked, Queen Gormflaith. You know, I travel a lot. I see many people. Do you know that when I was raiding in Leinster of late, I saw some Norsemen from Vedrafjordr? Though, and you might not believe this, they were pillaging their way around the Leinster clans and claiming to be Dyfliners. They even shouted things like 'Dyflin' or 'Kvaran' when they went into battle. Now I don't pretend to know why men would do such a thing. It's all beyond my simple mind. But, when I broke those bones, I realized that someone else must have sent those now dead men there to stir up trouble against Dyflin."

Gormflaith paled. Her cheeks, pink from wine, turned white. She said nothing while dabbing her mouth with a cloth. The queen quietly stood and slowly walked to the far side of the hall. Olaf twitched his head to the side and Ox-foot obediently followed the traitorous woman.

Mael furrowed his brow. He used a sleepy tongue to clean the film off his teeth. "Well, I hope you don't think I had anything to do with that. Before I met you tonight, I had no reason to be as sneaky as all that. Dyflin seemed ready to fall of its own weight." He now mimicked Olaf and leaned back in his throne, resting his hands in his lap.

"I make no accusations, High King," said Olaf. "It's only that the cracking bone gave me the idea that someone put the men from Vedrafjordr up to the task."

"Good for you. I'm glad the bones helped," said Mael. He closed his eyes. Soon his breathing became slow and regular.

Ox-foot hobbled back. "The queen just sent a messenger to Vedrafjordr. I heard her say now that the wedding is arranged they are to call off all attacks."

My lord shook his head. "So that's it."

"That's what?" I asked, my mind about as numb as one that is still conscious can be.

"I've figure it all out," he whispered so that Aednat could not hear. "The queen over there, the one you all accuse of being a puppeteer..."

"I think she claims to run Ireland all by herself," I said.

"She tries," agreed Olaf. "She wants her precious boy, Sitric Silkbeard to be not only King of Dyflin, but the High King of Ireland. Gormflaith wants her grandchildren to be the supreme rulers of the Irish Sea so badly that she was trying to do anything she could to force Sitric and Aednat together. If Leinster began attacking Dyflin, Sitric would take almost any terms from Mael and Mael would be willing to offer them if the Leinstermen began showing they had muscle. It's not a perfect plan, but I figured it out. Now Gormflaith scampers to call off her dogs so that they don't shit on her well-planned wedding. Mael!" Olaf shouted. The High King's eyes shot open. "What do you say we end the evening with some ancient words from my skald? My people love to hear tales from men trained to tell them. We long to hear the poetry that comes directly from our one-eyed god, Odin."

The tired king shrugged. Mael nodded while again closing his eyes. The High King's monks and priests gathered up their skirts and quickly moved to the door. They wouldn't listen to our old stories. One of them said, "They parade their sin like Sodom." How different these holy men were from Killian, the first Christian priest I had ever known. He immersed himself in our Norse culture so that he could convert us. In many ways he failed. Killian had become more like us. It was his lust for battle that got him killed alongside King Godfrey. And in fairness to those men who filed out of Mael's hall that night, our people had ravaged their churches for two hundred years. We'd taken, we'd killed. I'd not want to hear about my conqueror's present or ancient glories, either.

  Ottar stood and mounted the table so that his boots scattered a bowl of small bread loaves. My sea king at last appeared ready to truly relax. He again leaned against the back of his seaman. Olaf folded his arms, closed his eyes, and readied himself to listen to the work of the gods.

  The skald told the tales of heroes. He began with Sigurd, the slayer of the dragon. That's where most skalds started, for it was a terrific yarn. Though I knew almost every word of the long story, I listened intently. So did the rest of our men. Even the Irish men and women perked up to hear the strange words. Aednat alternated looking up at Ottar and over to me. I smiled, in my numb brain pretending that the young woman viewed me as her model of the heroic Sigurd.

  The hall grew quieter as Ottar went on. Most of the audience did not sleep for he was a fine storyteller. When Sigurd's tale ended, the skald said, "I'll leave the table after I say some words of poetry. Of all the wisdom gained by the mighty Odin when he sacrificed his own eye, the knowledge of poetry is the greatest."

> Praise the day at evening,
> The wife when she's cremated,
> A sword when it's tested,
> A girl when she's married,
> Ice when you've crossed it,
> Beer when you've drunk it.

> Chop wood in the wind,
> Row out to sea in good weather,
> Speak to a girl in the dark;
> The day's eyes are many;
> You need a ship for gliding,
> A shield for protection,
> A sword for striking,
> A maiden for kissing.

Ottar said the last at almost a whisper. My head swam. I dreamed of kissing Freydis, my always enchantress. She morphed into Aednat midway through the locking of our lips.

"By Thor's weak goats!" called Olaf, sitting upright as Ottar sat down.

"What is it," I slurred.

"You've much to learn, Halldorr," said the warlord. I looked around, dazed. Aednat and I weren't kissing. The princess slept peacefully in her chair. "When a skald speaks, it's not just about adventure and lies. Odin speaks to a man through those words. Well, Odin just spoke to me."

"What did he say?" I asked dumbly.

Olaf tut-tut-tutted. "He said what you heard, what Ottar said. He just told us to be cautious in our praise. And what have I done tonight, but praise myself? I thought I had it all figured out about Gormflaith. Odin tells me no." He cursed under his breath.

"What more is there?" My head ached. I wanted to sleep. I thought about sneaking over to Aednat and leading her to her bed where we could hold each other the rest of the night. It was a silly idea.

"I don't know! I know only that Gormflaith had better tread carefully. She's mixing her spirits. She tries to control people and people," Olaf said with a balled fist, "don't like to be controlled. She stirs. Gormflaith tried to brew a skirmish between the Leinstermen and Dyflin. When you involve men's hearts and their ire, little battles can blossom into war."

"How does that help us? What do we do?" I asked. I think my lips moved even slower than my mind.

Olaf sighed. He grinned. "I don't know how it helps us. Ottar's words may not help at all today. And what do we do? I don't know. I'm going to sleep."

The warlord shoved men to the side and made room on the bench so he could lie down. Vigi sensed that his master was resting and crawled out from under the pile of children. He skulked under the bench and spun in a circle three times before lying directly beneath Olaf. Ottar closed his eyes. The other Greenlanders closed theirs. The entire assembly went to sleep in the hall. Mael and Aednat slumbered. Only Gormflaith was gone.

I picked up a cold bit of pork rib. It may have been the remains of another man's dinner, but there was still a mouthful of fat stuck to it. I gnawed on it. When the last was torn away, I held the sticky bone. I shrugged. Why not, I thought. It took all my strength to snap it in two like my lord was wont to do. I waited for five full heartbeats for wisdom or the future to hit me. When they didn't, I sucked the marrow from both halves and threw them to Vigi. He sniffed at them and rested a single paw across what had become his property.

Sleep came on like the thick fog rolls into Greenland's fjords. It was fast and dark.

• • •

I was alone in the forest. It must have been day, for I could see. But the sun's light was hidden behind deep fog. The mist was so choking that I felt its moisture pressing on my brow. My eyelashes dripped. My cloak was soaking through, though there had been no rain. The road beneath my feet was hard-packed dirt, but my toes suffered with sloshing water in their midst. Trees, gnarled alder, ash, and whitebeams, lined the path just a fadmr away. They appeared as a web of faint bars keeping me on track. The woods were silent except for a haunting song that came from ahead. I was drawn toward it.

Slowly I crept down the way that wound through the trees. It was hard to breathe. Everything was tight – my jerkin, my helmet, the air. With every passing step I hoped to understand the words being sung. I could not. They were foreign. Yet, the ghoulish chant's meaning was clear enough. The band of women singing it sounded as if they reveled in its wickedness.

I stumbled over a crooked root that snaked across the road. I didn't fall over completely. My foot slapped the earth with a thud. My weapons rattled against my armor. The song stopped. I froze, afraid to breathe. My knees quaked.

After countless moments, the song resumed. Since I stood silently in place, I noticed another series of sounds coming from the same place. They were quieter than the frightening tune. It was the same order over and again. Scratch. Thud. Thud. Thud. Then mechanical clatter like wood parts rubbing on one another. Repeat.

I laughed to myself. I had been terrified of a few women who sang while they worked on looms. Everyone who'd ever lived knew the sounds of their mothers, sisters, or grandmothers turning single cords into sheets of fabric. I stood taller and confidently marched on. The fog seemed to dissipate as my mood improved.

A low, hanging yew tilted toward the sound. It pointed the way. I rounded the final curve and was welcomed with a Norse longhouse surrounded by a clearing. The grey embers of last night's fire smoldered in the center. A group of looms formed a semicircle around the dying heat. Women worked diligently at each one, their backs to me. I noticed the song again. Shivers ran down my back.

The women numbered twelve. Each had hair as golden as the brightest ring worn by the richest queen. Their arms were as white as the fatherland's snow. They all wore cloths made of swan's feathers. These women were the choosers of the slain. They were the Valkyries.

I was dead! Panic set in. I looked down and breathed a sigh of relief. My sword was firmly in my hand. I praised Thor. The sword meant I had died in battle. Though I'd miss riding on the gazelle's of the storm through the mountains of the sea, these women were preparing to lead me to Odin's hall. I'd spend the rest of my days drinking and singing with Odin until he called us, his chosen men, to enter the world's final battle, the

Ragnorok. A horse whinnied. At the edge of the clearing rested the dozen horses the women would ride on our journey.

The women! The Valkyries were known to be beautiful. I slid my sword into its wooden scabbard and approached the nearest woman. She didn't sense my presence. Her song didn't stop. Her work didn't cease. Thud, thud, thud went the beater. Clatter as she changed the warp. Scratch went the shuttle as it carried the weft. I didn't have to watch her hands do the tasks, for I knew the sounds. I crept closer to steal a glance at her lovely face.

I smelled it then. Death. I've smelled death on the battlefield. First, you smell the stench of human urine and feces as warriors release their waste. Dead men do it when their muscles go slack. Living soldiers soil themselves when fear overtakes their control. As blood spills over the grass and as organs roll, the odor is not unpleasant. There is almost no stink at all. Add three days. The reeking stench is almost unbearable. Add two more days to a field packed with fallen warriors and Hel's perfume will kill you on its own. The noxious scent that hung around those women was the latter.

I saw the loom. It was not Thjordhildr's loom back in Greenland. It was not made of cord and wood and steel. The vertical warp was made of a man's intestines. So, too, was the weft. Rotting human heads acted as loom-weights. The shuttle danced from one of the woman's hands to the other. It was not an oblong piece of wood. A dripping sword was the shuttle. The Valkyrie's hands were drenched in crimson, wet and slippery. Arrows served as the reels.

The song of the Valkyries halted again. The woman nearest me jumped to her feet and spun to face me. Her golden hair momentarily covered her face. I thanked Friggas for giving me that extra heartbeat to regain my composure for the moment I looked on what was to be as near to godly beauty I had ever seen. The curling blonde hair settled in place, framing her face.

Her rotting flesh oozed down. Sheets of it, black and yellow, hung off. I saw tendons and muscles. I could see the cracked bones of her forehead in places. Though the woman's mouth was permanently gaped open, undulating words spooled out. The Valkyrie whispered, "Witches mounts will feast on mail-coated trees. We be the perverted metal's goddesses. You be the lowly valley fish, its head crushed under the warrior's root."

I have never been so cold. I was frozen solid with fear. Thor had forsaken me. Odin gave up. I wasn't being led to Valhalla. They were taking me to Hel's dominion, Niflheim. My chest quivered. My hands ached.

The Valkyrie slapped both of her hands onto my cheeks and rubbed them. The gloves of blood that she wore were wet and warm. I felt alive. The warmth moved to my lips. It was hot. It stayed on my face and expanded. Soon my neck, my torso, my arms, and the rest were warm. All went dark. I could see nothing, but I felt the touch on my cheeks.

It took every bit of strength I had left to push my eyelids open. I saw golden hair dangling in my eyes. I felt lips kissing mine. I tried to pull away, but found that I was no longer in the clearing by the longhouse. I was lying on the floor. I grunted and shoved the Valkyrie away.

She withdrew without a fight. Her face was no longer rotting. She was embarrassed, horrified almost. A tear came to her eye and the curly haired woman spun and ran away.

I watched Aednat spring across the still slumbering hall. The first shards of daylight filtered through cracks in Mael's hall. The bright beams sliced through the fleeing princess like a knife filets a fish. I didn't call after her. I said nothing as I realized that I had been asleep, or maybe passed out. I put a finger to my lips, they tingled.

"Ahem," came a grunt from above.

I turned to see Olaf awake, looking down at me from his perch on the bench. Only one eye was open. "A dangerous game, lad."

Before I could protest, his eye slammed shut. Olaf smacked his lips twice to chase away the desert that always followed a night of drinking. His face relaxed and he returned to his dreams with the rest of the celebrants.

Dreams! Forgetting the foolish notions of a young princess, I listed out all the imagery and events I had seen. I said them over and over so that I could tell them to the last of the soothsayers back in Dyflin. A Christian priest wouldn't be able to help in this. It would take a seer of old. There had been fog, ash trees, and yews. There were horses, Valkyries, and entrails. A kiss. My dream ended with a kiss.

Was it a dream?

Or, was it a vision? Odin and the norns worked in such ways. I had heard that the One True God did, as well.

I couldn't wait until we returned to Dyflin. I jumped to my feet and shook Ottar until he was awake. The skald, with his gift of poetry, was the man closest to the gods in our party. He swatted and swore at me while rubbing away a handful of grime from the corners of his eyes. At last, I convinced him to listen.

And listen he did. His face went ashen.

CHAPTER 6

For a man who served the greatest sea king of his generation, I did a lot of riding – horses, not the waves. I did a lot of talking, little raiding. I was tasked at being an envoy, which was bad enough. Now I had to lead the band of warriors who would meet, then escort Princess Aednat and her entourage back to Dyflin. We'd leave hostages to return to Mael's hall to ensure the princess' safe passage. Our men would return once the Christian wedding was complete and Aednat carried Sitric's child in her belly. Both sides cared about the outcome of this marital union and I was tasked with the depressingly mundane task of riding alongside a girl so silly that she was under the misguided impression that I was a suitable match for her.

Fools. I served fools. Olaf, whom I loved, I've told you that, drove me to madness when he sent me on this errand. He was rightly smitten with Gytha. She said that the same fearsome men who got the deal at last completed should be the ones who guaranteed Aednat's safety. Olaf didn't want to go off chatting with an Irish princess, so it fell to me. The sea king drank in the halls, outfitted his ships for another series of raids, and bedded his bride while I glumly rode through the wilds of Ireland.

In truth, they weren't fools. I was the fool and I knew it. They were intelligent, cunning, strong men – and women, if you count Gytha. They were self-made, like Olaf. They were royal, like Silkbeard. They were wise beyond their years, like Leif. I was the oaf, yet that didn't stop me from grousing. Along the way I perfected my sulking and said almost nothing to the other men. Even their jeering didn't get me to bite. They heckled all the more.

"Halldorr?" said Ox-foot. My frowning face stared at my palfrey's mane. For the first time in a while, I wondered why the norns made King Godfrey die. He was to be my ticket to greatness. With him I would have riches and eventually win the hand of Leif's sister, Freydis. Perhaps, Olaf would take his place, but not if he kept sending me on pointless journeys.

"Halldorr," called Ox-foot. He sat mounted just three ells away. I moped.

It took him shouting my name a third time before I realized he was there. "What is it?" I snapped.

"Watch your tone," Ox-foot warned. "You may command this patrol, but I serve Olaf the same as you. I've served him longer."

"Yet he gave me command!" I shouted.

"Of an expedition that is best suited for a woman!" yelled Ox-foot. His deformed foot hung low, unable to fit into the stirrup.

I jerked a spear from where it dangled in thongs from my saddle. Before Ox-foot could react, I rammed the spear's butt into his ear. It split. Blood squirted onto his helmet as he toppled off the charger. The beast skittered down the path a few quick paces. "Well, it seems a woman just dismounted you with a single blow." He rolled around in the dirt, clutching the side of his head.

"Halldorr," quietly said a voice next to me.

"I've got more!" I cautioned, cocking the spear.

Tyrkr held up both hands in surrender. "Easy," he said. "You ought to at least get his report before you make it so he can't speak." The German pointed down to Ox-foot, who was serving in the capacity of scout. He had made it back up to one knee.

"Shorn ram balls," I cursed. I stuck the hind end of the spear down at the scout. He grabbed it and I hauled him back upright. The man favored his head, holding it at an angle while dabbing his ear with his hand. Time and again the palm came away red. The topmost section of his auricle was sliced in two. Good, I thought, another man with an ear that matches my mangled one.

"Eel," said the man.

"Ass," I said back.

Ox-foot chuckled. Tyrkr tossed a torn piece of fabric down. The scout wrapped it around his head and shuffled to his charger. After remounting, he trotted it to me.

"What do you have to report?" I asked.

"Eel," he said again.

"Ass," I repeated. Soon the spear was again stowed in its loose straps. "Now, what is it?"

"A group of us met the Ui Neill scouts," Ox-foot began. "I told them just what you asked me to say. We'd meet them in the morning near Lough Ramor, past Kells."

"And," I said. "The way you say it, makes me think they had other plans."

"No, the scouts thought it was a fine idea. But the princess herself rode up."

I rolled my eyes. "She had a better idea?" I guessed. "Royals usually do, especially if they are pretty young females. Their schemes are much better than ours." I acted bitter toward her, but I swear to you that my lips still tingled from the touch of hers.

Ox-foot offered a knowing chuckle. He wiped away a trail of blood that seeped from his makeshift bandage. "Aednat says that we are to meet at the gnarled yew. She acts as if there is only one on the whole island."

I frowned. "I know the one."

Ox-foot shook his head. "She said you would."

• • •

I led our band to within an English mile of the site where the princess and I had first met. We had to backtrack to the east. I stopped short of the clearing where a very naked Aednat had been captured by Iron Knee because there was no sense in following the notions of a silly woman with my small army. I didn't trust Mael. I didn't trust Gormflaith. They were too conniving for my taste. Most kings and queens were. I didn't trust Aednat because she had proven that she let her passions drive her to folly. I'd keep my men a safe distance away that night. We made camp, set our sentinels, and nestled in.

I didn't sleep. I got up and stepped over the snoring men. Randulfr looked like he didn't have a care in the world. He cuddled his weapons and a lice-ridden blanket.

"I'll be back by first light," I said to the easternmost sentry. "And tell your relief that I'll be coming. I don't feel like having a javelin in my belly for breakfast."

The guard laughed. He tugged down his trousers and urinated on a tree trunk. Steam rose from his warm stream on that cool night. "Maybe the scout you walloped will relieve me. Ox-foot might go out of his way to run you through."

"Ass," I muttered.

The guard clamped off his flow and bent forward, showing me his pale rump. He slapped it. "What do you think? Maybe this princess we meet tomorrow will fall in love with this and show me her own. I heard that you were there the day good Prince Iron Knee saw her in all her glory. Was it wonderful? I bet it was wonderful."

I walked into the falling gloom of the thick forest. "Ass," I muttered again, this time laughing.

Behind me, I heard the guard slapping his backside again. "She'll fall in love with this, I tell you. Forget Sitric's silky beard! My pasty rump will send her reeling."

I left him. Men like him, perhaps crazy to your Christian mind, are true heroes. I loved him and others like him. They could be counted on when mere mortals fled to the hills. Refined men and women would think him crude. They'd be right. He was. But men like that sentry were fine. Like gold, they'd been in the smith's cauldron deep within the furnace. Out they came, tested and pure. When the tide of death crept close to the longhouse, when the mists and fogs of battle loomed in the darkness, it was that type of man whose elbow rubbed yours. He would stand in the shield wall and never think of running. He might nearly shit his trousers with fear just before the mayhem began. But once the blows rained down, once the missiles spurt forth, once the most holy of mankind's activities commenced, a man like that would plant his feet like the roots of a great tree. He would be as firm as an oak. He would stand like the ancient yew in whatever weather came.

I was going to scout out the gnarled yew. I'm not sure why. We were in hostile territory, under a banner of truce to be sure, but I walked on Ui Neill lands alone except for my sword, saex, and battle axe. I told myself I was making certain that we would not fall into an ambush. Over and over, I mumbled those thoughts out loud. But I lied to myself. All men lie and all men tell half-truths to themselves. In fact, I think if you counted all the lies we've told to all the other men in Midgard, the number wouldn't come close to the falsehoods we broadcast to ourselves. My own lies litter my head. That night, when I marched out on my own for the righteous goodness of my men, I went because I thought that is what Aednat wanted.

And as much as I thought the girl silly, as foolish as her notion was, I agreed. If she wanted me as hers, I wanted her as mine. My big, dull head and my bigger soft heart led me to certain destruction.

• • •

Though they were technically foreign lands, I was familiar with most of their hidden treasures. Iron Knee had seen to that when he led us on his countless raids. On the way to the gnarled yew where Princess Aednat had been bound, I passed two tremendous barrow mounds. I climbed on them. I poked around, completely unafraid of the ghosts, or draugr, that may hauntingly guard them for eternity. Godfrey and Aoife had made certain that I gave no thought to the danger specters posed. Godfrey had done so with his single-minded pursuit of riches, Aoife, with her ignorant fearlessness – and sense of humor.

I walked over the second mound. A tree sprouted from the top. I came to the southern side and saw that its once vertical wall of stone was overgrown with thorns. A hare darted into a crevice in the still-sealed entrance way. This mound was much like the one Godfrey's band excavated on Anglesey – though this one was several times larger. I knew that through the entrance, there would be some type of long passage leading to the bones of one or many great ancient men. Riches would lie with them unless, like the Anglesey grave, it had long ago been robbed.

I crawled over a richly decorated rock that lay on its side in front of the entrance. Many generations ago a master carver had tapped dozens of swirls into the stone. The designs reminded me of rushing winds or the constant motions of the sea. "Hmmph," I said. Those primeval men had been much like me. Perhaps they, too, had worshipped my old gods, Odin and Thor. I wished I still had Killian, the warrior priest, with me. He would know the barrow's history. He was the most learned man I'd ever met. But he was dead. "Hmmph," I said again. Every person of whom I thought on my walk from camp was dead. Iron Knee was only the most recent. I wondered who among my current companions would be the next to leave me or die. It was a fact that everyone I had ever loved or cared about beyond a fleeting moment was torn away.

My toe was wet. As I turned over the images of people in my life, I'd wandered all the way to the north bank of River Boyne, what was to be the new northern boundary of Dyflin. "Hmmph," I said a third time. I waded across to the clearing where I had first laid eyes on the very naked Aednat.

I skulked around its edges for a few heartbeats, truly seeing if there was an ambush ready to spring on me or my men. Neither a glimmer of mail nor a rumble of a man's stomach betrayed anyone. I stepped out into the secluded meadow.

The trees that had eyes were there at the perimeter. I grinned when I thought about Tyrkr's confusion as Iron Knee had told us about them. I saw the place where our fire had been that night. I sniggered. The blaze's smoke continuously circumnavigated our group that night, making man after man swear and move out of its path. The wind was persistent in its pursuit.

I knelt to where Iron Knee had died. Though it was fully night, the small light from the waning moon and twinkling stars made me think I could still see that the ground was darker from the prince's spilled blood. It wasn't.

That didn't stop me from scooping up a handful of the dirt. I stood tall and felt its weight, felt its coolness. I wondered if Iron Knee could look down and see us from his perch in Valhalla. Whenever he left Odin's hall to drain his manhood in the bushes, could he see that we still tried to live up to his dreams? It was a shame that such a warrior left us.

But had he not died, I would likely have sworn an oath to him by now. Iron Knee would one day be King of Dyflin, but he was no sea king. He was no Olaf. I pressed the dirt between my two hands and let it slowly fall away. I decided that both Iron

Knee and I were better off after his killing. The Irish bastards and whoever their assassin had been were good for something.

Folly. I acted with the giddy mind of a young girl. I meandered to the great stones that had at first shielded Aednat's nude body from my view. Her half-clothed handmaidens had spilled over the rocks in fear. So had Aednat, but she was defiant at the same time. The girl was strong and by now you should know I admired strength in a woman. A woman stout of heart was music. A woman broad with hips made my blood course. A woman whose mind rolled like the rhythm of the sea was poetry. She was a gift from Friggas.

Every woman I'd loved, lusted after, hated, or admired was stalwart. Though you are familiar with the names, I'll list them again – Thjordhildr, Freydis, Aoife, Gudruna, Gytha, Gormflaith, and yes, Aednat. Line them up and they'd look nothing alike. But powerful were they in their own right.

I walked to the gnarled yew where Aednat first heard me give my defense of women. I spoke in nonsensical terms back then. They were the words of my future faith in the One God, but they'd won over the princess. What was I doing? I was there to meet a woman who was smart enough not to come. She'd said she'd meet us here in the morning and she would.

"Hmmph," I mumbled while turning to walk back to our camp.

"Hmmph," came a soft reply from the forest's edge.

I didn't react with a start or spin around to face an unseen enemy. The spritely pitch of the voice told me I had nothing to fear. Aednat had come.

"You took my meaning," the princess said. Aednat walked out of the thickets. The skirts of her dress snagged on a thorn. She carefully squeezed the plant's runner between her thumb and finger and plucked it free.

"I've taken nothing from you," I said.

Aednat chuckled. I was frozen, suddenly unsure what to do. She approached to within an arm's length.

"Not yet," she answered. "But I hope you take something very soon."

"You try to sound mature where you are young," I accused. "What do you know?" In another writing on another sheet of vellum, I've wondered aloud about the complexities of women. Their minds are mysteries – emotions, more so. But what was I doing then with Aednat other than the very thing I accused women of doing? I was coy. I felt a tug in my heart toward the princess and as soon as she came to me, I was rude.

The princess appeared hurt from my outburst. She was quick to muster strength, though. "I know you've come. For now, that is enough."

"Ha! And what about a time after tonight? What about tomorrow or next month? You'll be married to a Dyflin pup."

"Will I?" Aednat asked. She walked around me and spread her arms out wide, balancing on a long, winding root of the yew.

"You have no choice in the matter. Even Sitric doesn't have much say. It is what has to happen. Your father has decreed it. Kvaran supports it and so do the other powers in Dyflin," I said.

"Other powers?" Aednat asked. "Do you mean Olaf and Gytha?"

"Yes. So?"

"So, our fortress is not so far from your hall. Merchants brought the tale of their marriage. They chose one another, not for power, but romance," said Aednat. She leaned back on the yew, teetering with both feet locked on the root. The princess closed her eyes and smiled.

I thought two things at that moment. The first idea that crackled in my mind was that the young woman before me was mad. She believed the fairy tales told to her around the winter hearth. The princess believed that a strong warrior of valor and a fine woman of breeding were destined to be together. The truth was usually something quite apart. The second impression I had was that for all her crazy foolishness, Aednat was the woman for me.

I suppressed the second image. "Then the story you've heard is wrong. Gytha has lands. Olaf does not. Olaf has ships and men. Gytha does not. It is a match made perfect in its political and military power."

Aednat hopped down. "There were other suitors there that day at your . . . What do you call your assembly?"

"Thing," I said.

"Yes. There were other powerful men that could have filled Gytha's political needs."

"But none had Olaf's heart! Gytha could see that!"

Aednat inched closer. I was unsettled. I stepped back. "Exactly," she said. "So if Gytha didn't pick the richest, most handsome man, she picked the warrior with the largest heart." Aednat reached for my hand. I withdrew it.

"He probably was the richest," I said in useless defense.

"A woman wants a man with heart," Aednat went on. "Olaf has the heart of a raider. He's won the trust of his men. That was plain to see in the way you all looked at him at the banquet. I know a man who is all heart. He is muscle. He is strong. He is dedicated. He is ruthless and he'll fight for his country and woman with the tenacity of a rabid bear. He is a rock on which God may build a foundation."

I chuckled. "Perhaps not the One God. My name means 'Thor's Rock.'"

"Then you already know I mean you. You've already felt the same way. I saw your gaze when you first laid eyes on me," Aednat prodded.

"You were naked. All our eyes were on you and your parts," I said, glancing down to the chest hidden behind her dress.

The princess cocked her head and smiled. "Fair enough. But you defended my ladies against Prince Iron Knee when it wasn't convenient. That's heart. You set me free on your own authority when he was gone. That's ingenuity. Why not marry me and we can make a union that will become legendary? Our love will be told in all the Viking and Irish halls for generations. The names of Tristan and Iseult will be forgotten in the tales." Aednat was waxing, though I didn't know either of those people.

I stepped back again. "This is something that cannot and will not happen. Neither kingdom will allow it." I spoke the truth. Then, as if my mouth was working against my sense, it said, "We'd have to flee."

"Then let's run," Aednat answered. She said it as if the act was as simple as two women trudging down to the river to do the day's laundry.

"And you'd no longer be the princess of anything. Life is hard. You'd switch to a life of drudgery. And, worse than that, I'd leave behind my oath," I huffed.

"Make a new oath to me, for our love." The princess was persistent. She stepped forward so that the fabric that covered her breast brushed against me ever-so slightly. I stirred.

Knowing that whatever I did at that moment would have consequences for the rest of both our lives, I leapt – not literally, not yet. I moved my hands to her trim waist, squeezed, and pulled her up to me. Aednat helped by pushing off the ground with the balls of her feet. I could sense that my tug and her force were knocking me off balance. I ignored the potential negative outcomes of what was coming. Our lips brushed against one another. It was a moment that lasted longer in my mind that in reality. The sizzle of Thor's lighting was in that brief kiss. The taste of the stout earthiness of Friggas was on the tip of my tongue.

I moved one foot back to regain my balance. My heel caught on a serpentine root. Back we went like a mighty tree felled in a gale. The ground smacked the breath from my lungs. Any air I had left fled when Aednat crashed down on top of me. She smiled, beginning to laugh. I wanted to join her but the blow had knocked sense into me.

I gasped and stuttered to scold both of us while she lay on top of me. Suddenly Aednat frowned. Her head darted up so that her long curls bobbed. Her hand slapped across my mouth even though no words other than grunts had come out.

Then I heard what caused her worry. I roughly shoved her off and rolled to one knee. Nothing approached, but I heard the definite sounds of clatter and men's voices. It was, in a word, battle.

We spun our heads in the opposite direction when a new set of sounds erupted. It wasn't *a* battle. It was a pair of battles.

I stood and set my hand on the hilt of my sword. It was wholly unnecessary since it was plain to even the dimmest warrior that the twin conflicts were some distance away. The second sounded like it came from my camp.

"Did you lure me here so that my men were without a commander?" I asked the woman. "I should have known better than trust the shrewd Ui Neill. I should have known Mael's daughter, Gormflaith's step-daughter, was just as cunning as her parents."

Aednat climbed to her feet. She pulled her hair back in place. "Or, is it you who've laid a trap for my men. The first battle erupted over the hill where my father's men camp."

We studied each other in the darkness. Her narrowed eyes reflected what light came from the sky. She betrayed no hint of withholding the truth. Aednat looked me up and down. My leap into love had led to a veritable fall. And it was the tumble over the root that saved me from ruin. My love, or lust, had fled. I could only think about what happened in the forest.

Aednat sensed it, too. The young woman didn't take the time to discuss it. With her lips pulled taut, the princess nodded. "Well, if you didn't plan an ambush for us and we didn't plan an ambush for you, what is going on?"

"That is what I mean to find out," I said.

• • •

Damn women!

I don't mean it as if I said, 'Look at those damn women.' No. I mean it like, 'Damn all women to the One God's fiery hell or to Hel's icy crotch!'

In truth, I don't mean either one. It is just that I can hardly control the minutest events in my daily life. Why do I continually make the mistake to believe that I can make an impression on women, to affect outcomes beyond my own person? I was a dolt.

The din of war rose. Two fierce battles were growing longer by the moment. I told the young princess that she was to come with me, for it was the safest course of action regardless of what we found. I could not let any woman go traipsing off into the raging wilderness in the midst of strife, let alone the future bride of Dyflin's puppy prince.

As you may guess, her response was less than helpful. After several heartbeats of frustrating arguments, I stamped off by myself. At least Aednat had agreed to hide in the secluded glen and not return to her camp until we understood what was happening. After stuffing her among the rocks by the river, I kissed her forehead. It wasn't from lust or even love. It was something I felt compelled to do. The kiss was something I would have given a sister or even a mother.

"Thor's burnt red beard!" I cursed to myself as I pushed past the silent barrows and toward where I had left the sentry who was certain the princess would fall in love with his perfect, bare hind end. Neither he nor his relief was in place. The legs of a dead Irishman stuck from behind a bush. I peeked at him. He had a gaping axe wound on his face. His cheek bone was shattered. A lull in the fight ahead brought sudden, disconcerting stillness to the woods. Still I marched on to the main camp. In my wake, I could no longer hear the crashing sounds from the Ui Neill camp, as they were too distant.

"Lying Irish bastards!" swore one of my men as I jumped into the clearing. Fortunately, I was behind Dyflin's makeshift line. Beyond them stretched a host of wild Irishmen. I say wild because I hated the Irish. Like the sea rolls, my hate was a given. I witnessed them kill my men so I hated them. They felt the same about us. We'd killed their men. We'd sold them into slavery. I called them wild. They screeched into the night air with their native tongues, likely calling us nasty, wild, Dark Foreigners.

"What's going on?" I asked as I slid into line next to Tyrkr.

"Where've you been?" he asked – a legitimate question.

"Learn your place, thrall," I scolded. I shoved him. It was the wrong thing to do to a man who had been nothing but devoted to Leif and me for our entire lives.

Tyrkr flashed no anger. In that, he was wiser than I. "That batch of Ui Neill goat turds sprang on us. Our sentries had just enough time to warn us. Our walls have come together twice," he answered in his efficient, yet mangled Norse.

"And now both sides fling curses at one another," I summarized.

"Lying Irish sheep humpers!" screamed Tyrkr toward our enemies. Then he turned to me. "Yes." He grinned and faced our opponents. "Shriveled ram acorns!"

"Are you sure it's the Ui Neill?" I asked. It was the question a novice warrior would ask. I was too experienced to have asked it while facing potential death. But there I was, asking it. Who cares who it was? Kings and jarls may ask those questions when they are safe and warm in their halls, far from the battlefield. They can use the answers to build out their political and military stratagem. When you are a simple man or plain commander with a sword in your hand and across the way is a group of men bent on slitting your throat, you kill them first. Who was it? Dung for brains!

"Who else would it be? This is their land." Tyrkr finished his answer with a string of curses in his native German – aimed at the Irish and not me, I think.

I shouted down the line to Randulfr. "Are there other Irishmen in the area? Is this it?"

"I sent two scouts out to the flanks. They returned and said this pack of wolves looks like it is a detachment from a larger force, but the rest is nowhere to be found," called Randulfr. I had a hunch where the rest of the army was. It was besieging Aednat's guard.

"What have you tried?" I asked.

"We met them with our shield wall. That's it. They outnumber us, but they broke against us twice," Randulfr said. He stood proudly in the center of our line.

"I told you that," said Tyrkr.

I set a hand on the slave's shoulder. "You did. I am sorry."

"For what?" he said. I squeezed his shoulder and smiled.

"Then let's finish this!" I shouted.

"We can't," said Randulfr. "If we move to them, they can envelope us with their greater numbers. It's best to wait them out. If they attack, we shove them off this little hill. When morning comes, they'll run away."

"When morning comes, the rest of their army may be here!" I shouted.

Randulfr nodded in agreement. "Then I guess we die tonight." He adjusted the grip his hand held on his sword.

"Tyrkr, bring nine men," I barked. The thrall reacted with lightning efficiency. We peeled off the back and assembled. I rattled off the imprudent plan that bubbled up into my head. It went against anything I had seen in war. Well, it went against anything I had seen work. I'd witnessed versions of my idea fail a few times.

"We're with you," said Tyrkr.

"We'll move when the time is right," said Randulfr from his place in our main line.

And off we ran. It was a slave, nine volunteers, and me. We ran toward, not away from perhaps one hundred frowning Irishmen.

• • •

We burst from the far right side of our shield wall running at a full clip. Some of us had our shields lofted high. I didn't. Mine lolled at my side. Thankfully, I had guessed one thing correctly. The Irish had already hurled whatever extra missiles they carried. I had seen a few of their spears and javelins stuck into the earth, several trees, and a few of our men's legs. The weapons our enemy held in their hands would have to take them through the duration of our engagement. They'd not be launching any more.

All of us, even Tyrkr, had grown up around a winter hearth where tales of the old heroes were told by men practiced in the art of storytelling. Every Norsemen knew what a berserker was. They began their lives as mere men. But when they came of age, they climbed into the god realm not by being selected for breeding or bloodline. No, those men who became berserkers made their ascent in the only respectable way. They did it by becoming more frenzied than others when the filth of battle visited their doors. A man who became known as a berserker could take the base disaster that was war and make it so utterly terrifying for their opponents that it became absurdly beautiful.

I tell you all this about heroes because in our own small way at that moment the eleven of us who rushed at the Irish did our best at capturing the berserkers' essence. I howled like a wolf. Tyrkr snarled and drooled like an angry bear. The rest screamed and spat. Our weapons clanged against shields. One man rammed the point of his spear against his own helmet. That image, coupled with his wrinkled nose and bared teeth, disturbed even me. We made the racket of a hundred men ourselves. We appeared crazy to even the maddest of warriors. As we pounded with unrelenting speed toward the left end of the Irish line, each of our opponents turned their heads to get a glimpse of what was coming. Those faces, heretofore pink with valor, blanched. Our detachment slammed into them. We were met, not with the white of gritted teeth and tightened knuckles, but the pallor of fear.

My shield rapped the chests of two Irishmen. Both toppled backward onto their rumps. My sword grazed the side of a third man's head, opening a gash from his forehead, through his ear, and to the nape of his neck. My blade worked so quickly that the blood took a moment to fill the wound. Before the crimson splashed out, the slice looked like a ragged dead furrow in a farmer's field.

On I pressed. My momentum took me into the sides of more Irishmen. I've told you I was larger than most men. I wasn't the biggest man I'd ever seen, but my weight, my girth, could overcome most. Another enemy crumpled under just the force of my shield. As he rolled to his side, I used the iron rim of my bark to bash his shoulder. The edge slipped off the joint and crashed into his windpipe. The conduit broke with a dull pop. Then blood-filled droplets whooshed in and out of the new, gaping hole.

By now, the Irish had regained their composure. I hated them, but I cannot say they were weak children on the battlefield. They were, at times, as tenacious as were we. The next man met me as an equal. It was like I ran headlong into an Irish oak. My velocity drained away. With a great heave, the Irish warrior thrust me back. Crashing into the man running behind me was the only way I remained on my feet. I took inventory of our progress.

We'd slammed our way deep into the left of their line. They'd suffered greatly, but were adjusting. Irishmen shifted from the opposite end of their line to meet us. This had the effect of shortening their overall line and creating a salient. By Thor's great, long, red beard! It was as if we danced with choreographed movements. I could not have hoped for a better response. It was only up to Randulfr to act.

I glanced left toward our main line. A devilish grin curled amidst my dripping moustache and beard. A stray hair lapped against my tongue. I could taste my own sweat and the blood of others. I sucked off the moisture before spitting the hair out. I smiled again. Randulfr and the rest had just smacked into the now shortened line of the Irish.

We would win.

I turned and faced my opponents on the new leg of their line. A shadow crossed my eyes. I felt a dull pain in the side of my head, just below the border of my helmet. I turned to see that an Irishman smiled at me with dirty teeth. He raised the club he held in both hands to hit be again. I told my legs to shift, my hips to pivot. I instructed my arms to tense and block his blow with an elevated sword. None of my parts obeyed. My body mutinied at that exact moment. My head was dim. My thoughts were jumbled.

I saw a look of surprise appear on his face. Good, I thought. When a man looks confused in battle that means he has received a death blow. No man, no matter how many wars in which he has fought, expects death to come to him. The Irish man was dying from a wound inflicted upon him that neither he nor I had seen.

I laughed. I put my hand to the throbbing pain on the side of my head. When I looked at the palm it was red. My hair suddenly felt sopping wet. The battle raged around me.

I blinked. Had I been able to gaze upon my own face, I would have seen confused surprise. By Hel's frozen crotch! I had received a death blow at the exact point when the battle had

inexorably turned in our favor. My comrades flowed around me like a torrential flood. The Irish line shrunk. I teetered.
    All went black.
    For all I know, I died standing.
    At least I held my sword. I'd awaken in Valhalla.

CHAPTER 7

Ahh. There was the shouting. Everything was still black as pitch, but I suddenly became aware of bellowing. Men's voices barked out words. Maybe they even roared songs. It was hard to tell. Women's voices screeched. That surprised me, as I had always assumed that Odin's hall would be populated with mostly men. I corrected my long-held belief there in the dark void. I'd seen plenty of fierce women who could fight in a battle as fine as, or better than, some men. Queen Gudruna had been one such woman. Perhaps her voice was what I heard coming from Valhalla's walls on my approach. If I had any face or muscles left in my new existence, they twisted into a happy smile. The company of women in Odin's hall would make our near eternal celebration all the better.

The clamor gained in intensity. Odin hosted the best of revelry, I thought. The party-goers would recite verse and drink and hump their way to the Ragnarok. Soon I'd be there with them. If only the slow set of Valkyries that led me through the fog would hasten their pace!

The noise increased. My ears hurt. I noticed that it wasn't merriment that made such racket. Men and women were arguing, vehemently. My ears throbbed.

The throbbing wasn't my ears. It was my head. Thor had cursed me and I'd lived through the battle that night. The wound pulsed. Perhaps I would soon die from loss of blood, a mildly pleasing thought. I moved my hand. To my surprise it responded and fell onto my injury. The maimed lump was now bandaged. The dressing felt fresh and dry. The long hair that spilled around it felt clean.

I tried to piece together what was happening. I opened my mouth and croaked once. The arguments around me halted. I planned to ask a question of whoever it was, but decided against it. Instead, I cursed the tits of Friggas and willed my eyes open.

Olaf's bright face greeted me. "Stupidest tactic I've heard!" he said. "Breaking a shield wall by breaking your own." He wagged a finger. "Just because it worked against the Irish flowers, doesn't mean you're to go using the idea again with my oath sworn men. Do that and it'll be more than a piece of timber that raps your head." He jabbed a thick finger into my forehead and stepped back.

The world opened up around me. I was in Kvaran's hall, to the side of the raised platform where the king's twin thrones stood empty. One was bare because Kvaran was still away in Iona, hoping for his city to fall so that eternity could blame it on his witless pup. The other was bare because, of course, Queen Gormflaith's rump warmed the seat of another. It helped me collect my thoughts to go back to these basic memories.

I shot up. "Aednat! Where is Aednat?" I scanned the large room. The dog, Vigi, lounged under a table. Soon my head felt light and my vision swooned. The people in the room turned to amorphous blobs. I slowly lowered myself back down.

"That's why you're here!" shouted Sitric. "We're the ones with the questions."

I swallowed a fist-sized dollop of my own vomit. "The other men were there, too. If I made it here, certainly we won the battle near the barrows. Randulfr could tell you. Tyrkr could report," I said.

"They did, lad," said Olaf leaning over me again. "What they say makes little sense and so I want to ask you."

"He's a traitorous bastard!" It was Colbain. By Odin's one eye, I had forgotten he even existed. I remembered that I had felt sorry for him for a fleeting moment. Once.

"You're the bastard," I said, staring upward. I was unable to locate him in the room. "What's the Irish worm even talking about?" I said.

"Can you quiet the rat?" asked Gytha of Sitric. It was more of a command than a request.

The prince held up a hand to his near-brother. "Colbain's right. Not in his outbursts, but Colbain is right to question Halldorr." Silkbeard reached to his long beard. He stroked it once, felt the cross he wore beneath the whiskers, and so reached through to it. Two or three of his fingers played with his sacred amulet. "It was my mistake to send a man better suited for the battlefield to negotiate for Aednat's hand in the first place."

"I said the same," I quipped.

"Hush," warned Gytha.

"At every turn he seems to be in the position to sabotage the union. He makes questionable moves. He offends, fights, and badgers." Sitric paced among the participants.

"What is he getting at?" I asked, looking up at Olaf.

The worm moved behind Olaf. He stood over the sea king's stooping shoulder. "You sacrificed Ui Neill soldiers in a pagan ritual, offending Mael Sechnaill and his priests."

"At Gormflaith's direction!" I protested. No one seemed to hear me.

"And he was right to be offended," said Gytha. Her arms were folded across her chest.

"You had your way with Gormflaith in the woods!" shouted Colbain. This so-called fact really seemed to tweak him.

"I don't think I did," I began defending myself again. For a second time, no one heard me. I gave up.

"Another affront to Mael," said Gytha. I looked to Olaf for help. He simply nodded his agreement with his wife.

"With all these insults to the High King of Ireland, I'd think that you'd be dead by now. I'd think that the Mael would send correspondence asking for your head in order to begin negotiations again. That hasn't happened," said Sitric.

My head still throbbed, but I forced myself upright on the bench. "Just accuse me of something so that I know what you are all talking about."

"Lad," began Olaf as he pushed himself to a standing position. Though I was a bigger man than the sea king, his presence and broad chest made me feel small. It felt like the time I was a child and was accused by my first father of stealing the neighbor's axe. It was a fine implement. I did take it, but no amount of their searching discovered its hiding place. I was guilty then, but couldn't think of anything I'd done wrong now. "I saw you kissing the princess in the High King's hall."

Prince Sitric's face was turning red with anger. His aunt rested a hand on his shoulder. The man-boy prince jutted his chin and nodded his understanding to Gytha.

"Now, both Tyrkr and Randulfr report that you disappeared from the night camp before the assault from the Irish. I was thorough and asked all the men who lived through the battle. A sentry says that he saw you walking alone east some hours before the encounter." Olaf stated the facts plainly. He showed no emotion, though I knew that if he came to truly believe whatever his suspicions were, he'd do nothing to shield me from them.

"And then," said Prince Sitric. "You miraculously appear and lead Dyflin's men to victory, receiving a near fatal blow in the process. You're a hero." Silkbeard didn't sound pleased with the last. He'd gathered his composure and stood next to Olaf.

"I'll ask again. What am I being accused of?" I asked.

Olaf frowned. "Making everyone spell it out doesn't make you look innocent. To the contrary, it makes you appear guilty. You're at least guilty of toying with us."

I didn't know what they were talking about. "Fine. I don't help myself. But just tell me what I did so that we can figure out what happened."

Olaf sighed. Gytha scoffed. Colbain cursed me in his native Irish tongue. Prince Silkbeard said, "It is fine, as you say, if you want to harm your own cause. From the outside you offend and prod the High King of Ireland and yet he doesn't seem to care. You kiss his daughter, the woman who was to be my wife, in his hall. You disappear after your scouts have come across Princess Aednat and her party. While you're gone, a mysterious band of Irishmen attack what's left of your men."

"And I'd think every one of my men would say I've always done my best to fight for them and with them," I said.

"Or strike them," said Colbain.

"That's true. Our interviews said that you hammered one of the men you commanded. Ox-foot, I believe," said the prince. That was a worthless accusation. What commander didn't smack his warriors now and then?

"And?" I asked.

The prince fought every inclination he felt toward losing his temper. I saw his hands leave his belt for an instant as if he wanted to flail them around. He brought them back so that they pinched the leather. It creaked. I was proud of the pup at that moment. His youth was fading and he was growing into the role. "You've worked for the High King since you've come. There's your precious accusation. You showed up, the only survivors of King Godfrey's debacle. You refused to pledge to the House of Kvaran." Sitric shrugged. "At least you have a small amount of honor and won't make a false oath. The High King may be crazy enough to think that he can put a stooge like you on Dyflin's throne with his daughter, but that doesn't mean it will work." The prince swept his hands in the air. "Halldorr, the hero of countless battles against the Ui Neill, finally finds love and ascends to the throne from his own valor."

I laughed and moved to stand. Colbain stepped in front of the prince, partially drawing his fat-bladed dagger. Olaf set a firm hand on my shoulder and set me down.

"I don't need to tell you what this means, Halldorr," said Olaf. He glanced over at Gytha who, like the sea king, appeared sad. "We've done the talking. Now answer."

"He should have his limbs tied between two longboats under full oar!" rumbled Colbain. His hand still clutched the dagger, but the weapon slowly slid home.

Olaf stared at the impudent Irish servant, who quickly retreated.

"Where do I start?" I asked.

"The accusation," said Olaf.

"Is false. It is misguided. I serve Olaf and that is all. Serving Lord Crack-a-Bone is more than enough, I might add. If Olaf chooses to offer assistance to Sitric and Kvaran, then I do. I am not in league with Mael Sechnaill. I can put it no plainer."

"And all your supposed slights toward him that he doesn't mind?" asked Sitric.

I shrugged. "Maybe he wants a union as badly as we do. I know he says otherwise, but maybe he's figured out he can prosper in peace. Kings and queens never say what they really mean."

Sitric and Gytha looked at one another. My words weren't all that convincing, but they listened, at least. I must have struck a chord. "Go on," said the prince.

"As for Princess Aednat, I'll tell it all. You may ask Tyrkr his version of events, but the night after we first found her when Iron Knee was still alive, she heard me rambling around the fire. I was opposed to," I hesitated as I looked at Gytha, "the men's raping of her ladies. Princess Aednat, because she is young, let her heart lead her. She developed a child-like affection for me."

Sitric wrinkled his nose. "And so you place your lips on hers."

"No, Prince Sitric. I was asleep, having the worst dream of my life. Ask Ottar about the nightmare. I awoke to the princess stealing a kiss."

"You're accusing the future Princess and then Queen of Dyflin of something reprehensible," warned Sitric.

I held up my hands in surrender. "I accuse the good woman of nothing. I merely say that just like all of us, as we make our way from the dependency of childhood into the responsibility of adulthood, sometimes we make a poor choice. Such was that small, harmless peck."

Sitric raised an eyebrow, as he thought about my words. "And your disappearance? I cannot wait to hear about that."

"I told you I would tell it all. Aednat told the scout to meet at the yew."

"That's what we were told by the men," said Olaf. "There must be a million yews in Ireland."

"I knew the one. I assumed it was where she'd been bound after we found her. Where the princess *thought* she'd fallen in love with me. I went there. I met her there." Again I put my hands up in surrender. "We spoke a few words. That is all. I told her to forget her childhood fantasies. I told her to marry you, Sitric. Just ask her. She'll tell you."

"I'm not sure how we are to do that, Halldorr. Not now," said Olaf.

"What do you mean? Just go to wherever her chambers are here in the hall and ask," I said.

"Now that is funny." Colbain said, a safe distance from Olaf. His words dripped with loathing. "You were the last to see her at your special yew tree. I would think that you would know she had no intention of coming here. After defeating the Ui Neill in the forest that night, Dyflin's warriors scampered home. It wasn't much of a wedding present for her men to attack ours."

"But they didn't!" I protested.

"Lad, you're being ridiculous now," said Olaf. "You were on Ui Neill soil and surrounded. It was Mael's warriors, either under his or his daughter's direction."

"Or Gormflaith's orders," said Gytha.

"No," I said. "Did any of our men come back with spoils? Did they grab an enemy spear or article of clothing?"

"Of course they did," said Colbain. "They're pagans like you. They take totems any time they can."

My face brightened. "Good. It's good. Find the spoils. Keep me here under guard. Assemble all the men who were with me that night. Have them bring what they took. Tell them you'll give them double its worth so that you get it all. Trust me it will be worth it to you!"

All of my accusers frowned. Sitric was shaking his head. "I should just listen to what Colbain said. I should watch a tug of war between two ships with your arms as the rope. But against my better judgment, I'll ask what we are to do with a heap of Irish shit?"

I pointed to Colbain. "You are to place it in front of him. I place my fate in his hands."

They all frowned. Well, except for Colbain. The worm smiled.

"Then you seal your fate," breathed Sitric. "I am not certain what this will prove, but I need to have a publicly defendable reason to see a *hero* killed. Whether you try trickery or not, Colbain will find the proper verdict."

The servant gleefully nodded his understanding.

And I hoped he would come to the right decision. It all depended on who exactly the bastard was. I thought I knew. I prayed that he was just a bitter slave and not truly evil.

• • •

"What am I to do?" asked Colbain. He stood on one of the few tufts of grass that grew in the city. Next to him were the rest of my accusers. I faced them, on my knees in the mud, hands bound behind my back. Between us was a small mound of battle refuse, taken by my men from the Irish we'd fought that night. Behind me fanned a crowd of citizens who'd come out for the impromptu show. Leif, Randulfr, Cnute, and the rest of our crew were among them. I couldn't see their worried faces, but could hear their words of support. My confidence swelled.

Sitric leaned in to the servant. "I've already introduced you. I've already said that this pile was evidence. Make a show of examining the heap. Then make your verdict, loud and clear."

"Not exactly," I said. "Colbain, don't look at the pile. Look at *each* item in the mess. Catalogue it in your mind. You'll come to the right conclusion."

He scoffed while stepping forward. Colbain carelessly bent down and picked up his first item. It was a sword. It looked like a Frankish blade of high quality, a fine prize for any warrior. He set it aside after barely taking note. The second item was a swatch of a fallen Irishman's shirt. Sometimes our men would take such an item if the dead man didn't have anything of value. At least we could tie an article of his clothing on our belts or in our beards to show the world we'd met battle and come away victorious. Colbain hastily tossed it onto the blade. My heart sunk. I suppose I knew who he was at that moment. Colbain was not the man I had hoped.

He picked up a spear then halted. He gazed at the weapon. His thumb scraped across the sharp head. It made a slight ringing sound that I could barely hear over the murmuring spectators. Colbain scanned along the ash wood shaft. He quickly returned his attention to the spear's head. He measured its neck, stretching the thumb and smallest finger of one hand.

"Good show," mumbled Sitric. "But you don't need to take too long."

Colbain ignored the prince. He measured the width of the flat edge of the spear's blade with his thumb. His head darted to face the swatch of fabric he'd so easily discarded. He drew it to the spear and studied them both together. Colbain slowly looked up at me. I nodded. His eyes narrowed and Colbain gently set those two items on a separate pile.

He went back to work. Colbain was more active now, jumping from one article to the next. After a rapid glance, the spoils would fall in one pile or the other. When he held the last piece of the plunder, he stood. His head shook in disbelief and he dropped it onto the second heap.

"What?" gasped Sitric after Colbain whispered in his ear. Silkbeard was nearly aghast. Olaf and Gytha smiled while they listened to the conversation. I grinned too, for I had discovered what kind of man Colbain was. He was still a goat's turd, a worm, a bastard, but he was in the process of proving himself to be capable of honesty.

Prince Sitric regained his poise and stepped forward. "I am pleased to announce that this bound man is a true hero." Some of the crowd jeered. They'd hoped for a gruesome show. Everyone liked a good execution. Leif and my friends cheered. "The evidence confirms his testimony. He is free to go." The assembly immediately began breaking up, its members grumbling about the lack of blood spilled or about the weather or their aching joints.

Sitric looked down at me as Leif cut my ropes. "Into my hall, now. We have to discuss what this means." His hand waved at the pile of booty on the ground and he marched off.

My crew came and slapped my back with multiple congratulatory blows that reverberated up to my ringing head wound. The slaps themselves soon stung.

Suddenly, I was lifted off the ground and squeezed. I craned my neck and saw that Olaf was the culprit. He laughed. "Oh, I didn't think you were a traitor. Glad to hear it!" He bobbed me up and down again, pressing his arms in tighter and tighter until I almost lost my breath. By the time he dropped me into the mud, I was panting.

I wanted to tell the sea king, thank you for believing in me when it was hard, but he was already marching up the small incline to Kvaran's hall. "Ottar!" he shouted. "Come. Halldorr quit playing in the mud. Move! Leif, Randulfr, Tyrkr, whomever! Run! We've got some bones to crack! We've got some plans to make so we can really break some bones!"

Tyrkr hoisted me upright. He violently batted and scraped at the dirt and muck that covered my clothes before jerking me toward the hall. We passed by Colbain, who stood studying the pile. He glanced up. The bastard bunched his cheeks and gave me a wary smile. It appeared forced to me. But his head nod was not counterfeit, for once. In it he said that he was sorry for accusing me.

Without a word, I accepted his apology.

Thor's beard, he was a worm.

• • •

"Why are we dealing with the Leinstermen now? Sure they raided our lands over the past few weeks, but to invade the Ui Neill, too!" barked Sitric. Every shred of clothing amongst the victory spoils bore the thread patterns common of the Leinsters. Each spear pilfered after the battle was manufactured in the Leinster smithies. The points and necks all wore the evidence as if the clan's name was painted on them. All someone had to do was look closely. It was even more powerful if the investigator had been born a Leinsterman and happened to loathe me for a variety of reasons. Colbain had served his purpose. He was able to set his personal vendetta aside.

"You know what happens when you give a stiff breeze a little too much sail cloth," observed Olaf. I knew. Leif, Randulfr, Tyrkr, and even Ottar, the skald, knew what it meant.

Sitric, Gytha, and Colbain stared at the sea king with confusion. "Colbain, run to Kvaran's yard. Bring in a hen. It has to be one that still lays. It can't be grubby. Make sure she's pretty," said Olaf. The servant looked at Sitric with pleading eyes, but the prince waved him away.

When he was gone, Olaf tried again. "You know what happens when you take a fiery charger from her stall after the winter. What if you immediately throw on a saddle? Then, what if you hop on and whip her, giving her every length of rein there is?"

Gytha answered. "She'll run 'til she drops. It won't take long either."

Olaf offered his wife a teeth-filled grin. "Oh, you're a good one. I'm glad I chose you."

"You chose me?" she asked with a playful sideways glance.

"No more of your banter," said Sitric, slicing the air with his hand. "What do your stories mean, Crack-a-Bone?"

"Yes, the woman is correct," said Olaf. He cracked his knuckles, one at a time. Pop. "But before the horse kills itself, what may happen to the rider?" Pop. Crack.

"He'll be lucky if he can hang on," answered Sitric. "The fool could well be killed when the beast gets out of control."

Olaf popped his last knuckle. "Excellent!" He paced around the central hearth where the fire that never stopped burning except only on the hottest of summer days, crackled. "That's just what we've got going on here with the Leinsters." A haze of smoke climbed upward and hovered in the rafters, creating a blanket that sank lower and lower.

"The Leinsters, they are the fool riders?" asked Sitric.

Olaf set a boot up on the hearth stones and scratched his inner thigh vigorously. "No, no. They are the horses. They've been quiet for a few years. Now someone has let them out of the barn and whipped them to a frenzied pace."

"What man would be such a fool as to spark a war?" Gytha asked.

"Oh, it's no man," began Olaf.

"Don't tell me tales of your old war gods," warned Sitric. "Odin this, Thor that."

Olaf giggled. "No. Wouldn't dare." He pretended to close his mouth like a sea chest and lock it with an imaginary key. "Wouldn't do it with such pious company." He dropped his boot back to the earthen floor and impatiently looked toward the door through which he expected Colbain to come. "So, as I was saying, no man would do it. Also, I assure you, it is no fool who has ignited this little fight."

"Who is it, then?" asked the prince.

"It's your own mother, lad," accused Olaf. Sitric opened his mouth in protest, but Olaf held up a palm. "It is not my attempt to drive a wedge into your happy family. The woman has done that on her own. I'm not even accusing the former Queen of Dyflin of treachery against her former kingdom. I say she is doing her level best to *support* it and support her son, you, by encouraging the Leinsters to attack us."

Olaf went on to describe our interaction in Viklow just a few weeks earlier. He explained how Gormflaith reacted when shrewdly confronted about the ploy. "And the woman hoped to whip up the Leinsters. They'd think Dyflin raided them. The Leinster kings would raise a small army in order to punish us. All the while we and the Ui Neill would be drawn closer together for this marriage and for our military as we, together, met the growing Leinster threat." He shrugged. "Well, the former queen," Olaf pointed to her bare throne, "has dropped a spark amongst the tinder. She's given the penned Leinster beast a little too much rein. The Leinstermen attacked Dyflin with a little too much force. And if what Halldorr heard was the Leinsters fighting the Ui Neill, I'd say Gormflaith's plan, though crude and brutal, will have just the outcome she desired all along. The Ui Neill and Dyflin will be bound more closely than ever. Mael will be forced into the friendliest of terms to wipe out the Leinster threat with us."

Sitric was stunned silent. The flapping and squawking hen that Colbain carried into the hall interrupted the moment of peace. "What do we do now?" asked the prince.

"You are the prince of this realm," said Olaf. "You'll be king soon. Kvaran wants you to make decisions like a royal, so you must do it." He snatched the hen. Her head was quickly tucked into his armpit. The sea king's forearm cradled the bird's weight. His hand clutched her shanks. She was instantly settled, almost lulled to sleep. "I have this work to do so that I may decide what I will do for you, though – what faithful Halldorr and I will do for you." Olaf gave me a wink.

In one sweeping motion he spun the hen so that its head ran in an arcing circle. Still grasping her legs, Olaf brought the bird down on the edge of the hearth. It didn't even have time to squawk. Her body went limp. Olaf proceeded to pop and break the animal's bones while they were still in the beast. With each new crack, the sea king listened and nodded his understanding at the tale the bird's bones told. When he was done and his hands and chest were sufficiently bloodied, he tossed the carcass onto the burning hearth. The feathers smoked for just a moment before bursting into flame and spewing their noxious odor up into the hall with the rest of the smoke.

We waited to learn what Olaf had gleaned from his work. He rubbed his wet palms on his filthy trousers. "Looks like I've got a plan. The gods say I continue to offer my services to you, Prince Sitric. At your command, I will take my ships and raid Leinster. Though they are the pawn in this game, they must be taught a lesson."

Sitric nodded. So did Gytha. "What will you do, nephew?" she asked.

"The marriage must still go on." It almost sounded like a question, but he gathered his noble footing. Silkbeard looked at me. "Aednat was merely an impertinent girl when she approached Halldorr. She'll mature into a fine and strong woman. Our kingdoms will grow closer together. Our militaries will align."

Gytha smiled. The pup was growing up. He went on, "I'll send a new batch of envoys to the High King. I'll tell him that the time for bickering has come to an end. I'll offer to Mael that I'll personally come to his hall. I will wed his daughter there under the services of his priests. I'll explain to him that united, our kingdoms will teach the Leinsters a lesson."

"Excellent plan, Prince Sitric," commended Olaf. "Why not send your diplomats with all that information, as you say. But instead of you immediately running off to your wedding bed, why not outfit for war now. Have your runners tell Mael that you will meet him and his army, next week. Together you'll march into Leinster and truly obliterate them. My men will come from the northwest. You and Mael will come from the north." The sea king slapped his hands together loudly. He squeezed them so tightly that the few drops of the chicken's blood that remained, oozed. "There will be no more lessons to teach the Leinsters. Her harbors and towns will be ours."

"You mean mine," corrected Sitric.

"No, lad, I don't," said Olaf, not giving up his happy mood. "You and the High King will divide the piss-poor Leinster kingdom up. You'll have to divide your lands further for administration. I'm partial to the chieftain and harbor at Viklow. I also know a brave farmer there that I'd rather not see come to harm. I'll take them." As if on cue, Vigi at last awoke from his slumber. He ran out from under a mead table. The dog sniffed his master's groin, then quickly moved to the fresh blood on his hands. The giddy beast lapped the last of the crimson. Olaf allowed it. The sea king even rubbed his dog's snout vigorously, leaving behind streaks of blood in the mottled fur.

Sitric stretched out his hand, undaunted by what covered the sea king's mitts. Olaf grasped it. "You've got a bargain, Crack-a-Bone. My aunt could have done no better in her hunt for a husband."

Our meeting quickly adjourned then. We scurried about preparing for our grand plan. In fact, it seemed to me to be the first time since I landed in Dyflin that we would follow anything beyond a tiny scheme. It had taken Gormflaith's backstabbing to drive us to true action. Perhaps her mad claims of running the entire island of Ireland were not so barmy after all. As I ran down to the docks to prepare *Charging Boar* for launch, I thought that she would see her son made, not only the King of Dyflin, but one day, the High King of Ireland.

But I had forgotten my dream, my vision.

You remember it, though – the one with the blood-soaked Valkyries who worked the gruesome looms. Apparently, Ottar the skald had forgotten it, too, for he didn't bring it up at our war council. He was too busy writing complementary verses about Olaf in his head, for the victories that would follow our meeting. It was so different from the night I told Ottar about my dream. There in Mael's hall, the skald's interpretation had been clear. We, the men of Dyflin, would suffer greatly at the hands of the Irish.

I suppose it doesn't matter that I had forgotten it. Had I recalled the dream during our council of war, I would have said we already had suffered. I would have shrugged off the omen because its time had come and gone. The Leinsters had attacked us in the night. They'd attacked us and many of our kind died. I had a head wound to prove it. That was enough suffering. Though the signs in my dream were true, they'd already occurred.

We'd already experienced the future foretold in my vision.

I was wrong.

More suffering would come.

• • •

The tub that we took to the seas that was known as *Charging Boar* was nothing more than a trader's knarr outfitted for war. It was fat and relatively slow compared with the beautiful sleek ships in Olaf's fleet. When compared to the handsome *Serpent*, Olaf's flagship, *Charging Boar* more closely resembled a decommissioned craft better suited to a pyre so that her iron nails could be redeployed. But I loved that boat. I loved her because, though she still belonged to Leif, she told the story of my life.

I'd learned to steady my feet on her wet planks as she crossed the northern waters from Norway to Iceland, and then from Iceland to Greenland. Erik, my second father, had laughed when, once we hit our first swell on our first voyage, I was sent tumbling into the bulwark. My head clunked a cleat. I came away with a black lump the size of an egg, but I allowed no tears. They wanted to come. The salty tears begged to be released. I kept them hidden from Erik and his family, my new family.

All I had to do was gaze up at *Charging Boar's* billowing sail as it clung tightly to the yardarm. In moments the sight could transport me back to Greenland where Thjordhildr, my second mother, had sewn the cloth one stitch at a time. The winter that particular sail had been made, she was joined by Freydis, whose agile fingers laced one sheet to the next. I thought of my enchantress, Freydis, whenever I looked at the sail. Its vertical white stripes reminded me of the pale flesh of her arms as they'd emerge from her coverings when the long days of summer arrived. The cloth's alternating red stripes, of course, brought back the image of Freydis' curly red hair. When the wind whipped and tugged just right at our sail, I swore I could see the girl dancing and singing around the summer hills when they briefly sprouted green in otherwise barren Greenland.

"Where are you?" asked Magnus. He held the rudder. A more trustworthy man you couldn't want.

"Home," I answered.

"Me, too!" he said. "I love the sea. Land is nice, but it should only be a place to resupply before again hitting the waves." Wind sent strands of his long hair beating in wild directions.

I had meant that my mind was at home with my second family in Greenland. There was no use in explaining that. Besides, the sea was just as much my home as any of the places I'd lived while on land. I sucked in a deep breath. The salt stung my nostrils. A stray strand of hair, wet from spray, slapped my neck. It felt brilliant. "I love the sea," I agreed.

"And we again have a lord who puts us to sea every chance he gets," said Leif, lounging among the heap of hudfats. We had travelled for some days. Our armada ran south out of Dyflin. We skipped Olaf's favorite haunt of Viklow. We had rounded Ireland's southeast corner and avoided the Norse settlement of Vedrafjordr. If the Leinstermen were pawns in this game, the Vikings of Vedrafjordr were pawns of pawns. We owed them no retribution. Even the southwest edge of Ireland came and went.

I plopped down next to Leif. "I'll say it again. I love the sea. But what is the point of all this running, if we get nothing in return," I said. I pulled out my first father's saex and began carving the shape of a woman's body in the ship's hull. Leif said nothing about my defiling of his property. Over our shoulders Cnute and Loki held out crumbs of stale bread to lure the gulls in close. Some of the adventurous birds would pluck them right from their fingers. When they did that, the pair would try to latch onto the birds. It was all for sport.

"What do you mean?" he asked. "The point is that we are Olaf's sworn men. We do his bidding."

"I know that," I said. The woman I carved was looking more like a series of chicken crates stacked on top of one another. The ship pitched and the tip of my blade scraped across her body. Now she had a spear piercing from her leg to her shoulder. "Hel's crotch," I cursed.

"Your woman there has seen better days," Leif chuckled. "Really. What's the problem? You love Olaf. I love Olaf. He's a better leader than Godfrey could ever hope to be."

"Yes," I agreed. "You'll finally have the leadership model you've been looking for."

Leif smirked. "Probably not. If I'm to turn my family's lineage from two or three generations of murders into one of respect, I'll need to be more moderate than Olaf, more thoughtful." He snatched my saex and quickly put a tail on my woman. In a heartbeat she looked like a dragon scraped onto a stone by a toddler. We both giggled like the same toddler.

The blade found its way back into its scabbard. "At least Godfrey worked for his own benefit. Every raid, every battle meant more power and glory for him – and for his men," I said.

Magnus allowed his hip and one hand to steady the rudder as it fought him using the sea's power. With the other hand he carefully pulled out a louse from his beard. "You're a baby, Halldorr. You care for personal power as much as I care for this little beast." He squeezed it between two fingers and flicked it overboard. "All you want to do is hump Leif's sister, Freydis."

An image of a woman gurgled in my mind. Surprisingly, it wasn't Freydis. It was Aednat. The little fire had a way of sneaking into my thoughts.

Leif was well aware of my infatuation with his sister. He ignored Magnus. "And besides, you're wrong. Olaf doesn't just have us fighting for Sitric's glory. This year alone, he gained lands when he married Gytha. When we crush the Leinster clan, he and his wife will lay claim to more. I am sure his favorite men will end up with farms or estates of their own. The wealth keeps skipping down the rocks. There will be enough for all of us."

I suddenly had a foolish image of Aednat and me raising a brood of children on a green Irish hill. It could never happen. The idea was preposterous, yet I grinned.

"See there," Leif said. "You finally get it." He slapped my back before sprawling out to steal a nap on top of the baggage. Other men had already done likewise.

Soon the sound of snoring joined the beautiful splashing of the sea against *Charging Boar's* strakes. Though Loki and Cnute had stopped their game – after snagging a half dozen gulls each – scores of the winged creatures still swooped over our wake. Some landed and bobbed in the water. The rest hovered, waiting for just the right twist of the sea's current to reveal their next meal.

In the stern, Magnus kept his scanning vigilance. In the bow, Tyrkr began setting out the slabs of smoked fish for our evening meal. He meant to feed us onboard tonight. There'd be no land camp because Olaf wanted us to push ahead – fast. We needed the vigor given by meat because in just a matter of hours we'd drive past the Norse settlement of Hlymrekr. We'd enter the River Shannon and sail or row upstream. Irishmen would surround us on all sides and we needed to be prepared. If we made it all the way up to Lough Ree unmolested, then the real fight would begin. Our battle from the northwestern fringes of Leinster would commence. We'd push to the center of the clan's land mass where we'd meet Sitric and his new military ally Mael Sechnaill of the Ui Neill, the man who would soon be Sitric's father-in-law.

I intentionally turned my head downward. Now was not the time to become lost in thought about Freydis' hips while staring at a sail cloth. Now was not the time to dream of a simple life with an unattainable woman like Aednat. Now was the time to begin the work of the coming war. It was in the wee moments of life when the activities that determined a battle's outcome were completed. As you may now guess, I slid my sword from his fleece-lined scabbard and slowly drew my whetstone along its length.

It made a high-pitched grating sound. Men frowned as I awoke them from their slumber. But without a word, my actions inspired them. They pulled out their own swords if they had them. Others hefted their spears. Soon, the sound of two dozen whetstones grinding away at steel echoed up from our floating tub.

Other men on other ships heard us. Their captains kicked them, ordering them to do likewise. In moments, hundreds of individual scraping noises coalesced into a grand song of praise to Odin. We paid him tribute that day. Even the Christian brothers among us did so without knowing. Our hymn rang into the clouds. Thor heard it. The Norsemen of Hlymrekr scampered to their walls to watch us pass. They listened to our tune and added their voices to it.

The entire scene made me proud to be a Norseman. I was a raider, certainly. But at that moment, I was more than a mere pirate. I was a seasoned man, a hardened warrior who had inspired hundreds of his brethren to prepare for war. I scraped my stone against my blade, carefully running it between the fuller and the edge. My song rushed ahead with the whetstone chants of all the rest and it would only be the first weapon that would strike fear into the Leinstermen.

The next set of greetings was to be my blade, my axe, my saex.

• • •

We pushed up the Shannon without incident. Fifty Irish riders quickly began shadowing us on the banks. They had rapidly cobbled together an infantry force perhaps one hundred strong. What they thought they could do against our numbers, I do not know, but it is proper for men to make all attempts to defend their homes, crops, women, and children. These particular Irishmen had nothing to fear from us that day, however. The lower Shannon passed through another set of Irish clans, principalities, and kingdoms that had nothing to do with our current war. As our flotilla passed from Munster to Leinster, our marching shadow faded into the distance. I'm sure it breathed a collective sigh of relief.

It took a long while to reach Lough Ree. Twice we had to send men over the gunwales to lighten the load. The keels of our ships were never deep, that's why we could attack so far up rivers in the first place. Yet, even the shallow keels of our ships scraped a time or two. The men sent over the sides splashed in the shallow water or trod up on the winding shores. Some captains had their men tug on long ropes to help propel their crafts to the lake that would be our base of operations against the Leinstermen.

Then Lough Ree opened up before us. It was a long, narrow lake with crooked fingers jutting away from the spine. We passed a few islands that weren't much more than elevated sand dunes or scattered rocks with tufts of scrub grass and sickly trees gripping the loose soil with all the might their roots could muster. The shore lines on both widening sides of the lake were blanketed with old growth trees as if the Irish had no idea what to do with them all. I, for one, would have harvested them and made longhouses, longships, spear shafts, and clubs.

At the van of our armada, Olaf's flagship angled sharply to starboard. His pilot led us to a fair-sized island that appeared to be perhaps half an English mile in diameter. It, too, was covered in trees, save for a clearing that housed a monastery. *Serpent* slid into the pebbled beach that led to the holy place. Her beard of iron spikes poked into a mass of bleached driftwood with an audible crunch. Olaf and Vigi leapt over the bulwark even before *Serpent* was at a complete rest. The pair was bounding up the shore, scattering smooth stones with every step. A lone spearman with a lucky aim could have decapitated our army at that moment. Olaf was aware of this fact. It didn't stop him from plunging ahead.

"Move, men!" he shouted over his shoulder. Ahead, a dozen monks held their dark robes up as they fled in the opposite direction. The faithful sprang over stone markers and other permanent monuments of their craft. "Grab those men!" called Olaf. "Try not to kill them yet."

Charging Boar rattled to a halt. I was already in my armor so my feet were quickly padding up the shore. Tyrkr and Leif were there with me. Randulfr and Magnus saw to getting the ship properly unloaded and guarded. We ran after our quarry. They weren't hard to catch.

They led us inland a hundred fadmr. We gained on them with every step. After one failed attempt to hide amidst the branches of two toppled trees, the monks again began to run. We were better fed and used to the exercise. It took the well-aimed toss of a single stone into the back of one of the brothers before they stopped their futile waste of energy. They dropped to their knees as we encircled them. We didn't have our weapons drawn. Though I had known one Irish Christian holy man who knew his way around a blade, these men didn't strike me as skilled in that way. That doesn't mean they weren't brave.

"You may slay us, you dragons," said the one who was the abbot. He spoke in my tongue which said that he'd met my kind before. "But our faith grows stronger with every single one of our number you kill." I thought about his words then. If true, then the Christian God was growing more powerful by the day as my people slaughtered them in their homes and fields from Ireland to England to Frankia to Germany. In hindsight, now that I am a follower of the One True God myself, I know he was right.

"Come with us," Leif said. "There will be no slaying here in the woods. Tryggvason has told us to take you back to him safely."

"Crack-a-Bone," breathed the abbot. He and his followers exchanged worried glances which showed that even men who were willing to die for their faith, retained the most basic of survival instincts. I thought at least one would try to run when fear set in. None did. They were resigned to their fates – Providence is what the Christians called it. They slowly stood and we picked our way back to the monastery.

"The Shrine of Saint Ciaran," said the abbot as we passed a flat stone with the depiction of two men driving a stake into the ground. Many of my Norse brothers, before they accepted the One God, made grand sport of Christian monks. They would say that such unarmed men invited disaster upon themselves. They said monks were weak. Those old warriors were correct about the first, for an unarmed man does nothing but bring about his own destruction. They were so wrong about the second, though. I've never met a weak monk. Any man can flail about carrying a spear. It takes foundational courage to face hardened killers with little more than ragged robes and open palms between your life and your immediate death. It showed even more bravery when the abbot tried to engage us in conversation or possibly even conversion while we led them to captivity.

"Tell us," I said, honoring the abbot for his tenacity.

He did. The abbot gladly told us about Ciaran's life. He chuckled when he told how the saint's fellow students used to call him half-Matthew. I didn't understand the reference. It had something to do with memorizing only half of one of the gospels. The abbot told about how Ciaran was so envied by the other holy men of his day that they prayed to the One God to come and gather him with his reaping tools sooner rather than later. The abbot was most proud of a miracle that involved the long-dead saint's cow giving milk enough for an entire Abbey in a single milking.

Olaf heard only the tail end of the tales and so the sea king made the abbot tell them all over again. He laughed with the abbot at all the right places as they all lounged on the heap of driftwood. Vigi stood nearby, knee-deep in the lapping lake waters. His head stared down at the surface and every so often it dove beneath in pursuit of a passing fish.

When the stories were done, Olaf scratched his beard. "You men are good at telling yarns! Unfortunately, I have no need for another skald. I've got my own poet. Ottar's probably rummaging through your things now, looking for inspiration to speak a new verse about me." Olaf laughed. "It's ridiculous when you think about it! The lies I pay others to tell about me."

"It is," agreed the abbot. It was said in a wary enough manner that Olaf didn't take offense. "But men of all races are wont to hear heroic stories of themselves. That is not peculiar to your people."

"No, it's not, is it?" said Olaf. "Now, I need you to work with me. There will be some unpleasant business, but it must happen as we mean to invade, harass, and overcome the Leinstermen."

The monks had expected a typical raid or pillaging of their monastery. This was something a bit different. "What do you need? If we can diminish the suffering of your victims . . ."

"Enemies, abbot. They are enemies," corrected Olaf. "If they be victims, it is because they've made themselves that way."

The abbot nodded, but it was clear he didn't agree. "We are set in this time and place to worship the One God and to aid others. What shall we do?"

"I'm glad you feel that way. Your actions and little sacrifices will help the Irishmen and women in the coming days." Vigi came back with a fish. He shook the slithering beast wildly while it jutted from both sides of his locked jaws. Olaf was sprayed with lake water as his dog's head rolled side-to-side. The sea king didn't seem to notice. "I'll need five of you men to cook for us. Do that and I'll leave your walls and roof intact."

The abbot suddenly appeared eager to please. "Happily, Lord Crack-a-Bone. That is most generous."

Olaf held up a gloved hand. "I'm not done with the terms, yet. It will do you no good to agree early." He gave a wry grin. "Verily, you don't have much choice in whether you consent or not, but you might as well know all I ask so that you can be proud that you had the fortitude to say yes."

The abbot wiped a large, thin hand from the top to the bottom of his face. It looked like he tried to use his mitt to wipe us away from his sight. His cheeks were tugged down so that the pink beneath his eyeballs showed. The palm inched along. He pulled on the slack skin beneath his chin. The abbot let the weathered flesh bounce back when he was done. While he said nothing to Olaf, it was clear that the abbot felt the weight of all of Midgard on his shoulders.

The sea king shrugged. He laid a hand on Vigi's wet back. The fish was half-eaten on one of his feet. Vigi was trying to share with his master. "Five of you will work for us during our stay. Six will be set free to the mainland to the east. They'll go running ahead of us, screaming about our cruelty and just how fearsome we are. They'll flee with terror in their eyes, telling the Leinstermen that it will be better to never take up arms against us. The shrieks of your fellow monks may actually save some fathers and sons from unnecessary slaughter."

The abbot's mood brightened. Olaf's terms weren't bad, at all. Yet, the head monk was puzzled. "Lord, Crack-a-Bone, you miscount. You've listed roles for eleven of us. We are twelve." He realized the significance of the number and sought to use it as a teaching moment for us, heathens. "Not unlike the original disciples of Christ. Perhaps we may evangelize to your men while we cook for you." He paused while offering Olaf a slight bow of his head. "And the six runners you send ahead will do as you wish – even though it is a lie – since it may help preserve lives. It's a fib of which even our beloved Saint Ciaran would approve. You've been most sparing so far and we have nothing to scream about." He giggled. "Except Brother Tomas, who will probably have a lump on his back from the stone that man threw at him." Brother Tomas forced a smile.

"You'll want to withhold your praise," said Olaf as he pushed up from his place on the logs. "The five of you who cook may certainly talk to my men about the One God if they wish."

"Thank you," began the abbot.

Olaf held up both hands to quiet the abbot this time. "But know that I didn't mess up my counting. No, one of you must be sacrificed here and now. The truth is that the six men we send running can tell a more believable story if they've seen it with their own eyes. One of you will be killed, brutally, I'm afraid. I ask for a volunteer in order to preserve your dignity. You men deserve it for telling such fine tales."

The monks blanched like vegetables dropped in a boiling kettle. The one called Brother Tomas looked at his feet and sighed. He pushed on his knees to stand.

The abbot shoved him down. "No, Brother Tomas. It is my burden to carry." He stood tall, arching his shoulders back and his bony chest out. Brother Tomas stared up at his master with a mixture of awe and relief.

Olaf rested a hand on the abbot's shoulder. "That's what I thought would happen. Alas, my new friend, we can't have it. I won't accept your sacrifice, you'll remain here baking us fresh bread. You see, when I listen to the mumblings of others, I hear that I am impetuous. I move!" He released the abbot and went to the water's edge so that both feet were planted in the lake. Olaf pointed to the south into Leinster. "By Thor! I move and I get things done, fast. But I'm not foolish. If I butcher a respected abbot, well, that invites anger, vitriol, and a host of other intense feelings from your Christian brothers over there. But if I take an unknown man like Brother Tomas who valiantly volunteered even before you, abbot, he will quickly be forgotten. It's hard to spark outrage upon the hearing of just one more dead man's tale. All I want is fear enough for Leinster's sons to cower in their homes. I don't need anger."

The abbot stared at Olaf's back with enough anger for the whole of Ireland. His fists balled and I almost thought he'd lash out. Since then, I've witnessed the peace that faith in the words of the One God can bring. That's exactly what happened to the abbot at that moment. His features relaxed as he slowly lowered himself to his knees. His fellow brothers, including Brother Tomas, followed suit. Soon their Latin prayers flowed.

"Halldorr," Olaf snapped as he spun around. "Let the others all continue their chanting. Grab Tomas! Move. We don't have time to wait until they are done."

The others kept right on praying as I pulled Brother Tomas up to his feet. He didn't fight me, but he didn't help, either. He felt as dense as iron. His legs were like eels. I had to treat him roughly.

I look back on it now. I want to feel ashamed at what I did. I snatched a tuft of his hair behind his shorn pate with two hands and heaved on him. Once he was upright, I jostled him in the direction Olaf led. As I say, I want to be ashamed for how I treated Brother Tomas. I am, after all, a fellow Christian now. I don't feel that way, however. You see, I wasn't a Christian. I was a pagan and that is what pagans do. I did not follow the Christ. Since learning to read, I've read God's words. A man named Paul used to kill Christ followers with stones hurled from his bare hands. Then one day Paul was overcome with the light and love of the One God. He stopped his old ways and became new. If Paul can move on, I suppose I can move on, too.

So, I don't feel remorse for jerking, pushing, and prodding Brother Tomas toward his grounds of execution.

No, I feel wretched for what came next.

• • •

I wrote across three parchment pages. All the details of poor Brother Tomas' death were delineated in horrid and vivid detail. I remember the scent on the air that day. It was the sweat of Norse warriors that was soon swallowed by the stench of a dying man's piss. The ropes, the axes, the trees, the slices, the contorted faces, and more, I wrote about in my hand in the Latin. It took me a full day sitting by the fire to get the facts straight on the vellum. I remember scraping away a word or phrase that just wasn't right in describing the horrors that took place on that remote island. I replaced those words with wicked words that better told the tale of the sacrifice of Tomas for our cause, the cause of Dyflin.

Each of those pages went into the flames. I threw the large, heavy leafs onto the fire in one motion. The blaze itself choked on their weight. The flames died. Smoke soon poured around the uneven edges of my self-made parchment. The suffocating, black fog filled my hovel so that my old wife came in and scolded me. The girl was right for yelling, of course, but I didn't want anyone to ever see those words. I've done horrible things to other men. I've tortured and been tortured. All of it, I've written on these pages and have shown to all of Midgard. Not this. No one will ever read about Brother Tomas' gruesome end.

Some things are best left unsaid.

• • •

We sailed packed tightly in just a few longboats for the short trek across the lake to the mainland. The rest of our ships stayed safely back on the island with the abbot, four monks, and a small guard. Our army set foot on Leinster soil just one-half day after what was left of Tomas was buried by the monks and our six criers were released ahead. I know that if I were one of the monks sent to scare the Leinsters into giving up, I would have conveyed just the message Olaf asked. Each of the faithful men appeared frailer and thinner since we laid eyes on them.

Rarely did Olaf take a mount anywhere. He had a few fine horses stabled in Dyflin, but clearly thought it best to walk with his men. The sea king didn't even care to have a small number of riders skirting our band as highly mobile scouts. Instead, he relied on the quickest and surest of his men to skitter up and down the hills on foot and provide him with constant reconnaissance.

I couldn't get the images of Tomas and his sad brothers out of my mind. I sulked.

Olaf, always on the move physically, clearly ran on to the next task in his mind. He'd forgotten all about what he'd had me do. "Oh, this is going to be something," he said cheerily. Several of his scouts came in from our flanks and reported no activity. Out they went again.

"Don't you worry about the monks?" asked Randulfr. "Sending a warning seems," he hesitated, not sure how delicate he needed to be to our new lord.

"Out with it!" demanded Olaf. "It seems what?"

"Hasty," Randulfr said. "Every sea raid I've been on has succeeded because of stealth, rapid surprise."

"Ha!" exclaimed Olaf. Vigi trotted at his heel. "You were once King Godfrey's chief man, right?"

"Yes, lord," was Randulfr's quick answer. I readied myself for the scorn Olaf would heap on Randulfr for being associated with such a very dead king's tactics.

"He was a good enough man," said Olaf. "Now that was a reckless king. I am downright thoughtful compared to him!" Here came the disdain – only it didn't come. "I heard nothing but good things from Godfrey about you. I met him a few times, you know – hard for two pirates not to bump into one another in the Irish Sea. He said that when he listened to you, he won. When he didn't take heed, well, he didn't win. And at least you didn't get yourself conked on the head in the woods like Halldorr here."

Feeling emboldened, Randulfr asked, "And the monks, lord? What about them and the warning they give."

"Odin's eye!" shouted Olaf. "Do you think I don't know I gave the Leinsters extra time to mobilize and assemble? Do you think me foolish?" Vigi's head darted to look up at his angry master. Man and dog kept marching. "Don't bother answering because you're too smart to say yes if you do think me a buffoon." Randulfr, experienced and strong, shrank with gritted teeth.

Olaf forcefully cuffed Randulfr on the side of his helmet. "Oh, shout at me if you must, lad." The two were about the same age. "I want men to question my tactics, surely." He snatched the heavy bag of arm rings that we'd stolen the day we raided Viklow. "I mean to pass these out to men who serve me. Most will get them for killing the enemy. Some, though, will get them for using their heads as Odin intended. So, stop shitting your pants like a child and listen. I raid for wealth. One day I mean to build a fleet and take my country's throne from those usurpers there now. I need power, prestige, wealth, reputation, all of it for that task. I don't need to kill a host of Leinsters to get that. They'll do our farming for us once we rule! The Leinsters, like the Norsemen from Vedrafjordr are pawns in this game. At best, we are knights." I had heard of the game called chess, but never played nor seen it played. I've heard it was similar to tafl games. Those, I loved. The specifics of Olaf's references were lost on me.

"I admit that it is a risk to our cause. We might even face a few more, rather than less, Irishmen. To me, it was worth slaughtering a monk to potentially save us for bigger days ahead." Olaf picked up a stick and hurled it out front. Vigi tore after it while it still spun in the air. Ox-foot, returning from scouting ahead, had to duck out of the small branch's way. "Besides," our leader went on, "Sitric and Mael will have most of the fighting to do. They should have invaded Leinster a few days ago. Every man worth anything will have been mustered to fight their combined armies. We are in the less populated regions."

"Sitric did well in recruiting his townsfolk into his army," said Leif. "The walls have never had so many capable guards. The drilling grounds have never been so busy."

"He did, indeed, do well," said Olaf as Ox-foot fell in next to him. "The little piss ant will make a good king someday. He proved he could take counsel when he listened to me and made himself be known and seen in his city. He recruited boys to make them men in his shield wall. Their fathers were proud. Sitric has been generous with gifts and coin – to be sure it was his father's wealth he gave away – all summer. He now has a happy city. They obviously were happy to join in his fight against Leinster. They were lined up when we left."

"Olaf," said Ox-foot. He was a long-time follower of the sea king and often called him by name.

"What is it?" Olaf asked. Two more scouts approached from the east. They dragged a bloodied and bound Irishman between them.

"You'll want to hear what our captive has to say," said Ox-foot.

"Fine, though I'm not sure what a man who tugs on the tits of cows all day can tell me about the Leinster army," laughed Olaf. We joined him.

"That man is no farmer," said our scout. "He led a detachment for the Leinster army. He holds authority in their lands. I guess he is kinsman to their king. We fell upon him and his men. They're dead. We've confirmed all that he'll tell you."

Olaf wrinkled his brow. "What will he tell me?"

"You won't like it," warned Ox-foot.

• • •

Olaf took the news better than I thought he would. Ox-foot nodded his agreement of the facts as the Irish leader spoke.

"You're telling me that through those oaks there, we'll find a creek, and on the other side of the water sits a tiny army of Leinstermen?" asked Olaf.

The Irishman stood tall on his knees. "Yes, and that is all the force it will take to destroy you."

Olaf smiled at his captive. "Perhaps so. At least you have some vigor. For crying out loud, you've got that! So the rest of the Leinster army is heading east to meet the threat from the Ui Neill and Dyflin, correct?"

The Irish noble laughed. His teeth were outlined in the red of his own blood from his earlier tousle with our scouts. "The rest of our army sweeps behind to crush you Dark Foreigners between our hammer and anvil. We came across a weeping monk a day ago. He told us you were coming."

Randulfr frowned at Olaf.

The sea king shouted, "I know. I don't want to hear it. Kill one, spare eleven! I should have done the opposite." He turned to Ox-foot. "In any case, is he telling the truth? Even so, we should just put up a defense, prepare to hold it for a day and send out runners to bring Sitric and Mael to us." The Irishman laughed all the more. "Shut him up!"

Tyrkr stepped forward from the crowd of men gathered around and rammed his knee into the Irishman's face. "Damn Irish," he cursed.

"Damn Norsemen," said the captive.

That brought another knee to his face. "I'm German, you Ziegen Urin." The captive went on laughing.

"What's this about?" asked Olaf.

"Well, he's lying about the rest of his army swinging around behind us," began the scout. "There is nothing behind us."

"How do you know?" asked Olaf. He grabbed the Irishman's matted hair and studied his face. "So he's a liar, huh?"

"Randulfr sent more scouts to the flanks and rear in a train to keep us all apprised. I thought you ordered it," said Ox-foot.

Still clutching the Irishman's hair, Olaf glanced over to Randulfr. "Nice, lad."

"Yes, lord," said Randulfr.

"You said I was going to be angry. We go sweep up their tiny army across a little creek. What's there to be angry about?" summarized Olaf.

"I know he's lying," said the scout. "I know he laughs whenever we question him. He's hiding something. You can see it, Olaf."

"I can, but he's just one more crazy Irishman. The place is full of them," said Olaf, flinging his captive's head back like it was refuse. "Is there a good place to ford the creek?"

"I thought you might ask." Ox-foot pointed southward. "Just four, maybe five, hundred fadmr over there we can cross in knee-deep water. Once across, we swing back northward and meet the enemy. By my count, we outnumber them two to one. It will be a slaughter." The captive chuckled. He did appear mad.

Olaf plunged toward the forest and ford. "Kill the Irishman. I'll not have him yapping into the ears of my men as we pass."

Without another word, Tyrkr slipped a knife between the bound man's ribs. His laughing became high-pitched. He slumped to the ground with a thud. His gurgling and writhing stopped by the time Tyrkr had his blade clean.

We went to meet the enemy.

We ran to a butcher's store.

• • •

We were the meat.

As silently as hundreds of men can be, we slunk through the cool waters. Many men took the opportunity to drink since the uncertainty enshrouding the coming battle meant that it might be some time before another could be had. Others urinated in the flowing waters, thankfully downstream from where the rest of us slurped.

The experienced scout led us on a direct path toward where the Leinstermen were camped. He had us wait and snagged a half dozen men to go with him to make sure all was as he'd left it. Randulfr sent more scouts out in other directions. He was a fine warrior, cautious, but far from paralyzed.

Ox-foot's group returned. "All's well," he said. "They have a few lazy guards. Those men look like farmers. They'll be able to alert the army of our presence only a short while before we arrive. It will be just enough time for the men lounging in the camp to slip on mail or cinch a belt. It will be over before it begins."

Olaf clicked his cheek. "I've heard that before." Then he turned to Randulfr. "What say you? Any word from your other runners? Should we wait for them?"

"No," said Randulfr. "If we're doing this, we best do it. Surprise is what works. If there are more Leinstermen out there, we'll have time to form up once these men are smashed."

"There you go," said Olaf in a raspy whisper, though we were too far to be heard by the enemy. "And here we go."

The sea king pulled out his mighty sword and pushed through the undergrowth. It was early to unsheathe the blade, but who would argue with such an experienced warrior? The rest of us followed suit. Our shields, our bark, we hoisted. Teeth gritted. Rumps clenched.

We were mere heartbeats away from the first of the Leinster guards when noise erupted from our right. It sounded like a lone runner. One of Randulfr's scouts burst toward us, but was greeted with a spear from an overeager Norseman. The missile sliced off much of the unarmored man's skin as it careened off his ribcage.

Ahead, the Leinster camp was coming alive due to the racket we made. "Damn!" cursed Olaf. "Too late now. We go." He dove into the last stretch of forest.

We all followed our lord without thinking. Olaf wanted us to be loyal *and* thoughtful soldiers. But when it is time for the blood to flow, she flows. A man's thoughts can focus on just one thing when he has a sword in his hands. Battle. And so it was with our minds. None of us paid any attention to the shouted warnings from the scout with the splayed skin who lay crumpled on the leafy floor of the woods.

"It's a trap," he groaned. "It's a trap."

But as Olaf said, it was too late. The norns would have their blood one way or another.

• • •

When I burst into the clearing I was indeed greeted by the sight of a tiny, ill-trained army. I had caught up to Olaf. Our boots pounded the turf like the hooves of chargers. Olaf shouted. I screamed something foolish like, "For Dyflin!" Vigi barked and barked between us. The rest of our heathen army raced on our heels yelling all manners of curses. We'd close on the inexperienced enemy and fell them in a moment.

Now, perhaps you know for certain that the shield wall is invincible. It is, for the most part it is. Though, in this very writing I told you about how I broke that rule in the nighttime battle that followed my meeting with Aednat. That was, as Olaf pointed out, a fluke. The shield wall was to be respected above all else. It was to be used.

Not so this day. We'd set our minds on a rapid attack. Nothing was going to change that. We smelled blood, even though just the groaning scout's had been spilled. He was already far behind us, dead. It would have been wiser to move slowly. We should have used the shield wall.

More of us may have survived. We may have even won, for the shield wall is a gift from Odin.

I deliberately picked out the first man to hack down with my sword. He was a big man. He appeared to know his way around a weapon as he braced for our tidal wave. I wanted to meet him while I was still fresh. The cowards and novices could wait. When I was six steps away from him, the forest to our right came alive.

In my peripheral vision the trunks of trees split apart and became two, then four, then eight Irish warriors. The thicket turned into raised shields. The breeze morphed into an Irish version of the shield wall. They were *Irish*, so I didn't panic. It was when I turned my head and saw their numbers that I was struck with fear.

I slid to a halt and looked at Olaf. He, too, stopped. My lord just gasped while surveying the situation. He was running forward again before I could even process a solution. "Run through these men. Hack through. It's all we can do!" My lord was screaming. "Don't stop. Plunge ahead." Then he added again as if trying to justify it to himself, "It's all we can do."

I suppose it wasn't all we could do. We could have stopped everyone, issued orders, conveyed them, and hoped everyone turned and fled to the river's ford. Or, we could have halted everything, begun to lock shields, and formed a curving wall to face the small army as well as the immense force rattling their way out of the woods. Either of those things would have invited even more slaughter than the bitterness we experienced anyway. We had momentum as we sprinted. We attacked an ill-equipped band of Irishmen. Our best hope was to flow through them and continue right on running until we found a suitable place to defend.

I chased after Olaf. He had already taken an opponent down. The sea king parried blows with the big Irishman I had picked out. We didn't have time for dancing. I rammed my shoulder into the enemy. Olaf squirted free. The Irishman fought to catch his balance. I didn't pursue the kill. I left him teetering. Behind me, Randulfr sliced a blade across the man's exposed arm. It was a superficial wound. Randulfr had the sense to keep running, too.

It was like that.

We killed a few of them to be sure. Everyone had a lucky stroke now and then. But for the most part we wanted nothing more than to continue on. Even the men in the middle and toward the back of our wolf pack understood this. Some of them were running so fast they pressed and prodded us from behind.

Olaf's split-second decision was adequate, no more. It was not the grandest of military tactics. He kept us moving. But the Leinstermen that attacked our flank had legs, too. They closed the gap. They were methodical. Those bastards fought like we should have fought. They set their shields together – a tactic they must have learned from us – and squeezed. Their clubs, swords, spears, and farm tools slowly inched the back of our pack closer to the river. Many, many men, fine Norsemen, died there against that river.

I know they fought with honor and with the favor of the gods, because they are the only thing that saved the rest of us.

None of us who ran were cowards. We sprinted because that was the only way to snatch away a complete victory from the Leinsters. Though we ultimately failed and were rewarded with an unarguable loss, we did follow Olaf and Olaf was right to lead us away. It leaves a sour taste in my mouth just to write the words.

Those Norsemen who died with shields and axes in hand by the river occupied so many of the Leinstermen for so long, we were given a reprieve. We padded to a temporary halt once Olaf judged we had come far enough. It was on a wooded rise. The terrain was not the best, but it would do to meet what pursued us.

They didn't come, though. We heard our brethren fighting. Clanging echoed off every tree creating a cacophony of fright for every man's ears. Those men were now fully cut off, enveloped. Clattering, cursing, and crying drove away every feathered creature from the forest. I was looking at the ground, panting to catch my breath, when a blotched shadow darkened the ground. It swept by. I peered up through the light-flecked canopy and saw all kinds of birds fleeing the carnage. From robins to raptors, they escaped. The black ones, the ravens, I knew would soon come back to feast on the bodies of my friends.

"We push down from here," I said, anxious to prevent a total slaughter. I still believed in heroes. I thought I was one.

Randulfr agreed. "We can cut a hole and get some of them out. We'll find another ford!"

Olaf breathed rapidly behind his shield. One side of his upper lip was curled into a snarl. He waited to see if anyone pursued us. Not so far. In a voice that was too soft for the battlefield, he said, "We can't, lads. I want to, but we can't." He quivered with anger.

"We're still hundreds right here!" I shouted.

"And that was thousands of Irishmen. Let the sacrifices of those men by the river allow us the chance to avenge them one day. To go down there now, means total destruction. I'll not have it. Remember what happened to Godfrey. He reached and reached until his hand and his arm and then his body were severed."

Olaf was right. Godfrey's hubris and greed killed countless Norsemen that day in Dunadd. A queen and a precocious Irish girl died on that slope, too. A brave priest was filleted. Olaf, damned Olaf, the bravest man I'd ever known, was right. We had to flee. We had to abandon our brothers. Thor's balls!

"Do we run east away from our ships?" I asked. "Do we go toward Silkbeard's army?"

"There may not be any Silkbeard's army," breathed Olaf. He lowered his shield as Vigi came barreling up the hill. His coat was filthy with dirt stuck onto the blood-wet fur. He was unharmed; the blood was from dying men. The dog's dripping jaws looked like he'd already rutted through the innards of fallen soldiers as he searched for warm, tasty morsels. "That Leinster army down there was as big as anything they could muster." The sea king swung his shield sideways so that the rim set a deep trench in a nearby tree trunk. "And if they're here, and if Sitric was to invade days ago, Sitric didn't invade. We're alone."

• • •

I carried a wood-bladed shovel over my shoulder as I followed Olaf into the woods on the island with the monastery. We, the survivors of the debacle by the creek trotted like little palfreys all the way back to our landing area. Thankfully, the Leinstermen were tardy in their pursuit. The few scouts Randulfr had left in our wake reported that our Irish hunters were a full day behind. By the time they arrived at the shores of Lough Ree, we'd be floating back down River Shannon with our tails between our legs. So much for our glorious invasion. Our cousins, the Norsemen of Hlymrekr, could watch us from their walls and snigger. Vanished would be their cheers.

We had time for one more task, however, Olaf said. He ordered me to stow my gear and weapons aboard *Charging Boar*. I've told you the only implement I carried was a well-worn shovel. The sea king had his ever-present mail, helmet, and laden belt strapped on. He carried the bag of pilfered arm rings. He also carried a sack that appeared heavily weighted with clinking metal – silver, I thought. It was likely from his personal sea chest aboard *Serpent*.

It was easy to see what was about to happen. I'd witnessed it before. By Hel, I'd participated before, only on the other side. Obviously, I was still alive. Soon, I would not be. I was to be the brave sacrifice demanded by the gods when a man buried a treasure. Olaf had the wealth that would soon be swallowed by Midgard. I had the muscles and shovel that would perform the work. I also held the blood that, when spilt, would appease Thor's anger. The gods clearly demanded something since they allowed such a misfortune to befall our raid.

I decided that I wouldn't fight it. Ha! In a perverse way, I was actually as happy and light-hearted as I had been in many months. My steps were buoyant. My thoughts were easy. I remember thinking about how peaceful life would be for the monks on that monastery's island. Well, whenever we didn't use it as a place to conduct a strandhogg.

"This will do," said Olaf when we'd traveled far from prying eyes.

Without waiting for more orders, I plunged the shovel through the eons' worth of litter cluttering the floor. It took seven clumsy scoops just to reach the dirt. Olaf meandered around the area while I worked. He muttered to himself. "From the shrine due north. Two grand oaks and a hill. Two fat rocks and under the third a hole." Olaf repeated these phrases over and again, ignoring me.

I dug the pit deep. The twin sacks could have been safely buried under an ell of soil and not been disturbed for generations, but they weren't the only items to be planted that day. I made the hole large enough for my body. I only hoped that Olaf would allow me the honor to hold one of his blades as the life ran out of me. I couldn't bear the thought of waking up in Niflheim rather than Valhalla.

"What are you doing?" asked Olaf when he finally stopped his pacing. "The bags are small."

I kept on digging. "I saw the track of a wolf as we walked. I want to be deep enough so that the contents of the burial aren't bothered by the hungry beasts." The water table was high on the island. The earth was becoming sticky mud and I was only waist deep.

Olaf chuckled. "I've never known a wolf to sniff out gold and silver."

He was doing his best to keep me from knowing my fate. I would have done the same. Well, perhaps not. I may have asked for a volunteer who understood the consequences ahead of time. But Olaf may have still not trusted a volunteer to follow through without a fight. A man's heart wants to beat, after all. Even if his mind has agreed to the honor of a sacrificial death, his heart, when confronted with steel, can will the body to action.

I played along. "You're right. I was being silly." I slapped the last shovelful of slurry onto my pile.

Olaf offered a hand down. "No, I'm fine here," I said. There was no point in making him drag my hefty frame back into the grave. "Hand me the bags. I'll stow them."

The sea king shrugged. He tossed the bag of arm rings at my chest. It stopped with a resounding thud when I caught it. I carefully set it into the corner of the hole. Maybe I could use it as a pillow on the next leg of my journey. When I again faced Olaf, he used both hands to hurl the bag of silver at me. I almost toppled over backward. He laughed. So did I, but as I thought about what was coming next, my laugh folded into an uneasy chuckle. I set the bag next to the first.

Olaf offered his hand again.

"I'll stay here," I said. His ruse was growing long in the tooth. I tired of it. "Just finish our business."

"I'm not doing all the work to cover the pit," said Olaf. "I'm the lord. You're the oath sworn man." He appeared perturbed.

Now I was peeved. "You're going to have to do the work whether you like it or not."

"Listen, rooster cock, I don't know what's nipping at your head today, but you'd better shape up," warned Olaf. He stabbed the finger of one hand into the air at my face. The other hand sat on the pommel of his sword. Good, I thought, he was getting close to finishing our deed.

"At least let me hold the handle of your saex as I go. I would have preferred to hold that of my father's, but yours will be enough. I understand if you want to wait until after you make the first strike," I said, tossing the shovel out of the way so that

Olaf didn't trip. "But know that I have no plans to strike back. If I do, it is a mere reaction."

Olaf pushed from his crouch, to a standing position. He set both hands on his hips and studied me. "So you go willingly?" he asked.

"I do, but be quick. It's all my head can do to keep my hands at bay."

"Hmmph," said Olaf. "I hadn't even considered that. But now that you mention it, lad, seems like a noble thing to do for the gods." He spread his arms out wide and twisted at the waist, acknowledging the spirits there in the forest. It wouldn't be long now. "The wood elves inhabiting this glen would welcome such a fine sacrifice, I'm sure. The draugr of the Norsemen who've invaded here before us will more easily forgive our failures if we leave behind a man like you." Olaf shook his head. "Odin, mighty Odin would grant me favor for the rest of my days if I provided him with such an excellent warrior for his hall."

Olaf bent down again. He offered his hand. "Lad, I'd rather be damned by Odin for eternity than to sacrifice a warrior like you to an early grave. Now get your dumb ass out of the pit and cover our treasure." The sea king laughed again. "I told you, I'm not here to use the shovel. That's why I brought you along."

I was truly angry now. "Just get it over with or else when the time comes I'll fight. I don't want to, but I will. End it!"

Olaf shook his hand for two beats. "Take it, boy. There's no sacrifice to be made. I'll swear on Gytha's honor if I must." His smart eyes sliced through me like an unblemished blade. "Let's not make it come to that."

I sighed and slapped my palm into his. After he hauled me out of the hole, Olaf moved back three or four steps. Warily, I bent to take up the shovel. I peeked over my shoulder at him. His weapons stayed safely in his belt.

One scoop went back in. I paused and looked at Olaf. A second measure slapped into the pit. When I halted again, Olaf yelled at me, "I told you that I intend to keep your skin closed, but if you keep delaying, my mind can be changed. Move!"

I laughed. There was his favorite command. I scraped heaps of earth back into the treasure's grave. "Then why do we bury this?" I asked. "If it is not for the gods, then why?"

Olaf had already begun heading back toward the monastery, so he had to spin around and return to me. He pointed to the ground. "Cover it well. Put the litter back on it so that it looks no different than the rest of the forest floor." His eyes suddenly sparkled with an idea. In one motion, he snatched his saex.

By Hel's frozen crotch, Olaf was a better liar than I thought. He had me fooled into believing I would survive. I saw the single-sided blade flash. I truly was going to die.

Olaf used the short sword to flick open the flesh on one of his fingers. He let the blood drip onto the turned earth of the hole. "Good idea," he said. "A little blood never hurt in appeasing the gods." The gash clotted quickly. Olaf kneaded his finger and pressed out a few more fat droplets. "As for why bury the treasure, it's for me!" He popped the finger into his mouth and sucked on it. He appeared to enjoy the iron taste of his own blood. "Never before have I suffered such a humiliating defeat as we experienced over there. If I can't beat a few dirty Irishmen in battle, then I don't deserve my own silver. I don't deserve to hand out gold arm rings to my men. Such men are too good for gifts from me. No!" he said as his fist rapped against an alder. "The only way I'll deserve any of that is to come back here again and win. We'll go back to Dyflin and see what happened to the pup, Sitric. When I've got his mess cleaned up, I'll rebuild my strength. Only then will I come back here, defeat the Leinstermen for myself and for Gytha – forget Silkbeard – and retrieve this hoard."

He spun and marched toward the monastery. Olaf repeated his mental map to the hoard. "From the shrine due north. Two grand oaks and a hill. Two fat rocks and under the third a hole." The sea king sang it like a song. The skald, Ottar, would have been proud of his master.

I, leaning on the shovel, watched him go. I loved that man. And now you know for certain that I didn't just love him because he always won. Olaf didn't always make the right decisions. He was impetuous at times. There was never a finer Norseman.

Since then, I've met a whole new people. We called them skraelings, generally. I live with them now. One or two of them measure up to Olaf. Ahanu, certainly. Kesegowaase, perhaps.

Soon the shovel was again scratching at the ground. I patted the soil in place. I jumped on it with my heavy boots so that it was almost at the exact level as when we started. Olaf was long gone when I knelt down and scattered leaves and twigs back over the hoard's grave. Thrice I started over because the results didn't appear like the natural workings of the forest.

When I was done, I stepped back and admired my work. I couldn't even tell where the hole sat. I smiled. My mood was glad.

Several meaningful hoards of my own have I buried in my life. All of them I had planned on retrieving. Who would bury a treasure with the thought of entirely abandoning it? No one! It would be better to dump coins or hacksilver into the hands of a tavern owner than to let them corrode underground. It would be better to pour them onto the white thighs of a whore than allow such wealth to waste away. It would be better to wager the entire pot on one roll of the bones than to shove it into the dust.

None of my hoards have I recovered. None. For all I know they sit there still, waiting for my greedy hands. Well, I am an ocean away with no means of getting to them. They decay.

I seized my shovel and walked back toward the shore where our ships sat ready to flee. We'd lost many men. Our grand invasion was a failure, but I whistled like the village simpleton. I was as happy as could be, for I served a splendid lord. What more could I want?

So what, that as I marched there in the forest among the oaks and elms, I knew that Olaf would never come back for his hoard. Time and events would get the best of him like they did every man, even sea kings. That patch of land was suddenly rich and it would remain so until a lucky monk found it. Then he, in his piety, would spend it all on the poor of his community. Crack-a-Bone may have already forgotten about the treasure. The sea king would soon be occupied elsewhere. He would not return anytime soon.

And he never did.

• • •

The abbot said nothing snide to us, though he was aware of our debacle. It would be hard not to notice that we returned with nearly a third less warriors. The chief monk audibly prayed for the souls of his fellow Irishmen lost in the battle he'd not seen. He even prayed to the One God for his holy spirit to encircle us, his invaders. He wanted the True God not to smite us, rather protect us. The abbot shook hands with Olaf as the sea king boarded *Serpent*. I never cared to ask for the abbot's name, but now wish that I had. He was a strong man.

We floated down the Shannon under the power of the lazy current. We were in no hurry, for that would have made us look like even larger disappointments. Our fleet was intact. Every vessel was sailing for home. Yet, none of our captains had to direct men to jump over the side when we crossed the shallows. We'd lost so many potent warriors to the weak Leinstermen that our ships floated right over the rocks.

This time I kept my weapons sheathed. I was tired of war. The feeling wouldn't last, but I was exhausted then. I didn't run my whetstone down my blades, thinking that I could inspire an entire army to greatness. The lighthearted mood had fled – they always did. It was replaced with anger.

I planned to run up the steps of Dyflin's walls and trample down her muddy streets. I'd kick in the door to Kvaran's hall and dig out Prince Sitric Silkbeard. If he was there and if I found him, that would be proof enough that he was not to be trusted. If he sat on his throne as safe as a hare in its warren, then Sitric was a coward who deserved to die. If he'd already wedded his new bride and humped the lovely Aednat under a pile of warm hides, that was an indication that he was going to be a wicked king. Similar to when King David of the Jews stayed home from war at a time when the king should have been with his army, Silkbeard probably pierced his manhood into a woman rather than his sword into his enemy.

Those hateful thoughts kept me warm for the entire voyage home.

What we found upon our return to Dyflin, however, shifted my passions. My blood was still up. My anger remained at a boil. My jaded foundation firmed. What played out next allowed Sitric to grow in stature before my eyes while the rest of mankind slumped into the depths before me. Young Sitric, the pup, was learning to adapt, to be firm when necessary and to be flexible like the hull of a longboat at other times. My heart hardened toward the rest of the world, save Olaf. Any amount of tenderness I held toward women bled away. My world became a cynical cauldron of war and profit.

The valor and heroism of the old gods was, for a time, a myth for me. I had believed in a martial spirituality since my youth. No longer, I decided when we returned to Dyflin. What I saw there made the good and evil, the right and wrong of the One God, cease to exist in a world bastardized by men. All there was – I knew the answer – profit and loss. All that survived – I was so certain because I still had no grey in my beard – was what a man could do. And what a man could do, a man would do.

And, of course, a woman could do worse than any man.

CHAPTER 8

The Ruirthech was choppy. Much of our thinned fleet remained onboard their ships, anchored in the river's center. They formed a line of vessels that stretched north of the city's walls with a tail extending downriver east. Olaf ordered several of the ships to sit in the curving River Poddle so that the backside of Dyflin was covered. It was windy and the planks on which our men stood buffeted. Yet those obedient warriors stood strong with shields and spears ready.

Facing them on the banks was an Irish host that had laid siege to our great city. They covered the banks. They covered the single mainland gate that faced southwest. The Irish did not control the waterways – no, that was still our domain – and so Olaf's armada slipped through. Only a few risk-taking Irishmen sent arrows or other missiles in our direction while we came to Dyflin. No Norseman was hurt. We did not retaliate. Yet.

Charging Boar sat next to *Serpent* on the banks. Many other ships joined them so that the city's defenders cheered when we came up and over the walls. We were greeted like saviors.

Olaf rammed a fist into a nearby Dyfliner. "What in Hel's iceberg tits is going on here?"

The man recoiled, but remained on his feet. He rubbed the chainmail on his chest, below which he would soon have black and blue skin. The mail was now smeared red with blood. I glanced down at Olaf's knuckles and saw that they'd been cut on the man's armor. The sea king didn't notice. He flailed his hand in the air. "That is not a bunch of Leinstermen who've driven Sitric back from his invasion! I thought I saw Ui Neill banners!"

"Lord Crack-a-Bone, it's been this way for many days. The High King came right after you left. He's besieged us ever since."

Vigi lapped at his owner's hand. "Mael Sechnaill?" shouted Olaf as if it was new information that was the High King's name. "May Odin's poetry say nothing but the truth about Sitric's piss-poor leadership!" He pointed to a group of us. "You men with me! The rest of you spread out on the wall with these defenders. Maybe the sight of my pirates will send Mael running. Let's move!" He bounded off down the steps on the inside of the wall with Vigi still scrambling for just one more taste of blood.

The air in the hall of Kvaran was heavy. Though it was no hotter than any other late summer day, breathing was a challenge. Melancholy had swept over the royal court.

Sitric sat on his father's throne. He was slumped forward with an elbow resting on one knee. His chin sat on the hand above so that his fingers stuck out from behind his grand beard. They nervously flexed and relaxed, alternately tugging and releasing his whiskers. The cross he wore dangled behind all the activity. Silkbeard didn't take note of our entry.

Gytha did. "Thank the One True God you've come!" she said as she ran to greet her husband.

They embraced with affection. She ignored the fact that he wiped the grime from his mission onto her tunic. Gytha allowed the still moist blood from Olaf's knuckles to despoil the back of her dress. He pulled away and patted her shoulder. "I tell you this, good woman. That is the first time anyone has ever seen me walk in and praised the One God." The pair's hands lingered together and their eyes locked for a few heartbeats longer before both knew it was time to move on to the matters at hand.

"Tell me, woman, what is really going on? I don't want to talk to the sulking pup over there," said Olaf.

Colbain hurried in, reading a swatch of parchment. He nervously shoved it into his jerkin when he saw our motley band. The servant quick-stepped over to the prince and the sometimes-brothers talked in hushed tones, Colbain sternly, Sitric resigned.

"You're no dolt, husband. I think you see the predicament," Gytha began. "Mael's forces shredded the handful of patrols Sitric had out. We had just a half-day's warning before they were knocking on our door. Fortunately, the goodwill you've had Sitric spread to his citizens over the past few months, coupled with the call for troops to invade Leinster meant that his army was already assembled. It occupied the walls. The men drove away one feeble attempt to storm the city. It's been that way ever since. It's a dung-filled siege."

"And the cause of this?" asked Olaf. Then he swore. "Thor's dead goats! What does it matter the cause? What are the High King's terms?"

Silkbeard stirred. With one last tug on his beard he stood and walked to us near the hearth. "I thank you, uncle," the prince said to Olaf. "It's too late, but I thank you for beginning to instruct me in the ways of state, how to motivate my men and subjects to action. Without your words, the High King would have swept over our walls opposed only by a handful of guards. Thank you." He offered a hand.

Olaf snatched it and shook it with a single obligatory beat. The prince's fingers came away red. The sea king swore about a mistress of Odin before saying, "Uncle? This here be your aunt. That doesn't make me your uncle, pup. Now, I'll take your thanks, though I've done nothing to help your cause. I'm afraid we met near disaster in Leinster. Now I see why. None of the Leinstermen was occupied by fighting you and Mael together. Instead, they were free to mass against me." He then cursed himself for sending the monks running ahead. In my lord's defense, the tactic would have had the desired effect had the Leinster army been away fighting.

The prince took Olaf's bad news in stride. He slowly ambled in a sweeping arc around the room, pausing at the small gold leaf carving nailed to the post. "My father is old and tired and jaded. But now I see why he so often retreats to Iona. This life can wear on a man. Peace-weaver! Fantasy. I was such a fool."

"There's still a chance," said Colbain, slapping a hand on the prince's shoulder.

Gytha brushed it off. "Raised together or not, a servant knows his place." I glanced back to Tyrkr and rolled my eyes. He shrugged.

Olaf rudely spun the prince around. Gytha made no move to correct her husband's affront. The sea king spat a word hoard into Silkbeard's face. "Kvaran is old and tired. But until the Battle of Tara, the man was a ball of flame. By Hel, I'm not-so-old and tired. I'll not let a setback or ten setbacks stop me. Let your father retreat to Iona. Let him sit with the monks on the windswept island. They can shear sheep together for all I care. But stop being so morose and let's right this! We've got men with blood in their veins! We've got steel! We've got heart!" Olaf had himself up to a full lather at the end.

Sitric shook his head. "Maybe this is my Tara."

Olaf slapped the prince's face with the back of his hand. The sea king was leaving a trail of his blood wherever he went that day. Splashes, blotches, and pools marked the places where he reopened the cut. Now Silkbeard wore Olaf's blood emblazoned on his cheek.

Colbain jumped to his ruler's defense by clamping a hand on Olaf's tarnished armor. Colbain's other mitt fumbled with the ever-present knife at his neck. Olaf scoffed and unlatched the man's grasp, tossing him to the floor with a single sweep of his arm. The unsheathed knife clattered across the raised dais so that it stopped in the shadows of the thrones.

"Now what are Mael's terms?" asked Olaf.

Sitric left the sea king's blood where it lay amidst his beard. Thankfully, the blow from Olaf had knocked some spirit into the man. "I don't know!" he yelled. "I sent a group over the wall under a flag marked clearly of truce. Only one was sent back. He had his tongue cut out. The others, I fear, are dead. I've made no other attempts to talk. Now we sit in here. Every time we go to the river to replenish our water supply, Mael's men send a hail of arrows. Even when we get that water, it is filled with the shit of Irishmen. They intentionally relieve themselves upriver so that we are left to drink their filth. We've got a pair of decent wells in the city walls, but we'll run out of that in a week or two."

"Don't worry about water anymore," said Olaf. "My ships have cleared a path for you. We can easily get to the river now. That will buy us some time."

"The Irishmen still shit in the river," said Sitric.

Olaf frowned in acknowledgement.

"And we'll run out of food soon," continued Sitric. At least he wasn't whining. Rather, he told us the facts. "It is late in the year and harvest is nearly upon us. Our storehouses are low. We expected to replenish them in the coming month. Traders and merchants aren't going to come to a besieged city – Crack-a-Bone or not." He sucked in a deep breath. "The worst is that I've heard of a block of families that show signs of the bloody flux."

"By the One God," breathed Colbain as he crawled back to his feet.

Olaf held up his hands. "Don't let your minds gallop ahead. Are we sure it's the bloody flux. Maybe a newborn just has an upset stomach."

Gytha shook her head. "I went there myself. It's the flux and it's bloody."

Olaf gave his wife a reprimanding stare. "You kept your distance?"

"I did. It's bad. A child is already dead. Her siblings look to be close behind. Their neighbors began with the same symptoms this morning."

Olaf gritted his teeth. He dropped his hands to his side and allowed his fingers to dance, one at a time, with his thumbs. Vigi sidled up to his master and attempted to swipe more of his favorite elixir. This time Olaf rapped the beast's nose so that it trotted off. Soon it curled up under the throne on the raised platform.

"I'm not going to tell you any stories. The marching shit is bad once it takes hold. Time is not on our side," said Olaf. He rested two balled fists on his waist. "I'll grant you that I prefer a quick, harsh sea battle over anything on land. But before leaving Valdamar's service for my own adventures, I spent my young life standing in the shield wall. We fought on the side of Otto and his Holy Roman Empire. We fought against him at other times. I've never been on the inside of a siege, but I've been on the outside. Let me tell you this," he poked a finger in the air, "it's no day of plentiful harvest out there, either."

"Tell me," said Sitric, listening intently. The young prince was searching for hope, a good thing.

"You say that you await the harvest. Well, so does Mael. His army is filled with farmers. He'll need to release scores, if not hundreds of them soon. They lie outside at night. We still have homes and roofs. When it rains, they sit in it. They have access to firewood, but we all know an open fire doesn't drive away the damp chill like a hearth." Olaf stuck his hands in the fringes of the hearth's coals. They blackened his palms.

Silkbeard nodded. "So time is not on Mael's side either."

"Exactly," proclaimed Olaf. "Since we've got the bloody flux already, we're in a tighter pinch, but the High King doesn't know that. We can also hope that his men have the same problem with their shit that we do with ours. Not unheard of, you know. Many a time, the men outside the walls, succumb just like those inside."

"So what do we do?" asked Sitric. The pup asked like a man who wanted advice, not like a clueless youth.

"We call for terms," said Gytha. Olaf smiled and waved for his woman to continue. "My husband is saying that Mael grows just as uncertain with every passing day. The trick is to not over-react and make ourselves appear weak."

"Won't we appear weak just by asking again?" asked Silkbeard. Vigi growled as he chewed on something under the throne.

"A risk, yes," said Olaf. "The fact is we are weak. But, you've just been filled with new men and supplies. We now have access to water – dung-filled, but water nonetheless. In any case, our arrival is enough to warrant a discussion with the High King." Olaf cursed under his breath. "It shouldn't matter at this point, but what happened? We had such a perfect reason for a union with Mael's people. We had an attack on both of us from the Leinstermen. We had a prospective marriage so that both sides could claim strength. We should be dining with the backs of Leinstermen as our tables. What happened?"

Gytha shrugged. The prince said, "I don't know."

Vigi trotted out from under the throne carrying Colbain's knife. The servant jerked his head down and saw that his sheath was empty. Horror showed on his face and he scrambled to retrieve the blade. The dog jumped away and came to me. He dropped the heavy weapon on my boot.

"Give me back the knife!" Colbain demanded.

I slowly reached down and snatched it up. "Take it easy, bastard," I said. "It's not like I'd want some ornamental Irish blade that breaks the instant you use it."

"The knife is not weak. It's killed men easily enough! Now give it back!" shouted Colbain.

"He said he'll give it back," warned Sitric. "We're trying to save the city. Stop crying." The prince looked at me. His eyes said that he was disgusted with the Irishman who was raised by Gormflaith along with him. They also said that I should just give him back the weapon so that we could move on.

"Aye," I said. I stepped around the group to return the knife to Colbain. "Stop crying," I chuckled. I grasped the flat of the blade in order to hand the grip to the Irishman. I cut myself and pulled it back. "Ouch."

I should not have sliced my thumb, but I did. I had clutched the wide, flat side of the blade. It was only then that I truly studied the piece. The blade was double-edged in the style of a dagger. Starting a thumb's width from the sharp point, a shallow blood-gutter ran down its length. That fuller was short, however. It stopped just over halfway up. There the blade flattened to a cheek that extended all the way to the guard. Sitting on each side of the cheek was another short blade, perpendicular to the main one. They slowly climbed from the fuller's end, finishing at the guard. It was these wings that had cut me.

The blade had been forged with great care and skill. It was also ceremonial and expensive, probably a gift to the servant from someone rich, a royal, perhaps. That explained the bastard's overreaction to seeing it carried away by the dog. I clutched the blade again, this time careful not to cleave my finger in two. I raised the handle toward Colbain and looked down its length at the servant's angry face. He grabbed it and quickly jammed it in its sheath home.

"Nice knife you've got there. Looks like an 'X' from the end." I didn't even know what I said, until I said it. An 'X?' Colbain knew what it meant, though. We stared at each other for two heartbeats before he bolted for the nearest door.

I followed after him. "What are those animal's doing?" shouted Gytha.

"We're working here!" shouted Olaf. "Halldorr! Irishman! Stop!"

Neither of us obeyed. The hall was long, giving me just enough time to gain ground. Just as Colbain's hand slapped onto the latch, I leapt. The door opened less than an ell before my weight slammed into the Irishman, whose body pushed the oak closed. His head smashed into the door. My head rammed into his. Colbain's hand clamped onto my face and shoved it back. He grabbed the dagger's handle, but before he could draw it, I had his forearm locked in my grasp. The true grappling began. Slaps, punches, kicks, clawing, we did all of it to one another in a span of moments. I bashed his head against the door again. He drilled a thumb into my windpipe.

I swung him, lifting Colbain off his feet, sending him hurtling onto a mead table. He scattered last night's dishes and unsuccessfully whacked at the tabletop with a palm to halt his momentum. The servant continued on and rolled off the other side. When he sprang back to his feet, he surveyed his path to the door. I was in his way. He dashed toward a different exit.

Colbain made it just one step before three of Sitric's guards tackled him. I breathed a sigh of relief before being knocked down myself by another set of men. They took the opportunity to lay some grand punches. I didn't fight back – strange for me – but I decided it was the best way to be done with the entire business.

"Put them both on the wall," said Sitric. "It will be good to have two more guards. And if they fight you or refuse to go, kill them and be done with it." It was a harsh command, but I respected the prince for showing strength.

I fought the grasp of my captors. "Colbain killed Iron Knee! I can prove it."

"Lies!" shrieked Colbain.

Sitric's brow wrinkled. Olaf and Gytha appeared confused. "Iron Knee's been dead for months! We're dealing with Mael now," the sea king said.

"Don't you care that there's a traitor in our ranks, a murderer?" I barked.

"I admire the fight, lad," said Olaf. "But keep it up and you'll get yourself killed. You heard the prince's orders just like me." He sniggered. "And I think you know that my ranks are filled with murderers. As for a traitor, I'd see such a man meet a terrible end."

"I followed Iron Knee. I'd have pledged fealty to him if he wasn't dead! Don't you care?" I pleaded.

Olaf's chest seemed to widen by an ell. His voice boomed. "No, I don't care! He was a fine man, had a fine reputation, but Iron Knee is dead. Dead! I don't care!"

"But I do," said Silkbeard. His voice was calm. "Gluniairn was my brother and I care."

"He was your half-brother," said Colbain, sternly.

"We don't have time for family drama," said Gytha.

"Iron Knee was killed, what? Was it by an assassin's blade?" asked Olaf. "We'll all be dead with the billowing shits and bloody flux in a week if we don't talk to Mael. We should forget about the past."

"Speak," said Silkbeard to me.

I sloughed off the grasp of the last guard. "It was a blade that killed Iron Knee. The blade left behind a distinct mark."

"X!" shouted Tyrkr. "I was there. The dead prince and the sentinels all died from a man's knife who plunged it in once, tugged it out, twisted it, and jammed it back in. It was like he killed them all in the precise manner he was taught."

"They were all stabbed just once, by the same blade," I said.

"I was there, too," cried Colbain. "The German thrall is right. There must have been a dozen assassins who were instructed in the way to kill a man quietly. They just followed those rules."

"No," I shouted. "Colbain's blade is shaped like an 'X.' He was well known by everyone. All the guards knew him. We'd gotten falling down drunk that night, so the traitor saw his chance. He went to the sentries one-by-one to make it look like someone came in from the outside. His knife killed them silently before the men even knew what happened. The bastard came back and killed Iron Knee. He slept right next to the dead man for the rest of the night."

"These are all lies," said Colbain. "You know me, Sitric. Mother raised us together."

"I do know you, Colbain. And you know me. I am *Prince* Sitric to servants. We were raised together, but I no longer call that woman, Gormflaith, my mother. She abandoned my father when it suited her."

"She only wants what's best for us," said Colbain.

"I don't care what she wants," said the prince. "Now if all that Halldorr says are lies, we can prove it." He held out his hand. "Let me see the knife."

The guards let Colbain go. He moved with uncertain steps, holding the dagger's sheath tightly.

"Come," said Silkbeard. "You have nothing to fear. If Halldorr lies, he'll be executed just for making the accusation. Now come."

Colbain's eyes flicked around the room. His hands trembled. Before reaching the prince, the bastard dropped to one knee. "Mother loves us both so much. She wants what is best for us. I obey her. Every command she gives, I obey. I correspond with her so that my brother, the silkbearded prince, can ascend to greater heights beyond even the throne of Dyflin."

"And that is my plan, too," said Sitric. "Show me the knife."

"I ask for your mercy, brother," pleaded Colbain. "I killed Iron Knee so that you could one day be king. He was too strong, too aggressive. Mael would never have allied with such a beast. But you are Christian, devout and true. You have that in common with the High King. Besides, you, not Iron Knee, are Gormflaith's son. Mother wanted you on the throne, not some monster with a malformed knee."

Sitric was quiet. His eyes became wet, but he didn't cry, praise Thor. "I used to have a mother," he said. "Now I know a queen named Gormflaith who probably sits out there among the men who lay siege. She humps my enemy. I had a mother once.

Likewise, I used to have a brother. He was strong, true, and a friend."

"You still have a brother," interrupted Colbain. "I am still here. I work for your benefit at mother's request."

"No," said Sitric. He was growing in stature by the moment. Trials did that to a man. If the roiling surf of life didn't swamp a man, they made him stronger. "I no longer have a brother. The one I had is dead, not figuratively, but literally. He was killed by a traitor." The prince stepped in front of the quivering bastard.

"Be careful, nephew," cautioned Gytha.

"I have nothing to fear from this man," said Sitric. The prince again extended his hand. "The knife that killed my true brother."

Colbain swallowed hard and stood. He slowly drew the X-shaped blade and suspended it between himself and Sitric. His grip suddenly firmed and Colbain moved to stab the weapon into his own belly. Sitric was too fast. With two hands he grabbed the servant. "You're not getting that honor," the prince said. "My father's old gods say that to die with a blade in your hands conveys a man to Odin's hall. My faith says nothing like that, but I'll not give you the chance. Now hand your prince the knife."

The two men tugged back and forth until the bastard relented. Sitric plucked the knife free and studied as I had done. Colbain stood with shoulders slumped and hands at his side. He examined his feet.

"Now that the family business is done, can we get back to making plans?" asked Olaf. He bent down to his mutt, "Good work, boy."

"We can," answered Silkbeard. He raised the blade then drove it down into Colbain's chest. I heard a rib pop. The knife's guard was the only thing that prevented the dagger from running deeper. Blood spurt onto the prince. The servant reacted with a start. He tried to scream but only muttering came out. Colbain stepped back with one foot, but his knee buckled. He fell onto it. Colbain moaned and vomited on himself. The contents of his stomach splashed onto the floor. He tipped to the side and had to plant a palm into the pool. Like his knee before, Colbain's elbow collapsed.

"Search his person. Search his quarters. I want to read whatever he's shared with that woman, Gormflaith," growled Silkbeard.

"Mother loves us. You'll be king because of her. You may be High King one day." Colbain's words were labored. The guards flopped him onto his back and rummaged through his clothes. The bastard's face was becoming pale. His hands lay cold like those of a dead man at his side. It wouldn't be much longer now. "She wanted me as her husband. Truly," Colbain said, crying. "Every tryst was only to bring us together again as a family."

"Do you want me to finish him, Prince Silkbeard?" asked a guard who had just pulled out the parchment Colbain was reading when he came into the hall. "So you don't have to hear his nonsense?"

"No," said Silkbeard. "Prince Iron Knee died with the hand of Colbain across his mouth and nose and the Irish bastard's knife in his side. It was a slow death. The traitor will go the same way." He snatched the vellum from the guard and scanned it. "Delusional bastard," Sitric huffed, throwing the parchment onto the floor. "Don't bother searching his effects. The woman called Gormflaith toys with his tender emotions. She promises this and that. She promises her hand in matrimony to him, a thrall. If only Colbain gives her more information, does her work for her, kills my brother, he can have all he desires – a servant worm can bed the prize of Ireland!" He said the last with not a little derision.

"So where does that leave us?" asked Olaf. "What do you want to do?"

"We go to Mael for terms. Only instead of sending emissaries, I will go. I'd like to look into the woman called Gormflaith's eyes when I accuse her of starting this whole mess," said the prince.

"Tell mother I love her," Colbain gurgled. "I would have made her an excellent husband."

• • •

After Colbain, the murdering bastard, died reeking of vomit, Sitric quickly organized the party that would ride out with him to the High King. I went, given the honor for having uncovered Colbain's treachery. In truth, I gave the credit to Vigi, the dog. Tyrkr came because he happened to be standing in the room. Fifty guards were called from their posts around the great hall and embankment. Olaf was invited because having Lord Crack-a-Bone at your side could do no harm.

"That's no place for me," said Gytha when Prince Sitric asked her to come. "I am man enough to take care of my own lands and those of my former husband. I am woman enough to find a dear and strong second husband, but I think you would bring nothing but scorn upon yourself for having a woman in your troupe."

"Aunt," said Sitric. "Nothing of the sort will happen. I need you to play the part of pleading with Mael for my blessed union with Aednat. And since Gormflaith will likely be there, I'll need you to combat her belligerence. I know that only a woman can properly defend against that." He slapped the buckle of his belt to make sure it was tightly secured about his waist. "Besides, it's an order." Silkbeard marched out toward the stables without waiting for her response. He was learning rule. I was learning to like him.

So fifty of the royal guard, an exiled Greenlander, a German thrall, a brutal pirate – and his dog a mere woman, and a pup prince went out to make Mael Sechnaill, High King of Ireland, believe that we were mighty and weren't just days away from dying with blood in our trousers. The massive timber gates creaked on their hinges as the watchmen shoved them outward. Perhaps one hundred infantry with shields lofted scampered out in front of us to protect the gaping hole from a rushing attack by the Ui Neill. None came and those men funneled back into the city once our band slowly trod past. The gate was shut with a thud. I heard the iron bars noisily slide along their straps inside to lock it tight. It was us against a few thousand angry Irishmen. If Mael cared more for the prince's death and less for the truce flag, he could have his way with a snap of his fingers. It would cost him, though. I and the other men around me were prepared to fight to the last.

The River Poddle was on our left. Though water crafts could maneuver in it where it curved around the east side of Dyflin, here on the southwest it was little more than a trickling creek. The tiny amount of Dyflin's farmland that lay on its southern banks was thoroughly trampled by the hordes of Irishmen who now camped there. I'm sure some of those Ui Neill had the sense to harvest a handful of the grain at a time. But most of the food would already be ground into the dirt, useful to neither army.

Farther to our right sat the Ruirthech. She was a pretty enough waterway made ugly by the Ui Neill warriors who camped on both sides. Carts and men crossed back and forth upriver at the Ford of Hurdles. I was always told the ford was manmade. It consisted of a series of frames made of wattled twigs that gathered debris and made the ford shallower. What was left of the original frames jutted up out of the flowing waters here and there. They looked like two rows of sentries lined up staring at one another. What they guarded, I know not.

Sitric caught my glance. "When I was young my father told me tales about that ford. The Irish call it Ath Cliath. King Kvaran said that after our ancestors built Dyflin up from the bogs and ruled for many years, carelessness set in. They worried more about what their fellow Norsemen were doing than what the real enemies were up to. The city fell to the Irish about ninety years ago. About fifteen years after that, my grandfather – his name was Sitric, too – he took it back. The Ui Neill weren't happy with the turn of events."

"I'd say not," giggled Olaf.

"They were so angry that they prayed to the One God for many days. They sat on the banks of River Boyne and prayed, not eating," continued Silkbeard, clearly wanting to tell the tale.

"Then your grandfather should have attacked them and chopped them to bits while they were weak from hunger," laughed Olaf.

"Perhaps he did, dear husband," said Gytha. "You'll not know if you keep interrupting the prince, though."

Olaf laughed again. We all chuckled, beguiling the gravity of our mission. We approached Mael's host and came to a stop at stern sentries who stood with prickling spears behind a hedge made of pointed logs and thorns. The prince continued with his yarn, clutching the cross at his chest. "The prayers of the faithful Irishmen worked. The One God allowed the River Boyne to give birth to a terrific sea monster. The waters churned, the silt bubbled and together they belched out a creature the size of a man. The tiny thing grew before the eyes of the Ui Neill, becoming bigger than any longship. The beast submerged itself and took its claws and sharp teeth out to sea." Sitric pointed back down the river. "It swam up the Ruirthech to attack us." A few of the Irish guards understood his Norse words and laughed wickedly at the thought of a great leviathan besieging Dyflin.

"What happened?" asked Tyrkr.

"Well, thrall, we are still here are we not?" asked Silkbeard. Tyrkr nodded. "My grandfather with just his sword and fifty men waded into the river to take on the beast. Out of spite for what the Irish could offer, he took his woman with him. Together that small company slew the beast. What you see sticking up at the ford are, in fact, the monster's remains. It died on its back and those sticks jutting up are what's left of his ribcage."

"And now you, with just your sword, fifty men, and a woman come to meet all that today's Ui Neill have to offer. How fitting," said Mael Sechnaill as he rode up to the picquets. The High King was adorned in chainmail and a helmet. A curtain of iron links dangled from the rear two thirds of the helmet's rim. Like Silkbeard, he was accompanied by his closest guard, and a woman.

"You look well, son," said Gormflaith. "A king you'll be once you remove Kvaran."

Mael gave his queen a stern look. She didn't shrink. "So is Dyflin's so-called king still haunting his life away at Iona," Gormflaith asked.

Sitric faced the High King directly. "I also bring Olaf Tryggvason, Lord Crack-a-Bone, with me. His countless men brought plentiful supplies upriver. They and my citizens eat merrily within those walls. With those provisions we will rest happily throughout the winter. We'll be warm in our homes. I might even develop a layer of fat." The prince rubbed his trim belly. "But, in truth, when the snows melt we'll be tired of peering out at your army dwindling day by day from cold, exposure, and disease. We'll feel compelled to swoop out and crush what is left. It would be the Christian thing to do, to put a foe out of his misery."

"Fine speech, son," said Gormflaith. "Where is Colbain? I'd like to see both of my boys together."

"Dead," answered Gytha. She stared at Gormflaith.

"Woman," said Mael. "You've said quite enough, I think. Allow me to speak." Gormflaith sat quietly for a time, clearly not from obedience. She toyed with her new husband and the High King knew it. He sighed and went on. "I do have terms for you, Prince Sitric, if that is what you seek."

"No, we do not," said Sitric. I was surprised, but had the sense not to show it. Olaf and Gytha beside him sat quietly on their horses. Olaf murmured soft words of encouragement to his beast while the prince spoke. "I've come to give you terms, High King. You've invaded my lands, unprovoked. Now you besiege my city. Leave behind one hundred horses to pay for the patrols you murdered. Leave behind fifty shirts of mail. Lastly, leave behind your daughter so that I may marry her in my own church. She will be my queen. Like the conditions to which we originally agreed, she and I will rule a new, expansive Dyflin up to the River Boyne."

Mael Sechnaill's face turned red with anger. He pulled back the corners of his mouth, bunching his cheeks as he prepared to speak. Gormflaith's words walked over him. "I'm on your side in this mighty Prince of Dyflin. I am on the side of my husband as well. The stipulations you just stated are what I tried to tell the High King, son, but it is too late for that, I'm afraid."

"I," said Sitric with a barely raised voice, "am no longer your son. My place is in Dyflin as was yours. Now, High King, what is your answer to my terms?"

The High King took on Sitric's icy voice. "I have always thought you a pup compared to both your father and Iron Knee, but I admit to all that I underestimated you. Your comely features and rich beard belie the evil mind that lurks behind those eyes. You claim to be a follower of the One God, but what Christian would do such a thing as you? I don't pretend to understand the game you play, but you must know that I'll stop at nothing in order to repay you one hundred times over for the pain you've caused."

"What pain?" Sitric asked. "It is you who've invaded my lands. Now meet my terms. Bring me my wife."

Mael drew his sword. "These are my terms today. Though my daughter is dead, she is still too fine a creature for the likes of you, her murderer!"

"Dead?" gasped every member of our command group.

It was too late. Mael spurred his horse forward, while Gormflaith allowed hers to retreat. The High King's personal guard rallied with him and plunged forward to attack us. We were fortunate that their own picquets hindered progress. Spiked limbs and poles, makeshift fences, and other obstacles had to be shoved aside for them to get at us. We killed the first two men who squirted through. That was just enough time to get Prince Sitric and his aunt moving back to Dyflin. With the precious head start, we fought a hard retreat toward the gate, stopping to face the massing enemy for a time before running ahead. We had to repeat the process for many harrowing moments before we were again behind Dyflin's strong walls.

CHAPTER 9

Sitric was back on his father's throne. "He broke a flag of truce!" Silkbeard barked while pounding his balled fist on the barrels of coins that adorned the platform to emphasize every other word. The silver contents rattled inside.

I sat on a mead table with my feet planted on a long bench. I was sick with regret at having done nothing to save the smart and lovely Aednat. The fire that drew me to her and made me love her in a fashion was what got her killed. I pictured her leaving the safety of the hiding place among the rocks near the gnarled yew where I'd left her as soon as I was away that night. The princess would have run toward her father's men, not out of fear, but to somehow command, aid, or comfort. Aednat was brave beyond her years and experience. As a result, she died at the hands of the same raiding Leinsters that whacked my skull.

Aednat disappeared from the world in an instant. In that she was like every woman of worth – or just worth mentioning – that I'd known. You may be tired of the list, but I'm not. Images of my mother, Thjordhildr, Freydis, Gudruna, Aoife, and now Aednat roiled my mind. Some of them were dead. Others were still alive, but all of them ripped from my life by the cruel norns, those wicked women spinning fate at the foot of Yggdrasil. Memories of nameless women from the villages in which I'd lived joined the familiar ones in my mental froth. Many nameless women had died in pools of their own and their newborn's blood. Every spring brought a new batch of children and a handful of new, dead women. It was as sure as waves wearing on a beach.

I remembered my dream where the Valkyries had worked so hard on their gruesome looms. Ottar the skald had given me an interpretation that was filled with doom. For a time I had set aside his predictions since nothing appeared to be headed in a fateful direction. In hindsight, I suppose everything was slowly spinning out of control. Dyflin was sinking from greatness. The Irish tide we'd kept at bay for so long was swelling. We'd been attacked by Leinstermen in the woods and lost fine men. I'd been cracked on the skull. Aednat died. We moved to assault

Leinster and were surprised, losing more fine Norse warriors. The blood that pumped through their brave hearts now fertilized Leinster land. Now we were besieged – hemmed in – and unless we wanted to flee like cowards, we'd die in that prison. The Valkyries in my vision would have their way. The capricious norns had caught up with me once and for all.

"He did, but I can't say that I wouldn't have done the same," said Olaf. He lay sprawled on the floor next to his dog. The man had his feet propped up on the hearth and gnawed at a chicken leg. The dog was on his back and greedily ate scraps from his master's hand. "He thinks you killed his daughter in the woods and then are cruel enough to act like you don't know. You torture him."

"I do no such thing! I didn't know," said the prince.

"Mael doesn't know that," said Olaf.

"So we sit here besieged because of a misunderstanding," said Sitric, throwing his hands in the air. "What about the last misunderstanding? Why haven't the Leinstermen come to lay siege?"

"The Leinsters won't challenge the High King while he is prepared for battle," shrugged Olaf.

"Isn't that comforting," said Sitric. "Misunderstanding and battles. Misunderstandings and war."

"Aren't they all begun by misunderstandings?" I asked, momentarily stirring out of my melancholy. I thought myself intelligent.

"No!" shouted Olaf, finally appearing engaged. Vigi twitched at the raised voice. "Some, yes. Not all. Here we swim in a sea of kings; all of them would be lords of battle. What other outcome could there be but a bloodtide? Misunderstandings? Ha! Other fights are because of true differences in principles. Take our long wars against the Christians. Or, theirs against us. We believe in different things and it won't change. Misunderstandings!" he huffed, speaking more rapidly as he got rolling. "Take the Muslims and their conquest of almost everything. They butcher their way across Europe because of Allah, the moon god. We butcher our way across the same because of a wish to be like Odin. The

Christians are stuck in the middle. It is the opposite of misunderstandings. The wars are because we *understand* one another all too well."

I shut my lips, no longer thinking of my intelligence. I went back to stewing. It was more comfortable anyway.

"I don't care about Allah," said Silkbeard.

"Who does?" asked Olaf, returning to his meal.

"You're not helping," said the prince. "What do you do when your enemy won't listen to reason?"

"You speak with iron and steel, young prince." Olaf propped himself up on his elbows. "I've said it before but that mother of yours plays in matters that she may understand, but she can certainly not control. Events moved past her."

"She is not my mother," warned Silkbeard. He walked to stand over the spot where Colbain's death had darkened floor.

Olaf groaned as he stood. "I meant no offense, lad. None at all. It was just my way of speaking of the woman who pushed you out from her belly a long time ago."

Gytha came in. "The food stores have been tallied with guards placed. All of Olaf's and the royal provisions have been placed in the common barns. The families and their men who guard the wall are grateful."

"That was a fine idea, Crack-a-Bone," said the prince. "It will do much for morale for the people to know they've got food for a time. For a time."

Olaf cracked the chicken leg and sucked out the marrow before throwing what was left into the fire. "I could stand to lose some girth," he said patting his midsection. "It will make me all the better with my sword."

A young boy sprinted through the door at the far end. His feet slapped loudly against the floor. At first I didn't recognize him because his clothes were relatively clean and his face was not bruised. It was my favorite comb salesman. Being a runner for Sitric's army suited him. At least it got him away from his quick-to-strike father.

"What is it?" asked the prince.

"News from the wall," the boy breathed. He gave me a familiar wave. "The High King sent your mother to call up more terms to us."

I watched Silkbeard's jaw clench at the word, 'mother,' but he showed mercy to the boy. "Go on," Sitric muttered.

"She says that she's proud of the display you put on as Prince of Dyflin," began the boy.

"I don't care about her opinions. Her puppetry has gotten us into all this – a dead brother, war with Leinster, a dead princess, war with the Ui Neill. What are Mael's terms."

"Battle, he wants battle. He says that it is the Christian thing to do and since you be Christian like him, you should agree. Your mother says that the High King believes that we have the bloody flux. The stench is on the wind. He admits that he has it in his camp, too." The boy shrugged the shrug of a soldier. His indifference proved to me that he would make a great warrior, if he survived. "Mael has a point, Prince Sitric. Why not meet him?"

"Because, lad, he has twice the number of men as do we," answered Olaf. "With what I lost in Leinster and the disease moving through the streets, we'd need fortune indeed. Or, we just need more men."

"Men!" said the boy, snapping his fingers. "I almost forgot one of the terms your mother gave. The High King wants you as a Christian leader to show your true faith. He'll allow you to send out the women and children from the city. They must go east, nowhere near his army, lest they eat his food and bring more disease. But they may go. They may go out to the islands where we house slaves before the auctions. They can go to the Thing-mount or beyond – anywhere. The men may stay and meet their fates, though the queen's word was Maker."

"He's no better than a one-nutted hog!" exclaimed Olaf. "He thinks that Norsemen and women will be separated at a time of the truest of tests! By Hel, our children will fight the Irish toads in the muddy streets before we let them go scampering into the woods."

"Lord Crack-a-Bone is right!" agreed the young boy. He knew nothing of which he spoke. Give him just a taste of the piss and shit of combat and he'd plead to run into the forest at a moment's notice. He'd make a fine soldier one day, but he had some experience to gain. And, remember, he had to survive.

Silkbeard sighed. "My father would not have sent out the women," he said. "None of my ancestors would have done such a thing."

"Rightly so!" said Olaf.

The prince hesitated. "I'm just not so sure. They wouldn't have done it because they followed the old gods. I'm a Christ follower, just as the High King says."

"In either case it's a trick, a trap," cautioned Olaf.

"A trap for what?" asked Sitric. "In many ways it makes us stronger. We eliminate mouths to feed during the siege. What could be Mael's trick?"

Olaf was now completely frustrated. "I don't know! Perhaps he chops our women up in sight of the walls to cause us to lose heart. Maybe it's a payback for the death of his daughter. Maybe Gormflaith wants all the men of the island to herself so she can more easily pull our strings. I don't know! He's the High King and an Irishman to boot. Mael can't be trusted." He waved a broad palm at the prince in anger and dropped down onto the hearth with folded arms. Olaf wriggled his rump a time or two before he settled in. The comb-salesman-turned warrior came close to the sea king and rested his thin hand on the man's shoulder. The boy patted it twice and offered comforting words that would have been humorous were our situation not so grave.

Olaf tapped the boy's hand gently. "Now, that's a good lad, Thrond." I never bothered to learn the salesman's name. Olaf knew everyone.

Gytha knelt to her husband. "When an enemy wants to spring a trap on you and you find out beforehand, what do you do?"

Olaf curled his lips into a forced smile for his woman. "I'm just saying that our people don't send out women and children as if they are frail. They are hardier than those Irish rodents out there."

"That's it!" I said as I hopped down from the mead table. Damn the norns! Damn the Valkyries, for now. Those beauties would have to wait a while longer before they'd escort me to Odin's hall.

Gytha stood, nodding. "That *is* it." She looked to me with her handsome grin and I beamed back at the woman. My boy-like crush on her resumed at that moment. I'd lost many fine women to sickness, swords, falls, drowning, and anything else the norns had devised. But Olaf's woman was still there and her mind worked wonders. She was Crack-a-Bone's wife, but we could all benefit from her presence.

Earlier, I stated that men do terrible things to one another. I also said that women could do worse.

Gytha was proving that women could also do better, much better than men.

• • •

Gytha and the comb salesman, Thrond, were among the first to make the extraordinarily brief trip across the Poddle. Twenty others went with them, children and women. They formed a beachhead, so to speak, on the east bank of the river that slowly blossomed all day long as more and more refugees left the city. They carried only small knapsacks slung across their shoulders with a day's worth of bread, a kit of essential tools, and an extra cloak. A few of the goodbyes to the men were tear-filled exchanges that did nothing to raise the overall morale of the deported host. Like a sickness is curiously transferred from one warrior to another, the crying begun by one woman traveled as quickly as lightning to those nearby. Children, too, soon had wet cheeks and snotty noses.

The terms of the agreement made between the High King and the prince from afar were that our women and children, girls of any age and boys under twelve winters, could flee eastward away from the Ui Neill host. Only a small number of men could be seen with them or else the Ui Neill would have no choice but to attack. Just the men required to ferry the mass across the Poddle would be tolerated. When the last group set foot on the east bank, our men would be required to immediately return to the citadel or else the Ui Neill would again have the right to massacre all in their path.

The many rounds of transport went without incident. I was among those allowed to shuttle the exiles since *Charging Boar* was beached on that side of the city. Perhaps two hundred or more crossings were made altogether and it took most of the day. A few companies of Mael's warriors lounged nearby watching our every move, looking for any excuse to run our women through with their blades or manhood. On one of my trips a senior Ui Neill man was talking to Gytha.

"It's none of your business where we go," said Gytha to him.

"It's the High King's business and you'll tell me or else I'll be within my rights to butcher the lot of you braid-haired ladies and red-haired runts," he said. The man dug a dirty finger into one nostril and produced a treasure which was soon flicked into the river water.

Gytha gave an exasperated sigh. "Fine! I lead them to Dyflin's Thing-mount where we'll camp tonight. It's not that far, but we'll be moving slowly with the babies and infirm."

"I know where your precious assembly hill is!" he snapped, wiping the finger in question across his leather mail. "I'm no fool. I've lived in this land all my life and my sons will live here long after we drive you Norse foreigners away."

"My Norse relatives have lived in this land longer than the last ten generations of your family," prodded Gytha.

"I ought to slam you down on the rocks right now," huffed her verbal opponent. He grabbed or scratched his crotch. "After I take you, my men can butcher the rest."

"You are not only charming, you're intelligent and strong," said Gytha, reaching for the man's bicep. He let her give it a firm squeeze. "Obviously, I can tell you all our plans because I know that you'll know what to do with the information. You're a man of action and importance." My last passenger dropped onto the bank, but I loitered, trying to hear more of their conversation.

"You there!" cried the Ui Neill soldier with the snot in his nose, itch in his groin, and large bicep. "Move back or I'll chop this lady to bits." He would do no such thing as the attractive woman had already graced him with a touch.

Gytha stepped toward the man. They were about the same height, but she stood on a short stone. The lady looked down at him. The ends of her fingers dug into his arm. "Try it," Gytha whispered. The confused man impotently fingered his sword, but ultimately did nothing more than blink stupidly. Gytha turned to me. "Stop lingering, Halldorr. The sooner you get us all out, the sooner you can defeat the castrated Irish sheep so that your fairer halves may return."

"A just point, Lady Gytha," was all I said. I nodded to Tyrkr who leaned his shoulder into the bulwark. His feet and the keel rattled against the shore's smooth stones.

"As I was saying," said Gytha to the Ui Neill soldier. He again scrubbed the underside of his nose. "We camp on the Thing-hill tonight. During the dark we will begin to load our young and ladies on a single longship that will be released from here and sail to one of the islands near the mouth of the Ruirthech. It will take countless trips to get the job done."

"Hey!" the man protested. It was getting hard to hear them as *Charging Boar* drifted across to get more passengers. "That's not part of the High King's agreement. You are not permitted to move any ships anywhere."

"Shh!" hissed Gytha. "I don't want any of our men to hear us. You see, I called you castrated sheep in front of them to give our warriors heart. In truth, we women and our younglings don't have much hope in the outcome of tomorrow's fight. We sail to the island for protection against what is likely to be a veritable rout of Dyflin. We're afraid of what the strong and powerful Ui Neill will do once their bloodlust is up from battle. You understand, don't you?" She set a soft hand on his shoulder.

The dolt looked at the graceful hand. "I do. I do, lady. War is no place for women. Too dangerous, you see. You go about your fleeing. We'll get to you on the island eventually, but it would be some days after the battle. Leaders like me will again have a hold on the men by then. You'll be safe."

Gytha sighed in relief and hugged him. His eyes blossomed into giant, happy orbs. The lady asked, "Then you won't butcher us if we have a single ship to move us on the river?"

The man pulled Gytha away tenderly and brushed a stray hair from her face with his filthy hand. "No, no, of course not. Don't fret." He studied her face. "I wish you were around when I searched for a wife many years ago. But you're not Irish." He sighed, "I'll tell you what, I'll have the men in our quadrant release a few more ships to carry you. That way you're all gone by morning when the battle comes. You'll be safe and pretty."

"The battle comes at dawn, then?" Gytha asked, speaking a little too loudly to make sure I could hear.

It was his turn to shush. "Shh," he murmured. "Of course it does. The High King said midday in his terms, but there is no sense at prolonging the inevitable. Now go, lady, Godspeed."

"Thank you, sir. You are a gentleman in a harsh world," said Gytha, bowing. She'd made his day.

She made sure those of us involved in our little scheme knew we had even less time to see it hatched. Dawn was coming.

• • •

When our human cargo was completely moved, the only non-warriors left behind were those weakened by the flux. The city was mostly desolate. A plot of land where a house was to be built was left barren except for the wooden drain and drainpipe that had been previously set. The disease-ridden were all moved onto that lot and into the houses of a single block. We needed them out of our way – for their safety should the battle spill into the town and for our protection against the trotting flux they spread. A half-dozen old women who volunteered to stay behind and tend to the ill scurried about carrying water and soiled cloths. The tunics they wore were splattered with the green, yellow, and brown contents of citizens' bowels as well as the black crimson that shot out with it. More than any man on the battlefield, those haggard women were stout of heart, for they entered their field of contest knowing in advance they'd lose a third of their soldiers. And yet fight they did.

The equinox was just approaching so we had and utilized as much of the daylight hours as we could to fortify our walls.

Even so, the time seemed to slip away and we had to finish our toiling long into the night. You see, we were outnumbered – heavily. We understood that fact with certainty. All we had to do was scan the horizon and count the Ui Neill host. No matter how many times we made the assessment, Dyflin came up short.

Mael would know with reasonable clarity that he held the numerical advantage. I am not sure how it happens, especially when faithful Norsemen are in question, but it always does. In every contest of arms of any length, there is always at least one person among the besieged who skulks through the kill zone and into the enemy camp. They sell the secrets of their friends holed up behind walls for the price of a warm piece of bread or the promise of protection. I don't know who did the act this time, but I was confident it happened. Therefore, Mael understood our disadvantage.

The north and east and some of the south sides of the city were protected by the rivers. Our ships still floated there with men elevated on their decks to provide excellent cover. The long northern wall had just a handful of defenders to serve more as watchmen than true warriors because of the Ruirthech's depth and breadth.

Not to be ignored was our floating fence of spears in the shallows of the curving River Poddle. We expected a few of the High King's attackers to slip through this barrier, so we could not leave the palisade there undefended. Thus, men adorned with spears in each hand and more in reserve guarded the southern wall.

The biggest risk to Dyflin was at the side that faced inland. That is where Mael Sechnaill had decided to camp because it was the surest, firmest, and broadest way to surmount our walls. With his numbers he would spread his men and simultaneously attack wherever he could. We would struggle to keep them at bay. Their bodies would pile up on the plain and on the earthen embankment. It would be bloody and terrible, to be sure. If we could hold and slaughter them long enough, they might lose heart. With that, we might yet win the day. However, it would take just one or two besiegers to set foot over our walls for our defense to buckle. We would need the capricious norns on our side.

We hammered and nailed or tied extra posts to the tops of the timber palisade to remove a few sections of their attack route. We hoped that these taller walls would funnel Mael's forces to where we could best fight. Our legs, arms, and backs were busy all night, trudging around by torchlight. Out in the High King's camp, other than a few dozen sentries, the rest of them slept like a fat man after a large meal. I swear I could hear them snoring over the racket we made. They'd be fresh at dawn, we'd be spent. At least we wouldn't be surprised when the attack came at first light. When I reported on Mael's treachery, both Olaf and Prince Sitric marveled at Gytha's ability to milk candor from the foul Ui Neill soldier.

In truth, we hoped that the coming clash would never make it to Dyflin's walls. But Sitric was being diligent in his preparations. He was prudent and even Olaf complimented the young prince for it. We worked all night hoping that none of our extra fortifications would be necessary. You see, we hoped that our own surprise would spring just before dawn. When the signal came, we'd slap open the iron bars that locked Dyflin's southwest gates and rush out en masse to grind the Ui Neill into the soil. The High King and his legions would be dead at the first cock's crow.

When the night was just over half done, we set down our construction gear and picked up the more familiar tools of war. War is a trade that has lasted longer than building. It is in man's nature to kill. Killing came long before our desire to develop and create. Since the siege of Dyflin I've learned of Cain and his brother Abel. Cain wanted the favor of God won by Abel. He murdered his brother out of jealousy. It is easy to see from such history that passionate bloodlust predated erecting great structures. It is as plain as a slap to the face that man is no different today. It is obvious that when I whiten my grip on the hilt of a sword and I involuntarily grin, I am no different from anyone. I love the mayhem of battle. The tools that adorned my belt there in the dark were as much a part of me as my hand itself.

Olaf leaned with his back against the city's grand timber doors. His armor was anything but regal. The sea king looked no different than the first time I saw him in the muddy streets. I think he even wore the same clothes. Torchlight from above produced flickering shadows down from his face. He laughed joyfully as he told stories to his men. Each tale became more animated with Olaf drafting spectators to play various parts.

Vigi and my fellow Greenlanders stood or lounged around their warlord. Vigi gnawed vigorously at a plank that he'd dragged from a section of the timber that lined Dyflin's main road. My friends listened intently to their lord, happy to have something else to think about before the coming conflict.

Some men lie and say they have no fear. Well, perhaps they don't lie. Maybe they tell the truth and are too stupid to feel fear when a war is nigh. We all have knots turn in our bellies just before the blood spurts. In some men, the tightening stomach means they shit or piss themselves. In other men, the same feeling prevents them from relieving themselves for the next two days. The trick is to accept the fear in your head. Just let it sit there. Point it out in your mind, but don't let it travel elsewhere. Prevent it from getting to your heart. Fear in your heart is as soul-sucking as living with Hel after death. Most importantly, don't let fear make it past your lips. By Odin and the One True God, don't let your real and deserved fear ever form words. For if it does, you are sealing the fates of every man you love. Your fear, given a voice, will soon spread at a rate faster than the bloody flux. Your friends will compound it. Your army will quiver. You and they will die in buckets full of your own stool complete with spears jutting from your chests.

Cnute wore his leather mail. He might never afford chain armor since he lost wagers now on a daily basis. A spear and hammer were his weapons that day. He probably pilfered the hammer from a barren smithy. Leif and Randulfr wore proper mail and carried richly adorned swords. Tyrkr's kit was functional and no more. His stout arms bulged. I could see that one of his biceps twitched, an indication of either his fear or his anticipation. In either case, I'd not ask him. Brandr, Loki,

Magnus, and the rest waited behind the gates, ready to run out and hew Mael's host.

Sitric sat as a stoic. It was right of him to do so, for he could never hope to compete with Lord Crack-a-Bone in the aspects of leadership and inspiration. His smart bay stood tall beneath the prince. Like its rider, the beast was braced for battle. Its hooves were filthy with mud, but the rest of the animal had been washed so that the deep brown coat and black appendages carried a fresh sheen. Man and beast cut impressive figures and did much to inspire us with nary a word. The prince's mail had been scrubbed by an Irish thrall until it appeared new. The torchlight it reflected was blinding. Win or lose, if Kvaran could see his fairer lad today, the old king would be proud. He might even say, honestly, that the task of protecting Dyflin had fallen to the correct son. At that moment, I missed Iron Knee for a long heartbeat.

That moment and many more lingered. The night wore on. Eventually, even Olaf tired of telling yarns. He summoned the skalds, Ottar and Grouse-Poet, to continue the chore while the sea king roughly rolled on the path with his dog. He tugged on the dog's chew-toy plank. Some of us fell asleep. Silkbeard adjusted his rump in the saddle more and more frequently.

Time, which felt so short at the start of the night, oozed by.

After a lingering eternity, Sitric quietly said, "Back to the walls, men." The first indications of light had just begun to blaze across the undersides of the night's clouds. They reflected purples and reds, creating upside down, billowing mountains interspersed with deep, shadowy valleys. "Join the guards. It looks like the signal is not coming. We won't be fighting on the plain today. No, we must cleave them from the safety of our palisade. All the better for us," the prince added out of necessity. In truth, it wasn't better for us, since our master plan had not come off. Now the day would be won or lost with brutal determination and luck, nothing more.

The first grumbles came as men climbed back to their feet. Some were just groans from a stiff neck or knee. Others were what may be termed concern for the coming fight. A slap from Olaf or a scowl from Sitric quickly subdued such talk.

We filed to our places on the wall. There was no bounce in our steps. Grubby hands clutched mjolnir amulets. Christians made the sign of the cross. Prayers were sent for what was nearly upon us. Even more entreaties were lifted for what had not happened. Since the predawn signal never came, that meant something had gone wrong.

Just how wrong, no one knew. Our plan had rested on chicanery and feint. Could it be repaired? No one dared think about it. There was no time for adjustments or further scheming. The slow descent of Dyflin in Kvaran's last years had finally reached a cantor. In a short while, the kingdom's plunge would reach a full gallop. Nearly two centuries worth of work would be lost.

All we could do was stand behind our palisade with spears bristling. Our archers and javelin hurlers stood at the ready. Sitric had dismounted from his bay, allowing the sleepy creature to return to its stable, guided by a young boy who may not survive the day if our walls were breached.

I wondered if the prince had the same images flashing in his head that I did in mine. Another man might ride Sitric's horse by nightfall – a pillaging Irishman on the Prince of Dyflin's fine bay. The thought angered me, but my best hope at preventing such a travesty was to remain shoulder-to-shoulder with my friends. If only we drained more blood from them than they did from us in the first moments. We might have a chance.

Folly. My heart was sinking, though I had the sense to pinch my mouth into a certain grin.

Joy.

I heard the signal. It came, I was sure. My eyes scanned the expanse to the west in the slowly growing light.

My heart slipped below the water's surface. It began its path to Hel's bedroom.

There was no signal. The only noise, the only activity was from Mael's awakening host.

They came.

• • •

"Forward!" I heard the High King's voice as clear as if he'd been next to me.

Mael was mounted. Barring the horse, it was still easy to pick him out. His banners snapped in the wind. The kit of his personal guard made the rest of his army look like simple farmers. Many were, but as sure as an old man's balls sag, a thousand angry shepherds can lick a hundred uncertain Norsemen. I didn't know our exact numbers or Sechnaill's. I understood only that we needed to be reminded of our warrior spirit.

Olaf knew it. From his place behind the wall, he growled. "Take heart! Stand fast! We've been in worse scrapes!" I don't think he had, but even the longest serving of his crew would not correct the man now.

Silkbeard understood what was necessary. The pup became a dog that day, a fearsome, feral beast. To my right, I heard the prince mumble a prayer to the One God. "Father, carry us this day. Make my words bold. Make my arms strong. Forgive me for my shortcomings. Forgive me for what I say next."

The measured pounding of Irish feet grew steadily louder. It was like a drumbeat that was in perfect time to my thumping heart.

Sitric cleared his throat. "Men of Dyflin! Norsemen! Danes! Swedes and Germans! Icelanders and Greenlanders! Hear my voice." He climbed up on the timber palisade with the help of two men. He defiantly turned his back on the approaching horde. "Who are you that you might be vexed by mere mortals? Men are but grass, meant to be hewed! Who are you and who am I? We are the besieged, soon to be unleashed. I am Prince of Dyflin, Sitric Silkbeard. I am son of our city's king, Kvaran. The prior king, Sitric, was my grandfather. I have the blood of conquerors coursing through my veins." He drew a saex and used its tip to prick his wrist. Crimson soiled his clean sleeves. "My blood is red, made thick from generations of breeding hardy men with stout women. Now pierce your skin.

Do it! Do it!" All around me I saw my comrades use their spears or swords to draw blood. "Do you see your blood? Is it not thick as the icy rivers of Norway? Is it not as red as the blood moon? Your blood is my blood. My blood is yours. We are all descended from royalty. I claim kings in my heritage, but all of us may claim to be the sons of gods! Odin gave us words and poetry and war. Thor's hammer dangles from chains around your necks. It rests on your chests. Today we are as close to perfection as we will ever be! Today we will bring more glory to this island than it has ever seen. Behind me the Irish come. Their blood is as loose as water. It evaporates like steam. They have no claim to our heritage. They are not warriors. They are pretenders!" Silkbeard spread his arms wide. I could see the cross around his neck. "You are terrifying, evil bastards. Morning breaks behind you! It rises from the Irish Sea. Coming at me are waves of Irish weaklings. They will come to our walls and they will crumple. Our earth, our timber, our steel," Silkbeard pummeled his chest with a clenched fist. "Our hearts will see that the High King's strength is sapped and his soul weakened."

His speech was greeted with silence.

Sitric briefly scanned his defenders hoping for a reaction. None came. The prince swallowed hard and set his hands on the shoulders of neighboring warriors. They lowered him down behind the palisade. It was nearly fully light now. The prince faced the morning sun. He had tears streaming down his cheeks. He didn't bother wiping them away.

A lone voice cried out. "Silkbeard!" A second and third joined in. Hundreds followed. The butcher who Olaf had overpaid was among them. So were countless other common soldiers, all inspired to follow a generous prince who turned out to be an inspiring speechmaker. The cries rang, "Silkbeard! Silkbeard!"

More tears washed Sitric as he mumbled to himself. Olaf muscled his way over to him. "One way or another, lad, you've won today." The sea king slapped the young royal's shoulder as our army's deafening chants drowned out the jeering cries from the Irish.

I grinned. Win or lose, Olaf was right. The prince had secured a victory that day. And we would win with him. By day's end we'd again be powerful in Ireland or we'd celebrate in Odin's hall. We had already won.

A flash of light shot over the wall and cracked into the prince's back. The force from the arrow spun the young man around so that he crashed into Olaf. The pair almost fell off the rear of the platform.

We were lost.

You may think me fickle. You may rightly accuse me of being led moment to moment by my emotions. To that I say you are correct. But when you've stood in a shield wall or when you've balanced on a longship's planks with arrows raining down or when you've remained tall behind a fort's wall while under assault, only then may you judge me. My emotions: anger, fear, greed, and more, sloshed around in my belly during a fight. What I felt is almost of no consequence, for I always fought. Always. Fear didn't stop me. Resignation couldn't make me falter. I cut and sliced. For as long as I could, and with a balled fist or a rock in my hand, I would pound my opponents into dust. Who cares that my emotions swirled and changed with every heartbeat?

So, we were lost. Olaf was down on one knee. Sitric lie sprawled across the sea king with his eyes closed. "Don't do it this way, Prince Sitric. This is no way to follow up a grand talk."

Silkbeard's eye's flickered open and he awkwardly reached with one hand around his back and jerked on the arrow. It came free, popping off several links of his mail. That chain and its weave had been strong. Not a pinch of blood oozed. "I'll have to reward the smith for this suit," the dog prince said. No longer was he a pup in my eyes.

Olaf laughed as more arrows began peppering the walls and men's shields. The clatter became great. Sitric scrambled back to his feet. "What are you bastards waiting for?" the prince screamed. "Release at will!"

Hundreds of arrows leapt up from our bowmen. The sky became thick with black.

The battle for Dyflin had begun.

• • •

The air was sucked out from every Irish kingdom as those missiles darkened the morning sky. Each of them hung there as if they waited for the man who would be their target to march into place. Even the hailstorm from the Irish seemed to await the results of our first volley. No one breathed. Or, if they did, I couldn't hear it over the beating of my own heart. That tangled muscle pressed on my ears from the inside out. Thunk. Thunk. Thunk, it went.

I heard the cries almost as quickly as I heard the telltale thuds of arrows splaying flesh, breaking bones, and driving into shields. Men fell into their comrades so that even the Irish left unscathed, teetered. The mass of advancing Irishmen was checked.

I've been under the onslaught of missiles sent from afar. It is nothing but disheartening. You can do nothing but make yourself small under your shield and hope that none of the archers sent an arrow at a lower angle. You can't spit in your opponent's face. Lashing out will do nothing. Moving at all isn't even the best option. A storm of javelins or arrows can break a man. If it fractures the spirits of enough men, it can shatter an army. Clack. Clack. Clack went the flying daggers.

I swallowed the dry, hare-sized knot in my throat, hoping that Mael's men would rupture after the first round. They didn't. The High King's voice echoed over the plain and soon his Ui Neill were back up and making the distance between us shorter.

"Send a torrent on them!" called Silkbeard.

Our men obeyed and those who had bows used them, unleashing arrow after arrow. I felt the whoosh of those missiles. It was better than a crisp breeze of the spring equinox. Hundreds of straight shafts rasped across the fat bellies of yew bows. It was louder than the crickets of deep summer. The twang of bowstrings snapped far to my right, they played far to my left. It made music sweeter than in any king's winter hall. Though at that moment I was still sure we would lose the battle, I found peace and tranquility in those familiar sounds.

Mael drew closer. I snatched the extra javelin of a man next to me. He voiced a protest but I just shoved him away with my elbow. I meant to be the one who ended this engagement before it became a roiling mess. I took one more peek at the High King, gauged his pace, leaned back, cocked my elbow, and allowed my strength to run. I stepped into the throw, cracking into the palisade with my knee. I didn't feel it at the time, but later found a throbbing brown lump that dwarfed my knee's cap. Nonetheless, the javelin flew true. I felt it when the shaft left my hand. The toss was perfect.

The javelin sailed over Mael's head as his beast stepped forward into a depression in the land. My hurl had been less than perfect. I began scanning for another weapon to swipe. It was to no avail, as every man was releasing them at a rapid clip. Mouths grunted. Throats groaned. Chests heaved. The Irish army was within range and we discouraged them. I watched Olaf, my Lord Crack-a-Bone, wind up with two arms. As he had the night of our drunken wager, he launched them at the same time. He was strong like the iron beard of spikes on his longship. Olaf's chest and arms were granite. Those javelins flew low, fast, and flat. I swear to you they lost no altitude while they raced one another to the target.

And by Odin's wisdom, they soared true. Mael was going to die. Only he didn't. Another man's javelin cracked into the ground just in front of the High King's dappled horse. The beast's nostrils flared and it reared. Olaf's shots buried themselves deeply into the animal's exposed chest. When it came back down on those front hooves, its legs gave way. The horse crumpled, driving one javelin deeper into its valiant lungs, breaking the other's shaft. The creature was dead before Mael climbed off as safe as could be, but swearing up a storm to his One God.

We gave a collective chorus of jeering shouts down to the enemy. I don't know exactly what others said. I heard Sitric say something about a made-up whore on the battlefield. He referred to his mother, who sat scheming back at the camp, I suppose. Randulfr strung together a host of curses in such a jumbled mess that I chuckled. It was beautiful. As for me, I called those Ui

Neill turds ghost soldiers. They wanted to badly to be true warriors, but they were nothing. They were apparitions, capable of achieving nothing.

Maybe seeing their High King dismounted so, would send them reeling. Maybe the Irish would shrink. They still had no bloodlust to drive them, after all. Ample crimson stained the autumn grasses, but none was Norse. They would smell their own piss. They would smell the iron scent of their comrades' blood. The stench of released bowels would invade their nostrils. They would break. They would run.

The host was, in fact, hesitating. They would run. It didn't matter that our trickery had failed. We would rule the field without a single loss. Mael would gather his oath sworn men and trot home with head dangling and tail tucked.

The High King stalked across the front ranks of his host. He screamed at them. Even though he was closer now, I couldn't hear his words. Our own taunts split the morning air. We had plenty of breath remaining, but were running low on javelins. Our onslaught of daggers slowed. The vanguard of the Ui Neill began to again form up.

"The Valkyrie comes," whispered Olaf. Ottar, the skald, heard him say it. He came to his master's side and followed where the sea king's finger pointed.

Coming from behind the mass of Ui Neill warriors was a small band of riders. They churned up sod and muck. Two carried banners. One held the familiar marks of the Ui Neill. Another held a flag of a Leinster clan. Ten guards followed behind, eating the splattering mud kicked up by the van. At the very center of the front rank was a woman.

"Queen Gormflaith," breathed Ottar. He looked at me, wide-eyed. "Gormflaith is the Valkyrie from your dream. She is the death bringer. She will lead us to Odin's hall."

His words sounded marvelous. They were all for which a Norseman could hope – a gallant death on the field of conflict. Yet his tone sent my heart plummeting to the depths of the ocean. Despair was a stone around my neck.

Gormflaith said nothing to the rear ranks of Irishmen who had begun to flee. She rode tall in her saddle, staring straight ahead to our wall as if the woman would single-handedly trot over to capture a kingdom. Those scared men, who for a moment sniffed safety and freedom, halted their retreat. They watched the woman go by. Her stern face betrayed nothing. Well, nothing but savage determination. To a man, each Ui Neill who had lowered his shield and arms, hefted them in place and spun to return to his spot.

The host did not break.

I smelled piss.

We'd fallen silent. A man had used the pause to relieve himself off the back of our platform. His stream pummeled the embankment below and ran like a river down into the muddy streets. It was simply a man getting rid of waste, but I took it as a bad omen. I smelled urine and that meant death.

I would smell much of it in the coming moments.

• • •

"You men are the finest assembly any kingdom of Ireland has ever seen," called Gormflaith. She marched her beast back and forth between our palisade and her men. She was in no danger. We'd lost our senses and the control of our muscles. The puppeteer performed. We, her marionettes, obeyed. The former Queen of Dyflin, the current Queen of the Ui Neill held court and we listened. She spoke in the tongue of the Irish, but a few men on our wall interpreted her words.

"You are a magnificent sight, terrible and frightening. But what good is it to own a fine sword and hang it on the wall? Does it not tarnish? Does it not become dull?" The High King stood in the front rank looking like any common soldier except for his finery and personal guard. He beamed at his woman. Or, perhaps he, like us, was bewitched by her beauty, transfixed by her tapestry of words.

"For a short while your valor is in flower." Gormflaith held up a finger of caution. "Soon, however, it shall be that illness or steel will strip you of your might. Fire may claim your home. The tide can draw you under. Or, worse yet, the dreadful toil of old age may cause your eyes to fade and fail. Death will claim you. What then?" I was stunned. The birds of the field were bewildered. None sang a morning chorus. None swooped in to pick at the eyes of the dying Irishmen. Her speech was as true as a singing axe, twining on the air, silencing all in its path. "I'll tell you one thing. Most men are defined by events of their time. I mean to be a woman who defines my time. Join me! Join me today in making your lives and, hence, your deaths, whenever they come, mean something."

The intent of Gormflaith's words was clear. The Irish host responded by bounding forward without a command. That first step was made in unison and was as clear as a thunder's clack. The second step was less organized but it came faster. By the army's third stride, all cadence was lost. It mattered not, for when the tide wants to roll in, it does. That tide of Ui Neill was rolling in faster and faster now every moment. It delicately folded itself around Gormflaith and her guard. As soon as it passed her, though, the roiling mass closed once again. They gained speed.

"What, were you just weaned from your mother's teats?" shouted Olaf. "Stem the flow! Cut them!"

As if we were waking from a dream a full heartbeat passed before men blinked back to their senses from the queen's talk and the sight of a charging army. Bowstrings snapped. Javelins leapt. The numbers of missiles was not enough. We'd spent our currency earlier. Now we dug into the corners of our purses, hoping to find just one more arrow, spear, or even rock.

The last arrow flew when the first Ui Neill reached the bottom of the embankment. It had been a fine or lucky shot, rupturing the man's cheek. He sailed back into his comrades. Our well-aimed missile did nothing to check the approach. A thousand such arrows couldn't have stopped them on that morning, at that time.

Mael Sechnaill, Ireland's High King, was at the center of his vanguard. He bounded up the hill toward us, to where Sitric's banners flew. Mael churned up earth like a plow as his knees pushed up and his boots shoved down. His nostrils, partially obscured by his helmet's nose plate, flared. He barred his teeth. At first I thought they formed a strange smile. No. Mael growled. Behind him, two of his guard planted hands on his rump or back and helped shove him forward. Other men did the same for them. They came. The Irish tide would swamp us. Our palisade would disappear like snow dropped into a boiling pot.

As soon as Mael made it to the wall's base, dozens of short, wooden ladders were passed forward. They swung up in an eye's blink and when I peered over the palisade's top, men were already climbing. The few rocks we had stockpiled rained steadily down on the attackers, bursting skulls and breaking necks. Tyrkr shouted madly in his native German. His stout arms hurled one river stone after another down at the Irishmen scaling the ladder immediately below. With two hands he'd clutch one from the pile at his feet. Tyrkr grunted as the boulder came up over his head. He screamed, sending spittle from his mouth, as he launched the weight down. Again and again Tyrkr did this until at last his two hands reached down and found nothing. His fingers involuntarily felt around on the platform for more ammunition. His eyes grew wide with panic.

It had come to this. Almost all battles did when two motivated sides came together. It wasn't about deception. It wasn't about intelligence, brains, or cunning. By the time two armies fell together, it was about just two things. The outcome was determined by gross brutality and heart. Everyone's heart could be turned, their determination drained, if the opponent remained unflinching in their atrocious cruelty. It had come to the time when steel in one man's hand would decide the fate of another man's life. We'd meet face-to-face. There would be places on that palisade where one man's fist would clout another. A man might have to jerk another's whiskers or his hair. Fingers would claw, saexes would stab, teeth would bite. It was going to be a chaotic, violent brawl.

Mael's sword came over the wall. The adorned head of the High King poked above as his blade arced across the tops of the helmets of Silkbeard's guard. It nicked two of the iron caps, sending sparks shooting into the air and likely giving the wearers ringing headaches. With one hand clutching the wall and the other fighting, Mael stood on the top of his ladder. He dropped a royal guard by splaying his arm. The High King parried a strike from his left, then right, before slicing both attackers in turn. Mael would have his feet within Dyflin's walls in mere moments. The Ui Neill would have a foothold.

More Irishmen mounted the tops of their ladders. Many of those first men died with their foreheads slashed or necks filleted. I killed one by reaching my hand around the back of his head and smashing his face onto the jagged point of a palisade timber. Still, they came. Gormflaith had sent their blood pumping and so they'd morphed into a tide that would not be stopped by outside forces. The surge would only ebb when the collective mass of the deluge itself wished it.

Ui Neill had invaded our city. Down the line, several of them now stood on the platform with us, creating a pocket behind them for their brethren to fill. In Ireland the lifeboat that was Dyflin was about to be swamped. Olaf fought against a man who had one knee on the wall, trying to sling himself over. The sea king helped him by grasping his leather mail and lurching the man forward. When he clattered to the floor Olaf's blade pinned his neck down while Crack-a-Bone's feet kicked the twitching corpse. Another Irishman appeared in the dead man's place on the wall. They were like rats in the bilge – never-ending. Olaf tugged his sword free and went to work on the next. It was becoming futile.

All of my surviving friends from back home – our quiet Greenland home – struggled on that wall. Magnus made repeated spear thrusts, draining several men of their life's force. Cnute used a borrowed sword for he'd lost his in a game of chance that very evening. His spear was gone. Even the hammer he'd pilfered was nowhere to be seen. Cnute's rusted blade performed well given its pocked edges and heavy, rigid steel. Cnute's arms bulged as he used two hands to control the weapon. Tyrkr and Leif, slave and master, fought side-by-side. It was mayhem, but the two appeared to enjoy the scene. One would approach, the other would cut the enemy. The pair alternated in this way to slay perhaps a dozen Irishmen. Still the tide climbed and pushed.

Randulfr, Brandr, and Loki, the men whom I'd met while serving King Godfrey, clashed with the Irish. Randulfr efficiently swung his blade in short bursts, cutting a man here, stabbing a man there. He gave orders to the men around him. They were more warnings than orders at that point. "Duck!" Or he would say, "To your right!" Other times he'd shout, "Parry!" Rarely could Randulfr scream, "Attack!" The Irishmen, bloody horrible fighters, were engulfing us. The turds were drenching us in our own blood and penning us in. All we could do was defend. "Shield!" Randulfr shouted to Loki.

Sitric Silkbeard, the man who would likely be the last Norse Prince of Dyflin, had stepped to his rightful place. He fought against Mael Sechnaill in a dizzying display of swordplay. Both men had trained for their whole lives for this moment. The High King had lived longer, but not so long as to be slow with his blade. It would only be a matter of time before the younger man, Sitric, found himself overwhelmed by experience.

An Irishman's club smacked into my mailed ribs. I clamped down on the weapon with my arm and stepped toward him, cracking his face with my forehead. We slumped into the palisade together and began clawing at one another like two teens fighting for the hand of the same maid. It was dirty and ruthless. His knuckles rammed my neck. My long sword was a hindrance in such close quarters. I dropped it and grabbed the first thing I could – the flesh at the back of his upper arm. I pinched and twisted. I pulled. He screamed and tried to strike me in the neck again. His blow missed its mark and his knuckles became red from rapping my helmet. We rolled together, bouncing over a dead Norseman. The Irishman took it as a good omen and laughed. But I write this tale and so you know it wasn't to be his day. My hand latched onto the dead man's saex as we went over him. I slid it from its safe home in the man's belt and swiped the one-edged blade across my opponent's now exposed belly. The skin and small layer of fat split wide open. Still the Irishman fought. He slapped his hand onto my wrist to prevent more attacks from the saex. I balled the fist of my other hand. Soon it pummeled the man's exposed innards. Strike after strike turned the bulging mess into soup. His grip weakened.

The life fled from his eyes and he died. I fell on top of him nearly exhausted.

I felt a rutting at my foot. I kicked and spun to meet the threat, but saw only Vigi the dog recoiling in pain. He showed his teeth and growled, but then recognized me. His demeanor changed. Vigi barked happily and trotted off toward where his master now fought against three men. The mutt nipped at the shins of the opponents.

I laid hands on my weapons before jumping next to my Lord Crack-a-Bone. We toiled under the pressure that swarmed over the walls. We were down to a single thread that held together our defense. If it snapped, the palisade would topple. The gates would be flung open and the city sacked. Still, there was that one thread and as long as it remained, the norns had not decreed that we would lose. We, the heroic defenders of the greatest Norse city in the world, held fast. Next to the man to whom I pledged my life, I fought as if I were Thor incarnate.

For nearly inexplicable reasons, I gained confidence in those moments. From the corner of my eye, I watched young Sitric. He had begun the year as a preening pup more concerned about keeping up the appearances of his fine silken beard and maintaining his piety in the face of a fallen world. In the spring Sitric was third in line behind his old father, the king, and his older half-brother, Iron Knee. A year that began with a puppy prince pretending to be an adult and a somber High King sitting in his hall would end in a gruesome fight between the two, between a rabid dog and warrior king, Mael Sechnaill. Sweat poured from both men. They panted and swung. They ducked and stumbled. I began to think that perhaps the longer the fight, the better for the younger man. Mael would become fully winded long before Silkbeard, the dog prince. It was almost certain. My confidence climbed. My heart swelled with pride. I killed next to my lord. The force of the Irishmen shoved us backward, but we cut them and we hammered them. We would show them what the dark followers of Odin – and even the Christian Norse – could do.

Then suddenly the pressure changed.

When you work outdoors for your entire life you know this in the fabric of your soul. You sense the weather. I was just a lad when my true father yet lived, but I remember broadcasting barley seed on a warm day. We marched in the field from one end to the other, dipping our hands into sacks and lightly giving up the contents for the gentle wind to plant across the turned earth. Even though I write these words as an aged man, I can still feel the change on my skin. You plant the seed and suddenly the breeze disappears. It vanishes and stillness inhabits Midgard. You look up from your work and see nothing, but your skin tells you. Your skin talks to you. The raised hairs on your arms tell you to gaze further on, to the trees and beyond.

Then you see it! While where you stand is deathly still, far away a wall of weather is coming. You see it! The treetops flutter. Then their branches begin to beat. Entire limbs wave. Then the peaceful tranquility that inhabited your world for only heartbeats disappears. A new, colder wind smacks your face and you are soon in the midst of a tempest.

The pressure on Dyflin's palisade fled. The air went with it. We all struggled to catch our breath.

Of course, it wasn't a weather phenomenon that caused the change in pressure. No. Some factor far away had steadily worked its way from the rear to the vanguard of the Irish advance. Slowly, it had ebbed away strength and sapped away movement. It had finally reached the embankment, climbed the mud, hit the palisade, surmounted the ladders, and soared over the wall. The Irishmen craned their heads and looked behind them. We peered over their shoulders.

I like to write in absolutes. 'Oh,' I huff and puff, 'a battle is won with vigor and grit.' I said something like that earlier in this tale. 'Angry brutality beats your opponent.' The truth is never so clean. The consistency of the mud may favor one side over another. The placement of the sun and the time of the battle may make it harder for the enemy to see. A bad batch of the night's ale may hinder one force. Anything may rule the day. Combinations of anythings may decide a battle's outcome. Sometimes when two armies fall together, chicanery does, in fact, separate the winner from the loser.

The rear of the Ui Neill attack had now become a front. They were now defenders as hundreds of our Norse women and boys ran from the trees around the river. They wielded spears mostly – spears cobbled together that very night from spearheads hidden in knapsacks and branches found in the woods. Some carried shields. I saw many clubs that amounted to no more than what a boy could pluck up from the forest floor on his march to the plain. The tricky timing of our scheme had not played out as hoped. The women and boys were to show up just before dawn and attack the still sleeping Irish camp. Yet they came. We'd used the Christian High King's and his priests' and advisors' deference to women to move an entire army in plain sight. Even the conniving Gormflaith couldn't see the force that left Dyflin and marched right under her nose. The strong, traitorous queen could not bring herself to realize that other women offered something of value.

Mael peered down the ladder that he'd climbed. It was empty as his army had turned to meet an uncertain, new threat. No more men were there to add to his position. It was a position that was already shrinking.

Sitric sliced his blade downward across the High King's side. Dozens of iron rings from his mail popped and sprang loose. Other than being immediately sore from the blow, Mael was left unhurt. He blocked another strike and kicked at Silkbeard's knee, sending the prince tumbling back. "Up the ladders!" cried the High King. "It is nothing but women! Into the city!"

His orders were swallowed up. Even his confused lieutenants weren't sure what to do. They fought to protect their king, but stole glances to their army's crumpling rear. The High King's personal guard began falling like wheat to the scythe. He had no choice.

"Retreat!" he called

His Irishmen, those Ui Neill rats, who made it into our Norse city turned and fled. They jumped over the walls and climbed down those ladders. We hacked them from behind. We hewed off their hands as they clambered onto the ladders. We cleaved them. Blood spilled and it was a fine sight. The aroma was beautiful for it was the crimson of the Irish.

Olaf rammed an arm across Sitric's chest when the prince moved to climb down the wall in pursuit. "You'll not be going out there, Prince Silkbeard. You'll give up your entire advantage if you do that."

Sitric, his hands filthy, peeled Olaf's arm away. "And what of our women and boys? They'll be slaughtered if we don't go."

Olaf laughed. "My Gytha's down there and I want nothing like that to happen, but I think you don't give our women credit – especially against the Irish. They'll be fine."

Sitric nodded and Olaf grinned. "See there? I knew you'd come around. Your task is to hold the city. It's what Kvaran would do."

"I'm no Kvaran. I'm no Iron Knee. Though they accepted the One God in words, they remained pagan." The prince pushed past Olaf and shouted. "Every third man comes with me out the gate. We fight toward our women and children. The rest hold the wall." Silkbeard faced Olaf. "If I recall it was a band of weak Irishmen, Leinstermen even, who nearly routed you mighty Crack-a-Bone. You may be pagan and think that life is a means to death, but I follow the One True God. I will save the women of my city."

My heartstrings played. My soft head for women turned to mush incapable of making sound battlefield decisions. Seeing the young, decisive prince drive back the High King made me willing to follow Sitric anywhere. I saw him stand up to Olaf's advice. I jumped in line behind Silkbeard as he made his way to the vast doors. Such an inspiration had Sitric become that day that he had to turn away equally eager volunteers. Somehow his actions on the wall had motivated men, heathen and Christian alike, to leave the strategic safety of the city and sacrifice themselves for mere children and women. Even Olaf immediately changed his mind, throwing up his hands and saying, "I'll not be left out of a good fight."

The gates yawned open, spewing us forth. We met Mael's confused host and sent them reeling back toward their camp. I bathed in blood. The Irishmen ran into one another as they fled. Some still tried to fight, but the numbers were no longer right. The norns had decided.

And once fate made up its mind, there was no changing it.

CHAPTER 10

Ravens covered the plain as thick as dew. I stood on the platform and stared out as the flapping birds picked at the bloating corpses. The carrion birds fought one another for the choicest morsels. They cawed, speaking in a language I understood. The tongue they used was of death. I'd been a raider, storming shores, towns, and gates. Now I'd become a true soldier. I had sworn an oath to a man who'd survived and would come to thrive again. I'd stood firm on the platform and pushed back on overwhelming force. I'd become all that my first love, Freydis, who slept nestled back in Brattahlid on Greenland, had wished I'd become.

I was still miserable.

Behind me, the clop of horse hooves on the main wooden road could be heard. A half-turn of my head brought the delegation from the Ui Neill into view. They had come through the main gates which were now sealed shut. Prince Silkbeard, Olaf, and Gytha stood outside the great hall waiting to receive them. Sitric wore his finest garb. He looked like a king though his aged father yet lived and had spent the summer hiding on Iona. Gytha's dress was magnificent, red and blue I think it was with colorful piping at the hems. Beads were sewn onto the fabric above her bust. Her braids were high and tight with two thick strands extending down her back. She had a single scratch on her cheek and a bandage on a thumb from the battle two days before. Olaf was clad in the same clothes he always wore. They'd been laundered since the conflict, but carried stains that would never come out.

"Olaf says you should come to the talks," said my little comb salesman.

I stole a glance at the field of carnage. "Why, Thrond?" I asked.

The boy looked up at me. His shabby tunic was open at the top. I could see where his chest was mottled green and black. Thrond received a great blow from the fat oaken club of an Irishman during the battle. Several of his ribs had to be broken, but the strong boy performed ably enough, walking while tipping to one side, never once wincing. The lid of one of his eyes and the brow above had been badly damaged by a second crack from the same club that hurt his torso. That eye would probably never work properly again. "Because your lord told you to go," he answered simply.

He was right, of course.

"Come on then, Squint-eye." I had taken to calling him that. It was a proper name for a proper warrior.

He led the way down the ladder and around a few small buildings until we came to the hall. We snuck in just as the doors were closed, slinking into the far recesses of the building. Obviously, the obligatory pleasantries were already exhausted.

"We are still willing and able to mount an assault. My men must answer for the insults you've heaped upon us." The High King stood in the hall's center. His woman, the former queen of this very house, stood next to him. She wore a knowing smirk, but said nothing.

"Oh, you do not!" shouted Olaf. "Our fine Norse women saw to that! I'd like to see an Irishman, let alone woman, muster that kind of strength. The gals were tenacious!" His anger subsided and he gave his wife a small wink.

"That proves the Dark Foreigners don't negotiate in good faith. Out of Christian beneficence we granted leave to the women, only to have them skulk around behind us!" hissed Sechnaill.

Olaf snapped his fingers and rapped his skull with a set of knuckles. "I forgot! You forgot, too, High King. Our children, they slaughtered you as much as did our women."

"Enough, already," said Sitric with strength that belied his years. He sat not on his father's throne, but at a mead table. He motioned for the High King and Queen to join him. "Sit. Dine with me. We will talk. We have much to talk about."

"Fine idea, son," said Gormflaith. She immediately gathered her skirts to make the short trek to the bench.

Mael clamped a hand on her arm. "We have nothing to discuss, woman."

Gormflaith wasn't used to being controlled by any man. She jerked her arm free. "We do and you know it. The Prince of

Dyflin who will be ruler once old Kvaran is dead has invited us here to talk. We've accepted. Now follow through."

Mael bit his lip. His woman had the sense to wait for him to nod. When he did, both walked to the mead table. Gytha and Olaf joined them. Several of Mael's lieutenants did likewise. Squint-eye and I stayed in the shadows with Vigi. It was a good place for a trio of mutts to rest.

The meal, which must have been the last of Sitric's stores due to the long running siege, arrived. It was bountiful. Eating knives rattled on dishes. Other than the sounds of cutting and chewing, the royal negotiators ate in silence for a long time. My eyes grew heavy out of boredom until I saw Gormflaith give her husband a sharp elbow in the ribs.

The High King cleared his throat and swallowed a mouthful of salted eel. Pride, I think, went down with it. "Perhaps we do have items to discuss."

Sitric smiled. He was a handsome prince, I've said that. His smile was not the sardonic grin of his father. It was genuine, as if the lad was happy that Mael would talk. And he was, for though we felled countless Irishmen, Dyflin remained under siege. Our citizens still suffered and spread the trotting shits. We had not yet won. "It warms my heart to hear you say that."

"How tender," said the older man. "My daughter was to be a peace-weaver. Now she is gone. How do you propose peace? We are natural enemies."

We were, but Mael's men ran more and more frequently to the woods to release their loose stools. They suffered from the bloody flux as much as did we. We'd slaughtered many. Terms existed that would allow both sides to save face, though I'm sure I didn't know what they were.

"I say that he proposes peace from strength!" said Olaf pounding the table. "I am here. I mean to stay here. I am Lord Crack-a-Bone and I carry that name for a reason." Olaf jammed a dirty finger into the prince. "Because he has me, you have to deal with me. I have ships and men so dedicated that they'll run naked into battle if I ask it."

I was surprised by Mael's response. Had I been the High King, I would have reached across the table to Olaf and thumped him. I suppose that is one of the many reasons why I was not any type of king. "Lord Crack-a-Bone, I'll not deny that your piratical army's presence does figure into my calculations."

Olaf rapped his knuckles in quick succession on the table. "Hear, hear."

Mael held up a finger. "But, Olaf, I think you must admit that save for the few outposts of your people on this island, you are few."

"Outposts?" Olaf huffed. "Dyflin, the finest city. Vedrafjordr! Hlymrekr! These are not mere outposts. By Hel's iceberg tits! Even tiny Viklow down south has a host of men of Norse descent."

"Yet you don't work together. Those cities you've listed don't coordinate. You act like a bunch of tribal ruffians," countered Mael.

"And what about you and the five hundred kingdoms in Ireland? Ui Neill, Leinster, Munster – need I go on? Every man who lives in a shit hole claims to be descended from kings." Olaf was getting worked up. His face reddened. Gytha set a hand on his. He looked at it and patted her skin before removing it. "And I'd say with our strongholds covering the shores and best mouths of the best rivers, it be you the Irish who are in trouble. You are surrounded." The sea king ran a finger in a circle around his eating plate.

Mael chuckled. "I believe I have an army besieging you that says otherwise." The High King mocked Olaf by copying the motion around his plate. When he had completed one full circuit, Mael snatched up a slab of meat and tore it with his teeth. The implications were obvious.

Sitric looked at Gormflaith. The woman nodded to her son. He tapped his silver cup with an eating knife. The sea king and High King turned to look at the prince who scolded both men with a slow shake of his head. I've seen many a disappointed father give the same look to a rambunctious son.

"I am sorry for my outburst, Prince Silkbeard," said Olaf. Though he overdid his apology by bowing deeply, it was important to demonstrate to Mael that Sitric was the undisputed leader while Kvaran was away.

Gormflaith's elbow again found the High King's side. "I, too, apologize for bringing anger into our discussion," he grunted.

The young prince found his footing and shoved his way up from the bench. He clasped his hands behind his back and walked straight-legged around the table. The High King's lieutenants reacted by setting hands on sword hilts. "No fear, men," said Mael with narrowed eyes. "The pup wouldn't dare."

Sitric smiled, again acting like a dissatisfied parent. "High King, we have had much unnecessary bloodshed."

"You captured and killed my daughter." Mael's eyes immediately shone wet.

"I did neither of those things. Iron Knee caught her in the woods. He is dead."

"And so is my daughter! She was to be a peace-weaver! And, I am not ashamed to say the words, I loved her as any father would," protested Mael.

I remembered the young princess. Sorrow welled. Squint-eye patted my shoulder.

"And I would have loved her as well. When she left your kingdom to join mine, peace would have been in her wake. It would have been off her bow." Sitric held up a hand to cut off the next outburst from the High King. "We did not kill Aednat. It was not what we wanted. It served us no purpose. You see, I admit to you that we were in decline. We did not want to fight the mighty Ui Neill."

"That's why Dyflin needed my husband," said Gytha.

"And that is why Dyflin needed Aednat. We did not kill her," said Sitric.

Mael let the words settle in his mind. His anger still burned. The pouring blood from the battle had not quenched it. Slowly, his face softened. He came to realize that what Sitric said was the truth. "Who else would have killed her on my own lands?"

Sitric, Olaf, and the rest of us looked at Gormflaith. We all knew that her actions had set in motion the events that ended Aednat's fiery life. Sitric quickly shifted his gaze to the floor.

"Our entourage was attacked that very night as well. It was by the same men who killed the lovely Aednat."

"Who? Who is responsible for all this? Who goaded me into attacking you and losing dozens of my men?" asked the High King. It was hundreds of his men, by the way, but every leader must lie here and there during negotiations.

I wanted to shout the name Gormflaith. For once, I held my tongue. Squint-eye looked on the scene in wonder with his one good eye. He'd not ever be able to return to the comb-making trade now. He'd tasted war and lived. Instead of witnessing poor peasants negotiate to save a sliced penny, Thrond watched kings, queens, and princes haggle.

No one said the queen's name. I suppose it was political. Everything on the island of Ireland was political. Sitric stared at the High King with a stern face. The dog prince aged ten years in that moment. "There is a clan to the south that plays second to the Ui Neill time and again. They want more. They heard of a possible union between the rich Dyfliners and the powerful Ui Neill. The Leinstermen hoped to leapfrog into the primary position." Gormflaith beamed with pride. She seemed to breathe a sigh of relief.

Mael's grip whitened around his knife. He ground the tip into the plate. "Of course," he whispered.

"I tried to tell you, dear king," said Gormflaith. She rubbed his arm. "Now what do you propose, son."

"I, Prince Sitric Silkbeard, son of Kvaran, King of Dyflin propose a union between the Ui Neill and this kingdom. It will be an alliance based in military might. We will fight the forces of the Leinster clan who killed Aednat and raided beyond their bounds. Together, we will crush them. While I wish in my heart that Aednat would have been the peace-weaver you wanted, High King, it is now up to us to bring peace through force of arms."

Mael eased his clasped hand. He let the knife clatter to the table. "You understand that I cannot simply break the siege and leave. That would do nothing to strengthen my hold on my kingdom." The cunning Gormflaith appeared to grin at the prospect of the High King losing his power.

Sitric began his pacing again. He walked to the platform where his father's throne sat and stepped up. The prince flicked the gold leaf carving that was attached to the great post. He thought about his father's scorn for peace-weavers. Sitric was too young to truly believe that a woman couldn't bring peace, but Kvaran's words echoed in his mind. He moved to the casks that were heavy-laden with counterfeit English pennies made by Dyflin moneyers from the dies I'd sold them. When Sitric spun to face us all, he wore a confident expression.

"That barrel back there is filled with booty. Take it as a tribute for your victory in the siege." Silkbeard hopped off the platform and veritably bounded toward the table. "You may claim success, for who takes away treasure from a fight but the victor? I may claim the win because I shed some of your blood, drove you from within my walls, and sent you home."

Gormflaith giggled with delight at her son's idea. "It's a fine plan, High King," said the queen.

Mael gave the woman a sideways glance. "I suppose it is." He climbed to his feet, followed in rapid succession by his men. Gormflaith lingered.

Sitric offered the High King his hand. Mael reached out and the pair made their accord. Details were decided upon and in moments the High King and his guard walked proudly from the hall.

Olaf stood and moved the bench out for his woman to stand. He took her hand and helped her up, placing a tender kiss on the scratch across her cheek. "Well, I suppose you don't always have to thump someone to get what you want," said Lord Crack-a-Bone.

Gytha giggled at her man. "No, but Sitric could have done none of this without your strength." The couple ambled out into the daylight, her arms interlaced with his. Gytha rested her head down on Olaf's shoulder. *Olaf, my lord, told me with his eyes and a jerk of his head to stay put.*

I sat there with my wounded comb salesman. I was wholly unsatisfied. Perhaps you are as well. Get used to it, I'd say! Gormflaith paid nothing for setting all this in motion – from Colbain's treachery and murder of Iron Knee to causing the

Norsemen of Vedrafjordr to invade Leinster which caused Leinster to invade the lands of Dyflin and the Ui Neill. All of it led to Aednat's unnecessary sacrifice and a siege and battle. We had lost many men. More would die from the flux. All of it was the turncoat queen's fault. And there she sat as happy as a new mother in the dark hall.

I set my hand on the handle of my father's saex. It would feel good to use it for retribution of that kind. I watched Sitric begin to walk toward a rear door. His conniving mother would be dead by the time the door closed behind him.

"Son!" called Gormflaith from her seat. Prince Sitric halted mid-stride.

"Come to me," said his mother. I cursed there in the shadows. The fire crackled in the hearth. I'd have to wait a few moments before I killed the woman. At least it would be fun to watch the prince scold his mother without the fear of offending the High King. Perhaps he would again tell her how he had no mother.

Silkbeard turned and came back to the mead table. He stood tall over his seated mother. She took one of his hands. "Did Colbain tell you everything?"

"He did," said Sitric.

Gormflaith peered up into her son's eyes. "You know that I used his infatuation with me to get him to do what was best for us, for you?"

"I do," answered Sitric. "And I killed him to shut him up and to put him out of his misery. He actually thought you loved him. All this was cruel for even you, mother."

Gormflaith shrugged with an uncaring air.

"I suspected, you know," said Sitric. "I suspected that he was or you were behind Iron Knee's murder."

"But you remained quiet," said Gormflaith, warily.

"I did. Though you left Kvaran for a more powerful man, my father had more to teach me. King Kvaran was not completely done yet. I've learned to take advantage of situations as they present themselves. I loved my half-brother, but his death meant power for me. I did nothing to implicate Colbain because that would implicate you. And that, mother, might implicate me." He tugged his hand away from her and turned to leave. All of this talk did nothing to calm me. I wanted to kill the woman all the more. I wanted to run from the hall and serve a sea king on mountainous waves.

"So you and the High King are allied now," said Gormflaith to Sitric's back. "That was a fine bit of negotiating. Together you will attack my people, the Leinsters. It is good for you and for your future."

"I can tell your words mean something else, mother. Just speak plainly," said Silkbeard without turning to face the woman.

"You'll have no heirs of Ui Neill blood now," she began. "Your grand military alliance is no stronger than any of the other alliances made by your father or grandfather in the past. It may last a season or perhaps two. In the end it will fail and you'll be with the Leinsters against the Ui Neill. You will not be High King. Your heirs will not become the High King."

"Mother," warned Sitric.

"To the point, yes. There is a man of the Munster clan. His name is Brian Boru. My sources say that he will be an important man in the history of Ireland."

"The Munster clan is as weak as a cow with the ankles of a hen," scoffed Sitric.

"Today, perhaps, but power is ever-shifting. Mael mistakenly believes that he holds sway in the north. May the lord bless his soul, but Kvaran, too, used to think he ruled his domain. As you've seen by recent events, even when they don't go exactly according to plan, it is I who command Ireland. It is my will that is done. Mere men remain unaware of this fact to their own peril. It won't be the same with you, because you now know. As for the Munster clan, I've already made overtures to Brian."

Sitric chuckled. "You already plot to find the next man's bed to share? The High King is not good enough?"

"He may hold that title. But as I just told you, I dominate. I am the High Queen, if there were such a designation. At any rate, Mael may not be the High King forever," said Gormflaith, standing. She walked to her son and held both of his hands in hers. "I mean to be a woman who defines my times. I'll take you with me. Boru has a daughter who will be of marrying age within a decade. Her name is Slaine."

The prince stroked his beard. His mother's hands joined in and she fixed a lone tangle in his whiskers. "Tell me more about this Boru," said Sitric. The pair walked out into the sun in much the same pose as Olaf and Gytha.

I was left stewing.

That was the moment. As I look back on it, that was the exact time when compassion fled from my heart. It would be nearly ten years before it would return. I was done trying to do right for anyone but myself. Queens didn't do what was right for their subjects. Gormflaith proved that. Princes didn't. Sitric demonstrated courage and an inner resolve when he fought the High King on the palisade. For a fleeting moment I believed in him. Now, I looked to Silkbeard as the finest model of a man who was *nearly* great. Another disappointment. I should have been used to it by then. Sitric fell short of greatness because of fear and greed. If royalty didn't have to look after its citizens, why would I have to care about anyone else?

Even Olaf, my Lord Crack-a-Bone, whom I love to this day, used his men. He supped with us. And he was often the first one to jump onto a foreign shore, displaying his mailed chest as if he dared the defenders to send the first dagger at him. Olaf, the man who was to become my third father, used his people just like others. His bravery and the camaraderie Olaf gave only mildly tempered his single-minded pursuit of riches, his drive for Norway's throne. I can admit it today. My third father grew to love me back. We nearly died standing next to one another many times.

Dead King Godfrey had made me a raider. His priest, the splayed open and dead, Killian, introduced me to the One God's gospel. Its seed was just beginning to sprout. Olaf made me an oath sworn man, loyal. Sitric, Kvaran, Mael, Gormflaith, and the rest of those who sparred for the ultimate control of Ireland made me tired and angry.

Bodies piled up in my wake. Fortunately, most were my enemies. Many, however, were loved ones. My heart shrank as does your manhood when you piss on an icy morning.

I was a raider. I was a soldier. I took from others so they did not have the means to take from me. I was a raider and I was hard.

THE END
(Dear Reader-See Historical Remarks to separate fact from fiction.)

HISTORICAL REMARKS

As with all of the previous adventures of Halldorr most of the characters and events are true. Kvaran was king of the Norse domain of Dyflin (present day Dublin) for most of the tenth century. By the exact dates of this tale, however, he'd already passed away on the famous island of Iona. In my mind's eye, his long and remarkable reign justified extending his life just a few years longer so that he could be included in *The Norseman Chronicles*. For two brief times he was also King of Jorvik (present day York) in England. Near the end of his life, he did lose the decisive Battle of Tara to Mael Sechnaill of the Ui Neill which forced Kvaran into religious exile at the Iona Monastery. Kvaran had verbally accepted Christianity and been baptized earlier in his career for political reasons, but never truly gave up his dedication to the old gods. After Tara, Dyflin's boundaries shrank. Kvaran's eldest son, Gluniairn, also known as Iron Knee, thereafter served as the city-state's king, but was mostly a client of the powerful Ui Neill. Adding further to the insult of the defeat was that Kvaran's then-wife, Gormflaith, fled into the arms of Mael Sechnaill. I'll have more to say on her amazing life below.

An Irish servant or slave named Colbain killed Gluniairn in the late 980's during a drunken brawl. It has been suggested that the act was no accident since there were so many who stood to benefit from his death. In my tale, I've simplified Dyflin's royal family down to just two half-brothers – Gluniairn and Sitric. The truth is more complicated in that Gluniairn and Mael Sechnaill were even half-brothers. There were a host of other half-siblings all over Ireland, from Hlymrekr (Limerick) to Vedrafjordr (Waterford) to Viklow (Wicklow) that could lay claim to some of Gluniairn's titles and power. His death precipitated a flurry of change and activity in Dyflin as factions fought both outright and surreptitiously for control.

The most immediate beneficiary of the mess was Kvaran's son with Gormflaith called Sitric Silkbeard. He wound up as King of Dyflin and ruled the kingdom as a Christian for forty-six years, making a long pilgrimage to Rome at one point.

Silkbeard was the first ruler on Ireland to mint his own coins – not the counterfeits moneyed by his father from pilfered dies. His fortunes rose and fell many times during that long reign. External stresses from the Irish clans were incessant. Dyflin was surrounded by the Leinsters on the south and the Ui Neill on the north.

    Early on, Sitric benefitted immensely from what he would call God's Providence and what Halldorr would call Fate. Olaf Tryggvason, perhaps the most feared and richest raider of his time, married Sitric's aunt Gytha (some scholars believe Gytha to be Sitric's half-sister) after her first husband died unexpectedly. The sagas tell us that Olaf arrived almost as an afterthought at the Thing called by Gytha and she was immediately taken by him. This good fortune benefited many. Olaf now had lands in England to draw upon, a fact that would help him secure the men and ships when he would later fight to take the crown of all of Norway. Gytha had a husband whose name and reputation alone would protect her lands and claims. Sitric had an in-law who could project power almost anywhere. Olaf set up his base of operations in Dyflin for the next six years. Though Mael and other Irish kings tried to finish Dyflin once and for all during that time, the flock of additional warriors Olaf brought kept them at bay. When Crack-a-Bone, as he was also known, left to become King of Norway in 995 A.D., Sitric's fortunes ebbed. By 1000 A.D. Dyflin was again under the High King's finger.

    Olaf did get a dog from a farmer in the manner described in my tale. He named the dog Vigi.

    Princess Aednat is a fiction.

    Gormflaith is not, however. In preparing to tell my yarn, I realized early on that this was a politically astute woman. By all accounts she was cunning and beautiful. Gormflaith was most likely of Munster descent though I've placed her into Leinster to limit the number of varying factions in the story. At a young age, she was wed to the much older King Kvaran of Dyflin. After his defeat at Tara, she moved on to marry the High King of Ireland, Mael Sechnaill of the Ui Neill. Several years after the events in *Norseman's Oath*, Gormflaith married her third husband, Brian Boru, one of Ireland's most famous of all High Kings, after he took that title from Mael Sechnaill. Though it is thought to be after-the-fact, literary conjecture, Gormflaith was said to have orchestrated the Battle of Clontarf in 1014 A.D. This successful queen to three kings also had the fortune of having three different sons by those three men who would themselves become kings in Ireland. Suspecting that such a brilliant tactician would have the means to assassinate Iron Knee and get her son Sitric on the throne was not a far stretch.

Hoards of arm rings and silver were discovered on what is today known as Hare Island in Lough Ree. They were buried in a hurry, suggesting that the owner expected to return and reclaim them. He obviously never did. Fate, as it so often does, intervened. On several occasions Viking fleets sailed up the River Shannon to raid further inland with Lough Ree and its islands as their bases of operation. There is no evidence that Olaf Tryggvason himself ever participated in that particular sport.

In truth, Lough Ree is a little far north to border with the Leinster clans of old, but the idea of a fleet of Vikings sailing so far up a river then burying a hoard, captivated me. It is a novel, after all.

Mael Sechnaill laid siege to Dyflin in 989 shortly after Gluniairn's death. It lasted for weeks and eventually it was lack of fresh water that caused the Norse to pay a tribute to encourage the High King to leave. I included references to the bloody flux, or dysentery, since both the besieger and besieged usually dealt with this scourge in the Medieval Era. The clash between the two armies that I've described near the story's end did not take place. I did, however, wish to convey the extra battlefield muscle that Olaf gave to young Sitric in setting the young royal up for several years of strength. It also gave me a chance to pit the political slyness of Gormflaith against the intelligence of Gytha.

Several main characters from Halldorr's other stories took a back seat in this episode. Leif Eriksson was, of course, a real person, though he most certainly did not ever defend Dyflin's walls. You'll have to read along in the original three of

The Norseman Chronicles to find out why he makes appearances in my tales at all. Tyrkr truly was Erik Thorvaldsson's (Erik the Red and Leif Eriksson's dad) German thrall. Men like Magnus, Cnute, Randulfr, Brandr, and Loki are fictional characters.

Hallfred Ottarsson whom I called Ottar was Olaf's personal skald or poet. He would travel around in the sea king's company and recite stories and songs. The most famous and best skalds came from Iceland and Hallfred was no exception. They were valuable members of the society, providing heroic stories, a bit of history, and entertainment during the era's long winters. Absent a seer, it would have been logical for Halldorr to seek out Ottar for an interpretation of his dream.

Men with terrific names such as Thrond Squint-eye and Ox-foot, among many others, are listed in the sagas as some of Olaf Tryggvason's closest and best fighters.

I used several fine sources to build this story. *Vikings: North Atlantic Saga* edited by Fitzhugh and Ward remains my indispensible, all-around source. *The Oxford Illustrated History of the Vikings* edited by Peter Sawyer is also useful for general information. For the specific events and characters in *Norseman's Oath – Scandinavian York and Dublin* by Alfred P. Smyth, *Irish Kings and High Kings* by Francis John Byrne, and *Viking Pirates and Christian Princes* by Benjamin T. Hudson provided much in the way of detailed history and archaeology. Ottar's poem is from the Poetic Edda. It meant that a proper Scandinavian should be cautious in his praise and appropriate in his actions. I must also acknowledge that some of the imagery in Halldorr's vision of the Valkyries was borrowed from the poem at the end of *Njal's Saga* called *Darradarljod*. Gormflaith's battle speech was based on a few lines spoken by Hrothgar in *Beowulf*.

I know with certainty that Halldorr wrote more of his life's tales down on his homemade vellum. What I do not know is whether or not any more have ever been unearthed. We will just have to wait and see. In the meantime, if you long for more adventure you may certainly read those of his yarns that have been discovered and published. The rest of *The Norseman Chronicles* can be found on Amazon.

Lastly, if you desire a change of pace from rampaging Norsemen, check out my three-book series entitled *The Wald Chronicles*. It follows the struggle of a rag-tag group of Germanic tribesmen against mighty Rome under Augustus.

ABOUT THE AUTHOR

Jason Born is the author of *The Norseman Chronicles*, a multi-volume work of historical fiction detailing the adventures of the Viking, Halldorr, who lived during the time of Erik the Red and Sweyn Forkbeard. *The Wald Chronicles* series of historical novels centers on the conflict in Germania between the Roman legionaries and their tribal adversaries over 2,000 years ago. He is an analyst and portfolio manager for a Registered Investment Advisory firm. Jason lives in the Midwest with his wife and three children. If you enjoyed this work and would like to see more, Jason asks you to consider doing the following:

1. Please encourage your friends to buy a copy – and read it!
2. Go to his author page (Jason Born – Author) on Facebook and click "Like" so that you may follow GIVEAWAYS or information on his next book.
3. If you think the book deserves praise, please post a five star review on Amazon and/or a five star review on Goodreads.com.
4. Follow him - Twitter handle - @authorjasonborn
5. Visit his website, www.authorjasonborn.com.

Made in the USA
Lexington, KY
30 April 2015